MOUNTAINS OF THE MOON

MOUNTAINS OF THE MOON

I. J. KAY

VIKING

VIKING
Published by the Penguin Group
Penguin Group (USA) Inc., 375 Hudson Street,
New York, New York 10014, U.S.A.
Penguin Group (Canada), 90 Eglinton Avenue East, Suite 700,
Toronto, Ontario, Canada M4P 2Y3
(a division of Pearson Penguin Canada Inc.)
Penguin Books Ltd, 80 Strand, London WC2R 0RL, England
Penguin Ireland, 25 St. Stephen's Green, Dublin 2, Ireland
(a division of Penguin Books Ltd)
Penguin Books Australia Ltd, 250 Camberwell Road, Camberwell,
Victoria 3124, Australia
(a division of Pearson Australia Group Pty Ltd)
Penguin Books India Pvt Ltd, 11 Community Centre, Panchsheel Park,
New Delhi – 110 017, India
Penguin Group (NZ), 67 Apollo Drive, Rosedale, Auckland 0632,
New Zealand (a division of Pearson New Zealand Ltd)
Penguin Books (South Africa) (Pty) Ltd, 24 Sturdee Avenue,
Rosebank, Johannesburg 2196, South Africa

Penguin Books Ltd, Registered Offices:
80 Strand, London WC2R 0RL, England

First American edition
Published in 2012 by Viking Penguin,
a member of Penguin Group (USA) Inc.

1 3 5 7 9 10 8 6 4 2

Publisher's Note
This is a work of fiction. Names, characters, places, and incidents either are the product of the author's imagination or are used fictitiously, and any resemblance to actual persons, living or dead, business establishments, events, or locales is entirely coincidental.

LIBRARY OF CONGRESS CATALOGING-IN-PUBLICATION DATA

Kay, I. J.
Mountains of the moon / I.J. Kay.
p. cm.
ISBN 978-0-670-02367-7
1. Women ex-convicts—England—Fiction. 2. Self-realization in women—Fiction.
3. Bristol (England)—Fiction. 4. Psychological fiction. I. Title.
PR6111.A935M68 2012
813'.6—dc23
2011043899

Printed in the United States of America
Set in Sabon Std

In memory of Lynn Robertson
who lost her life on Ben Nevis, January 2001

People with nowhere to go
do go, they go somewhere
and somewhere else after that.
They go somewhere else in the physical;
somewhere else in the mind.

PROGRAM

CAST

THE VELVIT GENTLEMAN: Anton Konstantin
MUM / SHUT-UP: Joan King
THE JOKER: Heath Crow
DADDY / THE FUCK: Bryce King
PIP: Philip Kendal-King
THE OAK TREE: Peter Eden
GRANDAD: Bill Burns
NANNY: Rose Burns
BABY GRADY: Graham King
WELSH SLAPPER: Gwen Llewelyn
THE SANDWICH MAN: Richard Draper
ROBERTSON: Lynn Robertson
NEIGHBOR: Norman Baldwin
THE JACKAL: Jimmy Smithers
ELLIE: Eleanor Smithers
ETON BOY: Quentin Sumner
IRENE: Irene Sumner
DANNY FISH: Will Withywood
THE ANGEL MICHAEL: Michael ?
AUNTIE FI: Fiandre Krammer
OLD GEORGE: George Hewel
POTTERY MANAGER: Tim Evans
TONY GLOUCESTER ROAD: Tony Williamson
SHEBA: Lucky

ALL OTHER PARTS ARE PLAYED BY INNOCENT BYSTANDERS.

Overture and Beginners

Three keys: one for the main entrance; one for the letter box on the wall outside and one for my brown front door, which comes complete with fist holes and crowbar dents around the lock. You wouldn't think it, looking from outside. The building is an old vicarage, tall and imposing in a horseshoe shape with a gravel car park at the front. Sideways onto the street, it overlooks a park. Well, a railed bit of grass with mature trees; it belonged to the vicarage once. There's a bench and a slide and probably a bird if you wait long enough. It's used mostly by dog owners and heroin addicts, who don't mind the dog shit or the discarded needles. I've never understood the bond between people and drugs, people and dogs, always wanted a real friend myself.

The intercom bell is violently loud, shattering. I skid into the hall and snatch up the receiver. Hopefully it's Tim from the pottery; he said he'd drop off some stuff.

"Hello?" I say.

"Special delivery," Tim says. "Sleeping bag, camping stove, sewing machine."

It is good of him. I volunteer at the pottery three times a week; it gives me something useful to do.

"Come up, Tim," I say.

I press the button to release the main door and run down the stairs to meet him coming up. The vicarage belongs to a housing association now; they have converted it, badly, into one-bedroom apartments. Perfect for people going back into the community.

"I see what you mean," Tim shouts.

He sees nothing; he freezes in my hall, stalling for time while his eyes adjust to the gloom. Migraine-patterned music is pumping through the floor.

"I've got built-in surround sound," I shout.

It's a hot and sunny July teatime but the apartment is like a cave; low ceilings compound the effect in booming echo and chill. The bathroom doesn't have daylight, just a vent to outside that comes on with the light, assuming your giro came, assuming you can afford electricity. In the bedroom there's a lumpy futon mattress that I hauled from a skip down the road and carried up two flights on my head. The lounge is vast and rectangular. It's got filthy walls of gutless green covered with holes and coffee stains. On the dominant wall, spray paint splutters "*Cunt*." Mustard paintwork screams at the gray tile floor and black doors scream back. It is the ugliest place I've ever seen. Tim surveys it with his hands on his hips.

"It's got potential," he shouts. "You could paint it all white to brighten it up."

But white paint in poor light always looks gray, I know that. The windows are small, tall and arched in vicarage stone, blackened with mildew and condensation. The tree outside is blocking most of the natural light.

"The tree is beautiful," I say.

Broad-leaved lime. The vivid soft leaves press against the glass; backlit, they seem surreal like stained glass. The housing association has given me a thirty-pound decorating voucher; I've spent half of it on filler and bleach.

"It's a good size, Tim," I say.

He flicks the light switch in the lounge but there's no electric.

"It's one of those key meter things; my giro didn't come."

"I can lend you a fiver," he says.

But I'd rather not owe if I don't have to.

"Does it stink in here?" I say.

I know it does, of something specific; I can't put my finger on what it is. The kitchen consists of two gray base units and spaces waiting for a cooker and a fridge. There's a walk-in larder.

"You've made a good start," Tim says.

The kitchen floor was a job for bleach and newspapers and wallpaper scrapers. There's no electric for the kettle but Tim has brought a camping stove. No tea or coffee or milk or sugar; my giro didn't come.

"Nice cup of hot water?" I say.

He has to go; dual furrows in his brow, his beautiful schizophrenic wife and pregnant schoolgirl daughter are waiting in the car. I thank him for the loan of the stove, and sleeping bag and sewing machine. And the anorak, which he won't take back.

When Tim has gone I realize I could slide down the wall and sit on my heels sobbing but I don't, I'm too tired for that. I salvage an old tea bag from the bin, then sit on my bucket in the lounge and boil water on the camping stove that Tim has left behind. The boom of bass from Techno downstairs is making the pan vibrate. I swing between gratefulness and disappointment. I've been a long time getting here, when I think about it.

Releasing me, the judge, slumped under the weight of his own wisdom, suggests I go to a bail hostel in Reading where I can stay temporarily.

"Please, milord," I want to say, "anywhere but Reading." But I don't say anything and a travel warrant is issued. I walk from the court to the railway station. The day is bright and bitterly cold—I don't have my coat. I go into the cafe on the platform to wait. The man behind the counter is happy in his work. When it goes quiet he comes over.

"Can I get you anything?" he says. "You've been here a while."

"I'm waiting for the train to Reading."

"You've missed a few, there's nothing now for an hour."

"Dragging my heels," I say.

"Can I get you something?"

"To be honest," I say, "I've just got out of prison."

He's surprised.

"I've got a pound note but I gather they went out of circulation." I show him. "I've got a one-way ticket to Reading."

I've got a plastic bag with Irene's letters in it and a closed-up piercing in my left ear. The man goes away to the counter, comes back with a mug of coffee, ham rolls and chocolate bars.

"I know how it is," he says.

"Thanks ever so much," I say.

He pulls out a chair and sits down.

"Where are you from?" he says. "You sound a bit London, south, Home Counties."

I shrug; I've no idea where the Home Counties are. I probably sound a bit Holloway Prison, a little bit Ladbroke Grove, a little bit Suffolk, Yorkshire Moor, West Midlands, Dorset, Sussex, Kent. A little bit of everywhere and nowhere you can name. He puts a pinch of tobacco on the table in front of me.

"I'm Bernie," he says. "What did they get you for, then?"

Through the plate glass I see people in winter coats and scarves and hats, collecting on the station platform.

"Colorful, int it?" I say.

At the bail hostel in Reading there's a single room for me, but the other thirty inmates are half my age, waiting to go to prison, and I'm just coming out. They don't know what to make of me, there's something not right about me being there. I'm an undercover policewoman, that's what they deduce. I walk in and silence the communal room. One warm spring day I find Heath in the lobby, visiting a bailed mate. It has been eleven years. His red and green leather jacket has faded to pink and gray with age, but the number 9 on the back is still bold and black. He hasn't aged a day, still has a beautiful face in profile, like a medieval saint.

"Hello, Heath," I say.

We always saw eye to eye. The four scars drawn on my cheekbone make me unforgettable. He smiles. Laughs out loud.

"You look good, Kim," he says. "Fuck, do you look good!"

He means my prison-gym physique.

"Punchbags and medicine balls," I say.

"Still hacking your hair with a knife." He laughs, invites me to spar in the open space of the lobby.

But I don't. He puts his arm around my neck, hard-sells me bygones and a lot of water under bridges.

I get a job in the bowels of a warehouse, mixing mountains of potpourri with a shovel. Every day I choke on a different fragrant chemical. My wellington boots fill to the rim with ingredients from around the world. The boss is pleased about having someone he can trust. I do deliveries to London in the van, serve customers in the warehouse and go to the bank with the cash. I work fourteen hours a day for the same money I'd get on the dole, and he makes sure he gets his money's worth.

"What do you want from me, blood?" I say.

The boss laughs; he thinks I'm joking but I'm not. I lie about where I live and where I've been. When the wage packet comes I send a fiver to Bernie in the station cafe with a note saying thanks. I pay rent for the room in the hostel and the use of the kitchen. It isn't great but it's somewhere to try and sleep. There's reporting in and out; a night curfew of ten o'clock; there's someone who shits in the showers and someone who's got a gun because the police come wearing bulletproof vests and break down my bedroom door by mistake. A member of staff gives me a list of organizations that help with resettlement and housing. I phone them up. They can help me if I've got children; if I'm fleeing from domestic violence; if I'm a refugee or from a minority group; they can help me if I've got issues with alcohol or drug abuse. I don't fit the criteria. I never have. The last one on the list balks when I mention prison.

"Our organization only helps and supports young women who have problems with their mental health."

"OK, sorry to bother you," I say and hang up.

Upstairs my room has been broken into and trashed. The wages I've been saving have gone from my hiding place. I phone the mental health people back. It's a different woman that answers my call. I lie about my age. She asks me if I have suicidal thoughts; I say yes, about four times a week. They give me somewhere to live, a room in a halfway house. It's in Bristol, a city I like, the city where my love lives.

I hitch to Bristol down the M4. The house is comfortable, clean and safe. Except that, on account of the other women in the house (who have problems with their mental health) it's only halfway all right. One mad old woman knocks on my door constantly, threatens to kill herself if I don't come out. I don't come out. Another girl phones the police all night, every night, to complain about raging parties next door but the elderly couple living there go to bed at eight o'clock, there isn't a sound. I am the love object of another, she gropes my breasts and between my legs at every passing chance. I ask her nicely to stop but she doesn't. I have to get assertive and shove her off but then she does it more, for sport, to wind me up. I could kill her but I don't. One day I find Heath in the kitchen and all of the halfway women laughing.

"How did you know I was here?" I ask him.

"The bail hostel told me," he says. "I had a look in their filing cabinet. I had a Bristol drop so I thought I'd come and say howdy-do, as you do."

Heath lives in Manchester now with a woman called Sharon and her kids. He can't wait for me to meet her. I don't ask about Gwen, he doesn't ask about Pete. We go in the street to look at his Scania parked up the road. The Rolls-Royce of lorries.

"I'm driving it myself," he says. "But this time next year I've got two on the road and the following year I've got four. And where am I?"

"At the dojo?"

"Fishing," he says.

Every hair on my neck stands up. I look at Heath; remember the story of the crossbow and the gun, the two killer boys in the woods. Witch's house makes me shiver. Bygones.

I have to serve extra time in that house, eighteen months, reducing my suicidal thoughts to once a week, then once a month, until finally the organization decides that I'm able to take care of myself and they fix it with the housing association for me to have this apartment.

I sound ungrateful, I'm not; a housing association apartment is, after all, a guaranteed home for life.

It's chucking-out time at the pub opposite; I hear a fight unfolding and a woman screaming. Through a gap in the trees I see the ambulance come and the landlord with a bucket, swilling blood off his doorstep. There's a payphone below my window, it's used as an office by a man with a taxi: he sits by it with his engine running and waits for work to phone him. When he's gone it rings. The phone rings and rings until he returns, and off he goes again. A street lamp across the road filters in through the trees. I light a candle and tackle another job application. Warehouse pickers and packers. Today's date? I don't know. July 1996. Title: Louise Alder. 9/19/65. Education and qualifications.

"None," I say, but write O levels in English, Home Economics and Biology. I give myself Cs. The school I went to, the work history and all the dates—I make them up. The entire form is a work of fiction, even my name.

The apartment above me has a stream of visitors throughout the night: internal doors crash and bang; there's thumping up and down the stairs, they ring my bell by mistake. Men knock asking for Veronique.

"You want number 24." I point across the landing.

Her name is Sally really. I met her on the stairs: she told me to be careful passing the park, there'd been a rape, a nasty one, she said. Everyone seems to get where they're going via me; lucky for them I'm awake. I pace around the apartment, knock my forehead on this wall and that, walk diagonally from corner to corner, alternate hips on door frames. It might have been a trick of the light but I thought I saw something run across the kitchen doorway. Every time I hear a car door slam I go and look out of the window; I'm waiting for Peter to come. I've left a note with a friend of a friend, of a friend of his, to say I've moved and where to, this time.

One time Jimmy Jackal Smithers seen me do it, said he'd give me his cats' eyes to do it gain but I never, I can't do stuff with people looking; sides, it int proper to make marbles out of cats' eyes, not when you could eat them. Mum says I got lucky legs, lucky they don't snap and stab me to death, that's how come I int cuddly. When Auntie Fi comes she always turns me around in the kitchen, wets her finger, tests to see what color I is underneath the dirt. She can't get over the color I go in summer, Six Weeks in the Bahamas Brown, makes my eyes and teefs go white.

Auntie Fi says I'm Long, Limbed and Lean but I is a Fine Tuned Running Machine. Running's important especial if you want to get somewhere and fast, like the phone box outside the Taylors'. I is fast, even in my jarmas. I always has to go cos Pip's tonsils get too big and he can't talk to the telephone. I wait out the front for the police and the amblance. Bare feets is best for running but I has to be careful in the Masai Mara grass cos there might be lions or broke glass. Mum says she int taking me to the hospital gain, next time I can bleed to death.

Pip bashes his face in the pillow, makes noises like a washing machine. That's how he gets to sleep, down a bumpy road. Sometimes bashes til his nose bleeds. We don't have to wash our sheets no more. Pip got a good idea and now we sleep on newspapers, stead. He goes to the shop and gets the yesterdays. One time he done my bed with newspaper sheets what was pink. Sometimes we get words on us. Still we has to wash our jarmas; Mum says "you wet them you wash them," which is right I think. We does them in the bath. Pip gets his arms right in the cold but I help him to wring them out and pass pegs for the washing line. Our sleeves get wet and stinky, in the wintertime they go crunchy. Sheba's in a curl on the end of Pip's bed, tending to be sleeping but she int. One ear is always watching me. I don't think Sheba is her real name cos when you call her she don't come. Her hair gets everywhere. Pip rolls it into sausages, stops cold coming in around the winders. And she don't like Pedigree Chum, Chappie is what she eats, which is good cos it don't cost much. Piss drips on the lino underneath Pip's bed and then I know he's faster-kip. Sheba waves her tail when I get out of bed. The wardrobe door squeaks like an agony and then the long mirror gets the light. Lucky we got a giraffe outside, looks in the winder shining oringe. Next giraffe int til Merrylands. I get the fat pen and careful nice does my face. When everything is black I wake Pip up. I squashes his lips up like a kiss, tells him "Say television." Good cos always wakes him up.

"Telli-wison," he says cos I squashes his lips.

He opens his eyes. Sees how I is.

"You're going to be in big trouble again, Lulu," he whispers.

Then he gets out of bed and picks me up, even though I is too big and carries me shush past Mum's bedroom. Bryce snoring sounds like growling. We close the bathroom door and Pip gets soap on a stinky flannel, rubs it hard on my chin.

"Big big trouble." It int coming off.

In our room I show him the pen.

"That's permanent ink," he says.

"What's perm-nant?"

"Means it won't come off."

"Not like charcoal?" I says.

"No."

"Not like poster paint?"

"No."

"Not like shoe polish?"

While we was in the bathroom Sheba pooped on the rug. Pip tries to get it up with newspaper but it's squishy and stinks so bad he gets hick-sick. Makes me go hick-sick. Even Sheba goes hick-sick. But nothing don't come up. We all breathe hard by the winder and try not to do hick-sicks.

"Hhuck!"

Terrible. Pip rolls the rug up and drops it out of our winder on to the porch. But it comes unrolled and hangs down over the front door. The porch int safe, bits of concrete keep dropping off it, the posts wobble stead of holding it up. I climb out. I is a feather. Pip holds my wrist, case, and I kick the rug off. Then Pip goes down the stairs and takes the rug over the road, dumps it with our old fridge. It's lucky to live this side of the state, with the trees and the Humps for playing in. It is a Leafy Lane and they named it good and proper. But we int allowed in the generator, sides it's got high walls and barbed wire with Sheba's hair on. Pip goes around the back of it case the Sandwich Man has chucked his packed lunch. Sometimes sandwiches is paste, sometimes cheese. Sometimes we get an apple or crips. Pip coming back shakes his head. It's too early for the Sandwich Man.

Now Sheba thinks we moved the rug for dancing, does creamy swirls chasing her tail. Pip sees me gain. Big big trouble. He goes under the drawers where he keeps his matches and bits of ciggi from Mum's ash-trays. Sometimes he has a whole new one. Calms his nerves. Mum don't know how come she got such a gibbering wreck. He lights one up. I sit up sides him on the windersill. We watch the milk float come and stop at the Baldwins' house. Pip arst the milkman for a job but he int old enough, not til he's fourteen, still got two more years to wait. The Baldwins only get one pint, now that James is dead. They got him the car for his birth-day, eighteen, red Mini with a ribbon around it. That's how come he drove to Portsmouth and jumped off the top of a big tall car park. No one knows how come it was Portsmouth. The milkman steps over the wall with the pint and walks on the big corner grass. Mr. Baldwin's grass int for walking on. Then the milkman drives long and stops on the corner of Merrylands, it don't go no where like a cold-sack. Smithers get six pints cos they live in the first house and there is loads of them.

Pip looks at me gain, I wishes I had brown curly hair, mine int no good. Auntie Fi says it's fine but Mum says it's a piece of piss. Don't know what color, they keep trying to work it out. On Saturday Pip's going to Powys, in France, to be with his dad what's different from mine and not as filthy dirty. Never seen Pip's dad, he arst for Pip in a letter. Mum arst Pip what he wanted to do. He must have give the proper answer cos now he's going with good riddance and a made bed to lie in. One time Mum said I should arst Father Christmas for a daddy, that's how come I got Bryce, I int arst for nothing else since cos now my name is King. Auntie Fi cheers

Mum up, says someone called King got shot. Mum says we can hope like it's only men what gets it, but I move fast, case, and keep my head down.

Auntie Fi int a real auntie, Mum found her crying on the steps of the DHSS. Now she's married to Uncle Ike, he's only got one leg and cos it hurts he's a helium addict and drives his car into chemists. Mum goes to all Auntie Fi's weddings.

"Will your new sisters be as good as me?" I arsts Pip.

"No," he says. Then he gets the big fat trouble pen and colors in the bits I missed. He turns my face to see the giraffe.

"Zulu-Lulu." He shakes his head. "Why don't you talk properly, Lulu?"

Can't tell. Secrit.

"I'm going away on Saturday."

I looks at Pip.

"Is it a secret?" he says.

I nods. He waits long time. He looks sorry, looks like he's going on Saturday, looks like my secrit should be a present, looks like he int my brother no more, looks like he's going back to bed.

"I wants to be *especial*," I says.

Surprises me. He stands up on the chair, gets a box off the top of the wardrobe. In the box is a string of conkers and he comes and ties them around my neck.

"Seven conkers," he says, "*cos* that's how old you *is*."

"Going into care," I grims at him. "Mum promised, if I done it gain."

"I think you've done it," he says, "this time."

He puts another conker, drilled and ready, in my hand.

"That's for when you're eight," he says.

Act One

He's always there in the dark, on the other side of the door to sleep. It's not the frenzy, not his hands trying to drag me from the foxhole, from the long narrow pipe; it's not the endless pursuit dream or the little girl dead in the storm-sewer nightmare. It's got nothing to do with physical pain or with the end of the will to live. It's the taste of the fly agaric, the sound of it screaming when I picked it.

The fog hasn't lifted. Daylight has a dark green tinge sapping the color from everything. It's my birthday, I've got seventeen pence. The heating pipes from a boiler in the basement bang and rattle. I pay the housing association a compulsory six pounds a week for the sound of central heating but no actual warmth. I have to get out of the apartment. I have to. Tim, at the pottery, lent me an anorak; I put it on and flip-flop down the stairs, meet Techno on the landing below, coming out of his front door with a dead rat on a platter.

"Dinner," he says.

"I'd want it cooked," I say.

I look to see if his ears are bleeding. Mine are, fucking bastard. I go into the park next door and sit on a bench. I sit and sit. I'm Louise Alder. I'm thirty-one today. I sit and sit. Voices come through the noise in my head.

"Will you please state your full names?"

"Kim Hunter. Beverley Woods. Jackie Birch. Dawn Redwood. Catherine Clark."

"You have at one time or another used all of those names?"

"Yes."

"Remind us. How old are you, Kim?"

"I was twenty-one in September."

"You have come into the police station of your own accord this evening?"

"Yes."

I sit and sit in the park. A kid is hurling sticks up at the horse-chestnut tree. Stick hits stick, like rattling bones. Rattling cold.

"Have you got a habit, Kim?" DI Wilson says. "Something that you've not told us about? Do you need to see a doctor?"

"About that blanket?" Mr. Book says.

"Can we turn this fan off?" DI Wilson wonders out loud.

I sit and sit in the park.

"Shall we get it over with?" DI Wilson says. "Are you OK to continue?"

Resume.

"Was it your gun?"

"No."

"Where is the gun now?"

"I threw it off the Suspension Bridge."

"When you pulled the trigger did you know what you were doing?"

"Yes."

"You intended to kill?"

"Yes, the person I was aiming at."

"Why did you want to kill the person you were aiming at?"

"I'm not prepared to say."

"You shot Quentin Sumner by mistake?"

"Yes."

"You were aiming at someone else?"

"Yes."

I sit and sit in the park. The horse-chestnut tree looks unreal, in this fog and green light, like a pantomime prop. One limb spreads wider than the others. Perfect for a noose. Perfect drop.

"Nice day for it," a man says, walking his hyena past.

Every day we begin again. I go back to the apartment and unpick stitches with frozen teeth and fingers, cut and pin together a patchwork of velvet from charity-shop dresses. The floor cushion is half made when the lamp dies, the sewing-machine needle stops mid-seam as my meter runs out of electric. My giro didn't come. I sit down and light the camping stove, it's running low on gas. A blue light starts casting around the apartment. Something has happened in the pub, an ambulance is in the street. I didn't hear any screaming, usually I hear the screaming. I sit down; imagine that I can see my bones in X-ray over the stove's blue flame. Out of the corner of my eye I see the woman in the mirror, flitting backward and forward to the window, like Madam fucking Butterfly.

"Sit. Down," I say to her.

A car door slams.

She doesn't listen. Techno music drones through the floor. Peter hasn't forgotten her birthday; he's never known when it is. There's a heavy knock on the door. The woman in the mirror goes.

"You want number 24," I hear her say.

I should write to Irene and give her my new address. I light a candle to see. My life—in a shoebox; I empty the contents on to the floor. I don't own a photograph. With the apartment comes evidence that I exist: I must be real, I've got a tenancy agreement and the first lot of paid bills. I feel my ear for the butterfly, get just the smooth lobe. I've got a folded one-pound note. I've got Irene's letters; beautiful handmade papers with flower petals pressed in them, tore a corner off one once and ate it. Her letters came from Scotland first, then America, Australia and Japan. I sniff at the bundle of letters, don't know if the perfume is still there but the idea of it fills me up.

I don't know why Irene kept on. She didn't believe the verdict when none of the jurors had a doubt. At first I didn't trust the kindness in the letters; she always asked for a visiting order but I thought she might attack me. Eventually I came to wish that she would attack me and requested a visiting order for her. But then, after all those years, when she came I was concussed, in the hospital wing. Women hunt in packs, like wild dogs, there was something not right about me being there.

A warden took me in a wheelchair. I'd always imagined wire mesh and glass screens, but the visiting suite was a big hall, with spaced out tables.

My mind caught on a thread of scent; it was clean, intensifying, glorious. I knew it. I closed my eyes, went chasing after fluttering names through scented fields of memory.

"She's not all that coherent," somebody said.

I looked across the table; saw a posy of spring flowers that formed into a face.

"Lily of the Valley," I said.

It made me cry.

"Visitor, sit back down, please," the warden ordered. "Sit back down."

"No." A pink lady with a lacy collar was kneeling down holding my hands.

"Let go, please," they ordered. "Let go."

"No."

"Let go." It had a final tone.

"No," she said. "I will not let go."

They lifted Irene up and away, her legs pedaled in mid-air.

"Put me down," I heard her say. But she must have ducked back under their arms because I saw her little forget-me-not eyes. I looked down; saw my palm and her wrist pressed swirling against mine.

"Yardley," she called. "Lily *of the Va-lley*!"

It was faint, from a long, long time ago. But it was sweet and it lingered.

It lingered.

Dear Irene, I think she imagines what she wants to see. She must be seventy now, more, seventy-five. She had Quentin really late in life. A shaman is working with him now.

"If that's Grandad tell him to fuck off."

That's how come when we got the phone in I had to answer it. It was always Auntie Fi, or Uncle Ike looking for Auntie Fi. The one time it was Grandad I wasn't ready. He said, "Is that little Lulu?" I said, "Yes." He said, "Is that the African Queen of the Mountains of the Moon?" Don't know how come I started crying. *Grandad, Grandad,* Mum said, in my voice cept smaller. There was only one word for it: *Path-e-tic* and *Dis-loy-al.* After we looked them up in the dictionary Mum wrote *Judas* with her finger in the steamed-up back-room winder. I climbed up on a chair to write it underneath. Especial lesson, case I forget, and it don't matter how long it takes, she does me with words til I drop. And she still int talking to them.

"Just ring the doorbell and wait on the doorstep."

The hospital shaved a lump of her hair off, stitches looks like done by a learner.

"What if they don't know who I is?"

She can't hear me cos the car's Big N's start knocking. She's going to a battered house what's halfway to Chiswick, case the baby comes. I close the car door and go up the path and presses the bell. I wave to Mum as she pulls way but she int looking. Then the car backfires a cloud of black smoke and stops dead where it is. I see the light go on in the hall and the shape of Nanny and Grandad through the bobboldy glass. Nanny's got giant boobies. When she hugs me the whole world goes deaf. Grandad squeezes me so hard I int got breath, has to hold on to the wall in the hall til I come back into view.

"Where's your mum, pet?" Grandad says.

I point to Mum's car smoking outside Mr. and Mrs. Pennywells'. The lorry coming out of Nestles factory honks at Mum. Lorries always honk at Mum.

"Bastards," she says.

Grandad holds my hand cos of the traffic. Nanny walks side to side; she needs a hand behind her for going forward. We go long the pavement to where Mum's under the bonnet. I wait for her to say f-off. She don't say nothing. Airplane goes over and we all has to duck cos they uses Grandad's chimney for finding the runway. Car int starting.

"Have you any oil in it?" Grandad says.

"I can't tell, Dad, there isn't a dipstick," Mum says.

Nanny's voice goes up and down like a siren.

"Bill, wiilll this do, Biiiiiillllllll?" She's waving a snapped-off branch of privet.

"Nay, Roose," Grandad says. Nanny's name is Rose, that's how come there's a rosebush in the middle of the concrete garden, cept Grandad says it Newcastle. Mum gets back in the car, next thing it goes bang and she roars off down the road in a cloud of black smoke.

"Head gaskit," I says.

I'm having poor man's oysters with Grandad. First you cut the white off the fried egg. Then you get the yellow balanced on your knife and tip it in your mouth, you has to let it slide down your throat. Mine falls off the knife and drops splat on the plate, me and Grandad got some on us and Nanny's dress hanging on the back of the door.

"Oh Biiiiiiiiiillllllll. Biiiiiiiiiilllllllllllll."

Mum says Nanny was an opera singer once but now she's a steric.

"Roose," Grandad says, "we can get the dress cleaned."

Nanny does her crying in the front winder so the Pennywells can see she int happy.

"Sorry, Nanny," I says.

She dries her eyes on the curtains. I got egg on my eyelashes; Grandad says I got the touch of Juncty-Vitis; African Voodoo Doctor gives people eye infections when they don't look at things proper.

After we cleaned everything up Grandad goes in the sideboard.

"We've been saving your presents for you, pet." He puts them on the table all wrapped up in Christmas paper. I arsts him if I has to wait til Christmas.

"Nay, pet, these are from last Christmas and the one before."

I open the big heavy one first. Africa it says. I turn the pages over, looks at the land and the animals in big shiny colors, and then comes the tribe peoples. On page 156 there I is, *got red cloth, spear and everything*. One time I seen a Masai on Grandad's television.

"Grandad," I says, "when the new baby comes, spects I can carry him on my back."

I show him the African lady on page 205.

"Is Mummy having a baby, pet?" Grandad says.

"Uh-huh. I arst Jesus for another brother, now Pip's gone, don't know if I'll get one, Grandad."

"Isn't Philip at home with Bryce?"

"Pip's gone."

"Where, pet, where has Philip gone to?"

"France. A new baby is coming."

"Champion," Grandad says. He looks sad about Pip.

"Oh Biiiiiiillllll," Nanny says.

So busy with my Africa book I forget to open the other presents. We save them til tomorrow. When I go to the toilet there is some newspapers there, so I tear some up and pack it in my pants. I know that Grandad pisses a lot, down the drain and up the wall, don't know if he's thought of using newspapers. The box room at the front int friendly, case an airplane comes in, so I sleep on a camp bed long side Nan and Grandad. They pile up so many coats on me I'm like a jumble sale.

"Did you ever hear the story about Hiawatha?" Grandad says.

"No," I says. "Is Hiawatha in Africa?"

"Yes," he says. Tells me how things is with that little African girl. In my Africa book he finds me where Hiawatha lives. There's rainbows and Living Stones and Victorian water falls off the edge of the world. Hiawatha is brave, wonders if she does handstands on the edge.

When I hear Nanny and Grandad snoring loud like hogs chewing, I creep out on the landing with my book. In the box room there's junk and might be mice and lights from Nestles lorries come in. Auntie Valerie's bedroom is locked. One time I arst Mum where Auntie Valerie was.

"Same place as your father," she said. Normal she does me with words, but slaps is better cos over quicker. I int never to say "Auntie Valerie" gain. In the bathroom I read the pictures in my book. *I need a shield, more clay and beads. Patterns is what I need.* When I hear the milkman out the front, I go back to bed and put my legs down in the arms of coats.

In the morning I get in bed with Nanny and Grandad. I does a run and jump to get up. We has tea from the Teasmade and wait for it to cool down fore we put the milk powder in. They does the crosswords and I sit tween them with my book. When they get dressed I rummages in the box room, finds a moldy handbag with raffle tickets and a pearl necklace. I make the pearls double and put them on with my conkers. In the kitchen I sit on the draining board and help Grandad shave, case he misses a bit. The razor blade int sharp so we has to put a new one in. Conkers is like my eyes, Grandad says, and pearls is like my teefs.

"Has you got any string, Grandad?"

"Why-eye, pet."

"Eight conkers is too tight."

In the back room downstairs I find an instant shoe shiner with a dabber on the end. I get to work. It dries nice on my legs. I has to do three coats on my face and keep my teefs smiling so it don't crack. Then I polishes me up with a pair of tights. I int got my red cloth, weren't time, so I has to do it with a tablecloth. Good cos done me a spear with cardboard and a bamboo cane. I take them by surprise in the front room.

"Oh Biiiiiilllllll, Biiiiiiiiillllll." Nanny hides behind the curtain.

"Make way, make way," Grandad says. "For an African queen."

He bows down but his back gets stuck and I has to lend him my spear to lean on.

"I int a queen, I'm a warrior," I says. I has to get the book to show him.

"Ooga mooga wonga donga," Grandad says.

"Wonga jonga longa," I says. Teefs clacking cos cold.

"You come, we go jungle," Grandad says.

We run down the hall and through the kitchen and down the garden path into the greenhouse. It int green, it's blue. It int cold, it's all steamy and jungle grows like heaven.

"Remember the seeds you and Philip sowed when you were here last?" Grandad arsts.

I nod even though I forgot.

"This is them," he says, smiling up.

They climb all cross the roof. He lifts a little pot down from the shelf.

"See this one here," he says. "I grew it specially for you, pet."

The leaves is tiny, it looks all trembly like a bird what is caught.

"What's it called?" I arsts.

He writes it for me on the newspaper and I write it on the stick with big fat perm-nant ink. *Sensitive Plant.* I kisses it gentle and it curls all up. That's how come it protects itself, mustn't kiss them more than once cos they get wore out. All long one side is plants what I done called Coleus, they got patterns, red and pink and yellow, minds me of paisley and Auntie Fi. Nanny comes like a weeble down the path; she gets scared at all the cracks.

"Bill, Biiiiiiillllll, it's Bryce on the telephone, wants to know where Joan is. Oh Biiiiiilllll."

I looks up, wonders who Joan is. Surprises me, my mum's name is Joan. Mum says her name is Vivienne but it int, it's Joan.

"Bryce wants to speak to Luuuu-luuuu."

I feel sick. I stop smiling and my African face cracks.

"Did you want to speak to Bryce, pet?" Grandad arsts.

I reckon he int phoned for nothing.

"Best had," I says. Don't know if my mum is dead. Grandad puts his coat on me. In the hall cold blows under the front door. I take the phone, it's cold.

"Hello."

"Hello, it's Daddy," Bryce says. "Do you know where Mummy is?"

I int forgot my lesson.

"No," I says.

"Do you want to come home?"

I don't know what the proper answer is. I go from feets to feets. Nanny and Grandad is watching me, standing in the front-room doorway.

"Sheba misses you. You can come home and go to school."

"Can't," I says. "I got tonsillitis."

"You had your tonsils taken out when you were five."

"I still got tonsillitis."

"I can come with Sheba and fetch you, would you like that?"

Even if I wants to talk, can't, tonsils is too big.

"We could go in the car and visit Philip."

Don't know how come I starts crying. I put the phone down and swallow my tonsils.

"Cold," I says.

Int sure if I done a disloyalty. Nanny's in the curtains crying.

"Wicked," she says.

Don't know if she means me.

"Roose," Grandad says, "best we have a cup of Special African Warrior Tea."

"I . . ." She's all sniffling. "I don't think we've got any, Biiiiiiiilllllll."

"Well, FIND some, Roose," Grandad says.

I sit at the table on my cushions with Grandad. Warrior Tea turns out black with four sugars. The phone rings sudden and we all slops our Warrior Tea. Grandad goes, closes the door behind him. When Grandad comes back in the room his face is red, with blue worms under his skin. Looks like his tonsils is up. He sits down next to me but he can't pick up his cup cos his hands is shaking and his knee goes knocking like a Big N under the table. Nanny's sitting in the corner; her rocking chair keeps bashing gainst the wall and her knitting needles is clacking.

"Roose," Grandad says, "you haven't got any wool attached."

She starts gain. Then I see she int crying but laughing stead. Her big boobies bounce up and down, false teefs drop down and she pushes them back up with her tongue. Then her face goes like Coleus and she starts to cry. Grandad and me holds our heads. He turns the telly on. It takes up nearly all the table. Horse racing is on; he finds the list of the horses in the paper.

"Pick one out, pet," he says.

I read the list, pick a name can say.

"Open See Same."

"Open Sesame," Grandad says.

When the race is on I watches the oringe hat with the yellow star on it. It comes from the back and wins easy. Grandad tears a piece of white bread and squashes it with his finger and thumb. The bread turns back to dough, gray with sweat and finger skin as he learns me what an outsider is.

Turns out I'm good at horses. I sit on the crossbar of Grandad's bike and we go to Ladbrokes. After we made our bets we ride long side the Grand Union Canal and talks to boat people and gypsies and fishermen. Big horse with hairy feets has got its head over the fence, int scared cos I kisses its nose. Girl comes long with steps to brush it, lets me give it one of her carrots.

"What's it called?" I arsts.

"Grand Union Hayes," she says.

I reckon it's a good name.

In Cranford Park the trees is sleeping but we see a cedar from Lebanon; Grandad wishes I could see it one time beautiful with snow. Monkey-puzzle tree always puzzles me cos it int got no monkeys. Hemlock is the beautifulist, feathery ferny conifer, terrible poisonous, Grandad says, same as yew. When we passes elderberry we has to tip our hat, case the old lady of the trees curses us something bad. We get leaves in a plastic bag for looking up after dinner, then I names and presses them and keeps them in my scrapbook. Grandad reckons we found a rare one, *Metasequoia glyptostroboides*. On the bridge by Hayes railway station we get cockles and winkles with our winnings. Trees in Nestles Avenue is just

London plain; rains and airplanes come racing over our heads. Then I see it's Bryce's car, parked outside the Pennywells'.

The bread factory is on a trading estate in Rose Green. No roses. No green. The new bloke at the jobcenter has arranged the interview for me; he's drawn me a map on four sheets of paper taped together. It's taken me an hour to walk here and half an hour walking around the outside of the factory looking for a way in. I hate the wind, the crashing and bashing. Now I'm late, chewing on split ends. I check the jobcenter paperwork for the name, and then ask at reception for Brian.

Brian's office is suspended, apparently on nothing, up above the factory floor. There's a heavenly flight of lightly floured steps; nobody has been up before me, there's a resting platform at the halfway stage. Each wooden step has a bounce; they're not quite deep enough for a forward-facing foot. Brian follows me up, through the layers of heat and noise and yeast, through the clouds of flour that my flip-flops produce.

"Sorry, Brian," I say.

The factory looks like a scene from James Bond: vast chrome tunnels, steaming pipes, hundreds of little people in pajama bottoms and white wellington boots. Brian leans against the door frame for a minute, fanning himself with paperwork. It isn't natural to sweat pus. Finally he sits down behind the desk.

"So." He drags a dry tongue around the crust of flour on his lips. "What we need Ashley, is someone for doughnuts."

"Louise," I say, "Louise Alder?"

"Are you sure?" He tilts his head to keep another festering sweat from rolling down into his eyes. It is seriously hot. He hands me a blue application form with a flour footprint on it.

"Don't fuss over pages 2 and 3. We need someone for twilight shifts—6 p.m. til two in the morning, five shifts a week, four pounds an hour, can't say fairer than that."

I must have nodded some kind of continued interest.

"You do right by us, Ashley, and we'll do right by you; back in a minute." He disappears through a door that I thought was a bookshelf; nothing on it, except a can of lighter fluid and a Thompson's Directory.

The pen doesn't work. His desk-tidy is full of betting-shop biros and flaky pastry. The pegboard on the wall spells out that more people are *Out* than *In.* He reappears, closing the bookshelf behind him.

"Now listen, is there any chance that you could do a few hours right now? Being as you're here, just til lunchtime, Ashley."

"Louise," I say.

"Right you are," he says. "Why don't you do a few hours and see how you get on, then you'll know if you want the job or not? You'll be paid for it of course."

The supervisor, Elspeth, is waiting for me at the bottom of the stairs. I stop on the halfway platform and wedge my flip-flops on tighter.

The changing room is vast, bleak. Whoever painted the concrete floor only did it the once, with a small brush and not enough paint; at the base of every locker it has worn smooth away; the women have made tracks, into the toilet cubicles and out again, to the door and back. I sit down on a bench in a slat of light coming in through a broken vent. Elspeth has given me a pair of white wellington boots, size eights, they've run out of sixes and sevens. I wrangle with the *over-apron* for about fifteen minutes; it has all the devices of a straitjacket. *Jesus*, I say into the back of the stupid hat, but the word spreads along the lockers, travels the room like a Mexican wave. *Jesus!*

"The veil goes at the back," Elspeth says.

I follow Elspeth to the hand-scrubbing bay, along a path worn in the concrete. We wade through a tray of disinfecting fluid, turn corners in the machinery maze. There's a wall of doughnuts in shallow crates stacked by the machine. It has two sharp protruding nozzles, a foot pedal.

"Take a doughnut in each hand," Elspeth shows me. "Push them on to the nozzles, and then press the foot pedal to inject the jam."

I stand in her place. Something behind me crashes, I see the flying twin arcs of jam arrive in each of my wellies.

"You should aim to get the doughnuts on before you press the pedal; that is the skill of this particular job," Elspeth says.

In the vicarage car park by the bins, there's a box, a record player, good old thing with a valve. It's got a plug; the wiring is disconnected at the arm. I wonder if it is fixable, if Tim at the pottery has got a soldering iron. I was out before the post this morning so I check my postbox on the way in. There is a primrose letter from my solicitor. Once upon a time the letters were palest gray, the aqua years were OK, the change to pink was a mistake. This latest "primrose" is cheery at least.

My compensation claim is doomed, again.

I take the record player upstairs. The clock says ten to five; I might just catch my solicitor.

The phone is ringing in the phone box. I open the door and answer it. A woman wants a taxi to Clifton Village.

"Try in half an hour," I say.

I make my call. His secretary answers.

"Can I speak to Mr. Mac, please?" I say.

She knows who I am.

"Can you hold a moment?"

"I've been holding for a decade."

The letter says Legal Aid has withdrawn its support. My compensation claim rests on the consistency of mud, a substance my solicitor has never encountered and cannot fathom. To help him understand how clay soil could stick to a rubber boot, I had to mock-up a clay-laden wellington and take it into his office in a black plastic bag. We've been debating this mud for so long he's got fifteen addresses for me including HM Prison, Holloway.

"He'll call you back, Beverley," the secretary says.

I sit up on the vicarage stone wall. The pub landlord sorts out a bottle delivery, he's got smasher written all over him. The phone rings.

"It's risky," Mr. Mac says. "They're prepared to go to court; proving liability is the difficulty." He has a basketball hoop in his office, I can hear the ball scuffing against the wall and bouncing back. Assertiveness usually requires rehearsals and weeks of preparation but this has become a matter of principle.

"It was an accident in the workplace," I say, "and they are insured to cover accidents in the workplace." Bastards, they want me to give up. "Tell those fuckers I'll see them in court, put that fucking ball down, Mr. Mac, and phone them up now, tell them to bring their chequebook." I hang up. It's not me talking; I got it from some courtroom drama.

But I know what is fair and what is not. Fuck it. You'd think that nothing would faze me now, not in the scheme of things. My guts churn to liquid, they always know something I don't. Or I've lost my nerve. Finally lost my nerve. I crouch down in the phone box and sit on my heels, waiting for calm. When I open my eyes, through the phone-box glass I see the dark gray Audi Quattro, coming toward me up the hill. Read the nearside kicked-in wing and the number plate. It's Gwen's car. But is it Gwen? Of course it's Gwen. The car passes; Panda is laid on the rear shelf looking out. I'm surprised the dog is still alive after all these years. The phone rings and makes me flinch.

"Can I book a taxi to the airport?" a man says.

"No." I hang up.

Gwen stops the car just up the hill and reverses into a side street. I climb up on the vicarage wall. Can see a chink of the Audi paintwork parked. Through a gap in a privet hedge and a missing section of the wall I expect she can see the vicarage gateway. It didn't take her long to find me. A blade of rage cleaves up under my ribs.

But it isn't me she's waiting for, it isn't me she wants.

I wait out the front. Giraffe turns off and birds start up. Baby Grady's crying.

"What service, please?" the lady arst.

"Police, police," I said, "1-3-8 Leafy Lane."

"They're coming, Lulu," she said.

Then Bryce seen me, pulled the phone out the wall. He took off so fast the air still smells of skid marks. Mr. Baldwin's curtains is nervous. I spects the police has stopped at the garige cos Roger, normal, brings me chocolate. Uh-huh, it's Roger.

"Gone, has he?" he says. Gives me a Milky Bar from his pocket.

Never seen this other policeman, he must be practicing, cos he knocks his hat off coming in the back room and Sheba won't let him have it back. Mum calls the back room a den, but it int. People love the sofa cos it's got lion's paws. All its guts was hanging out, but me and Mum pushed them back in and done it posh with red velvit. We was lucky, got the bridesmaids' dresses at a jumble sale and Mum learned me how to unpick stitches. That's how come people stroke it and make patterns on it and Auntie Fi always cuddles the curtains. Our house is the London Palladium, even the banisters is gold.

"You OK Mrs. King? Need to go to the hospital?" Roger says.

They want to sit on the sofa but it's soggy with coffee and bits of broke cups. Stead they sit on the arms like riding horses. Radios keep calling Roger but he don't answer cos he's doing the forms. Other one pats the sofa. I put the table and chairs back up, dog-ends is everywhere with flied knives and forks and fish fingers and peas. Surprises me my dinner is still together on a plate. Sheba's squashed under the sofa, her face is guilty tween the big feets of policemen; she wants my mashed potato but her tongue int long enough. I lights Mum a ciggi on the gas stove cos she stays where she is, longsides the skirting. Don't know how come I take an ashtray. Mum's top lip is getting fatter and her toofs bleeding down her chin. I got her a cold flannel but she int used it yet. The one what's practicing looks at me.

"What's your name then?" he says.

Police makes my tonsils big.

"Lulu," I says.

His ear comes over and I has to say it gain.

"Lulu?" he says case it's a lie. "How old are you then, Lulu?"

"Nine," I says. "I got conkers to prove it."

Roger tells Mum they can't do nothing cos she is married to Bryce. Case they missed it, Mum crawls down the hall, shows them that the front door is smashed in good and proper.

"What chance have I got?" she says. Even though it was her what done it.

"It's a job for the courts, Mrs. King," Roger says.

But I reckon we needs to phone the council and arst them for a carpenter. Now the policemen look like Wombles, they both got Sheba's hair on. Roger says it's best that they take the axe way with them. Un-adulted bastards, Mum says when they go to their car. One time Auntie Fi was married to a policeman and that's how come she knows. Then I try to get the front door over the hole a bit and shout thank you to Roger cos he give me chocolate. Mum's face is dis-gust.

"*Thankyou,*" she says. "*Thankyou, Thankyou. Mr. Policeman*—you make me sick."

Her finger pokes me gainst the wall. Ouch.

"I'll tell you about policemen."

Ouch.

"They."

Ouch.

"Tell."

Ouch.

"Lies."

I try to make uh-huh but my tonsils is up bad.

"Do you think *Mr. Policeman* goes home and kisses his wife? *You don't know.*"

I needs the toilet.

"There's only one word for policemen, know what it is? Deceit-ful. Corr-upt."

She's chucking up loads of stuff looking for the dictionary, never can hear Baby Grady crying.

"It's by my bed," I says.

"Well, go and get it," she says. Upstairs I go to the toilet quick, bring Baby Grady and the dictionary down. I turn the sofa cushions over and he goes to sleep holding on to my finger. Mum reads me what corr-upt means, one of her eyes is closing up.

"Uh-huh."

"Know what POWER is?" she says.

While I has my lesson I get fish fingers and peas up with the dustpan and brush. In the kitchen I make cups of tea. Mum don't eat when she's talking and her face is smashed. Sheba done my dinner when the police was going. Uh-huh. Mum can't see me in the kitchen eating what bits I can from the dustpan.

"You don't fool me, you behave all *timid* and *don't know* but I know your scheming plans. Yes, you. You're the worst kind of enemy. I know your treachery."

She walks about, nodding like it's true. One of her eyes has swelled up closed, swelled up terrible.

"You humiliate me, you embarrass me, your mission in life is to destroy me but you won't defeat me, not you, not Bryce, not those fuckers in uniform. Social workers and dis-loyal daughters are the worst enemies of all."

"Uh-huh."

Kids is going to school, sees them through the front door, still smashed and hanging off. Coldness is making frost on the inside of the back winders, cept now I int got nothing for chopping sticks with and the Rayburn don't light just with paper. Lucky one of the chairs is broke to bits. Uh-huh. I get the fire going.

"Dr. Shaw. Do you think Dr. Shaw is a nice man? Don't know much, do you, I'll tell you what Dr. Shaw is, Dr. Shaw is a pedophile. Know what a pedophile is?"

Some warm is coming now from the fire cos *treachery* has started melting and running down the winder.

"P-E-D," Mum says.

"Uh-huh." I look down the dictionary pages but all the words is black and swarming.

Warm int a good idea. Mum sees I'm falling sleep, I int allowed to sleep during lessons.

"Stand up," she says.

I know the spot cos carpet is wore out. Sheba gets up and stands sides me, she always thinks she done it.

"Let's see how smart you are. What do you think Bryce does in Holland?"

"Pipes," I says.

"What Bryce does in Holland is a Dutch woman called Henrietta. Where do you think the food money is going?"

My face does thinking.

"The money is going on a Dutch slut with a name like a chicken."

Outside it goes dark. My knees keep dipping like I've got a hoop. Uh-huh, my feets is on hot coal. Words come in and out like ghosts. Uh-huh. The room starts spinning around and around, looking for the way out. Normal lessons stop when I drop but my legs int giving up. I wishes they would but they won't. Mum has to find worster words to kick behind my knees and drop me down on the carpet crying. Uh-huh. Milkman comes gain.

"You think you're so smart but I'm the adult. I sacrificed everything for you and Philip. Know what a sacrifice is? You owe me. You owe me everything. It's called a debt. Know what a debt is? It's in the dictionary."

"I'll pay you back," I says, "when I'm growed up."

"Will you? The truth is—if it took your whole life you wouldn't ever be able to pay me back. I was in the Royal Ballet for Christ's sake, my name was in lights at the Royal Opera House."

Lucky, just when bells start ringing and I is total deaf and blind, Mum runs out of Embassy and I has to go to the shop.

Sunshine stabs my eyes and the pavement puddles is icy. I sleeps walking on the way to the shop. I get the Embassy and a jar of food for Baby

Grady but there int enough for bread or Chappie. When I get in Mum has gone to bed. Sheba is so tired, fast sleep snoring, tending to be a rug. Wishes I could sleep but can't cos now Baby Grady is wake, spects I has been up three days.

"Oo-Lu!" he says.

I grabs him fore he falls off the sofa. Then phone the council, arsts for repairs.

"Is the lock also broken?"

"Uh-huh," I says.

"Who has done this damage?"

"Don't know," I says.

Mum int done the nappies. Baby Grady's all like a stinky puppy. I does him with a tea towel, stead.

"Hhuck!" Makes me hick-sick. "Hhuck!" Terrible, has to flap my hands, tend there int no poop in the world. I get the twin-tub out for the nappies. No soap powder so I has to use washing-up liquid. Baby Grady loves bubbles. His top teefs int coming but he's got four good ones long the bottom. He grabs my necklace cos the conkers is shiny and smooth.

"Oo-Lu!" He slaps on his own leg. "Oo-Lu!" Good joke.

His chops is chubby, that's how come I keep on kissing them. Someone is knocking on the front winder. I think it's the council come quick to fix the door but it int. It's Mr. Baldwin from next door, minds me of a stick-insect. He's got a shovel, with a poop on it.

"It was on my grass," he says. "I believe you are responsible for it."

"I int pooped on your grass, Mr. Baldwin," I says.

We look at the poop on the shovel. It is Chappie-colored, must mit.

"Sheba probably done it," I says, "cos we got loads out the back the same."

"Can you call her in so that she doesn't do it again?" He's all airy-ated.

Sheba is over the road, sniffing around the giraffe. I call her but she don't even look. She runs down the middle of the lane, lucky int much car our end. Her tail goes down the ditch and under the wire and off cross the Masai Mara.

"Sorry, Mr. Baldwin," I says.

"I'll leave it here for your mother." He tries to leave the poop on our silly grass but it won't come off the shovel.

Has to look the other way.

"Shouldn't you be at school?" Mr. Baldwin says.

"Hhuck!" I says. "Got Hhuck! Tonsillitis."

Mum's bedroom winder goes open sudden. She always talks so posh, sounds like a music box.

"It's got nothing to do with you, you dreary gray old cunt. Now fuck off."

Mr. Baldwin goes home like a red cross. Mum shuts the winder, goes back to sleep.

I hang the nappies on the line, then tie Baby Grady on my back and take him over the Humps. One time machines come to make a school. They put a high fence around the field and dug terrible deep holes for all the posts. All the dirt from doing the posts they tipped in the middle, humpty-hump. But then the school weren't allowed and that's how come the Humps is here, under all the wild. The wire fence has all gone. Smithers got it for they's chickens, Tinker patched his hedges with it and we got some for the back garden, keeps Sheba out of Mr. Baldwin's. The metal fence posts is still up though, like spears in the bushes under the trees, I magines they got me surrounded.

Kids make camps tween the Humps, somes got branches and turf, somes got bits of tin and plastic. The Jackal has got a mattress in his, can see through a crack in his door. It int proper to go in someone's camp, cept people does. That's how come I got my cave on Big Grin rock, where no one can get. Wishes I could go there now, but can't with Baby Grady, it int proper safe for a baby. I walk up and down the Humps, swinging one arm.

"Trumpetty–Trump–Trump–Trump." I is a tired elephant.

Baby Grady laughs. I ties him tighter on my back. Then I spies the Sandwich Man coming cross Tinker's fields. All the horses stop eating to watch him. Late today. He lives around the back from us but he don't park his car outside his house or anywhere near. I seen him, he parks it in Millbrook Close and then he gets the bus one stop. I spects he works at night cos he always comes home in the morning. Pip seen him one night in camouflage clothes. He had a gun and especial goggles for seeing in the dark, told Pip he was going to shoot some rats. Me and Grady stalks him stead.

He takes his shoes and socks off at the river, goes in the water with his trousers rolled up. Icy cold makes him gasp. I know how cold it is cos I always wash my clay off in it. He bends over, like looking for something in the river stones. Fishing sticklebacks with his hands. Wonders if to tell him under the bridge is best. Too cold, he sits on the crocodile's nose and puts his shoes and socks back on. I spects him to go around over the bridge but he don't, he swings over the river on the rope. He likes it so much he goes back over and does it gain. Puffing in the cold air. He runs up and down the Humps, tends he's an airplane. Gone behind the generator. He don't never eat what's in his lunch box, he chucks it all, then he steps out on to Leafy Lane and goes around home. Spam sandwich and a banana, me and Grady has it.

I make a nest for Baby Grady in the scraggy grass and climb up in the old oak tree. I walk out long a level branch, oak tree int never going to drop you. Baby Grady, he's good at laughing. His hands clap together with citement. I hang upside down on a branch and make monkey noises for him.

"Oo-oo-oo," I says.

"Oo-oo-oo." His lips is a kiss and his arms try flying.

I disappear, lay thin long a branch. Shush. He don't know where I is.

"Oo-oo?" he says, testing.

His eyes float up like big bubbles with windows in. Sometimes they is gray, sometimes blue. Sometimes they is see-through. I wonders how Baby Grady would be like, if I never come down. I could easy sleep wrapped around with one leg dangling. My eyes is tired like the *Jungle Book* snake, swirling same as "*Trust in Me.*"

The doughnut job is much the same as all the other jobs I've had: stupid footwear; stupid hat; the people don't have faces, only the clock. The factory noise is loud enough to distort thoughts, loud enough to prevent chat. The workbenches are too low; I have to splay my legs like a drinking giraffe. My feet swell up to fill the size eights; the flour and sugar content in the air has already split my fingers and lips. The heat in here is somehow chilling, with the loading bays opening and closing. I get a rhythm going, cruise into full speed, try to think of the eight-hour shift as a moving thing under my feet, if I slow down I might fall off it. Eight hours, who am I kidding? Ten. Fourteen. *No one goes home til the doughnuts are done.*

After seventeen minutes an icing bride comes marching over from the pink volcanoes. She's furious.

"You slow down." She waves her palette knife in my face. "You're mucking up our piecework rate."

My mind goes back years to Mr. Smith, enraged, shaking and shouting: "NO BODY! NO BODY! NO BODY WILL EVER LOVE YOU!" It takes me back down a cobbled high street. Don't know where they are, the girls, Hope and Faith and Charity. I'm on my own with Mrs. Smith; we go into the jeweller's on the corner. The bell tings on the door as Mrs. Smith closes it.

"I remember," the lady says. "It is done! Mr. Johnson!" She calls out the back. "It's the girl for the earring!"

"The girl with the diamond," he says.

"It's beautiful, Catherine," Mrs. Smith says.

The corners of the tiny box dig deep in my palm. In my fist. We walk further along the cobbled high street and turn left down a narrow alley. Smell the hairdressing salon so strong. Ladies are sitting reading magazines with hairdryer helmets on their heads. No appointment necessary. At the back of the salon I sit in a chair and Mrs. Smith sits by me. The girl chews gum, snaps on white rubber gloves.

"Now," she says, "Sonia tells me that you only want one. Is that right?"

"Left," I says.

"Unusual, you, aren't you unusual? I said to Sonia how unusual you are."

She gets a special pen and dots my earlobe, holds a mirror up for me to see if I like where the dot is.

"Yes?" Mrs. Smith says.

"Yes," I says.

"Yes!" the girl says.

I start to cry, I don't know why.

I wipe a tear away; get doughnut sugar in my eye. The icing brides are off up the machinery aisle. Elspeth is over my shoulder.

"Finish that tray," she says. "Then come for your break."

In the canteen there's a line for the drinks machine. I'm not in it; I'm twenty-three pence short of the thirty pence required. The tables and chairs are all occupied. A seat has been saved for me, the icing brides wave me over. I sit down at the end of the table. The nominated question asker coughs.

"So, Ashley, are you married?"

"No," I say. "I guess I'm just lucky."

"Just lucky," one woman says.

"Any kids?"

I brace myself; try to support the weight of all the things I haven't got.

"Boyfriend?"

That's that then. They think I'm aloof. Next break I stand outside, carved up by sheets of wind coming through the fire escape. A loof: not quite man, not quite woman. Not quite back scrubber. My lighter runs out of fuel before I can light the cigarette that I picked up off the pavement on the way here. I throw them both down, disgusted. In the changing room I slurp water from the tap using my hands as a cup.

Something has gone wrong on the bread-baking conveyor belt. The bread is coming out of the ovens quicker than the man on the end can catch it, though he's been trying for six hours. He's down to his vest, has the meat colors and the pumping veins of a body that's been turned inside out. Loaves of bread which he's dropped or missed get kicked aside or return to dough under his feet. Usually there are two people offloading. I see Elspeth coming for me. I'm to help Bart with the ovens. He can't look away from the bread conveyor long enough to say hello or give me instructions. We stand side by side, facing the front line of a hot wholemeal army. Every forty-five seconds, when the oven flap opens, Bart and I bow down to each other so that the heat doesn't punch us in the face.

Eight hours? Ten hours and forty-six minutes. I walk outside into the blinding headlights half alive. Men come, husbands, to collect the women. They've sat and waited. I get a lungful of exhaust fumes and fall into the flow of let's-get-home. I've got a violent shiver trapped inside me. My every fibre is cross-wired. I'd like to faint. But I can't. Someone mistakes my anguish for a smile.

"All right." They cut across me.

I need something to eat, that's all it is. I need to sleep. That's all it is. I'll get something to eat on Thursday; it's only two more days. I'm shattered, that's what it is, can't sleep in the apartment, keep thinking I've got something on me. I work hard at walking, these shoes are crippling; that's why I'm so skint: I bought the shoes from a charity shop; toilet rolls and bleach; a light bulb for the landing; I paid my water rates. I bash into a chain-link fence and bounce back on track. Someone in a car has stopped. Maureen's face unrolls in the window, I think it's Maureen. She gestures me a lift. Fueled with gratefulness I run around to open the door and get in the passenger seat. She drives like someone who has never done it before.

"Where are you going to?" she says.

"Montpelier."

"Oh dear! What a shame!" She stops the car, seems really disappointed. "We'd be all right going but I'd have to drive back through St. Paul's on my own, my husband wouldn't be happy about it. I'm sorry, Ashley, I really am."

Not as sorry as I am, Maureen.

"That's OK," I say, "I understand—thanks for stopping all the same."

I try to be kind; it's my only chance at beauty.

Curb crawlers light up the backstreet route. When I don't look up they drive off, replaced immediately by another. Go home, man with baby seats. It's too late and cold for the really bad bastards, there's insufficient prey on the streets. I step out of the shoes, leave them striding out on the pavement. At the hill before the vicarage I wake up and wise up passing the park.

The pub landlord has long since finished chucking the empty bottles in the tall metal bins but the last smasher is still ringing out. Taxi work below the window has dried up; the driver is sleeping on the backseat like a child. Techno underneath is still going strong with his pair of sub-bass woofers. No, it's the idea of a van door slamming in the car park that wakes me up. The intercom blasts a tune, I know it's him. I know. I feel my way to the door like a diver with the bends. I live and die and hear him coming up the stairs.

"There you are," I say casually.

He doesn't duck under the door frame and stride in to inspect the place; he takes my hand and pulls me out on to the landing. I'm not dressed, my door is wide open.

"Door, Pete," I say. "Keys. Trousers."

He has my hand; I trip along behind him down the stairs. Techno's door is wedged open; his music is so loud and thick on the stairs; it's painful to breathe, to swallow.

Outside is warmer than in, balmy and perfectly still. The mammoth van is abandoned on the diagonal, blue-white in the security lighting. Pete has no inclination for parking. We stop; he lets go of my hand. I look to him for instructions. He points to the van with his eyes. I look; it's still dirty and falling to bits. The engine gives the tick of cooling metal and drip-drip-drips oil on to the gravel. I look to Pete for another clue. I follow his gaze to the metalwork of the door wing mirror. Something is on the wing mirror. A bat, hung like a parachutist up in a tree. It's dead, I'm sure, with its head at an obscene angle.

"Listen." Pete cocks his ear close to it.

I don't know what he takes, to make his eyes this wide, to fix this open-mouthed wonderment. I bend with my hands on my knees and strain my ear at the bat. I hear my pulse; synapses snapping, nerve fibres crackling with static; a bird in the park is singing its heart out, pausing now and then, ever-hopeful of an answer. I squint at the moss-green pixels in Pete's eyes, search for some kind of picture. His hair is dripping wet and his face is dribbled with sweat, he would have me believe that the bat is singing, conducting it with his little finger. From the bat I hear nothing but out on the street the payphone is ringing; the taxi man—I hear him yawning, "*Half an hour.*" Up the hill Panda starts yapping at some four-o'clock-in-the-morning person, passing Gwen's car.

Pete sketches a spooky laugh in the air. I think it's a laugh reserved for me.

"Come on, Amazonia," he says. He turns, goes back in the main entrance and takes the stairs ahead of me, four at a time, disappears around the turnings. On the wrong landing he ducks under Techno's door frame, strides into Techno's lounge.

"All right, mate?" I hear Pete say. "I've just popped in to turn this down—don't get up."

In my apartment, the quiet is breathtaking. I make coffee, without milk and sugar, handy because I don't have either, while he checks out the airing cupboard and the bathroom cabinet. His shoe leather explores the painted landscape in each of the rooms.

"I didn't know you were an artist," he says.

I pretend I can't hear him; my voice would give me away. I make him coffee in the bone-china cup and saucer that we stole, years ago, from the Swallow Hotel. I thought coffee was doubtful. It was half past four in the morning, Pete was in his market clothes, looked like he'd slept in his van for days. I was tragic, barefoot and fresh from treachery. The van was still shuddering long after he turned it off. Sure enough, the ferocious little doorman strode out from under the awning and opened Pete's door for him.

"Hello, Mr. Eden, sir," he said.

We had coffee in the drawing room, sat on identical sofas at opposite ends of the room. Then we went to Ashton Court woods. I remember the scene with the blue flowers, birch-leaf shadows draped like lace on Pete's bare shoulder. Even now, waiting for the kettle to boil, it tips my head back against the wall. Villeroy and Bosch. He found the china cup and saucer a few months ago; they'd been under the passenger seat of the van, rattling for twelve years.

Now for the first time he's in my place, arranged on the cushions like Valentino dragged through a wet hedge. The cup rattles on the saucer, amplified by silence. The lounge goes on forever. He chews on a matchstick and stares at the rattle; it rattles all the way to the floor beside him. I strike a match to light the candles; my hand rattles left and right of the wick, needs my other hand to steady it. I sit in the shade of a painted thorn tree and try to roll a cigarette, it's tobacco butt end and tea-leaf mix, a trick I learned in prison. His voice is pitter-patter.

"I like the apartment; I like how you've done it."

"What—like an empty stage with a few symbolic props?"

He sketches that laugh again and skids his packet of Silk Cut over. I take out one cigarette and crumble it into the mix. His eyes flit between the illusions of the room. He gazes into the candle flames licking the wet shine on the painted floor; I hadn't wanted the high-gloss finish but beggars can't be choosers, as it is six candles become twelve and then twenty-four in the mirror, multiplied again in the open polished window glass. Lamplight puddles, here and there and there. His eyes cast off across a painted promising sky. Double windows, double trees, double me.

"Was the mirror already here?" he says.

Can't raise the spit for licking the cigarette paper.

"No," I say.

I think about Pete's van and the struggle I had with the huge mirror. It took me six hours to move it half a mile, from the skip where I found it leaning. The trees are breathing in and out. He lets out smoke on a sigh.

"Sanctuary." He lies back like a great tree brought down in a storm.

I blow across the floor to the record player. The needle rips across the grooves; eventually I get it on the start of the title song. Edith Piaf stirs "Exodus" up, thick in the vast empty room. I don't know where Pete goes. I see a woman in the mirror watching him, watching me.

Mirror, mirror against the wall, who is the fairest of them all?

Pete is aptly named, dark and earthy, unnervingly handsome, as winter woodland is, as an oak tree in a plowed field is. I still try to kiss him. I like to see him turn his face away.

"Exodus" plays. I don't know where Pete goes. When the song ends he looks for me in the illusions of the room, finds me distant in the mirror glass. Waves me over. I crawl all the way to him. He has no interest in my breasts or body, has never undone my shirt. Ours is a skinless thing about joints and limbs, my long light bones. My legs: he goes about them like something treasured, a pair of heirloom rifles, puts my feet against his shoulders, checks the pair are straight, blows dust from off my shin bones, polishes my calves, smooths and views them from different angles and cocks them at the knee. He ponders the scar on my right calf like a shame, a careless dent reducing my value. I'd be touched—if he wasn't stroking the hypersensitive fray of severed nerves. He smooths a little air where a toe once was.

"Stand up and walk toward the mirror and back," he says.

His arm has me do it half a dozen times; I feel silly. His eyes bid me continue; I do my best one foot in front of the other. He lies on his stomach to see my legs coming and going.

"Put the kettle on," he says.

In the kitchen I lean on the cold wall, turn around to face it, close my eyes and rub my temple against it. He plays my nerves like harp strings, the tension fit to sing or snap. We know how easily and how happily we could kill each other. Air just isn't working. I put my head down between my knees; feel like a plane coming in to crash. In the kitchen he stops me falling, pins me up like a wall hanging. My legs keep dipping like I've got a hoop. I'm spinning. I'm spinning out.

"I don't know whether to fuck you or call you an ambulance," he says.

"Call me an ambulance," I gasp.

"You're an ambulance," he says. Takes me down, drapes me over the work surface. Pete had a vasectomy. For all his presence I can't feel him, I can't feel his hands. Listen, the kettle clicks off. Listen, Pete's trouser zip. Listen, in the cupboard under me. Pellet poison, rattling, in little silver-foil dishes.

On the cushions in the lounge, Pete drinks his coffee. I put my foot across, try to snuggle it on his ankle. He moves his foot away, chews lazily on a matchstick.

"You ruin it when you do that," he says lightly.

Dawn light starts to show the apartment for what it really is. Brush-strokes. The sparrow lands on the branch closest to the window. Does its morning stretches, one leg then the other, seems to roll its shoulders back, opens one wing then the other. It chirrups and lets out a plaintive song. Waits for a reply.

"Are you happier here? Better than with those nutcase women?"

No reply comes. It chirrups. I wonder what the sparrow is saying to itself.

"I went around there to see you," Pete says. "A few weeks ago; Tin-tin forgot to give me your note."

"Was it four in the morning?" says the woman in the mirror.

"A mad old woman spun me around on the doorstep. 'Well, fancy that,' she said, 'we all thought she made you up, but she's gone now, gone.' "

"Gone," I say.

Pete's car keys jingle-jangle and he stands up.

"Put that song back on," he says, "so I can hear it as I'm driving down the road."

Pete goes.

I stay where I am. I sit and sit. There's five coats of paint on the dominant wall but the word *Cunt* still shows through. Panda starts yapping up the hill, at school children passing the car. *Enough now.* I sit and sit. I'm back at Park Lane. The lounge is upstairs at the front of the house. I go up and open the door. Gwen is on her hands and knees, the two kneeling either side of her head have divided her hair between them and flick her back and shoulders with it, like horses' tails. Her tongue is frantic, licking the air between them; in turn she swallows their cocks whole, spewing them back up again. Someone is suckling underneath. Heath behind her bangs away, looking up at the light fitting, at the jagged edge of a broken bulb, hanging there. Her face is twisted and ugly; she laughs and throws back her head. "We're teaching Quentin how to do it, adequately," she says. I see him then, fully dressed, curled up in the wing chair. Tears are streaming down his face. I step back and close the door.

Cars keep honking cos Mum's got shorts on and all her hair pours down like custard. I bashes my head on the sump.

"Bastard." Mum bashes her head on the bonnet.

"Stuck," I says. "I needs the hammer."

Mum passes it down through the engine. My fingers is good at fiddly. Water pumps is easier on a Hillman Imp, this Sunbeam Rapier int no good, Bryce got it especial for Mum so we run out of gas and can't get no where. I hold the spanner on the stuck bolt and bash it. Slips. Ouch. Terrible. Lucky cos knuckles does grow back. I get the water pump off, crawl out to fit the new gaskit. Baby Grady's eating daisies on the grass edge, we don't mow it; council does.

Good thing is Auntie Fi turns up. I see her feets; even though she's giant size her shoes is tall and pink. Mum hugs around Auntie Fi's legs. Uncle Ike is on his crutches, got his trouser leg tucked up in his belt. I crawl out from under the car. Auntie Fi's glasses is like a joke, but they int. Mum says Auntie Fi is always happy cos she don't know the seriousness of the situation. Long as she's married to someone. She gets Uncle Ike's leg from off the backseat and throws it over her shoulder. It's got a different shoe on from what Uncle Ike is wearing. She always brings Mum flowers cos Auntie Fi does flower ranging. They loves each other, it works good cos Mum talks and Auntie Fi cooks us dinner. Afterward they does the Beverley Sisters and see how long it is fore Mr. Baldwin bashes on the wall. Good job Bryce has gone back to Holland. Auntie Fi don't come when Bryce is home, cos Mum gets mouthy with Auntie Fi behind her and we has to go to the hospital.

"Lulu," Auntie Fi says, "you're the oiliest person I've ever seen."

I never knew she brung me flowers.

"Gladioli," I says. "Thank you, Auntie Fi."

Uncle Ike is on the grass with Baby Grady, eating daisies like delicious. I try not to look where his leg int. I put my flowers by his nose for smelling but he takes one, eats it.

"Mmmm," he says. "My favorite."

Don't know how come, Uncle Ike always goes in the front room, lays down under the piana. In the back room I waits ages to arst, Mum don't breathe when she's talking. I make questions small so they fits in.

"Out?" I says.

She's got Auntie Fi, she don't need me. Her arm says—yes! Sheba wants to come but I has to shut her in the alley, case she gives me way. I get under the wire and I'm wild in the Masai Mara, long grass int stinging cos I is an impala, my feets don't even touch the ground. I could run all day if had to, never knew no one so quick as me. Where the cows get water, I get my clay. Then I climb the fence by the sign.

M25 LONDON ORBITAL MOTORWAY
DANGER—KEEP OUT
ROCKFALL, FLOODING AND LANDSLIDES

I got a rope down from the back of the post, buried in the tall grass. Big Grin int easy. Rocks is bad shapes done in granite, dirts crumbly and stones run way. I has to be steady. Blood gets drumming. Fingers and toes knows this cliff, I squashes my face on the rocks. I is a leopard, I lets go and leaps the gap. When last I get on this big smiling rock, I shake my spear and roars at the gods. Surprises me how lucky I is. The Great Rift Valley is down below and Big Grin Rock int going nowhere. I crawl into my cave, got everything nice and dry in a box, checks still there, my Africa book, scrapbook, I-Spy books. I put the red cloth on, ties a knot on one shoulder. Straight way drumming gets louder. Clay's red and squishy and spreads on easy. I rubs it in my hair, ties it up like sausages in knots. My spear is long and straight but it int proper sharp, cos Jimmy Jackal Smithers got my penknife. Int proper. It int. The dirty Jackal said he'd tell bout Africa and everything. One day, when I get my penknife back, I spects I can kill him with it. Int proper, Pip give it me. Pearls go on with conkers, then beads done with acorns. I know when I'm ready cos I stand on the edge, int scared, int scared. I got a rope for the worstist bit, then down and down I skids, once it's started the drumming can't stop, like Africa here I come.

Wildebeest has all gone home. Elephants is fast sleep. I run through lakes and flamingos swirl up, they minds me of *Carousel*. I'm clouds of dust. Sand, I kicks it up. When I'm running I is sure and fine-tuned, so shush as a Rolls-Royce. Only sound is the drumming bashing and the warrior song what I got. I sees where a hyena has been and that's how come I track it.

Come so far, can't see Big Grin smiling no more. Don't know where Africa ends. Wonders if it goes by Grandad's cos airplanes is low going over. I has to be in fore dark, fore the lions stretch they's claws. I stalk around some hippos in the Okavango Delta. Racing long the ridge I is a pack of wild dogs. Listens—hyenas laughing in the car park, behind the Portakabins. I is the wind in the Mara grasses. The sun don't want to go in. I slip over the edge and back down to Big Grin Rock.

In my cave, the animal herds done with chalk seems like moving over the rock. They kicks up dust in my eyes but it's just a trick. Clouds is small and by them selfs, going fast like film cross the sun. One time went to Saturday morning pictures with Grandad. Me and Pip. I seen everything. Pip arst for a job as an ush-rette but they said come back in eight years. I look in my Africa book. Uh-huh, even on the page, the Bushmen's animals looks like walking. *Mig-ration.* Wildebeests has all got knees up, don't know how many knees up, I done mine the same. I turns the pages looking at Africa patterns, zigzags, swirls. Best is little lines, going long, sides by sides. The sun is like another planet, red. Razor blade is golden oringe. I is brave. Still I bites three conkers in half.

Mum got contempt of court and I has to go to school. Tonsillitis int working no more even though they still is big. Mum says they won't teach me nothing, she learns me what's important, sides we int no good at mornings cos Mum does talking til the milkman and I stay up and does listening. Now Pip's gone I has to do it every night, fore we done it taking turns, long as someone looks like listening. Stories is always the same about London Palladium and olden days. One time Mum was Al Jolson for the King, even though she was little and her arm was broke. *How I love ya, how I love ya, my dear old mummy.*

When Mum was Cinderella in rags, her tights got stuck on the safety curtain, that's how come she went up with it and done the song from on the ceiling. Tiny ponies pulled the pumpkin coach, good, cept they pooped all over the stage. Mum done dancing with Prince Charming and got loads under her dress. Twelve o'clock came at ten past. Other Cinderella come on when Mum weren't off yet. Lew Grade said, "You're all fired." After that comes Madam Butterfly, weren't no fun, Mum had to sing "One Fine Day" and stop keep mucking around. I is a good audience. I always know what the next line is and claps in all the proper places.

Pip's like a little boy in a story, gets his head stuck in the balcony bars. Mum always sings the song she sang while they was waiting for the firemen. *Watch for the mail, I'll never fail, if you don't get a letter, then you know I'm in jail.* Don't member that apartment, with balcony bars. I spects we has moved so many times we int sure where we is anymore. Stories go on and on in a circle, there int no place for stopping or starting. My dad int never in them. I like the one about Auntie Fi's baby girl. She was born the week after me but Auntie Fi gave her up for adaption. I wonders what her name is, case she goes to my school. My tonsils is up bad.

Mum learned me how to iron my school shirts. I stayed wake especial but then I fell sleep. Normal Grady yells at eight o'clock cept today he oversleeped and Mum don't get up til the sun is around the front. That's how come I'm late and school is in Addlestone. I don't go the long way around, Lowry Road and School Lane; I is a cheetah, cross the Mara. I races clouds in the Great Rift Valley. Stop to put my shoes and socks on fore the gate, looks like there int nobody here cept for teachers' cars. The school gate sounds so loud as late. Magines can still hear Baby Grady crying. Wonders if eyes is watching cos my feets can't work these shoes. The floor in the corridor is so slippy like a mistake with kids. Can't stand up. Big lady comes out of the office, makes me jump. I hang on to her trousers to stop from going over.

"Why are you here—who sent you?" she says.

"Magistrates," I says.

"Speak up, girl, don't make me come down. Who sent you?"

She's got a ginger hair growing from the wart on her chin.

"Magistrates," I says.

Grunt brings her ear down and that's got ginger hair as well. Hairy ears, like a pig.

"Magi-strates," I says.

That's how come she brung me to Miss Straight's class and her hair's in a doughnut. I sit down where she points me, in the middle. Kids look like trouble.

"Do up your top button and tie, " Miss Straight says and all her words is by them selfs.

I try to do the button.

"Stand up," she says. "Do up your shirt and your tie."

Chair falls back. My fingers is tied up, I got one stuck in the buttonhole.

"Can't," I says, "my conkers is too big underneath."

Miss Straight's ear comes around the tables.

"Conkers is too big underneath," I says. "Can't do up my shirt and tie."

"Take them off." She walks way.

I undoes my tie and put it on the desk. I take my shirt off and fold it up. Here I is all conkers and teef. Eyes go over my patterns like a blind man's fingers.

"The *conkers*—take off the *conkers*," Miss Straight says.

I is boiling water. The bell goes like a mergency.

"Stay where you are," Miss Straight says.

Kids go past me like Uncle Ike's leg. Never knew Jimmy the Jackal was here. He nods like he knows me. I put my shirt back on. Miss Straight comes over, looks for the knot in my conkers. She's got scissors in her desk drawer. When she cuts the string the conkers drop off and bounce, all cross the floor. She helps me to pick them up.

"Should be ten." I count them and put them in my bag.

Playtime, I tie my shoelaces together and make a longer necklace hangs down inside my shirt cept now my shoes is more useless. Teacher in the corridor arsts me where the laces is.

"Gone," I says.

"Gone?" he says.

It's a mystery and I has to go to lost property, case they got some shoelaces.

I go for dinner but my name int on the list. Only person missing is called King. I member that's who I is, but the dinner lady don't believe me. After no dinner we got PE, cept I int got a PE kit, lucky I know where lost property is. We play rounders, girl with a head like a box throws to me, I'm backstop, I catch and throw it. Girl on first base looks like Auntie Fi cos of basin haircut, I throw low, case I break her glasses. When it's my turn for batting, I hit the ball out. Surprises me. Ball comes back in Sheba's mouth, and she won't drop it, stead she gets five rounders. Miss Parker tries to grab her but she's left holding hair. Even when Sheba drops the ball, no one wants to pick it up. I tends I don't know her but then she comes and sits on my feets. When I'm upstairs having history, I see Sheba playing netball. Wonders how things is with Baby Grady. Zebras is chasing a rabbit on the football pitch, vultures is waiting, case, high up on the rugby posts. Mr. Brownlow talks like history is all a terrible shame. Lucky Mum learned me how to sleep with my mouth and my eyes wide open. Class ends like waking up.

Mum's singing Kismet, so beautiful sound in the alley hurts my heart. I leans gainst the wall to listen. Now Pip's gone she has to play the piana and sing. Piana takes all the front room but I int allowed to touch it. One time Pip said Mum was scared case I turned out good at something. I open the back door and listens for Baby Grady but he int crying. I run upstairs, he int in bed but Sheba is. I spects he's in the front room under the piana. While Mum's a Stranger in Paradise, I go in the kitchen and has five slices of bread and jam, stomach thinks my throats been cut. I make Mum a cup of tea and waits for her to sing my favorite. Uh-huh. I love this song cos it hovers and swoops, high as birds and glass bells . . . *So that–someday–he may–buy me a ring–ring-a-linga–I've heard–that's where it leads–wearing baubles, bangles and beads* . . . I wait til the last bird has flied so high that it can't be seen any more, then push the door. Baby Grady is under the piana, eating the rubber off his slippers. He's pleased to see me cos his hands is chubby and claps together. I puts kisses in his dimples, once I started can't stop, never knew nothing so soft. Now Mum is Calamity Jane, she sits up on the piana top, tends it's the whip-crack-way wagon. I sit on the windersill; look at the beech trees over the road.

Mr. Baldwin told Pip one time that the beech trees is two hundred years old. I reckon up there you can see the Mara and all of Africa. Keep trying but can't get up. There int no branches lower down, just bushes in the way and fence posts. Yesterday I got stuck. The Sandwich Man from around the back came past, trousers was wet from the river gain. He seen me there halfway, hanging on a hole like a woodpecker.

"Having trouble getting down?" he arst.

"No," I said, "got trouble getting up."

After "Secret Love" I claps and then arsts to go out. Mum don't answer. She lights a cigarette, smoke all come out one nostil.

"So," she says, "did they teach you anything?"

I int sure what the proper answer is. I get off the windersill and then back on it. My fingers is cat's cradle. I look for the answer in the beech trees. Mum's tapping her lighter, waiting, lucky Baby Grady chokes on a bit of rubber off his slipper. By the time we has brung him back to life, Mum's forgot what she arst me. And now she's doing *The Jarma Game*.

I see Jimmy Smithers in the Humps; he comes cross the road trotting like the Jackal he is. I spects him to go past home but he don't. He comes to where our gate used to be, looks like he's coming in. The winders is open, I try to tell him with my eyes that I int coming out but he knocks on the door like a bay leaf. Then I members. He seen my patterns at school. My tonsils swallow me whole. Mum wraps her dressing gown around tighter and leans out the winder.

"Is she coming out?" says the Jackal.

He int never come around fore.

"No," Mum says. "She's busy."

"Oh." He rolls a stone under his feets. "Is she coming out later?"

"No," Mum says.

Jackal always looks like the sun is shining in his eyes, hands in his pockets makes his trousers half down.

"Is she coming out tomorrow?"

"I haven't decided yet," Mum says.

"I'll come back tomorrow see if you decided," he says.

"Will you?" Mum turns in to me. "Your little boyfriend is ballsy," she says.

I folds outside in. Mum shuts the winder cos shows must go on.

"Coffee for the road!" Tim says.

I finish packing away the last of the clay, the jars of slip and glaze, and wash the brushes at the sink. Twenty-five people made a terrible mess. Brilliant terrible mess, days like today make it worthwhile. The group from the hospital really enjoy it, pleasant chatter: news of people not present, plans already on going home at Christmas; Radio 4 reassuring in the background, people coming in and out of the conversation, in and out of the tea room, in and out on their medication. It's better since we pushed all of the tables together, we can see each other. Some people can't get on with shaping the raw clay, they prefer to paint. I always make a selection of pots and bowls and plates for them to decorate. We've got amazing colors now. A couple of weeks ago we had a stall at Redland fête, sold off loads of abandoned items. We spent the proceeds on a drum of white porcelain clay and beautiful powder colors. The two are mixed together with water to make this clay-based paint called slip. Twenty-seven colors now, red and black was driving us mad. The illustrated seed catalogue I bought from a charity shop is proving really useful too for flower colors and petal shapes. Today they painted green Christmas roses, sunflower splashes, purple pansies with black eyes, blue campanula bells, pink tulip cups, double delphinium rosettes, raspberry dots and seed pods. A wave of tiredness goes over my head. I've got three hours more to kill before I have to go to work. I dry my hands. We've done it. The workshop is shipshape. Loads to do tomorrow though. Coffee for the road.

I sit down in the tea room with Tim; he's still cobalt blue like a genie from a bottle. He dropped a paper sack of blue slip—the powder exploded like a bomb in his face. The patients from the hospital loved it. Terrible mess but good stuff, everyone was well engaged and inspired. We are becoming victims of our own success, can't really cope with such large groups but days like today make us proud, working together as we do. Tim chuckles, shakes his head.

"Bloomin heck, I'd still have been here clearing up at nine o'clock. Are you working at the factory tonight?"

"Start at seven."

"Bloomin heck," he says. "It can't be right. I need you here, paid and full-time, the people need you here. I told them again at the meeting last night."

He keeps asking and means well, but if there was an official paid job, it wouldn't be me that got it.

"I'm not qualified, Tim, not with clay or mental health."

"No one would know," he says. "I mean, look at me."

I look at him. He is a blue genie. Loves his job, his beautiful schizophrenic wife and pregnant schoolgirl daughter.

"So what did King Cuckoo say?"

"No money." Tim shakes his head. "And there you are putting bloomin jam in bloomin doughnuts."

"There I *was* putting jam in doughnuts."

"Where, why, what?"

"I shouldn't have done it, Tim. I was supposed to finish at two last night; it was quarter to five in the morning. The thing is: they said I might be asked to do an extra hour occasionally, but it's not occasionally, it's two or three hours every night. I've already done fourteen extra hours this week. I'm going home, I said."

Tim likes the way I tell them.

"'*That's it—you just think of yourself*,' the Blue Icing Bride spat in my face. '*I'm sorry, Elspeth, but someone's got to tell her, I don't know who Ashley thinks she is.*'"

"Who's Ashley?" Tim says.

"Search me. I'll come in for my shift tomorrow, I said, I'll work eight hours according to my contract. I'll do an extra hour occasionally, but now, I said, I'm going home."

"Well, if that's what your contract says," Tim agrees.

"'*No one's allowed to go!*'" Elspeth was screaming at the back of my head as I parked the white wellies in my locker. "I just walked out, Tim, past all the icing brides."

"Heart in your throat then tonight?" Tim says. "Icing brides."

"They were sharpening their palette knives, in the gaps between their teeth."

Stupid. Principle isn't going to pay the rent. Volunteering at the pottery isn't going to pay the rent. I notice the time.

"Fuck! The kiln, Tim!"

"The kiln!" He stands up and runs to reduce the temperature.

If I get sacked Unemployment and Housing Benefit won't pay me a penny for six weeks; they like to give you a massive financial slap as punishment for your courage or stupidity. I rummage about in my bag for a crumb of tobacco that I know doesn't exist. A primrose letter from my solicitor is still in my bag, didn't have time to open it this morning. Bastards. I rip the letter open and prepare to spit tacks. Re: your accident, in the previous decade. Phone urgently. Pain and suffering. Eight thousand pounds. I check the letterhead; it's definitely addressed to Beverley Woods.

"Eight thousand pounds will put some electric on your meter," Tim says.

It will. It will pay the rent if I get fired at the doughnut factory. That's not the point. Eight thousand pounds isn't meant for paying rent. I want to smile but it slides away from me. Tim hands me a sheet of kitchen roll.

"It's just a shock, that's all, Tim," I say. "Now that they've backed down, on principle I feel like telling them to shove it."

"You can fix your apartment up now," he says. "Get a carpet; get a fridge, a cooker—washing machine."

"A machine gun to shoot the neighbors."

I read the letter again. Phone urgently, to accept, says Mr. Mac.

Tree commotion wakes me up. There's a lorry with a container outside my window, outside everybody's window. It's Heath; he's trying to park the lorry on the pavement, tight against the vicarage wall, tangling with trees. The taxi man doesn't know whether to guard his car or the telephone box, but he needn't worry, Heath is good at parking lorries. The hydraulic handbrake hisses. Heath climbs out of the cab and stands up on the vicarage wall. I open the window.

"Come in, number 9," I call.

He climbs from the vicarage wall on to a fixed ladder, then up on to the roof of the lorry's blue container. He's got something to show me. He does a handstand on the edge. A one-hand handstand. Balanced upside down on the one bowed arm, he is perfectly still. I can feel the stress, the tension, in my diaphragm, in my eardrums, in one particular heart valve. *Breathe.* The sycamore tree is shedding its helicopter seeds. He's still upside down. He doesn't know how lucky he is. Gwen has been watching the apartment for nearly two months but she doesn't do alternate Tuesdays, probably has to sign on in Wales or something. Heath is still upside down.

"Come in, number 6," I call.

He's such an arsehole, somersaults off the end of the lorry and lands on his feet. I hadn't seen that Sharon is with him, she appears with little Jennifer on her hip. Tarka, Heath's Alsatian dog, is barking bonkers in the road. I see the boy, Gavin, slip behind them into the pub, with a little bastard backward look. I know he's only nine years old but I wish they'd serve him a pint of Guinness and keep him in there. Heath goes in to get him.

I can hear them coming up the stairs and suddenly wish I was on the ninety-ninth floor. I open the door. The dog stands up like a bear to greet me.

"Tarka! Get down!" Heath yells. I skid through the hall, no traction on the slippery floor. The dog slams me against the lounge wall. I'd like to yell myself but it's got its tongue down my throat. Heath hauls it off me. Usually Heath is white as Basildon Bond but the upside-down stunt on the lorry has left him pink and puffing. Hasn't been training. All of their hot breath steams into my freezing lounge.

"I had to go to Windsor to pick up this container," he says. "Legoland was great."

"We thought we'd call in and see you for a change," Sharon says. "Don't touch that, Gavin. Gavin! Put it down!"

"I want the toilet, Mummy, the toilet, Mummy, the toilet, Mummy," Jennifer says.

"Gavin!" Sharon yells. "Mind the mirror!"

"What do you think of my new beauty?" Heath says.

He means the Scania, I gather.

"Well, it's a big apartment," Sharon says. "It'll be nice when you've done it. Gavin! I won't tell you again! Sit down on the sofa and don't you dare move."

"There isn't a sofa," Gavin says.

"He's got a point," Heath says.

"Sit down under the—tree," Sharon yells.

"Tarka!"

Tarka has gone in the bathroom, sounds like he's on to something behind the bath panel. He's clawing at it.

"Gavin! I won't tell you again."

"Nice cup of black unsweetened tea?" I say.

"I'm all right thanks," Sharon says.

"I've got some coffee in my cab. Shaz, go and get the coffee from the cab."

"Yeah, but babes, we're not staying that long."

"How was Legoland?" I ask.

Heath doesn't hear me because Gavin is trying to climb on his head. The emptiness of my apartment seems to recommend a bout of contact sport. Sharon joins in, throwing punches and her pigtails. The dog skids in, taking the paint off the floor with its claws and joins in.

"Bloody hell, babes," Sharon says. "That really hurt."

"You think that hurt, try this."

"Babes!" She clutches her dead arm.

It gets too painful for the dog, it skanks back to the bath panel.

"I could go and get the coffee," I suggest.

"Now that is a stonking idea," Heath says.

I take the Scania keys downstairs. My bare feet melt a sifting of frost on the pavement. The lock is smooth. I climb up in the new Scania and sit at the wheel. I sit and sit. The phone box starts ringing; the taxi man gets out of his car to answer it, and then takes off up the hill. Tim reckons it won't be long until everyone's got a mobile phone. Heath's black holdall is on the bunk bed behind the seats. Same stuff in the bag: white karate outfit; the black belts; his other jeans; green designer suit with zip pockets; worn-out *Lord of the Rings*. The gold-colored plastic canister is still in the bag. I shake it and listen, light bone fragments of Heath's dad rattle on the surface of the heavy ash. Remember the witch's house, every hair stands up. Think about the two boys, playing in the woods, the crossbow versus the gun. I find the jar of coffee at the bottom of the bag. Then loiter by the bins and breathe before going back in.

Jennifer is immune to the sport, sucking ferociously on a round lollipop. I skirt around the fight action in the lounge and pick her up, take her in the kitchen. She sits on my hip and helps me make coffee.

"I got sacked last night," I tell her. "Brian gave me my P45; *troublemaker* was the word he used."

Jennifer pulls the lolly out of her mouth. It pops.

"*Troublemaker.* Uh-huh. It made me laugh."

She doesn't believe me.

"That wasn't *trouble*, Brian, I said, it made me laugh so hard. Trouble. Unfair dismissal. Another thirteen-year fucking battle."

Jennifer looks worried.

"It's OK," I say. "Between you and me I've got some money coming. Eight thousand pounds. Are you having a coffee?"

"I'm three," she says.

"Babes!" Sharon says. "That does it, babes; you're too rough, you've really hurt him this time."

"He isn't hurt, are you, little man? Come on, little man? Gavin? Ouch! You little bastard, you'll pay for that."

We get the coffee made. Jennifer's hair is palest auburn; I could kiss her silky crown. I'm afraid to kiss her, in case I can't stop. She is so warm on my hip. I lean on the door frame, watch Heath in the middle of the lounge performing the Seven Swords. He can still lift his foot way up above his head, and hold it there; playing with air, with tall man's ears, with light bulbs. Memory sees his toes toying with light bulbs at Park Lane. He smashed bulbs all over the house, left us constantly in the dark.

"Mind the mirror, Gavin!" Sharon says.

He says he hasn't trained for years but he's still deadly. Even his penis goes in like a dagger.

"You all right?" Heath says. "There was an old lady that swallowed a fly. Hee-ha, catch me if you can, little boy, little boy."

Sharon takes a breather.

"You OK?" she says.

"Bit tickle stomached."

"Hee-ha, little boy, you'll have to do better than that," Heath says.

Gavin, flying through the air, lands a butterfly kick on his jaw. They're all sweating and panting now, snorting steam.

"Mind! Gavin! The mirror!" Sharon says.

"Come on, you lot," Heath says. "We'd better get going."

"I made coffee," I say.

"We'd better get going," Sharon says. "Long drive back to Manchester."

Tarka starts barking. Heath puts his jacket on. These days he wears a gold stud in his ear. Memory hears Gwen's voice, clear as an elocution lesson: *what is there to lose?* I close my eyes, hear the blast, and smell Quentin's blood, all over my hands, all over my lap.

"Last one to the truck's a woozy," Heath says.

They go. I sit. I look again at the letter from Mr. Mac. Eight thousand pounds. I look at the gaps in the kitchen; try to imagine a cooker, a fridge. I look in the bedroom; try to see a bed with pillows and quilts. A car door slams. The phone box starts ringing.

"Sit down," I say.

Techno's music drills through the floor, my bass backbone. I sit and sit. Hear voices through the noise in my head.

"Kim has been offered witness protection and has declined it. Is that true?"

"Yes."

"Why have you declined the offer of police protection?"

"I don't believe the police can or will protect me."

"Why should you take all of the blame?"

"I'll take the blame for my part."

"What was your part?"

I take Baby Grady to Africa. We has to go the long way around, cross the Mara and over Lowry Lane and down by the ridge and the slope, where the heavy plants go. Can't do warrior running; Baby Grady is too heavy. Stead he sits on a termite hill and I run circles around him, case lions get him. I give him two sticks and a hollow log cos he bashes good and makes drumming and he don't stop. Grady looks up in the sky, thinks drumming moves the clouds long. Dance goes backward and sideways, I jump high and run in and out, Grady loves the warrior dance cos my legs go on and on. One time a man came in a yellow elephant said Africa weren't safe for playing. Grady kept on drumming like the man and the elephant weren't even there.

"We *int* playing," I said.

The man still told us bugger off.

Can hear Mum screaming. Bryce is home. He's got a new car, white Ford Escort Estate. Don't know how come he's got a trailer and a racing car as well. Mum's over his shoulder, laughing so loud as couldn't care less. He tends to throw her on the sofa, out the winder, on the piana. Her legs is wild doing scissors. Sheba's barking, doing swirls on the carpet.

"Help!" Mum is upside down tween laughs. "Help me, Lulu!"

Bryce tends to run the bath and throw her in it. Then they go in the bedroom and slam the door. Baby Grady don't know it's joking, his face is on the edge of something. Roast potatoes is on fire.

I take Grady out to look at the racing car. The Sandwich Man steps out on to the road, been in the bushes under the beech trees. He's got a saw and a hammer, don't know how come, and a bag of nails. Mr. Baldwin is in his side garden guarding his greenhouse cos kids on the end triangle is playing football, got jumpers for posts. When the football bounces in the road, the Sandwich Man aims careful, kicks it. Surprises me he gets a goal and all the kids go wild.

"Mr. Draper! Mr. Draper!" kids is yelling. "Mr. Draper!" Both teams want the Sandwich Man to play for them. He puts his tools down, plays long enough for a goal both ends, then he waves and goes off home.

Indoors I get the table out full. It was down an alley in Chertsey, me and Mum brung it home on the bus cos it wouldn't fit in the car. Table legs is barley twist, we done it good as new with sandpaper and hogany varnish. I iron the white tablecloth and set the table nice with buttercups. We int got enough chairs left so I has the piana stool. When they come down Mum is dressed up being somebody else, got perfume and earrings on.

"Hey, son." Bryce lifts Baby Grady up so he can touch the ceiling.

Bryce makes him high and low, all up and down the hall. Spects I'm too big for flying. Grady flies around the lampshade, lucky cos he likes it. Then Bryce lays him down on the sofa, tickles him with his fat moustache til Baby Grady's squealing for mercy. I has to baste the potatoes.

When I look they has gone out the front, left the door wide open. Bryce's hat says Formula One, but the car on the trailer int. TR7, ugly car. He gets in it with Baby Grady on his lap.

"Brummmm, brum." Grady turns the steering wheel.

Mum's eyes is bluer than the sky and so is her silky princess dress. Her teefs is perfect when she smiles. All the kids come over to look at the TR7, 'cept Ellie Smithers. She's come over to look at Mum. Ellie's eyes is popped; one time she whispered wet in my ear and arst me if Mum was real. No, I said, she come off the top of a Christmas tree. I stand on the doorstep, has to keep going and checking the dinner. Ellie's got a new coat, two colors yellow with a frilly neck, she minds me of a daffodil. Spects if Mum said something Ellie would beam and fall over backward. Stead Mum steps up on the trailer, gets in the TR7 with Bryce and Baby Grady. Lady walks past in black trousers, they got big lumps of Sheba's hair on.

From Holland, Bryce has brung Southern Comfort and Embassy. Sheba don't like his brown leather jacket cos she growls at it on the sofa. And he's got a new belt what's so fat I spects the edges would cut. Good job Pip int here. For dinner we has chicken and it int even Christmas, Mum got up especial to cook it. We sit down at the table and start. Bryce has got bread sauce on his moustache.

"How's school?" he arsts.

Don't know what the right answer is. My fingers is churches and steeples, words is dried over words on the winders, buttercups is dropping petals, lucky cos Grady chokes on his stuffing.

Mum and me does the wishbone and I get to wish. I wishes for Big Grin after dinner.

"The fork should be in your left hand," Bryce says.

They talk about gas pipes in the North Sea cos Bryce does drawings for engineers and that's how come he works in Holland. He used to work for Bentalls, driving furniture, but Auntie Fi got a three-piece suite and Bryce got pretty larciny. Now he's doing North Sea Gas. Mum don't reckon the pipes will meet up, said she'd eat hay with a donkey.

"What's funny?" Bryce says.

"Baby Grady," I says.

We all looks at him, lucky his bib is over his face, got the mouth hole sucked right in like a ghost.

I washes up, dries up, cleans the cooker, wipes the cupboards, sweeps the floor, clears the table quick ready for when I arsts to go out.

"Get the Monopoly," Mum says.

I int going NO where.

"I'll be the banker—and the Car," Bryce says.

Pip's the Iron.

"I'll be the Boot," Mum says. "Whoever the shoe shall fit I'll marry the boot." She always does Cinderella wrong. Game is good til I get Mayfair and Bryce tips the board over. No one don't say nothing. Then Baby Grady laughs like a best joke ever and Sheba comes out from under the sofa, does swirls on money and hotels. I try to make polite.

"How long is you home for?" I arsts Bryce.

"How long *are* you home for," he says.

"She speaks badly on purpose," Mum says, "just to show me up."

"I'm amazed she gets to talk at all with you around," Bryce says.

I take Baby Grady up to bed quick cos Mum int going to leave it at that.

Downstairs words is swarming. I has to stay wake for school case I misses it, cos done the story what I promised Miss Connor. One time she read my story out in class, reckons I got a good way of putting things. I done her a new bit same, bout the Mountins of the Moon. I read it to Baby Grady and he went sleep. Downstairs things get louder and smash. Mum's screaming. I get out of bed and listen at the top of the stairs. It don't sound like joking. It int joking cos now she is screaming for me. I run downstairs and push the back-room door.

"Shut it! Shut it! Shut it!" Looks like rabies and his shirt is off, case he gets the blood all on it. He loosens his hands on her throat, to see if she's learned yet.

"Feel like a man, do y—" Her words get wrung out.

He turns to throw her on the floor. Never seen Sheba's teefs fore, not proper, nose is wrinkled and fangs is out, she's brave but scared and comes forward like to bite him. That's how come he kicks her. She goes up like a terrible pain and down the wall in the corner, lampshade comes down. Sound comes from her, int proper, int proper like her lungs is stabbed. She tries for standing up but only her front legs is working. She wants to get in the garden, I try to help her out but she growls like she don't know me.

"Shut your fucking mouth, fucking shut it, shut it!"

Mum smashes over the table and everything is crashing and screaming.

Sheba falls down the back step, drags long the path. Sound from her int proper, like her lungs is stabbed. Underneath the elderberry she tries to do a swirl but falls over like a person dying. I tell her sorry with my eyes, feels like what they done to Jesus. I hears glass smashing in the house, Mum screaming gain.

"Lulu! Lulu! Help! Help me!"

They roll around on the kitchen floor, fighting and biting and slipping on blood; don't know whose it is. Mum's hair is twisted like a long thick rope, that's how come he swings her around and bashes her head on the corner of the oven door. I get past them, does 999 but no one talks quick enough and Bryce pulls the phone out of the wall. Mum's eyes say Do Something Quick cos now her hair is around her neck and her face is purple, strangled to death. I jump on his back but he throws me off, like nothing. I smashes into the sink. Mum is half up on her feets but he still has got her hair, strangles her back down to the floor. I look quick for an idea, sees Sheba's lead on the back door. It's heavy, got leather and fat choke chain. I jump on Bryce's back gain, try to get the choke chain over his head but he easy throws me off cos there int nothing to hold on to. That's how come I stands back, and slams the chain down on his back.

He yelps up.

Bends backward.

Arms go out like on a cross.

Int no air cos it's all sucked in.

"She didn't mean it, Bryce," Mum says.

I stand still. Wonders how he'll kill me, if he'll do me like he done Sheba. He grabs me, drags me and carpet burns. Baby Grady fills my ears.

"No, Daddy! No, Daddy! No, Daddy! No, Daddy! No, Daddy! No."

The choke chain is done around my ankles and I'm hanging upside down from the banisters. Arms int long enough to reach the stairs. Nosebleed has dribbled down cos Bryce swung me gainst the wall; lucky my teefs still in. Baby Grady is looking through the stair gate. His face is snot and stripy with crying and his fingers is stuck as wet knots.

"Oo-oo-oo," I says. "Oo-oo-oo." Til gets a wonky smile come.

Chain digs in bad on my ankles; I get one arm up and hang on that. I keep changing arms til I sees Bryce at the front door. His shirt is in his hand, chain has done like a tractor track, cross his shoulder and all down his back. He comes up the first stairs.

"No, Daddy!—No, Daddy!" Baby Grady squeals.

Bryce is upside down to my face.

"Next time," he whispers, "I'm going to kill you."

Then he goes back down to the door and closes it gentle nice behind him. We listens for the car. Mum checks in the front room, makes sure he's proper gone. She holds me on her shoulder so I can get the chain off, can't stand up cos feets is dead.

"You shouldn't have done that," she says. Both her eyes is like a boxer and blood is black in her hair. Door knocks.

"Everything all right?" Roger shouts through the door. "Everything OK, Mrs. King?"

Mr. Baldwin must have called the police. Mum talks through the letter box.

"Fine," she says.

We listen. Radio crackling and calling Roger. They goes way.

Mum goes upstairs to bed. I make the sofa cushions a nest for Baby Grady, sings him lullaby to sleep. Then I pick up chairs and hair and Monopoly money and clean the kitchen floor, sweeps up glass and blood and dog ends. I go upstairs every now and then, check case my mum is died. She's just laid in bed, staring into no place. Int got nothing to say. I take her up a cup of tea but it int no good cos she needs a straw. Can't find one so I break a pen. When the mersion water is hot I run Mum a bath and help her get in it. I washes her hair, then combs it out, gentle nice, sees what the cut on her head is like. Int cut, just bashed in and ouch from all the hair pulled out. Worstist cut is on her eyebrow and it don't want to stop bleeding. I look downstairs in the kitchen drawer for butterfly stitches Auntie Fi brung us, save going all the time to the hospital. I does Mum's eye and then dries her hair.

"Sorry about Sheba," she says.

But I don't hear her cos the hairdryer's loud. She stays on the bedroom chair while I make her bed with clean sheets.

"I'm going to get an injunction," she says. Then she falls sleep.

Downstairs I look in the dictionary see what an injunction is.

I try to lift Sheba. She's fixed in a swirl, eyes is open gone milky, empty like paper mache and woodlice is underneath. I tie Baby Grady on my back; drag Sheba down the alley and cross the road on a bit of plastic. Then I go back for a shovel. I pull stingers out and start digging, takes ages cos the handle on the shovel is broke. I keep trying Sheba in the hole but it int no where near big enough. I looks up, sees the Sandwich Man, standing with hands on his hips. He nods like he knows me. Next time I look up he's gone. Baby Grady crawls over and kisses Sheba's nose, he don't know how come she int licking. He squashes up the side of her mouth.

"Telliwison?" he says.

"Sheba—gone way," I says.

His eyes is puzzled like twin bubbles.

"Sheba—gone way," he says.

Lucky there int no kids, everyone's gone to school. Next thing the Sandwich Man is back, brung a sharp spade with him. Hole comes deep quicker cos he chops and I scoops out. I make a bed of leaves in the hole fore we puts Sheba in. When we put the dirt back on her I wonders if I should be crying. I tries but there int none in me. The Sandwich Man and me get some stones for putting around. He sits down and rolls a cigarette; I make a cross from sticks and long grass. It goes cold and dark sudden, clouds is deadly nightshade but behind the sky is yellow. It's a proper grave what we done, don't know how come the dirt looks purple. Int no vultures going to get her.

"Shall we say a prayer?" the Sandwich Man arsts.

I throw the broke shovel in the stingers.

"Int no God," I says.

Cabbige whites fly up, never seen so many.

"Int no Dog," says Baby Grady.

Surprises me I starts crying, lucky cos the rain falls down like coming from a buckit.

I'm with Edith Piaf, in Paris, by gaslight, it's gay; it's so gay it makes me brave. The intercom bell blasts through the music. I turn the record down and answer it.

"Hello," a bloke says. "I just saw your postcard in the shop window? It said to ring the bell?"

"Oh, brilliant. Come up," I say, "second floor."

I only put the ad there yesterday. It feels like a sure thing. As if by appointment Techno turns his music off and goes out, slamming his door, jumping down the stairs. I hear the bloke coming up. Will he pay the rent?—that's the question. He doesn't know how important he is to the plan.

"Ah!" he says.

He shakes my hand.

"Danny," he says.

"Come in," I say.

He will say yes. He will pay the rent. He has come to make it easy for me. He's wearing a green denim jacket with an Aztec lizard panel hand-stitched on the back, though he's not the least bit Latino to look at; he's a golden type of bloke with faded jeans and silver jewelry.

"Fantastic," he says. "I'll have it."

He has green DM boots. I'm not supposed to sublet.

"There's no fridge," I say. "You don't need one—it's so fucking cold in here."

He doesn't seem fazed. I lie down to show him where the warm strip is under the floor. He lies down to see what I mean. He sees how if you cook your toast on the camping stove you can warm yourself at the same time. He checks out the bathroom like a clever and totally new idea; examines his tongue in the mirror. He moves like someone that can dance.

"There's a twin-tub; I got it out of a skip." I open the larder door to show him.

We settle down on cushions around the camping stove. He likes the painted landscape; asks me about it, talks about Turner's use of light; the way the painted sun strikes the yellow bark, explains about the cubist nature of my painted thorn tree. There's a fish skeleton printed on his T-shirt. I find myself in Machu Picchu, a place I've never heard of; in ancient civilizations in general, in hieroglyphics and rock engravings, in the weave of llama wool, in the filigree of silver work and methods they have of smelting. He rolls an elegant cigarette with beautiful hands, pinches a stray tobacco thread from his tongue. We're on to Colombian pots.

"They burn a special kind of bark in the kiln, which produces the smoked black finish."

I don't think the way he dresses is fashion; more a collection of fond memories, everything about him is somehow original. Edith Piaf is still playing.

"Listen to this, Dan," I say.

I turn the crackle and volume up. We listen to Piaf's live applause in 1954. She warbles "Autumn Leaves" for us, and them, one verse in English, one verse in French. Danny seems at home. He's been working in Colombia for six years, teaching, but now he's doing an art foundation course.

"Everything is coming up *fish*," he says. "I've got some savings; I'm working part-time at the Language School, teaching beginners' conversation."

Music to my ears.

"I love it. Today a lovely man from Italy came in. 'Hello,' he said. 'My name is six o'clock.' "

I see the woman in the mirror laughing. *Here—life is beautiful; zee girls are beautiful, even zee orchestra is beautiful.* She's very animated. *Leave your troubles—outzide.*

I realize Danny Fish has been here several hours. We're on to Doctor Dolittle, via llamas and push-me-pull-yous.

"I shared an apartment with a doctor once," he says, "a plastic surgeon."

"Could you tell he was a surgeon from the way he carved his meat?"

"No—but when the fish arrived, it did look *remarkably* like Cher."

There's mischief in the set of his teeth; I imagine one fang, but there isn't one. Piaf sings a tightrope walk, and a flying trapeze, no safety net, the accordion worries about underneath. Danny picks up the small brown phrase book.

"Jambo," he says to me.

"Jambo," I reply.

"Mzuri?"

"Mzuri Sana."

"Jina lako nani?" he asks me.

"Ninitwa Louise," I say.

"Karibu Louise," he says, "hakuna matata."

"Hakuna matata?"

"No worries," Danny Fish says. "I think it's amazing what you're doing."

"One chance, Dan," I say. "One fritterable amount."

He's interested in the map.

"Five feet by seven feet," I say. "Thirty-five square feet."

Same size as my cell.

"PADAM, PADAM, PADAM," Piaf kicks arse in a circus parade. "DADA DUM, DADA DUM, DADA DUM."

I reckon the Sandwich Man done them for me. Wooden blocks, bashed up with nails around the back of beech tree number 4, in the bushes where no one can see, less you looks proper. The wooden blocks work like steps up to where the trees get busy. Beech trees is the beautiful-ist. Green leaves going gold around the edges, minds me of Pip's eyes and the bark is smooth and gray, not silver, not slippy like the silver birch. Beech trees is easy now, up and up and then long. They was planted close together and some of the arms has growed together. Sometimes has to jump a bit, can get from one tree into the next. Int scared.

Mum and Auntie Fi is hiding in the bedroom, case Uncle Ike comes. Mum's bedroom comes true in the sun, sactly as we magined. Don't know how many reds there is, bossed with gold on the wallpaper. Must mit it was a bastard, never wanted to stick on the ceiling. Furnitures was all different so we done them the same with hogany varnish. I done all the gold leaves swirling around the handles cos I is good at careful and edges. We was trying for *Boodwaa* cept the curtains turned up jumble-sale satin, in black-and-white stripy. Then Mum got a good idea so stead we done it *Monay* with mirrors and pink paper peonies for clashing. We had crêpe paper left from *Carousel*, when Mum done it at Pip's school. I try to member where we was, in the olden days, fore Bryce. Don't know if we done *Carousel* in Bedford or Taunton or Norwich, I spects the place with hydrangeas.

All the winders is open cos it's last chance warm. Auntie Fi's laughing. Baby Grady's learned to stand up, holding on to the chair with his chubby feets in the *fuck-me* shoes what Mum got from Marilyn Monroe. They done him a feather boa and sparkly boob tube. His face is lipstick and black massacre. Mum puts on the short black wig. Then comes black gloves, she unrolls them up her arms and sits on the chair the wrong way around. Uh-huh. Girlfriend known as Elsie. Mum sings big so the gods and Liza Minnelli can hear it.

"SHE WASN'T WHAT YOU'D CALL A BLUSHING FLOWER, AS A MATTER OF FACT . . ."

"SHE RENTED BY THE HOUR . . ." Auntie Fi sings like a choirboy. They hold on to each other cos laughing.

"BUT WHEN SHE DIED THE NEIGHBORS CAME TO SNICKER . . ."

"THAT'S WHAT COMES FROM TOO MUCH PILLS AND LICKER."

"BUT WHEN I SAW HER LAID OUT, LIKE A QUEEN . . ."

Auntie Fi, quick, lies down on the bed being Elsie dead, but I can only see her legs.

"SHE WAS THE HAPPIEST CORPSE I'D EV-ER SEEN . . ."

I never wants to go like Elsie. Mum's got all of the song. Auntie Fi gives up, finds Mum's mauve dress in the pile on the bed and strokes the silkiness and tries to put it on but it won't go cos of big bones. She's stuck; caterpillar in a cris-lis. And Mum int even looking cos high kicks is coming up. Baby Grady copies Mum, that's how come a fuck-me shoe goes flying out the winder.

"AND AS FOR ME. AND AS FOR ME . . ."

A parcel man turns up in a van. And he's going to ours. He waits by the front door, puts the parcel down on the step and then he picks it up gain. Mum does a *Cabaret* finish and he don't know if to knock or clap. He knocks hard. Auntie Fi can't side where to hide; Uncle Ike int happy cos she's been doing Escort Agency in the afternoons. He don't want her working with cars. Mum looks out the winder. Then she opens the front door still in spenders and takes the parcel in, I spects it's from the catalogue, stupid shoes for going back to school. The court says gain, *I has to go*. I wishes they int black patent. My feets is good as leather, could just draw the laces on and shine them up with polish. Bare feets is made especial good for climbing beech trees. I has to learn every tree and sactly how they is.

I find a way to the next beech tree easy where the branches kiss. The Baldwins' house is different from ours cos the bathroom is at the front. It int proper watching Mrs. Baldwin, she's like a dressing gown hanging on the back of the bathroom door, looks like crying. James went to Portsmouth to die. No one knows how come Portsmouth. Mr. Baldwin is mowing his side grass, it's more greener than anything else; the end triangle grass is dead cos of football and it still int rained. It int rained. Spotty hyena from number 96 lies down all the time on Sheba's grave and he won't get off. The Hump grass has gone all yellow and shaggy.

The last beech tree is older, bigger and fatter than all the others. The branches spread out and open wide. Africa fills my eyes. The Masai Mara grass is rolling, golden, golden over golden; running way from the wind, don't know how big it is. Pip said one time he found a manhole cover with a big empty sewerage underneath. Magine, a manhole cover in the Masai Mara grass, big sewerage underneath it. Somewhere this side close by the hedge and the wire. Pip said he couldn't find it gain and I can't find it niver, I spects he dreamed it, a manhole cover in the grass. The Rift Valley lakes has dried up, showing all the bones. Dirt is red and the sky is pink, more bigger than anything else. Sometimes the sun makes me blind. Africa goes on forever. The Jackal is in the Mara, don't know how come he int at school. I spects he's been sniffing at the top of the cliff, wants to get down on Big Grin. I seen him cos I stalked him fore, he even lifts his leg to piss. He goes down over the edge but then he comes up quick, too scared to jump the crack. But every day he gets more braver. Feeling says move my camp, my book and everything. Sides the dirty Jackal, I got Baby Grady all the time and I can't go to Big Grin with him. I look at this end beech tree, its arms is strong and out like welcome. I sees Mum on the doorstep. She blows the whistle for me to come in, sounds like a penalty, lucky the kids int playing football.

Uh-huh: a parcel is on the table with brown paper ripped off it. Definite shoebox. I see the writing on the label. Surprises me, says *Zulu-Lulu*. Grandad learned Pip how to write copperplate. Post office stamp says *Powys*. It int proper Mum opened it.

"It's from your brother," Mum says. "Traitor."

She goes upstairs with Auntie Fi cos Baby Grady's screaming, too loud for noring.

I open the shoebox. It int shoes. Pip's made me binocliars! He's done them good with toilet roll tubes. They got bits for turning and a string for hanging them around your neck. I look through them at the sky. Eagle! Eagle flying on one lens! And he's done me something else, wrapped up small in tissue paper. Conker number eleven, beautiful, and even the hole is drilled ready. Looks like he done me a card; envelope is ripped open and not even nice. He's done the drawing with felt-tip pens; giraffe is saying: *Happy Birthday*. He's done me words in a letter. Reckons they got six sheep dogs but they int so good as Sheba. New sisters int so good as me, that's how come he sent me binocliars and the conker and five pounds. I look in every place, can't find no five pounds. Mum, I spects. It int proper, it int, I needs it for razor blades and stamps. Least now I got Pip's address, place name like an alphabet. Auntie Fi has come downstairs, forgot her glass of wine.

"When is my birthday?" I arsts.

"September the 19th, darling," she says. "I remember the day you were born."

She rummages in her bag and finds her diary, got sunflowers on it. We find September. We int sure what day it is today. Auntie Fi works it out.

"It was yesterday, darling," she says.

Loverly; eleven, I spects, is better than ten.

"Auntie Fi?" I says.

She's stops with her wine on the stairs.

"Yes, darling?"

"Can I wash your car?"

I has to go indoors to fill up the buckit. Mum and Auntie Fi is talking in the kitchen now. They gave up on Baby Grady, he's still screaming upstairs. Wishes I could get him but I can't, not yet, got busy-ness to do.

"You must be doing a fine job, Lulu," Auntie Fi says.

I has been washing her car all day.

"Uh-huh." I try to look like not sweating.

They don't know. I int washing the car, not proper. Stead I run over the road and pull stuff up in the beech trees quick; got towing ropes from Auntie Fi's car. It int easy. I has to be fast case somebody sees where my new camp is; kids come home from school soon. I got planks up, don't know how many. Tinker said I could have the wood and the wavy tin, they was overgrowed with brambles behind the stables. He reckons I more than earned the planks for helping him with his horses. Don't think nobody seen me pulling stuff up in the trees.

"We'll do something for your birthday tomorrow," Mum says. "Where do you want to go? And don't say *Grandad*, we aren't going to Grandad."

My face does thinking; don't know what else there is sides from Pip and Grandad. I wonders if to say Pip. Last time I went to school I seen the map in geography class, Powys int in France, it's in Wales which is good cos you don't need a boat. Still, I spects it's a thousand pounds in gas. Sunbeam Rapier, we can't get no where; sides, saying Pip is probably a *treachery.* Mum is waiting. My fingers knit and my tonsils grow. I wonders if tomorrow is really Thursday, and if after dinner, is still Miss Connor. Don't know if to say it, case of a *disloyalty*. My face is trying on ideas.

"Where do you want to go?" Mum's airy-ated.

"Could go to school," I says, "it won't cost nothing."

Mum does despairing.

"I'll think about it," she says.

I has to get Baby Grady, has to, cos his crying is so terrible sound, case he thinks he is the last person live on the earth. I get him and the buckit and take them out the front. Has to bandon the tree camp today. Looking up you can't spect all the stuff is up there ready. Now I wash the Cortina proper, got too many bubbles. Baby Grady stands on the driving seat.

"Brum, brum, brum brum brum brum," he says.

Auntie Fi comes out in her gray bear coat, looks like going. I get her car keys ready for her.

"I'm just walking down to the shop, darling." She knocks three times on the gate post. Sometimes she gets halfway home to Ealing, then members she never knocked and has to come all the way back. Now I always mind her fore she drives way, case. But now she's going down the shop. She walks like the land of the giants and her shadow goes all the way to Merrylands. Wonders if she'll get me an I-Spy book. Don't know if she will, they is thirty pence.

I shine the car mirror and sees her coming back. Uh-huh.

"Happy birthday, darling." She gives me the little brown paper bag.

I-Spy Hedgerows.

"Int never seen a stoat, Auntie Fi," I says.

Or a red mushroom called fly agaric. It's important to know what's poisonous, case one time you wants to kill yourself.

Good thing, I can get Baby Grady easy up in the trees. I has to tie him on me tight so he don't fall out. He don't mind cos he stays still, cept sometimes he gets cited, bounces up and down, "Monkey oo-oo-oo," he shouts, makes me wobble. It's a long way up and then cross to Africa camp. I got planks for the worstist bits. Surprises me, I made a floor where there weren't one fore, up in the beech tree over the road. People walk and drive long underneath. No one thinks as high up as us. I jumped up and down and tested the edge. Strong. At the jumble sale Saturday, I got a strappy leather thing for walking toddlers. Fits Baby Grady nice, he can't fall off, the rope int long enough. He bounces up and down on the floor.

"Oo-oo-oo."

"*Shush*," the beech trees say. "*Shush.*"

Tree Camp is the bestist, I spects I could live in it. Done me a bed with sacks and straw. Pip would climb up easy. He'd sit down on my bed and smoke his cigarette. I got one for him, case, and if it rained we wouldn't get wet. I got the skull of a crocodile and lions' claws hanging on fishing line, and spoons that jingles together. Baby Grady would bash out six-eight time and Pip would play the spoons, I spect, and whistle a happy tune. I could learn them the warrior song.

Pip int coming.

Three times he was coming but then he never, cos Mum's titled to change her mind. Don't spect he even knows that we got a Baby Grady brother. Now he sent my birthday parcel I got his address in Powys, now last can write him a letter. I done a rummage under the stairs and found a photo for him. Mum don't know the photographs in plastic bags under the stairs. All of her pictures is in the album or framed up on the piana. I reckon Pip took the picture with the camera Grandad give him. Sheba's doing a creamy swirl but Bryce is stupid, on his hands and knees, wagging with a stick in his mouth so I fold the photo nice and careful, tears him off. Sheba looks like smiling. In my scrapbook I write *dead* to see how it is. *Dead* don't seem like the proper word. I does *dead* big letters, then small copperplate, I does *dead* curly and swirly joined up. Dead. Don't know if to tell Pip, cos of when they came to take him way.

"Please, Mummy, please, Mummy!" He was on the doorstep crying and hanging on to Sheba's neck.

"We could take the dog." Pip's new mum was crying.

Pip's real dad looked surprised.

"We can," he said. "We can take the dog. The dog could come. It's a farm, Joan, the dog could come."

"Malcom, you're such a wanker," Mum said. "The dog stays here."

Then she went back in the house. Bryce dragged Sheba in the alley and closed the gate. Then he dragged Pip cos he was kicking and screaming and throwed him in the car. Cept Sheba got over Mr. Baldwin's fence and come out the front gain and cos the car was driving way she tried to jump in through the winder. Pip's new sisters was screaming. Don't spect Pip's got a photo of Sheba so can send him this. Baby Grady sits on my bed. I give him some paper and a crayon to eat. Letters int no trouble. Grandad learned me how to make a story so that anything can happen.

Deer Pip,

Sheba still sleeps on your bed but she int crying so much now. I spect you is good at sheepdogs cos of being good at whistling. My new camp is in the beech trees case one time you is looking for me. We got a new brother what's called Baby Grady, he's good at drumming. And he's always got his bum in the air, listening what's under the floor. He don't say much but when he does it all ways is a nice surprise. Sorry sisters int no good.

I int a Zulu no more, two much war and trouble getting

> leopard skin. Stead I'm being Masai tribe, we herds cattle. I got three hundred cows with big horns down in the Masai Mara. The others help me to around them up. We has to be careful case lions get them. We got spears. We ware red. We int scared. Thanks for the binocliars cos now I can see every thing better. Conker number eleven is on my necklace. Int spent the five pounds yet. Uncle Ike has been Born Gain but shame cos he's still only got one leg. Auntie Fi is here cos Bryce went back to Holland yesterday. Good job you weren't here.

I sees Dolly sitting on my box. She likes the spoons jingling. First I thought she was a mouse, cos scared me, but she int. She's a little jenny wren but I call her Dolly, stead. Surprises me, so little she is, but she sings BIG with her hands on her hips.

I like making letters. I make one for Big Chief I-Spy, Wigwam-by-the-Green, 382–386 Edgware Road, London W2 1EP, arsts him if there's any chance of me being Africa Masai tribe. Tired.

"Shush," says the beech trees.

The beech trees is hushing and gentle nice rocking. Baby Grady has gone to sleep. Spoons stir music in to my mind. Lulla-by. Grady's face is still wrung out, from crying all afternoon. And probably he'll cry tomorrow. Only if I go to school. I take off my red cloth and lay it on him. Sometimes scares me, he don't seem like breathing, so small it is.

So hush, little baby, don . . . 't you cry.

I kisses the end of his fingers, don't know how come.

I'm at the bank when it opens. The cheque for eight thousand pounds has cleared. I go directly to Trailfinders. She adjusts her tinsel halo.

"Hello," she says. "Have a seat. What can I do for you today?"

I sit in the chair and tell her. She taps on the keyboard in front of her.

"December the 15th is the earliest, a week today."

I see me outside, nose and palms squashed up against the glass.

"Ten fifteen in the morning," she says. "Two hundred and fifty-four pounds."

I nod.

"What name?" she says. It takes me several minutes to recall who I am.

"Catherine Clark." I stand up and count the cash in twenties on to the desk, put the rest away, then show my empty hands to the CCTV camera and her colleague. Dip, suddenly faint. Locked elbows are holding me up; see myself in the shine on the desk.

"Are you all right?" the woman says.

"Spending power," I say, "nearly knocked me over."

The drumming is so loud and so clear.

In *Cash-Converters* small valuable items are displayed in glass cabinets. The staff are all busy, converting in electric-blue shirts.

"Do you know about cameras?" I ask a man beside me.

"Well," he says, "a bit."

"I don't know where to start."

"Well," he says, "it depends really on what you want the camera for and how much you want to spend."

I tell him. He points through the glass at the pros and cons. He's very earnest. The assistant comes with a key and opens the cabinet. My man detects sand in one lens and a scratch on another. He turns them over, literally weighs them up.

"This is good, this is very good, this Pentax body," he says. "Before you decide we could look over the road and see what they've got."

We look at all the options on the Gloucester Road; nothing too fancy to make me a target, nothing too heavy. Zoom and wide-angle; polarizing filter; aperture; shutter speed: it's an education. He's been with me all morning, this wise adviser. I remember I'm rich and offer to buy him a coffee. In the cafe he writes a list on the back of a receipt, to make sure I've got everything.

"So now it's just a matter of whether you want to carry a tripod."

"What sort of thing might I need it for?"

"To keep the zoom or the camera still, for low-light situations: dawn, dusk, night shots, dark places, caves; dancers around a fire." He's been stirring his tea for fifteen minutes. "Fireflies, but then a tripod is a pretty cumbersome thing." He clasps his hand on the table and awaits my thoughts.

"Will I be all right?" I ask him.

"Definitely," he says. "Just try and hold the camera steady; your biggest problem will be overexposure."

To malaria. Dysentery. HIV.

"Just watch out for your aperture." He gives me his phone number in case I need to ask him anything else. He'd love to see the photos when I get back. Nice man. He has to go.

"You've got everything you need," he says.

I thank him. He waves from the door. I look at the scrap of paper he's given me. That was *Tony Gloucester Road*; I've no idea what he looked like.

At the health center, the nurse is a nurse. A December bluebottle is caught in a vortex above her head as she prepares the vaccinations.

"I'm a bit queer with needles," I tell her as she tightens the tourniquet.

"It will soon be over. Clench your fist for me, Louise. That's lovely."

The fluorescent light strip is everywhere, painfully clean, liquid in the white floor, solid in the black window, curving on the metal kidney dish, in the arms of the chrome tubular chair, turning lethal off the needle. Brilliant light, Armageddon white has finally come to take me out.

"Stay with us Louise," the nurse says.

Please, Catherine—Catherine, please.

"Are you with us?"

I'm sideways on an iodine-scented slope. Typhoid dashes past the back of my eyes.

"All done."

The bluebottle lands on the sonic zapper.

Catherine.

Catherine.
Everything is flashing.

I take Baby Grady over the Humps, sees the dirty Jackal, standing up on Tinker's gate. Horses is waiting by it, swishing tails. The Jackal int no good, Biscuit int old enough for riding! She does bucking bronco all down the field, with the Jackal riding on top of her head. Reckon she'll throw him off, might even trample him to death. I tie Baby Grady on tight and we fly up and down the Humps and swing over the river on the rope. In Tinker's field we walk about, don't know where the Jackal is. Somewhere sounds like crying. That's how come we find him, in the ditch, under all the blackberries. I get a stick and bash a path. His arm is so plain snapped as a twig.

"Tinker's gonna kill me," he says all sniffling. "An me dad."

Looks like agony.

"They're gonna kill me," he says. Tears is squashing on his eyelashes.

I try for an idea.

"Could say you fell off your bike good and proper."

He wipes snot on his shoulder.

"I'm gonna," he says. "You won't tell Tinker I was on Biscuit?"

"Biscuit," Baby Grady says.

I has to think about it.

"I won't tell . . ."

"Promise?" he says.

His bottom lip is a wobble.

"I won't tell," I says, "long as I get my penknife back."

We get him out of the ditch cos I kneel down and he stands on my back. Then I wheel his bike from by Tinker's gate. The Jackal keeps stopping like to faint. We do it slow ten steps at a time, we has to sit down on garden walls. His trousers is halfway down; shirt is ripped and runckled up; Biscuit kicked him hard in the back cos the bruise is horseshoe shape.

All of the Smithers come to the door, don't know how many there is.

"Car nearly hit me." The Jackal starts crying, looks sideways at me.

"Uh-huh," I says. "Lucky his bike is still in one piece."

"Biscuit," Baby Grady says.

And Mrs. Smithers gets him one. Custard cream.

I make me and Baby Grady a jam sandwich and we take it with us. We wait for a car to pass then we cross the road and go in the bushes and disappear. I tie Grady on my back and climb up the tree, easy on the Sandwich Man's blocks. Then walk long through the hearts of the trees, got the planks tied nice. Grady int no trouble, he stands on the edge of the floor and leans out on the end of his rope, tends he's flying like Superman. He int scared. Makes me nervous. I check the rope gain; it's proper strong, won't break or come undone. Then he sits down with his sandwich; he don't eat it, just licks jam off. Dolly comes flipperty-jibberty and I makes her seeds of bread.

Grandad sends Mum letters; she puts them underneath her mattress. He always does a page says *for Lulu* on it. Last one said that the coleus plants is taller than me and my presents is still in the cupboard. Retired weren't no good cos Nanny give him headache. Stead he's being a park keeper, the trees at Cranford Park is his for looking after, and the flower beds. He was planting daffodils, ready for Lonely as a Cloud. And when the kids fall off the swings he calls amblances for them. He reckons he seen a monkey in the monkey-puzzle tree. Seen it proper in the colors of black and white. Don't know if it's true. Gypsies by the canal has gone. He sent a list of horses for the Derby. I picked Nijinsky, don't know if it won.

Wonders if to write and arst him case Nanny can make the monkey a sandwich, case he can send my letters separate. I don't get much chance for under Mum's bed cos normal she is in it. And tell him I don't need no more presents, my Africa book is good enough forever cos now I read the pictures and words. Don't know how many there is, side by side, surprises me: they all mean something. I looks up *tetanus* in the dictionary. Then I final gets it, that your jaws can lock together. I looks at the Masai baby smiling in the Africa book. I looks at Baby Grady. I looks at the little bottom teefs. I looks at Baby Grady's teef. Don't know if to knock one out case one time his jaws lock. I could easy save him then by blowing water in the gap.

The Great Rift Valley got a river of stones. They roll over, changing color, yellow, oringe, mauve. I look in my Africa book. Wildebeests is thousands, moving silky side by side, gray-brown looks like purple, more wider than a road. The sun is finished soon, rain clouds is starting to gather over the Mountins of the Moon. Feels lectric in the air. Beech trees is shivering. And me. Baby Grady cuddles on my lap, lucky I brung a blanket up. Africa Tree Camp is the sky of the world. Ellie Smithers is playing on the end triangle grass, sprightly dance, counting steps with a magined friend. *Seven and twenty, ten, one, thousand million and freefty-free—no you have to follow me!* She left her doll's pram on the pavement but it's rolled and tipped up in the gutter. Sees the Sandwich Man coming walking, wonders where he's been. Behind him sees the flock of starlings come swirling cross the Mara. Magines if the sky is water. The starling flock swims together like don't know how many fishes. They shift and shape and swirl and come to land, on Mr. Baldwin's roof. He's working in his side garden, he don't like them, bashes his dustbin lids together to scare them off. They shift and shape way. Ellie's on the verge by the ditch, telling time with dandylion clocks. The Sandwich Man gets to the wire, is standing there watching Ellie, case she goes in the road. He calls her over, there's something in the Masai Mara that he wants to show her. The starling flock is back, especial beautiful cos the sky behind has gone dark pink. Beautiful! Beaut-i-full. They gone. The Sandwich Man is back on the lane, waves to somebody he knows as they drive past in a car. Spects Ellie ran off home. Or one of her brothers came by and took her home the other way. Forgot her pram, still there, tipped up in the gutter.

The pottery people were excited about it. A great adventure, Tim said, a great adventure for all of them. In the gateway to the vicarage I step out of the way for the postman, it's second post, he blats around in his van. I check my postbox on the way in.

Lily of the Valley.

Airmail from Irene. Airmail paper, hurried. I wrote to give her my new address. There's other post, businesslike; I take it all upstairs and make a coffee; a whole coffee with milk and sugar. Final payslip from the doughnut factory. They've deducted fifteen pence for the doughnut I ate on the way out. See what tricky bastards they are; fifteen pence is the retail price when I actually ate a wholesale doughnut. I didn't get the job at McDonald's. I open Irene's airmail letter with a knife. It is unusually brief, purple pen, a flowering paragraph. *Irene.* I walk with the letter to the front door. I take it into the bedroom. Hold it filling the kettle. Read it sitting on the edge of the bath. I walk around with it, getting lighter with every step. Think I can hear a tolling bell. I find myself sitting where I've never sat before: against the airing cupboard door; up on the draining board. I eat three bowls of cornflakes and use two pints of milk and drink the sugary dregs from the bowl with tears streaming down my face. Then wash up the bowl for what seems like hours, before going down to phone Heath.

"What compensation, what accident?" he says. "When?"

"I'm going the day after tomorrow."

"Stop! Stop!" he says. "I don't think you know what you're taking on; I don't think you've thought it through. You could be raped or murdered there, no one would know, no one would even know where you were. It's not safe; a woman was murdered and left for the lions only last week. I heard it on the radio."

"Yeah—but I'm not a woman, Heath." It's a joke of course, a long-standing one about how I'm not really a woman—apparently I don't behave or react to things like a real woman would. That's my trouble—I'm intimidating—I'm just too tall—I just won't play the game.

"Why Africa of all places? What if you get sick, what about armed soldiers and bandits everywhere? I don't think you understand you're putting yourself in serious danger."

He waits for me to say something. I wait for him to say some more.

"Where exactly are you thinking of going?"

"Kenya, Uganda," I say, "Tanzania."

"You're going to fucking Kilimanjaro."

I hear his *tiger* roar and his fist hits the wall; the crunch of plasterboard.

"Bloody hell, babes, I've only just painted that," Sharon yells.

"Fuck-ing Kilimanjaro. I want you to take my dad's ashes."

"No," I say. "Take him yourself."

The coins run out and the line goes dead. Up the hill, the Quattro won't start, can hear it turning over. I wait and wait, to see if Heath will phone me back but he doesn't. Gwen has flattened the car battery now. No engine, no heater. It's bloody freezing. I'm halfway back to the vicarage gateway when the phone rings. I go back to answer it.

"All-righty?" Heath whispers, doesn't want Sharon to hear. "I was thinking I could fly out in a few months' time and meet you in Tanzania. We can climb Kilimanjaro together and leave my dad on the top."

"Yeah?" I say, eating hay with a donkey.

"I hope you know what you're doing," he says. "A year is a fucking long time, out in the wilderness, it'll be hard."

"Not as hard as ten years in prison."

I hear him drag on a cigarette. I thought he'd given up.

"I don't suppose we'll ever know exactly how that happened." His stock line, he coughs, chokes.

"We might."

"What do you mean?" he says smokily.

"Quentin woke up."

I wait. He waits. He draws in smoke. Blows it out. Coughs. Moves the receiver to his other ear.

"They switched his machine off, years ago."

"No, they didn't." I write *Q* with my finger in the condensation on the phone-box window. "They changed their minds; they took him to the States."

"How do you know?"

"Because his mother wrote to me in prison. I've always stayed in touch with Irene."

"Where are they, then?"

"Now?"

"Mmm."

"South Africa."

He draws on the cigarette. Exhales.

"I don't expect he's up to much—let's face it, half of his head was missing—he wasn't all that bright to start with."

"I've got to go, Heath; the phone-box windows are icing up."

"Kilimanjaro," he says, "phone me when you—"

"Bye-bye," I say.

I hang up.

Miss Connor chooses my story and she don't even know that coming to school is my birthday present.

"Will you read it for us, Lulu?" Miss Connor arsts.

My tonsils blow up and I dies in all the eyes.

"I could read it for you," she says.

I nod. We push all the desks back and make a horseshoe shape with chairs, stories is made for sharing Miss Connor reckons. She comes and talks to me especial and gives me a list of words for learning: There I is: *There I am.* When she reads the story out she'll say it all proper so that I can hear the difference. Miss Connor sits forward for stories, with skirts all around her muddy boots and paw prints on her denim jacket. Her hair is dark brown velvit curtains. Shame Miss Connor int got no ears.

"So," she says, "this is the second part of Lulu's story, I think we all enjoyed the first part last year?"

Kids int saying. She holds the page a long way way. Wishes I never done it on wallpaper cos the words is wonky where the pattern is bossed.

"*Mountains of the Moon—Part Two*," Miss Connor says in her story voice.

Kids look like they believe it already.

"*It's true. The rain is purple but the sky is gray and doesn't give anything away. The lions are coming, they're hungry again. They're coming for my other leg—*"

It int proper, it int me. Surprises me, Mum comes in the classroom and she don't even knock. Don't know if Baby Grady is dead. Then I see she's being Bonnie, cos of the beret and her hair all smoothed under and the cardigan with fur on the sleeves and the collar.

"Wha, honey, I searched all over for y'all," she says American.

Kids look around to see who she's talking to.

"Is it urgent?" Miss Connor says. "There's only ten minutes of class left. Are you Mrs. King?"

Mum don't answer. She takes her time to look at the blackboard and walks over to look out of the winder. Kids is glued. Mum's stockings has got seams in. She sits on the front of Miss Connor's desk, ankles crossed, swinging her legs. Don't know how come she's chewing gum. Kids and Miss Connor is spell bounded. I wonder if Mum will change her mind and be the Sound of Music cos it all looks like perfect for "Doh-Ray-Me."

Lucky cos she don't.

"Wha don't y'all just take a look at my little ol' honeybee?" she says.

Everybody looks at me.

"Wha, she's just as happy as can be to see her little ol' momma."

I sees me in the shine of stupid shoes, teef is out but they int smiling. I don't know if to sit back down. Stead I bite my conkers. Miss Connor tries to find words.

"Mrs. King, I don't know—"

"Exactly," Mum says. "You don't know." She gets up and wipes the blackboard clean. Then she gets the chalk, writes big letters, HOME TIME.

"Come on," she says to me, "let's get out of this little ol' dump."

Mum's high shoes clack all down the corridor. The ginger warthog lady comes running out of the office.

"Mrs. King, you can't—" she says.

Mum don't stop or look back, stead she blows a big fat raspberry and the corridor makes it ripple.

Bryce is waiting in the car with Baby Grady. Mum got a Degree Narcissus, said marriage is finished, but it int. Degree Narcissus don't mean nothing. I spect he's come to do me, cos he said *next time* he would. Tonsils nearly stops me breathing. We must be going somewhere. The Escort State is loaded up. Don't know how come we still got a dog guard. He don't look at me, when I get in the car.

"Honeybee, would y'all be so kind as to drive us away from this dreary ol' place?" Mum says cos she's still being Faye Dunaway.

"Soitenly," Bryce says.

I look out the winder; see me running on the verge, got red cloth and conkers on; got patterns; got spear; got bare feets, drumming so smooth and easy as breathing. The car int so fast as me. When we get to the top of a hill, there I is, standing waiting under a tree. There I is, red dash in the yellow field. There I is, at the roundabout.

There I am.

I run so fast through the market nobody even looks up. I sees me silky in the woods, red ribbon through the black pine trees.

Here I is, here I is, running, running on the verge. Now and then I look to see, case I'm still sitting in the car, looking out of the winder. I smiles. Sometimes I run close enough for one hand fingers on the glass.

I am real.

When we get to the seaside, I int even wore out. I sees me in the parking lot, standing off to one side. I nod like understand, *wait here*, I says.

"WE JOINED THE NAVY TO SEE THE WORLD, AND WHAT DID WE SEE? WE SAW THE SEA."

Mum's stockings and shoes is off in a pile with the blanket and the picnic bag. Bryce tends to throw her in the water. He puts her down and she runs way in shapes of eight, all pointy-toed and getting no where.

They go holding hands, looks like stopping the land from blowing to France. Tide is out; sand is wet and bumpoldy with swirly worms. Baby Grady is Superman, got red pants over the top of his trousers and the Superman cape that Auntie Fi brung him. He looks at the sea; shakes his head like can't believe it. I spects him to run at it, but he don't, stead he gets down, puts his ear on the sand. He still is chubby, don't know how come, he don't eat nothing cept Weet-a-bix. I always give him two cos he's growing more than me.

"Boom. Ba-ba boom. Ba-ba boom!" he yells, waving his plastic shovel like in charge of the music.

We walk out to find the water. The tide is coming in cos it rushes up to meet us. Has to be careful, kids can get drownded even in puddles.

"Here comes a biggy." I flies Baby Grady over little waves. The water is too cold; I get ouch cramp and my toes cross over. It's too cold for getting wet, stead we go back up the beach. I find a stick and write our swirly names in the sand: *Lulu Grady Pip*. Baby Grady runs up and down with invisible strings cos he thinks the seagulls is flying kites. Mum and Bryce is coming. Bali Hai is calling on the wind. I hates *South Specific*.

Mum's waving my swimming costume. I thought she forgot it but she int.

"It's too cold for going in the water," I says.

"*Too cold*," she says in my voice, cept smaller.

My swimming costume is blue-and-white stripy, got a little skirt sewed on it. Looks silly; I int five. I go into the sand dunes and put the costume on and wear my school shirt over the top. Gainst the sand, I is Bahamas brown.

"Come here, Lulu," Mum says. "Look at her pins, Bryce."

Uh-huh. She feels down the back of my legs and I int even a horse.

"Dancer's legs like mine," she says.

"Shame about the two left feet," Bryce says. "What happened to your face?"

I done three lines, sides by sides.

"Barbed wire," I says.

"She won't dance," Mum says, "or sing. She's too fucking tight, not like this little bundle."

She sits down and pulls Grady onto her lap, ready for singing Happy Talk.

"Talk-in talk-in talk-in talk-in talk-in talk-in," Baby Grady says. His little fat fingers is blinking, "talk-in talk-in talk-in . . ."

"TALKING TALKING HAPPY TALK—TALK ABOUT THINGS YOU LIKE TO DO . . ." Mum does the harmony like a nice lady.

Bryce is bent over his *AutoTrader*, got Formula One hat turned sideways so he can get close enough to read the page. He int taking his shirt off niver, cos of the pattern I done on his back. He looks up and calls me.

"Come and be a family." His voice is friendly but his eyes could kill me.

The wind blowing hard makes me deaf. There I is, in the dunes, singing and dancing the warrior song, *come on*, I says and we starts to run, ripping the beach under our feets.

"Bor-ing!" Mum yells.

We beats the word to the lighthouse and back.

Jam sandwiches has all gone. Baby Grady is burying Bryce in the sand but the hole int no where near big enough. The sea is coming in fast, starting to rub our names out. Wonder how long it will take, for all of us to disappear.

"Shirt off," Mum says.

I has to keep my patterns hid. Don't know how many I got; thin and white and side by sides. They minds me of a prisoner what's marking off the days. Last night I seen the starlings flock and land on Mr. Baldwin's roof. I seen him bash his dustbin lids to scare them off. I seen Ellie Smithers, her sprightly dance. I seen the Sandwich Man call her over.

Danny Fish has been and gone. Final arrangements. The gas in the camping stove fut-futted and ran out. I've opened all of the windows; it makes the cold more honest somehow. The wind has frozen stiff. The candles are at the end of their wick. There is money on the electric meter but I don't want to see too clearly.

I've never noticed before, I only breathe out; see the woman in the mirror, sitting up on the windowsill. I don't know how long she's been there. Listening. The freeze is keeping everything still. The city seems to hold its breath. For one heroic motorbike. On the ring road. Risking it. Loving it. Hear a slow heavy van, rattling down City Road. Exhaust throbbing at the traffic lights. First gear, then second gear, up Stokes Croft, turning right at the car showroom. A fine point of heat starts to burn. Foot down for the hill; third gear, second, grinding. Can't find a gear—make one. Pete.

The vicarage car park is full. He backs quietly into the bins. Softly scrapes the stone gate post, swings back gently into the road just missing a parked car. While he's searching for a forward gear the van rolls backward down the hill. Something gets a grip, the accelerator sticks, and the van rages up onto the curb, plows on scraping the wall and then impacts; the phone-box glass explodes in the headlights. Spectacular. The van stalls. Shudders. Pete gets out, leaves his lights on and his door open. The ruin shifts position. The world holds still again. He's in the road like something planted. Somewhere in the debris under the front of Pete's van the telephone starts ringing. He puts his head on one side, then the other.

"Hello?" he says. "Hello?"

The phone keeps ringing. He follows his ear to it, bends down, peers into the wreckage; finds it under his front fender.

"I'm sorry, mate," he says. "It *was* a phone box a few minutes ago, but it isn't one any more."

He seems to enjoy the caller's words. The caller wants some sort of favor. It's probably Heath. Pete has heard enough.

"It's four o'clock in the morning, you cunt," he says. Reaches into the wreckage to hang up.

Headlights dazzle the silence. He seems raptured by the light and the prettiness of shattered glass. A black cat walks into the scene, along the top of the vicarage wall. It sits down to survey the damage.

"Have you ever thought of getting glasses?" I say.

Pete looks up at the cat on the wall. He thinks the cat is talking to him.

"I'm night-blind," he confesses. "In the dark I can't see anything."

"Is it a good idea to drive the van, Pete?"

He scribbles a laugh in the air, surprised and delighted that the cat knows his name. We all listen to the faraway train. The cat splits through the light and disappears in the darkness. Pete seems sorry then. He's looking up through the bare trees but his blinded eyes can't find me, or the cat.

"I'd like to stay and talk to you." He turns a full circle. "But I've come around here to see someone."

"Some other time?" I say. "If you happen this way."

"I'd like that," he says.

The intercom blasts as I close the window. I release the main door and open mine to listen. Something urgent brings Pete up the stairs. I hold on to the door frame to keep myself from falling over. Close my eyes. Open my eyes. Close my eyes. He catches a breath beside my ear, spreads it out along my cheekbone; takes the breath from out of my mouth, lays it hot on my neck. His eyes turn my face away, and bring it back and bring it back and bring it back. I could kill him. I could savage his face. He sniffs along my hairline.

"There you are," I say casually.

He strides into the lounge. Stops short. Wide-eyed. Open-mouthed. The expedition equipment is still laid out across the entire floor. I look at him sideways; see him looking at me sideways. I bite my bottom lip, nod my head. His laugh skates the icy air, flourishes. His eyes ask the question. I look at the clock.

"In four hours," I say.

He nods his head, calculating all of the odds. I show him the way around the map, to a floor cushion in Libya.

"According to the compass," I say, "north is in the airing cupboard."

Rounding Cape Horn we get caught in a storm of mosquito netting, hanging from the light fitting: I've been practicing. I move the purple backpack and the medical kit so that he can sit down.

"I've run out of heat; can still boil the kettle, though."

I make coffee for him in the Swallow Hotel cup and saucer, spilling it everywhere. I hear Pete tapping a Silk Cut cigarette out of the packet; smell the sulphur from his match. He's messing with the camera; hear the slow shutter click and the film winding on. I hear him put it down and then the pages turning.

"Tourniquets and sucking out the poison are now comprehensively discredited," he says. He puts the guidebook down. I rattle the cup and saucer into the lounge. Rattle all the way to the floor beside him. He's found the freaky gadget in the medical kit; he's holding it up like a dead thing, a large polythene bat, with a tube and a plastic orange, oval face.

"According to the leaflet," I say, "it's a face mask for mouth-to-mouth resuscitation."

He nods his head in a "fair enough" way. He puts it down. He picks it up.

"If you're unconscious," he says, "how would you ask somebody to use it?"

I snatch it off him; put it back in the medical kit. We look at the dictionary opened at P for *prophylactics* and the fizzing anti-malarial tablet spat out on the side-effect leaflet.

"That was probably Heath on the phone," I say. "You didn't recognize his voice?"

Pete doesn't know what I'm talking about.

"The phone—the phone box—it was a phone box a minute ago but."

There's a dawning as Pete remembers the demolition outside.

"Heath—how is he?" Pete says. "I haven't seen him for years—nine, ten, eleven, twelve years?"

I remember introducing Peter and Heath, in the kitchen at Park Lane. They recognized each other from the night in Davros' Cellar; they stood there in the kitchen gleefully insulting each other. That first time Pete came to the house, Gwen didn't quite stress the "t" of his name, her elocution lessons dropped off with an afternoon bottle of Scotch. It's PeTer, actually, he said. I loved him, I loved him then. While the kettle was boiling I went in my room and rolled around with a lion skin, didn't know he had followed me in and was leaning against the door, watching. I try to remove the memory like a sticky thing from my eyebrow.

"Heath's back doing haulage." I say. "I phoned him yesterday, to tell him I was going away."

"Is Heath still married to Gwen?"

"On paper."

"You didn't ever get in touch with her again, you don't still see her?"

"I see her almost every day, Pete. She's parked in the side street just up the hill."

He's charmed and delighted by the notion; *poison dwarf* he used to call her. He's smiling at a candle flame dancing in the floor shine. I reach for two flat nylon pouches, pencil cases really with zips. He watches me put them side by side on the floor in front of me.

"Two pouches," I say. "One red. One black."

He's rolling a matchstick between his fingers and lips.

"One pouch contains two thousand pounds in US dollars; the other contains a wad of airmail paper. Red or black?"

"Black."

He's smiling at me, that slightly open-mouthed smile. I twist a matchstick lazily in my lips. He tips his head the other way. I slip two new batteries into the flashlight; Pete's eyes follow the beam to the wall. I turn the focus tight, to a sharp particular point of light. On the wall I write Q, in two clean sweeps. I turn the flashlight off but the letter remains, glowing like a ghost of itself.

"I got a letter from Quentin's mother," I say and count to ten. Then decide to count to twenty. "She wrote to tell me that he'd woken up."

Pete doesn't flinch. He looks up into the dark corner as though something magical is occurring there. When his gaze returns, I'm not sitting where I was. He finds me in the mirror. Waves me over.

I pretend I'm asleep. He gets dressed, loose change spills out of his pockets onto the painted tile floor. A sparrow in the tree outside mistakes the sound for song and repeats it back. He takes ages putting on the layers: it's cold on a market stall all day. I hear his shoe leather go into the lounge. His heavy set of keys jingle-jangle. And there it is, the sound: the short "zip" of a pencil case, opening.

Closing.

Twice.

There isn't any money in either of the pencil cases, just two wads of paper, one says *bye*, the other says *bye*. Friends and Family parade as favorites but you get better odds with strangers, I find. The front door opens.

He's gone.

No.

His shoes come back in, creak in my bedroom doorway. I feel the body of his heat above me.

"Be careful," he says.

And he lets himself out, closing the door with a click behind him. I stand up straight away. Relearn gravity. Stuff everything into the backpack. There's a tap-tap on the door. It's Pete, jumper half off over his head. He's getting undressed again. Off comes the sheepskin waistcoat, the sweatshirt, the moss-colored velvet shirt. He holds it all between his knees. Off comes the vest. It's bright white, like a new one out of a packet. He hands it to me and then he's gone, in a garment struggle, out of sight and down the stairs. I bury my face in the soft hot vest. Then get to the window just in time. He drives slowly down the hill, dragging a payphone on a curly cable behind him in the road. Fucking bastard. I'd like to see it ring now.

I've got twenty minutes. I move from room to room with a laundry bag, gathering my remaining possessions: the shoebox of paperwork; a few clothes, the dictionary, bits of tat. I stuff it all in the airing cupboard, out of Danny Fish's way. I copy Heath's address in Manchester from a notebook onto a scrap of paper and tuck it into my shirt pocket.

This is it. I put the backpack on my shoulder. My booming heart. I close the door behind me and bump down the stairs. Danny Fish has the postbox key; I drop the apartment keys into it, for him to pick up later. Don't care if there is post, don't care what it says. It's a filthy, cold, horrible day. I turn left up the hill, past a heap of warped metal and shattered glass. Panda starts her pedigree yapping. There's an empty bottle of Scotch on the passenger seat.

"Shut-up, Panda!" Her eyes are closed. "Enough now! For pity's sake, be quiet!"

The quilt over her legs is filthy. I tap on the car window. Yes, wake up, Gwen. Her hand flies to the door-lock button. It's locked already. Green piggy eyes set close together. Dirty-colored skin. A raptor's nose. She winds the window down a fraction.

"What the hell do you think you're playing at?" she says.

"I thought I'd save you the wait." I slip Heath's address in through the gap in the window. She lifts a grubby hand to take it. I pull it away slightly, make her reach, make her overreach for it.

"For God's sake," she says. "You look ridiculous—where the hell do you think you're going?"

"Africa," I say.

She laughs with her little stained, pointy teeth. I could never see her beauty.

"I'm off to visit Quentin, actually. You remember Quentin, Gwen?"

She sits back. Panda starts yapping at me.

"Don't be ridiculous," she says. "Quentin is dead and buried."

I slowly shake my head, lean down to thread the words in through the window.

"Apparently, he gestured for a pen and, after a little bit of practice, wrote *Hello, Mum—Can I have a cup of tea?* I've got to go, Gwen, plane to catch."

I don't look back.

I sit at the front of the coach, with a high view of the filthy motorway. I look sideways out of the window. See the cows in black and white, lying down. The fields in fallowed brown. Sheep all facing in one direction, as though strategically placed. A stubble field. A black pine wood. Rain clouds raging overhead. Window wipers doing their thing. I think about

Danny Fish, feel a pang of guilt about the apartment, the noise; the rats. His parting words were so nice, regret that I was disappearing when we'd only just met.

"I'll write to you, Danny Fish," I said. "I know where you live."

He's someone to look forward to, when I get back. If I get back.

Lorries buffer past the coach, chucking up sheets of grease. I shift sideways. I lie back. I wipe sweat from my forehead with the back of my hand. I think about Gwen and where that began, in counties all over England. I'm on the coach, so cold. We pass Swindon. I close my eyes. Wake up passing bloody Reading. I close my eyes. I wake up still passing Reading. I close my eyes. Wake up as a plane goes over the coach, coming in to land at Heathrow. The drumming is so loud and so clear. I see the slip road and the signs; all roads bring me back to here.

You asked to see me, sir.

I'm sorry to delay you, Sergeant, I appreciate your holiday should have started yesterday.

That's all right, sir.

Dave, is it?

Yes, sir.

DC Bryant has been taken sick.

I heard, sir, trouble with his ticker.

I'm picking up his threads.

Have they found her, sir?

They're still looking. Where did she go?

Well, sir, we just lost her, she was there and then she wasn't.

Who's we?

Sergeant Coot and I, sir, and one of the witnesses, do you mind if I consult my notes?

Go ahead.

Mr. Richard Draper, he lives around the back from the girl, he joined us in the chase.

Chase?

Well, a running search if you will, sir, it was almost dark.

What was happening when you and Sergeant Coot arrived?

Well, the brigade and the ambulance team were doing their best, as you'd imagine. A large crowd had gathered and were blocking the lane.

Where was she when you and Coot arrived?

Still up in the tree, sir, way up above the road. The brigade were using their hydraulic platform, sir. She was clearly visible in a red cloth. Mr. Draper—

The neighbor from around the back?

Yes, sir. Mr. Draper, he said she dressed all the time like an African warrior, red cloth, spear and everything, sir.

Where was the mother?

On her knees in the road: several bystanders had been sick, sir; it appeared that she was playing to the crowd.

Playing? What was she saying?

Demon seed, sir, bear with me, sir—it's in here somewhere. She said, *demon seed*, sir, *She couldn't stand it, I loved him, she's killed him, poison*, something about a *vixen*, sir, I couldn't catch it, sir: it sounded to me like Shakespeare. She yelled at the crowd and then at us and turned to scream up at the trees, threatening to kill the girl.

Did the girl respond?

No, sir, she seemed terrified rigid. The wind was fierce, the treetops were swaying. It was almost dark; the street lights hadn't been adjusted for the changing of the clocks, with the search teams returning and the headlights in the lane and the blue lights flashing and spark flying: the brigade had to use an angle grinder, sir; it must have been very confusing.

Why didn't the brigade get her down?

They were about to, the platform was on its way back up to get her. I was distracted, sir, a fracas broke out when a man in the crowd stepped forward and slapped the mother, a Mr. Baldwin, sir, the next-door neighbor, he made the initial call. The girl's aunt, who was visiting at the time, slapped Mr. Baldwin; he's a retired gentleman, sir. When I looked back up the girl had gone. The brigade hadn't seen her go either; they were searching through the treetops with their spotlights. There were planks, sir, running from tree to tree.

What happened next?

Well, sir, while Coot moved the crowd back and redirected traffic, I walked to the end of the lane following the line of trees. I thought the girl might be hiding or fallen and hurt, sir. Mr. Draper searched on the other side, in the waste ground. He must have flushed her out; I thought I saw something run across the lane.

So you went after it?

No, sir, not straight away. I ran back for assistance—Sergeants Prichard and Pine had arrived by then so Coot came with me, sir, and Mr. Draper, he showed us where to get into the field, a ditch, sir, and barbed wire. Like I said, sir, we couldn't really even see her.

It had got dark?

The sun was sitting on the horizon; I saw a jumping silhouette, fleeing, well, like an antelope, sir. Then I wasn't sure if I'd seen it all, it was more like chasing an idea. Mr. Draper seemed to know where the girl would run, we followed him, sir, not being familiar with the landscape.

How far did you chase the *idea*? What sort of distance are we talking here?

I should say half a mile, sir, of waist-high grass.

But you couldn't see her for sure? Not even in a red cloth?

No, sir, everything was black and red. It surprised me, sir, because the field just ended suddenly, there's a low fence with wire and Keep Out signs.

She went over the edge, down into the motorway works?

No, sir, it was a sheer drop, a hundred foot or so. One of the Smithers boys was there, sir, smoking a cigarette, and he pointed left, in the direction she went.

She went *left*?

Sorry, sir—toward Weybridge.

Junction 12. Clockwise.

Where is the search now, sir?

Watford, Junction 19. Which Smithers boy was it that sent you *left*—Digger or Jake?

No, sir, one of the smaller ones. Whichever one's got his arm in a plaster cast.

How long did you pursue that line, Sergeant?

It became clear within minutes, sir, that there wasn't enough light to find her.

You all went back to Leafy Lane?

Yes, sir, DC Bryant had arrived by then and we reported back to him. Coot and I took all of the witness details and then we were replaced by Sergeant Rawlings and Sergeant Lake. Sergeant Rawlings is familiar with the girl; there's a record of domestic violence. I hope they find her soon, sir—they've forecast snow.

Thank you, Sergeant, for your help; be sure to write the details as you've described to me—they found the other girl's shoe this morning.

I will, sir.

Have a good holiday. When you go past the desk tell Rawlings I want to see him.

Yes, sir.

What is it, Sarah?

Mrs. King is at the front desk again. Sorry, sir. Says she's got evidence that proves intent.

I think about falling.

I think about the plane and flying. We were so above ourselves. I wasn't scared. I didn't care if we crashed. I was looking forward to it. *We haven't come all this way to die out in the ordinary.* I was invincible. The hostess brought me a glass of water. I rolled up my sleeves. At twenty thousand feet I was closer to the gods.

"Come on then, you fuckers," I said and felt the drumming.

The beat was so loud and so clear.

The white cotton is fine and soft. I tug at the knees, settle the long white drape over my hands and feet. I don't like clothes, I never have. I bought these pajamas yesterday from an Indian stall in the market. Feel cool and monumental in them.

"Lawrence of Arabia?" says the woman in the broken mirror.

"Trust me." I shake out the bright African cloths; tie a tangerine swag around my waist and hips like a sash. Well, it will save the arse of the white tunic every time I sit down. I drape the finer brick-red cloth over my head and around my face, with the long ends twisted over my shoulder.

Does she look like a twit? Sitting on the roof terrace yesterday has turned her face and shaved head the color of teak and whitened her teeth, and eyes, and drawn straight and bold the four white scars, side by side on her cheek. Close to the bone. Like someone who has traveled far.

"On a camel?" says the woman in the mirror.

She thinks I care what people think; besides, what part would you rather play: Backpacker or Lawrence of Arabia? I don't really want her to know exactly how excited I am.

"Are you ready?"

"Uh-huh."

Mr. Iqbal is awake. Vital. I hadn't expected an Indian man here; India to Nairobi, via Oxford.

"When you come next time," he says, "maybe we are playing chess?"

"You'll have to teach me how to play, Mr. Iqbal, and how to win."

"I will begin straight away to whittle the pieces."

I pay for my tab and give him back the room key.

"You're not taking your bag?" he asks.

Oh! Yes!—That big heavy purple bastard that I'm supposed to carry and never leave out of my sight. He's laughing at me. He has to give me the room key back.

"Why are you running?" he says. "Late is not an African word."

I fetch the bag and he comes downstairs to see me off.

"Thank you, Mr. Iqbal," I say. "I've had such a nice time."

"What is your name?" he says. "What is the 'L' on the score sheet standing for?"

"*Lucky?*" I grims at him.

"In life, but alas not Scrabble," he says. "And what about love?"

"Don't ask." I laugh and turn away, stepping out into River Road. I ran this ramshackle gauntlet yesterday.

"Muzungu!"

It's me, I thought.

"Muzungu!"

I'm rich.

"Muzungu!"

Limited-edition rich.

"Muzungu!"

I'd got something to give.

"Muzungu!"

And something to lose. It was a whole new place. I moved fast and kept my head down; saw dusty dark legs and white calloused feet; passed through the burning smells: corn roasting on the cob; hot seat PVC, fan belts searing, metal smelting, a light high: aviation fuel in my hair.

"Muzungu!"

Beware the scam.

"Muzungu!"

The instant crowd technique.

"Muzungu. Tzzzz."

A small boy was running to keep up with me.

"Muzungu muzungu muzungu."

I had to stop and bend down; waited for someone to cosh me over the head.

"Muzungu," he said. "Give me pen."

He had tiny green shorts, a little willy hanging out.

"Pen?" It sounded odd, unfamiliar, surely a small thing. "Pen?"

He pointed at the smudged route written with biro on my hand.

"Pen," he said.

"Pen!" I floundered in montage confusion: goat; old Singer sewing machine, red fabric streaming through it; in the gaps between the traffic a silver arc of blade was hacking into something. Over the road. Over the boards. Over the steaming holes in the road. Cars. Buses. Pineapples. Dark men in dark doorways. A wall of exhaust. Tzzzzzz. The taste of banana skin. The devil I didn't know.

"Pen," the pot belly said.

I gave him a shilling from out of my pocket. As I walked away I looked back; saw him running down the street holding the coin up like an Olympic torch.

But today it's Sunday and very early and much more relaxed. The rain a moment ago was so short it left dark spots in the red-red dirt; they're disappearing before my eyes.

My shadow leads the way. I don't know why I keep looking over my shoulder; it's only the sun and the backpack looming up behind me. Street sellers are setting up for the day.

"Muzungu!"

Good-humored.

The road turns from crude red dirt to lilac asphalt and widens out. I suppose they'd call them *boulevards*. Tree-lined. Shady arcades, a glitter in the smooth walkways.

"Jambo, madam, welcome to Kenya!"

I know where we're supposed to meet: in the wide boulevard with the mauve tarmac and the china-blue flowering trees. Only four other people had booked—it is the short-rains and off-peak season. Plenty of room in the minibus. The company are gathered. Isaac sees me coming, isn't sure if it is me. I wave and cross the road.

"So fine. So fine!" He marvels at my pajamas and the dash of orange sash.

"Jambo," I say to Isaac who will guide us. "Jambo," to Benjamin who will drive us. "Jambo," to Lawi who will cook for us, imagine that. I've got a sudden thirty-year hunger—I gesture to him as much and he's going to see what he can do. I hadn't expected an elderly lady in the group. She's tiny, in a linen suit with her white hair pinned in an elegant knot. I pan from her face to a paunch with a belt around it. A curly giant bends down, offers me a huge hand.

"Vernon Pennsylvania USA," he says. "This here is my mother Margaret."

Her hand is tiny, arthritic, I'm afraid to crush it, for some reason I find I've bent and kissed it. She curtsies, I don't know why. The other two people are a couple, his and hers khaki.

"Jeff and Alison, Wolverhampton; we've renewed our vows."

"Ah," I say.

They seem like nice people, all looking at me. Me, who comes from who knows where, in white pajamas and colored clothes, apparently by camel. The shadow of Vernon sits down on the minibus step, leaving me exposed.

"Louise." I squint into the limelight.

I talk to Vernon and Margaret. This trip to Kenya is a gift for her seventy-fifth birthday, a dream come true from Vernon.

"We're both pretty darn excited about," he says.

We all help to load up the minibus, with our bags and the boxes of supplies, bottled water and sacks of charcoal and Lawi's pots and pans.

Then we're in. And we're off. My heart becomes a lark. I wonder if special occasions feel like this. That's what I'm having, a five-day special occasion. Before I get raped and murdered for all this money I'm carrying.

We are away now from the city, climbing, always climbing, overtaking laboring buses in the face of flying downhill traffic. Little black-and-brown patchwork goats are herded on the verges by herds of little raggedy boys. Not verges. No boundaries, just clearings that the tarmac passed by. The trees are out of this world in scale, dwarfing people, dabbling in light and shade on thriving plots. Shambolic leaves of banana trees, tall tasseled corn and glimpses of mud huts in between. Mud shacks set back, *Smirnoff* and *Coca-Cola*, kiosks I suppose. Food, I can see, will be found at the roadside. Two tomatoes. Something yellow with green spots, melon or pumpkin, I don't know. Green bananas. Surplus fruit with minders, waiting to sell under sticks and woven shelters.

"Say, Louise? Would you like some gum?"

I would. I sway forward.

"Thanks, Vernon."

Something for my nerves to chew on. In five days time I'm out there, on my own. I think I see me on the roof rack of a bus, in with the luggage, in with the sacks and the chickens, in with a chance of being thrown clear, in with a chance of having a cigarette. Umbrella up for shade. Uh-huh. The temperature is perfect and blowing with the roof propped open. I lift my face into the slipstream, offer it my neck.

I see me striding through shadow and light. I buy a bottle of fizzy pop from a kiosk and sit down in the shade to drink it. I see me asking the bright women about the stuff, spread on the mats. Coffee? Beans? They pour through my fingers hot from the sun. I see me arranging my pillow hands and laying my weary head on them. I see my fingers feeding a suggestion of food into my mouth. I've got a Swahili phrase book. I don't know about water. We've got bottled water in the minibus but I don't know about water out there. Only that it is red, and people are shifting it, in plastic water containers, distances, on bikes, on heads, on donkeys with little traps. So many colors of water container. Children are what I see, war parties of them with spears, in shot-through dresses and straining shorts. Terrifying. My heart booms.

Wake up on higher, drier, dustier land. I look up my side at dramatic crags; imagine eagles and leopards in it. Didn't expect palms or giant mouse-eared cactus. The other side is an ocean of sky. Clouds tower up like galleons on it. Armadas, unfurling and sailing off.

"Now we are stopping for lunch!" Lawi says.

Vernon turns around to check I heard. We park by a wayside shack with threadbare grass and three picnic benches. Stepping out I feel light, like a dream, suspended in space and pale blue air. I can't see anything, just balls on a scarlet pompom tree. It has no leaves but it's down on one knee, trying not to drop its pompom flowers over the edge of the precipice. I don't know the name of anything.

"The Great Rift Valley," Isaac says.

My eyes follow the arc of his arm. Stagger a bit. Suck in at the blue vapor. Everything shifts. Isaac is pointing at something hundreds of miles distant. It looks like a flat-topped purple cone protruding from the valley floor. I go and stand beside him.

"Logonot," Isaac says. "She is finished now but everywhere in the Kenya there is volcano underneath, getting ready for coming up."

"Terrible hellfire is burning under feets," Benjamin says.

A man after my own heart; I've always enjoyed language liberties.

"That volcano," Jeff says, "is bigger than our Ben Nevis, looks like nothing down there, does it?"

We sit down on picnic benches, positioned for a falling-off sensation. Brilliant. I love it when sandwiches are cut on the diagonal. It's a wide-angle lunch, laid out on a white tablecloth. Lawi has changed into a chef's hat, white apron and vest.

"Nut roast," he says to me. "Bean salad. Quiche. Avocado. Banana. Papaya. Watermelon. Mango. Passion fruit." A whole new language.

Isaac and Benjamin have some business with an old man in the shack. They've fetched him some supplies and are busy carrying boxes in. Margaret is happy to sit on the bench beneath a rustic woven shade. Come up into the air. Breathe deeply. I know that it is the East Wind, the same wind that on the coast they call the Monsoon–King Solomon's favorite horse. But up here it's just the resistance of air as the earth throws itself forward into space. Out of Africa. I remember every word. Up in this high air you breathed easily, drawing in vital assurance and lightness of heart. That Danish lady, she wasn't wrong. The others are standing on the edge, taking awed photographs of the view. I lift my camera to my eye, try this and that, but the Great Rift Valley makes a nonsense of zooms, wide angles and volcanoes.

"Say, Lou—are you about ready to move right along?" Vernon is at my elbow.

I'm fixed on color and clarity. Scarlet pompoms. Black butterflies. They came all at once and landed to sip on the tubes and drips of scarlet pompom juice. Slide film. Macro lens, the shutter is a sure and steady thing.

"That's it now," I say. "I've done a whole roll of film."

Before Vernon can get a shot himself, the black butterflies lift together and in a series of rapid blinks disappear as quickly as they came. I walk with Vernon back to the minibus. Jeff and Alison reappear from a toilet shack yonder. I help Margaret up the minibus steps.

"Don't they do hip replacement operations in America?"

"Waste of tight-anium," she says.

"It was this trip or a new hip," Vernon explains.

We set off again. Benjamin takes a careful track, hairpin bending down the steep valley side. Beyond that the hours start to scuff, we run through ruts until the ruts run out. Hit the gray grit of a thrown-out road, spraying it wide in banks behind us. Benjamin knows this road, settles us into a swaying slalom around the craters and the meteorites that made them. The land is overexposed, shimmering with heat mirage. Blown and ripped with crooked thorns and green splints of short rain leaf. The road grit starts firing under my feet. Seeing red, see it, red, blurring through the bass lines, a drumming running stitch.

"Masai," Isaac says.

"Say, Isaac, where do you think he's coming from—where would he be going to?"

Nobody knows. I close my eyes, begin to spin. Out of the black, and into the red, and into the blue. Flashing. Shar. Shar. Shar. Shar. Sharp with burning sparks.

"Stay with us, Catherine!" they call, they shout, they arsts her nice. "Stay with us Catherine! Catherine, please!"

They keep on calling but she don't come. One man is angry now cos he wants her more than anyone else.

"Fight, Catherine, you have to fight!"

Statement of: Mr. John Nesbitt,
42 Ellend Road, High Wycombe

November 22, 1976

Taken and transcribed by PC Pine 0867

I am employed by Templar Construction as an FBD driver. It's a large earth-moving machine. On Monday November 15, I was working on the foundation stones laid between Junctions 13 and 14 of the London Orbital (M25) Motorway. I finished work at five o'clock and parked the FBD back at base where we leave our cars. It was my first day with Templar and I chatted to the site foreman in his Portakabin for about an hour. When he locked up and we went off to our cars, I realized I had left my car keys in my work coat pocket. I had left the coat about a mile along the works, on the rock where I had eaten my lunch. The foreman offered to take me home and pick me up the next day since he lives my way. Sadly my wife had miscarried our first baby the day before and I was in no mind for going home. I said I'd walk back for the coat and keys. It was dark and the wind was biting. I picked my way back through the motorway works. Everything was frozen up and difficult to walk on, there were stars in the puddles. I got there eventually but my coat wasn't where I left it. I didn't know what to do except go back to base and walk up to civilization for a telephone box. There was a broken down JCB-752 parked off to one side. It's a big digger with a wide beam bucket. I passed it on the way up and on the way back tried the cab door, to see if there was an old coat inside I could borrow. The cab was locked so I walked around and tried the other side. It was open but there wasn't a coat. I found a packet of cigarettes and sat and smoked a few, glad to be out of the wind. The sky changed from black to green and I saw the blizzard coming. I was too cold to stay any longer and the snow was settling thick and fast. The bucket of the JCB was facing down, rested flat on a heap of sand. When I climbed down to leave I saw a hole, like a badger or something had dug under it. I got the matches from the cab and tried to see if there were paw prints in the sand. It looked fresh-dug and I was curious what was underneath but the wind kept blowing the matches out. I put the last lighted match down in the hole and recognized then a small human foot. I called into the hole but there was no sign of life. Next thing I was tunnelling like a badger myself. When I tried to pull the child out, it was then that the spear went through my hand. The doctor says I won't be able to work for six weeks. And though I am very happy that the little girl is alive, my wife says six weeks' wages are hard to find. Also my back is playing up from running so far with the girl in my arms. I am not a big man.

John Nesbitt

". . . Masai killed the black rhino and all of the lions to prevent that land from being designated as a National Park as well. Say, Lou, would you like a humbug?"

Vernon Pennsylvania USA is talking to me. Would I like a humbug? I would, to rid the taste. I sway forward to get one.

"Thanks, Vernon."

Something for my nerves to suck on. I go back to my seat. This relentless never-never-ness, our eyes run off with glare. The afternoon sun is scorching in my lap. I close my eyes. Still see red.

I open my eyes. Vernon has left his seat to kneel nearer the front, where he can see the road ahead and talk to Isaac. Margaret is sitting alone. Something's coming. A feeling, like a double bass bow string. I don't know what it is, but it is . . . what? Going to be fine. Something is going to happen. Something always does.

"Margaret." I move down the minibus to sit beside her. "Margaret. We're going to the Masai Mara!"

Her small hand punches the air. Then life explodes beside the road, goes off, like flying sparks, like fireworks, like the greatest show on earth. They disappear.

"Very fine!" Isaac says. "Thomson's gazelles! I have never before see so many-many together as this. Very fine!"

Come on, something, come on in, don't be shy—pull up a chair.

Hello, Mum—Can I have a cup of tea?

Irene said he would need time. More time. I posted a letter in Nairobi yesterday to say I was here, in Africa.

I'm here, in Africa.

I said I was six thousand miles away, coming very slowly, overland. I think about where it might end. I think about where it began.

"Masai Mara," Isaac says. "Only five more hours to go!"

Act Two

Can't get the hang of his name: Mr. Mac-Kiddeley-Pullet-Something. Even got it written on the palm of my hand but it's smudged with nerves. I just call him Mr. Mac and he thinks it's a sign of affection.

"Explain it to me again." He shoots at the basketball hoop fixed above the door. Nearly. The ball tips off the rim, drops and sends my crutches flying. I get the ball and hold it.

"You can no longer do your job?" he says.

I shake my head.

"Which was?" he says.

"Running around plowed fields like a nutter with a spade, digging sapling trees in and out of the ground."

He has to close his eyes to see it. I try to make it vivid for him.

"It's a winter mail-order business. I've got a team of part-time ladies that stay in the shed and pack them. I have to stay outside in the rain and put the orders together. We've got two hundred and fifty different makes of tree, in two foot, four foot and six foot sizes, spread out on seventy-six acres." I wonder if to say on a slope. And all of the roots tangle around your legs. And some people order one of each.

"Go on." He does a swirl in his chair.

"I have to carry heavy bundles of plants and shift big trees about. Spring, I run around all day with trolleys and unload lorryloads of plants and garden pots and statues and building sand and bales of compost."

He opens one eye.

"Sounds to me like a penance."

I close one eye.

"Well, Mr. Mac," I says, "if I keep my nose to the grindstone it might improve my looks."

Nothing. He starts chewing gum, even though he int got any.

"Actually, you look fit," he says. "Like a powerhouse. Fighting fit."

I wonder if to mind him I can't actually walk.

"This second operation hasn't repaired the damage?"

"I won't know til this cast comes off."

"I was wondering about that—the cast—nothing is broken, is it?"

It would help if he read the consultant's notes.

"No," I says. "It's the severed nerves; they've tried to fix the motor nerve: the one that moves your foot up and down, the cast is to keep all the tendons stretched."

"Are you in pain?"

"If I'd had a car last night I would have driven it into a chemist."

"So, we've got Pain and Suffering. Expenses. Loss of Career and Income. I take it you're single," he says. "Remind me, how old are you?"

"Twenty," I say.

He wants the ball. He int having the ball.

"Where is your file anyway?" he says. "What was your name again?"

"Beverley Woods," I say. "W, double O, D, S."

As solicitors go he's brilliant, he's just such a cunt at his job, that's all. Can't get these crutches level, odd pair, makes me look like a crippled cripple. I hobble through the market square, know he's at his winder watching me. Don't want him to see me drop the paperwork, case I has to crawl about on the pavement. And he says Negligence gainst the Cottage Hospital won't stand up. They may well have treated the stab wound like a surface cut and stitched loads of grit inside, and sealed in the blood seeping from a nicked artery til my foot was the size of a fucking elephant's but no medical practitioner will testify gainst another. Don't know whether to spit or bawl my eyes out, too tired to concentrate on either. I fall down on a grassy bank by the river behind the abbey. Spring is sprung. The grass is riz and damp. Should be looking for another place to stay. I lie down. Wait for my heart to stop bashing, sun shattering through my eyelashes.

Makes me laugh. A white ball of fluff with a pink tongue comes, licks my eyelids inside out. Makes me laugh so rude, I grab the little maniac bundle and hold it up.

"Hello," I says.

It squeals, hope it don't piss.

"Panda!" a posh voice is yelling. "Panda. No!"

I squint sideways through sunlight; she's wearing white pedal pushers and navy pumps. In training for summer.

"The idiot lead wouldn't retract." She sounds as clipped as box hedging.

Rapunzel I think cos of her hair, hanging forward over one shoulder in a long fat orange plait, magines yanking it, see if bells start ringing. She seems mused cos the puppy loves me.

"She'd be just the same if you were wearing your best clothes," she says.

I wonder if to tell her.

"This is much more like it," she says.

We look up, at blue sky through the blossom branches.

"Aren't they pretty," she says, "the cherry trees?"

These are almonds actually, but I nods all the same. She's got a sailor shirt with stripes and rope bangles, handbag and everything. I sit up and put the puppy down sides me. It goes bonkers in circles trying to get my hand to stroke it, spreads and shuffles all of my paperwork.

"Watch she doesn't—Oh dear," she says, "it's what they call a tinkle."

"It's what they call an eviction order." I look at the piss on the paper. "Soaking in nicely," I says.

"Oh dear?" She's on a back foot, intrigued.

"Well, not sactly *eviction*. His Lordship has sold the manor, that's all. It's notice to get out of the Gate House, find somewhere else."

The puppy shoves up under my jumper, comes out at the neck. Finds a mole under my chin needs especial cleaning.

"I'm trying to rent a house here myself," she says. "Is there a weekly property paper? I need stabling for a horse as well."

"The *Post*, tomorrow," I says.

It is warm. I take my jumper off with the puppy still inside it. Dog laughs, loves me more.

"What's its name?"

"Officially, at the Kennel Club she's *Pandora's Ice Star Galactica* but I call her Panda Bear, don't I? Don't I—nah?" she says. "So, pray tell, what is the highlight of this town?"

"Leaving it," I try for a joke.

"Quite," she says, little and wicked.

She looks at her watch.

"My car is parked on a double yellow. I'd better go." She says, "I'm absolutely sick to death of getting parking tickets."

"Bye," I says.

She drags the puppy, it don't want to go, like stubborn fluff. On the bridge by the abbey she picks it up, stuffs it under her arm. Can still hear it. Wailing. Terrible. The river is shallow and running fast with yellow ribbons of weed. Duck. Coot. Swan. Kennel? Never heard someone say the word: kennel.

Dog's house. Pray fucking tell. Can smell witch hazel but there int one in sight. I breathe. I sit and sit by the river.

"Five more minutes, Mr. Nesbitt." She squeaks way.

So close he is, over my face. His watch is ticking by my ear and his coat smells of roads. Crying, gain. One of his tears drops on my cheek and rolls down into my eye.

"Catherine," Mr. Nesbitt says. "My princess, my girl."

I move my head and pour the tear out from my eye, but stead it goes in my ear. Tickles. Makes me laugh.

Makes me laugh. Funny.

Int funny. Can't stop.

Can't stop.

"Nice and calm, nice and calm," the fat nurse says. Her hands is mad as marshmallows. Makes me laugh.

Makes me laugh.

"Nice and calm," Mr. Nesbitt says.

My policeman starts laughing. Int funny.

"Nice and calm!" He can't stop laughing.

Mr. Nesbitt pats my policeman on the shoulder.

"Nice and calm," he says.

My policeman laughs so hard his heels is up on the chair and tears is running down his face. Laughing, can't stop. Makes me laugh. Int funny. I close one eye, leave the other two open.

"Don't worry," the fat nurse says, "it's just the mushrooms in your mind."

Int funny. Makes me laugh. Two men come long tending to be doctors. They stop at every bed; one splains it to the other, sounds like bah, bah, bah. The edges of my brain goes frilly.

"Bah," one says to Mr. Nesbitt.

"Flygaric," I says.

"Hello." My policeman moves his chair out of the doctors' way.

"Catherine Clark, hypothermia—critical, five times we lost her and got her bah-bah back."

"Riley?"

"Exposure. Starvation. Dehydration. Frost-bah-bah bite."

Other words whisper behind the curtain. Lions' whiskers.

"Riley?"

"Loss of liver and kidney function. High measure of pst pst psilocybin in her bah-bah blood."

"Riley?"

"She's must be pretty trippy." He smiles, cos happy to have a sheep's head.

Makes me laugh. Int pretty. Int pretty.

"Back from the bah-bah brink, Catherine?" the doctor says. "Nice to see you've warmed up."

They done mistakes. I int Catherine. I int warmed up.

"How are you feeling?" the other one arsts.

I has to close my eyes. Cabbige whites fly up. More whiter than green, more greener than white. Can't hold them or keep them, if you does they die. I has to go with them. I has to go now.

Blue is moving. Baby Grady finds me, I get his good surprise. Smell of sunshine and calamine lotion. I breathe his skin and feels his elbow in my ribs, got his chubby feets on my hips and his soft weight laid down on me. I know he's smiling cos I get his little laugh and fingers squashing up my lips. Baby Grady. I open my eyes, spects his little button teefs. Blue starts spinning, I hears the screaming, makes me sick inside, I got the taste.

"I'd run, girly, if I were you."

Nobody here. The bashing is so loud and so clear. I buries myself and breathes through a straw. A lion gets up on my bed, sniffs around my face. Int sure if there's anyone here. The curtains move and more lions come under. My policeman tends he can't even see them.

"I'd like to take a little more blood from you, Catherine, if that would be all right?"

I look in the lions' eyes.

"Go on then," I shout but they don't. They take the lady from the next bed and drag her down the ward, she don't say nothing, surprise made her heart stop. Mine stops all the time. I lay in a swirl and wait.

"Would it be all right, Catherine, to take a little more blood?" the Blood Lady says case I bite her.

I nod my head.

"Good girl," she says but I int.

Blood won't come out cos it's froze, needle hurts with antifreeze going in my other arm. Starts crying don't know how come. A man tending to be a vicar comes in holding up his dress, does the cancan at bottoms of beds, steps over the bits what the lions has left. I members what they done to Jesus, makes me chuck up sick.

"Nurse!" my policeman yells.

Curtains is whispering all the time. I hangs on a terrible pain.

I hangs.

I rears up in my mind, agony makes me deaf and blind.

"There we are, smashing toes," the Bandage Nurse says. "That nasty old Jack Frost bit the little one off, didn't he?"

I sees the paw prints in blood on the floor and up all over my sheets. The lions took my toes, they done it so I can't run way. I listens. The curtains' whisker.

My duffel bag is packed. I go slowly on my crutches, down to Betty's transport caff on the trading estate. But I'm hours early and Bob int here yet. Don't know if I'm clever enough to live in a student house, but the room is cheap and they know I'm coming, all thanks to Bob who comes from Sheffield. He's going to give me a lift. He int here. Just a few plumbers.

"Hello, goddess," one of them says.

Another one has got a gammon steak on his fork and a ring of pineapple.

"Body made for loving," he says.

"Why does you have to be so fat?" I says. But it's just my magination.

I move on crutches around all the tables and sit down over in the corner. Tyrone brings my coffee to me. We always has a cuddle cos he's got the Down's syndrome.

"Where's Bob?"

"No Bob. No Bob. No Bob today," he says.

A couple of customers followed me in and he goes back to the counter to serve them. I smoke and watch the plumbers eating. One slaps a slice of bread in his gravy then eats it with a knife and fork. The door opens and the rich girl from yesterday comes in. She's wearing jodhpurs and a hacking jacket and long black rubber riding boots. Mad fluff puppy wedged under her arm.

Everyone stops chewing to watch her, mugs is halfway to lips.

Today her hair is loose, like an orange cape shining red in the kinks from yesterday's plait. Surprises me how someone so little can look down her nose at people, it's like she's still up on her horse. I look outside, see if she came on it, but there's only a dark gray Audi Quattro and the plumbers' vans parked. Nice car, Audi Quattro. She goes straight to use the payphone on the wall. Gets in a mess with the dog and the leash and her purse and the pen and the address book with the phone number in. Coins keep dropping through.

"For God's sake!" She puts the dog down, tries gain to make the call.

Dog looks around bored, sees a bit of fried egg under a table, goes off on a weaving adventure, around table legs and chairs. When it sees me it goes mad, brings everything dragging and slopping with it. Leaves a trail of piss, knocks my crutches over. Wuthering Heights drops her purse and all the coins spill out.

"I need to speak to—hello—oh for pity's sake; can you ring me back. Hello?"

I hobble over on the plaster cast and take the *idiot* lead from her hand; it's gone around her legs three times. She's got through to someone.

"I'm tired of this now," she says. "Tell him it's urgent—it's Gwen Llewelyn."

I pick the puppy up and start untangling mess of legs and tangled furniture. When she finishes on the phone I've got everything straight and cleaned up and the puppy has gone up my jumper.

"It's ridiculous," she says.

"You should sit down have a cup of sweet tea. Cigarette," I say, "calm your nerves."

"I had no idea that people actually spoke like you in real life."

I could say the same about her, sides no one speaks like me in real life. If I didn't speak the way I does I wouldn't even exist.

"Don't you think it suits me?"

"I mean where in London would I have to go to end up talking with an accent like that?"

"I int ever lived in London," I says. "Lived everywhere else. You want a cup of tea? I'm having another one, since your dog knocked the first one over."

"I suppose I ought to thank you and buy it."

"Yeah," I says. "I spose you ought."

It's unusual, red hair and olive skin. She's grubby around her neck, in the creases on her wrist. Uh-huh. That's what I sides, she's a dirty person in clean clothes.

"Did you get through in the end?" I offer her a cigarette.

"Finally," she says and takes one. "The tragedy of working for a living."

"What does you do?" I says.

"I'm a private investigator," she says.

"No shit," I says. Likes it, wishes I could say it gain.

I light our cigarettes and hold the match while she blows it out. Tyrone calls that our tea is ready; he's too scared of her to bring them over. She goes to the counter, seems like the whole caff goes with her. The puppy is hypnotized by my thumb stroking tween its eyes. I remember that yesterday she was looking for a place. She brings the tea and sits down.

"Any luck in the paper?"

"Eh?" she says.

"House Hunting, Horse and Hound."

"It looks as though I'm not staying after all; my case is moving to Rotherham of all godforsaken destinations. Did you find anywhere?"

"I'm going this afternoon," I says. "I've got a room in Sheffield and a free ride up there."

"How odd."

Don't know what she means.

"We'll be practically neighbors," she says. "Do you know the address?"

I get the piece of paper out of my pocket. Chippenhouse Road, Nether Edge, Sheffield. She reads it.

"When I get up to Yorkshire," she says, "I could give you a knock. We could go out on the town."

It int something I can picture. I spects she will forget the address.

"If you like," I say, feel a bit faint. The painkillers make me woozy. Feel really faint.

"Has to put my head down." I lift the puppy.

She reaches over to take it from me.

"Is it pain from your foot?"

"I int been feeling very well," I says.

"How long have you been like this?"

"Twenty years," I says, ducking.

"Soppy," she says.

"Five more minutes, Mr. Nesbitt."

"Nurse!" he calls.

She rolls back like a person on tracks, her smile and elbows and wrists is clockwork.

"Mr. Nesbitt?" Her head tips sideways.

Mr. Nesbitt looks up at her.

"It won't be tonight, will it?" he says. "They won't decide tonight?"

"No, Mr. Nesbitt, nothing can happen until Mr. Abraham has seen Catherine."

He holds his arms out, like carrying something heavy and dead.

"Where will they take her? I'd like to know."

I wonders what he done to his hand.

"Mr. Nesbitt," she says, "it really is a matter for the police, for close friends and for . . ."

Lions eat the rest of her words, ripping up under her ribs. Her leg int coming off easy, but she still is smiling as they drag her all cross the floor.

"Don't worry, Catherine." Mr. Nesbitt breathes on my fingers one at a time and rubs them, case he can warm them up. "Don't worry," he says.

I tries to tell him, *I int Catherine*, but the first word ties a knot. Stead, I smell the freesias and eat a grape to cheer him up.

"You really must go now, Mr. Nesbitt," says the clockwork nurse.

"Could you not hear me, Catherine? I've been calling you," the nurse says. "This man has come to take some photographs of you. He's come especially."

He looks like sorry for being Scottish. He's got a kilt on with a long safety pin and socks with tassels. The nurse pulls the curtains around and my policeman stays the other side.

"Hello," the man says. "Ken Dooley at your service. I understand that you've got some ve*rr*y special patterns?"

"Would it be all right, Catherine, for me to undo your gown so the man can photograph your front?" the nurse arsts.

I make them all nervous. Case I bite them. I nod my head. The nurse undoes my gown and pats for me to lay down flat. I got blue pants with daisies on, don't know how come. Nurse folds the sheet so that the man can see.

"Yes indeed," he says. "Ve*rr*y, ve*rr*y interesting."

They pull one curtain back on the winder side and roll me about ever so nice trying to get the light right. The camera's nose comes out, elephant wants a currant bun, don't know how he does it, can't see no strings or nothing. He don't even want my face. I int allowed to stand up.

"Aerial view," he says.

He stands on the plastic chair and the nurse holds it steady cos the floor int level but she int allowed to look up his skirt.

"I was wondering," he says, getting down. "Would it be all right to take some close-ups?"

They both stand looking at me.

"What do you think, Catherine? Would it be OK for this man to take some close-ups of your front?"

I nod my head.

"Good girl," she says.

He has to come down almost level, to get the sun and shadow proper. The film runs out so fast he has to put a new one in. He turns the camera one way, then the other, runs around the bed, side to side.

"Beautiful," he says. "Beautiful."

And it's true, my patterns is beautiful. I wonders if to tell him I done them with a ruler. The sun goes behind a cloud.

"We'll have to use the flash," he says.

"Weston-super-Mare?" I say to the ticket lady.

She gives me an irregular look like I stole the coat or something.

"Return?"

"No."

The coach is filling up, last winder seat is mine. I think about Gwen. Surprised me, one Saturday night I found her on my Sheffield doorstep. She dragged me out to the Ritzy, we went a few times. She danced around her handbag and all the men in the room. I always slipped out on the fire escape and sat up on the roof, until it was time for Gwen and me and some bloke to leave. She was living in Rotherham, renting a caravan in Maurice's yard. He's got a shed and a polytunnel and a flower barrow in a lay-by, I did some pricking-out for him and minded his shop while he had a day off. Gwen's *case* was living just up the road but three months later they moved again, to Weston-super-Mare, so Gwen and her horse and her dog moved too. She tried hard to tempt me at the time, but I'd already promised Maurice I'd help him with the run-up to Christmas. My hands is still shredded from making the holly wreaths. I went over there this morning to say I was moving south, catching up with Gwen. He was in a good mood, "Go on, ask me," he said. Went out last night with an air hostess that Dateline sent him, "Cunt like an allotment," he said.

Sometimes think me and Gwen are friends only because she insists. I don't know how people get good friends; I only seem to get other fuck-ups and freaks. That int fair, it don't sound kind. We did have a few nice times and even when she left she rang me every week for a chat. I feel a bit sick actually, with impending doom. Christmas and New Year was desolate in the student house, just me and the ferret in the kitchen. Last night Gwen caught me off guard.

"Come on!" she said. "What are you waiting for?"

"I don't know," I said. "Listen." I put the receiver down on the floor so Gwen could hear the Pennine wind chewing under the front door. Students kept climbing over my threadbare shoulder on the threadbare stairs.

"So what are you waiting for?" Gwen said. "Why stay in Sheffield?"

Students is such filthy bastards.

"I've got to get a job, Gwen."

"You can look as easily down here," she said. "Come on! It will be a crack!"

"I don't know," I said. "Member the policeman's boots?"

Have you nowt better to do than tiptoe through bloody tulips?

"It's much warmer down here," she said, "positively temperate."

Sold to the lady with the mouth full of marbles.

"OK," I said. "I'll get the coach tomorrow."

I heard the long-distance words, traveling down the line, and instantly wished I could get them back.

Now the coach is making sounds like leaving. Sheffield has been kind to me, everybody gave me cake, but winter came the first week of September and all I did was thrash about with tears freezing on my face. Cept now I've got Soyoko's coat. Reckon it has saved my life. And security guards don't follow me around. It's a new year. Now I'm going to Weston-super-Mare. Seaside. Gwen says her aunt bought this place as a property investment but she's gone to Leningrad for a nose job. Holiday cottage. I magines spring, creeping over me windersill.

Warm face.

Warm hands.

Warm feets.

"Lovely." A bloke sits down sides me. "Last seat. Roasting in here."

We pass the hospital. Physiotherapy has finished now. It's so hot on the coach we has to take our coats off, whether we want to or not. The Lovely bloke stands up to put them in the overhead rack; holds my coat over his arms like a beautiful fainted lady. Change is as good as a rest. I think about Piggy, Gwen's horse, great chestnut clod with his white socks around his ankles, his great white face, his great big heart. I get really excited then, like going to see an old friend.

Warm, salty wind slaps hair all over my face, int sure which way I'm facing.

"It walks," Gwen says. She's never seen me without the crutches.

"It limps long."

Panda jumps right up into my arms. She's grown a lot in the six months since I last seen her. She finds the mole gain, under my chin. The coach driver gets my bag out from the stowage.

"Here you are, Miss," he says.

Surprises me how a coat can change your bloody what's name.

"Is that it?" Gwen says. "Your worldly chattels?"

"My worldly dictionary."

"What about your clothes?"

"I'm wearing them all. Minus nine in Sheffield. It's definitely warmer down here." I look around. "No car?"

"Poor Betsy's sick—I've offered sweet words and kicked seven sorts of shit out of her but she won't start. It's only a stroll along the prom. I use the word 'stroll' loosely," she says.

"Glad to get rid of the crutches. It int just your foot you lose, it's both your bloody hands as well. Where's the sea?" I arsts.

"Good question."

We go to the promenade wall and lean on it, looking out. See the seagulls, they is so citing playing on a wind. Wonders which one is Jonathan Livingstone.

"Never knew mud could be so beautiful," I says. "Is the pier open? I love them sliding shelf machines where you drop the penny in, there's something mesma about all that moving metal and shine. Have they got the Six Horse Race machine? Is it open now?"

"No, Soppy," she says. "It closes at three in the winter." She always seems to jig around me like I was up on a plinth or something.

In an avenue of stately old people's homes, we turn down a leylandii conifer track wide enough for a car to scrape through. Wedged between garden fences, on a tiny plot behind, is her aunt's holiday cottage. Gwen's used the word "cottage" loosely, looks like it's made of wet hardboard. The gray Quattro is parked in front, next to a muck heap.

"I think it was cheap," Gwen says, "and it's not costing us anything, so that's good, isn't it?" She does a jig of good fortune on the breeze-block step. The front door is warped with wetness; she has to kick the bottom of it. I'd like to say she's done us proud but it looks to me like a damp, poky old hole with concrete floors and woodchip paper on hardboard walls. Polystyrene ceiling tiles. Stick-on floral dado rail. The caravan Gwen had in Rotherham had more substance about it. The hall has plastic pine folding doors, sticky with fingers and flyblow. One clatters back.

"Ta-da."

Freezing ugly hole of a bathroom. Pitchfork in the shower cubicle, out of the way. We step over a shit in the hall.

"Panda," she says, case I never knew who done it.

"Ta-da."

Kitchen.

"Compact and bijou."

"Loverly close-up of a fence," I says.

"Food hatch." She flaps it down on a broken hinge and it won't close back up. Falls down. "For God's sake," she says. "A little maintenance wouldn't go amiss."

We shuffle around peeling our shoes off the lino and come back out.

"Ta-da."

Gwen's bedroom, same as usual, bridle hanging on the bedhead, straw all over the carpet. Bales piled up around the winder. Another nice close-up of a fence.

"What's that noise?"

"Ta-da."

"Fucking. Hell."

Piggy neighs, always does when he sees me.

"That's Piggy's end of the lounge and this is ours." Gwen is jigging on a carpet so wet with horse piss it actually splashes. He looks pitiful, with his big head hanging down. I move his saddle off the sofa and sit down. Can't look. He clonks a stride forward, puts his head over my shoulder.

"Hello, big fella," I says.

He breathes hard into my hand.

"He int got any headroom, Gwen."

"Well, I know that," she says. "It's not bloody well my fault that I got him in here and now he won't come out. I have to put him somewhere. What am I supposed to do?"

Silence rings with a petulant pitch. The dog gets in her basket, tramples around in circles trying to dig a deeper hole in the denim jacket. My voice is lit and sparks in the air.

"Tomorrow we're going to get him a field," I says.

"How can I be expected to pay for everything?" She wuthers on the edge of tears and some dark moors above the dado rail, pulling and clawing at her plait, always lets her hair down for it. Now she's going down the hall, me and the dog get up to see. She slams the front door behind her, but it's damp and bounces back open. When she kicks in the nearside wing of her car, the dog yelps. She storms off down the track.

I feels sick, guts has gone, int got the stomach for my heart bashing. I feels faint, finds my way back to sit on the sofa. Don't want to touch it, try to breathe. Horse hooks over my shoulder, pulls me in, and closer. I clutches his whole head in my arms. Softness and warmth of his throat almost hurts and he stands so solid still. Don't know how long we close our eyes, waits for calm, til we got one breath and one heartbeat. We listen to Panda hounded, in her basket, in her sleep and rain drumming on the chalet roof.

Gone dark, I don't want to disturb this horse, to get up and turn the light on, but he lifts his head to let me. I grope about for switches. A fluorescent tube flickers on, then its twin the other end. I see a horse in the strobe, top lip turned up, sad mock-up of a huge joke. I know. What kind of cunt puts fluorescent tubes in a lounge diner? I look at the big stupid horse, the ceiling making him low down and humble. Toe down and dip-hipped. It int proper.

"You want to lie down?" I arsts.

When everything is done I turn off the lights. Listens. Our hearts all boom in the dark. Water falls from guttering. The front door sticks and kicks. Gwen back, with butter. She talks to me from the dark hallway.

"Ingredients for toast," she sniffs. "You've got the Calor gas fire going; it won't ever light for me. Why are you sitting over there in the dark, why don't you sit by the fire?"

The horse is giving off more heat. She comes then, stands in the doorway and flicks on the lights.

"Oh?" she says. "You've moved my belongings about?"

I've moved the dented rusted ugly fuck of a Calor gas fire, and the total bore of a Paris painting that she always hangs above it. I've moved the nylon-covered soggy chipboard sewing box.

"I've moved the sofa forward so the horse can lie down behind it if he wants to. I hope you don't mind but I gave him some straw to lie on and a wedge of hay and filled up his water bucket."

"Spoiled Piggy!" She jigs around into the kitchen. I can see her through the food hatch, doing a piggy jig with the butter knife.

"There's six stables listed in the Yellow Pages," I says. "In the morning we could try phoning them for a start. We could have a drive out to somewhere green; arst at a couple of farms or something."

"There isn't any money," she says. "Which part of that don't you understand?"

Oh—that clinking clunking sound.

"I can get a bit from the bank."

She's burned the toast, it's on fire.

"You cook it, I'll scrape it," I try for a joke.

"But we can't drive around anywhere, Betsy won't start."

I know the script, we done it so many times fore.

"I'll have a look in the morning."

"God, it's infuriating. Is there no end to your talents?"

I wonder if to tell her I'm crap at choosing friends.

"How many slices does The Body want?"

"Five." I spit on the saddle soap. I always like to clean the saddle and run the stirrup irons smooth up and down long the leather.

We was sposed to be going out on the town and I'm glad we int made it. She's pretty harmless indoors, pissed, playing air guitar and throwing her hair backward and forward to Nutbush City Limits and here we fucking go: Quo. The more pissed she gets the closer she comes, smiling at me and calling me Soppy and doing jigs like Rumple Stiltskin, inviting me to let down my hair.

"It int going to work the same, Gwen" I says. "Not with my piece of piss."

"You shouldn't worry," she says Welsh. "Who the hell needs hair with a pair of legs like yours?"

"One of them don't quite work," I point out.

"With a body like yours, hell, you don't even need a face." Off she goes gain, rocking all over the world.

Four hours later she's on her damp knees miming midnight and not a sound from the pavement. I wonder if to kill myself. Always does when I drink.

I'd shoot the Paris painting and track down the man that done it. I'd shoot him three times, for lack of color and magination and one last time for wasting paint and ripping off tourists. I'd track down Gwen's ex-fiancé, Ian, and shoot him for taking her there. I'd shoot the Calor gas fire and the stereo tower. And the car. I'd shoot the horse, clean in the temple, and the dog; I'd save Gwen for last. I'd give my right arm for a gun. I'd need my left to shoot it. I'd press the barrel hard up on the roof of my mouth and pull the trigger.

Why do the leaves–on the mulberry tree–whisper–differently–now?

The sun is holding my face. So warm it is coming through the winder. I try to get it on my tongue and on my wrists. Dust is sparkling, in the air, over Detective Cooper's shoulders. They glitter. *And gleam*. So, I close my eyes. Lights float by like petals on a pool.

Drifting, I listen to Detective Cooper, talking so soft like reading a story.

". . . you do not have to say anything, but anything you do say, may be taken down and used against you."

I open my eyes and close my mouth. I nods like understand but my shadow on the wall don't move.

"I am your barrister," Mr. Lawson says. "I will be representing you in court. Do you have anything that you want to say, Catherine? Catherine?"

And why is the nightingale–singing a tune–on the mulberry bough?

"We'll see you again tomorrow, Catherine," Detective Cooper says.

My policeman coughs.

"What kind of flowers should I plant along the fence?" the nurse says. "I thought maybe hyacinths. Oleanders?"

My fingers are laced up under his mane. His head clamps me in, his chest is so warm. I look down at my bare feet on the straw and his great plates of hooves; he's standing on my toe that isn't there any more. I turn my eyes sideways at the stereo tower, record still spinning and the needle scuffing. Stale cold smell of morning. And horse. In a lounge dining room. I've still got my beautiful coat on. I move the curtain; see raindrops on the roof of the car and the muck heaps steaming hot in the air. Stopped raining. No sound of Gwen or the dog. I find her car keys on the side in the kitchen and let myself out of the front door. Horse wearing a net curtain, watches me from the winder. It's warmer outside than in, can smell the sea. I open the Quattro with the key. It's full of hay and takeaway rubbish, empty half-bottles of Scotch.

She has to have three cushions to see over the steering wheel and the seat pulled so far forward I can't even get my legs in. I put the car in neutral and turn the key in the ignition. Listens. It int the battery or the starter motor.

The engine clattering wakes Gwen up. The dog hops up on my lap. I pull the bonnet release lever and get out.

"You stay in here, and drive," I tell the dog and she does.

"What's the diagnosis?" Gwen is wearing her nylon dressing gown; sight of it makes me shudder, the ditchwater color, the stains on it, the melted cigarette hole in it.

"Shit in your carburetor," I says.

"Why," she wuthers, "does it always happen to me?"

"Well, you always is driving on dregs."

"I always *am* driving on dregs."

I don't say nothing.

"Poor Betsy," she says.

"I left the Yellow Pages open, ready," I says. "Are you going to ring the stables or am I?"

"No—no, I'll do that." She does a jig. "As you were."

The carpet squares keep shifting sideways. My teef is upside down.

"Catherine Clark is here, Mr. Abraham," she says. "That's it, dear, through that door."

I hobble in. My policeman comes in with me.

"I think you can wait outside," Mr. Abraham says to him. "Leave the door ajar, would you?"

My policeman goes back out. I sit down in the daddy bear chair.

"Catherine?" Mr. Abraham says.

I shake my head.

"Who's been sitting in my porridge?" he says.

"Sorry." I stand up to come back out.

Through the open door I see the lions. They smells the secretary underneath her desk. Three lions together shove it over and rips her up like sheets for bandages.

"Sit down, Catherine," he says. "I have to write a report, about how you are, in yourself. Do you know where you are?"

I stay looking at the door. The drumming is so loud and so clear. A clock ticks but breathing int a certain thing. So sick, so sick, the taste. Knees is locked but I sinks straight down into the floor.

"Marion!" Mr. Abraham yells.

The secretary's shoes come in.

"I'll fetch a blanket, Mr. A," she says.

"And a pillow, Marion. And a cup of tea. Better bring a bowl. Yes, bring a bowl too."

There's a hole in the bottom of Mr. Abraham's shoe, yellow sock shines through. He's fallen sleep in his chair, spects he needs a holiday. I stand up and hobble, fold the blanket up and put the pillow on the table. Been sick in a bowl. Shiver nearly throws me over. Don't know if to wake him up. He's still holding his pen. It's dark outside but the lamp is shining on his desk. I look to see what he writ but all the pages is done Chinese. See two cups of tea both cold. I flick the skin off one with my fingers and flick it in a plant pot. Terrible taste. Thirsty, drinks mine and his as well. Shame he over-dunked his biscuit. The office is dark cept for shine from the corridor. The secretary has gone. My policeman int allowed to leave me. I look out in the corridor. He's with a man in a dressing gown and slippers, long way up by the coffee machine.

"It's criminal," the man says.

My policeman has to bash it. Then I get the whistling tune, in my ear and under my skin. I know it. I know it. Listens, the whistling, louder left. All of the corridors look the same, gray filled with doors and whistling. I close my eyes and sniff the air. The whistling is fresh as air. Don't know which way the lions is, but Pip's coming.

Uh-huh.

He is. Whistling and drumming on the change in his pocket. I slide down the wall, wait for him to come around the corner. I wipe at my eyes with the sleeve of my dressing gown, don't want him to see me crying.

It int Pip.

It's the newspaper trolley man. He stops whistling and looks down at me.

"Bit lost missy?" he says. "Do you know where you're from?"

I wipe my eyes, on the bottom of my dressing gown. He looks about for a wheelchair but there int one.

"Well, that's not a problem," he says. "We can nip past reception and they can look you up, have you got your plastic bracelet on your wrist?"

I look up my sleeves.

"There we are," he says, "your hospital number is on it."

I sit up on his trolley tween the *Sun* and the *Mirror*. We go in the lift and long past all the arms and legs and crunched bones. The newspaper words come off on my hands, bout a little girl they can't find. At accident and mergency the lady on reception writes down the number on my bracelet and looks through the records.

"Catherine Clark: Ward 7." She smiles at me, then at the newspaper man.

An old man in the waiting room wants to buy a paper from him so he wheels me over and gives him the *Mirror*. Every feeling in me stands up and the drumming starts to bash. I got the taste. That's how come I look around. The Sandwich Man is at reception.

"Lulu," he says. "Lulu King."

"I'm sorry." The lady checks one more time. "We don't have anyone of that name."

We found a field with good grass and a shelter, out on the road to Bristol. Lucky I had the money saved thanks to half-price rent in Sheffield and holly wreath cash-in-hand from Maurice. Gwen waited in the car outside the bank while I went in and got the money. Hundred quid for field rent in advance, forty quid for the hire of this horse trailer and twenty for gas.

I've been two years saving that money, now, gain, back to scratch. Principle is always costly, Anton learned me that.

We leave the car and the trailer out on the road and walk down the track to the chalet. Gwen goes in to make happy tea. I climb up on the muck heap out the front, look at the fascias. Then I go in, stand in the lounge doorway; look at the door frame and the turn in the hall. I look at the horse behind the sofa. Shake my head. Gwen leans through the hatch.

"How in God's name are we going to get him out?"

"How sactly did you get him in?"

"He just put his head down and breathed in, and slipped under the door frames. He's scared of the folding doors, idiot. So much for 'bomb-proof.'"

I look at the graze on his withers and the rip long his tender flank where the door catch caught him and the horseshoe-shaped dents in the wall where he kicked out, frightened. I look at the horse, nibbling sad hay. Scuffed knees. He looks up at me. I walk and whispers in his back-turned ear, he mustn't panic or try to rear up. I see the car keys on the kitchen counter; lean in and pick them up.

"Where are you going?" Gwen says.

I tends deaf.

"But you can't drive." She follows me with mugs of tea. "But you're not insured," she says on the step. "But you don't have a license," she yells.

In the street I turn the tow-bar handle and drop the horse trailer onto the road. Then reverse the car down the track and park it as close as I can to the chalet.

"What are you doing?" She spills tea hot on my heels down the hall.

I touch the horse on the shoulder and he shifts to where I want him. The winders open when I bash them and the tow rope threads through the frames.

"But," she says in the front doorway, "I don't understand?"

"Understand?" the dog says.

I tie the rope to the car and then get in and start it. I look at the chalet in the mirror, reckon it's only rested together like a house made out of cards. The wheels spin, the tow rope strains. Uh-huh, the front wall of the chalet falls down. Gwen wants to say something but can't, mugs hang limp in her wrists. The wall is laying down on the muck heap with the front door and winders in it and curtains still attached to the rail. Four-inch nails stick up from the frame, clean pulled out. I grab the wall and drag it wider out of the way.

"You get the horse in the trailer," I says. "And I'll bash the wall back up."

"Nice one, Macduff," she says Welsh.

"Macduff!" the dog says.

I don't know what it means.

The horse can hardly walk down the track, his joints so stiff, but he holds his head up noble and stumbles up urgently into the trailer, like he knows the ordeal is nearly over. The chalet wall bashes back up so neat, from outside you wouldn't know. I find Gwen in the dining room looking at the corners where the wallpaper tore.

"My aunt's going to have a fit," she says. "You've destroyed the decor."

I look at the black mold growing long the coving, at dog shit in the doorway, at the puddle of bright yellow horse piss collected in the corner.

"If your aunt dies of a fit," I says, "it will be the phone bill that done it."

She members then, the nine hundred and forty-seven pounds she's spent private-investigating the whereabouts and new life of her ex-fiancé, Ian. He's getting married to somebody else, cept Gwen int going to allow it. Her *case*.

"Oh well," she says. "Hi-ho."

Gwen mucked out the dining end with a wheelbarrow and I borrowed a fuse from her hairdryer to get the wet and dry vacuum working. Sucked up buckets of horse piss and then water and then disinfectant with Panda mad attacking the nozzle. The carpet has come up cleaner than it ever was and almost dried overnight. Have I ever noticed, have I ever learned, if I watch the toast it don't cook and if I don't it all gets burned? Can see Gwen through the hatch, sitting on the sewing box in front of the Calor gas fire. She reads me what the advert says, is going to set fire to the newspaper or melt more of her dressing gown.

"Have you ever been in one?"

"No," I says.

"No, I haven't either."

I reckon you has to be pretty.

"You should go for it, Gwen," I says.

"I may just give them a call and see what they have to say for themselves. What is there to lose?"

"Best had quick then, fore they cut the phone off."

Must mit, it is curious. I put our cups on the food-hatch ledge and walk around with our plates.

"Good morning," she says. "I'm phoning about the advertisement in the *Western Daily Press*, for Trainee Croupiers."

She's got the dog on her lap and a catkin of ash on her cigarette. Young men and *young women*, the advert says. I feel like forty and a car mechanic and Gwen looks like an old cigarette, one that got wet and dried out twice.

"Yes, I'll hold," she says.

Someone comes to the phone and she listens.

"Yes," she says. "This afternoon?" she says. "Right," she says. "One o'clock. I'm phoning on behalf of two of us, as a matter of fact. Yes," she says. "Both twenty."

I pass her the ashtray.

"Oh dear," she says. "What kind of tests?"

My tonsils blow up, feels sick, don't know what she's getting me into.

"No, I'm afraid I don't. From Weston-super-Mare." She gestures for the pen. "Quite," she says.

She tells our names. Then she writes *Casino Royale* and draws roundabouts and traffic lights on the margins of the newspaper.

Her hair's hopeless, lifeless, frizz.

"For God's sake," she says. "What am I supposed to do?"

She's still got a black suit from when she was a sales rep. It's covered in horsehair and stinks of gasoline.

"Black court shoes," she says.

I find them under a bale and some mold and fallen plaster.

"I keep meaning to get them repaired, they need new heels."

Plastic. Fucked.

"Shall I give them a wipe?"

"There's some polish under the sink," she says.

I find an instant black shoe shiner with a dabber on the end, does her shoes and my army boots. She's smearing foundation on her face, wrong color really, too orange.

"Black or tan tights?" she says.

"Black," the dog says.

I rip at her suit with strips of sticky tape.

"I'll come with you for the drive," I say. "I can wait in the car; just say I changed my mind."

"Don't be such a chicken!" She slings me one of her knee-length skirts. "We need to get you smartened up and businesslike."

The skirt looks like a pelmet on me and even though I'm twice her height she's wider than me on the hips.

"Oh dear," she says.

The blouse is seven inches short in the arm. The trousers . . .

"Maybe not," she says.

It's too bloody cold to be undressed. I put my old jeans back on and my lumberjack shirt and my beautiful coat.

Funny, Gwen has decided not to notice my coat; int said a word about it. Soyoko in the Sheffield house was learning Fashion Design. One night late she tapped on my door, surprised me, said the mannequin weren't no good, she needed to see the cut moving. The project was a full-length coat. The challenge, she said, was to get real warmth and beauty without any bulk. She paid for the black lambskins and all the pale broidery silks, come in the post from Italy. Every stitch was made to fit me. It took her three months and she nearly went blind hand-stitching the pale butterflies and flowers on the fluted cuffs. She came into my room and stood on a chair and kissed my cheek, got First Class and Exquisite. There was a show at the end of term and she arst me if I would go on the night and walk up and down in the coat. I had to keep flashing, people wanted to see the shantung lining. After, when we got back to the house, Soyoko gave me the coat to keep. It made me cry, so chuffed, and when I finally stopped, she came with me out in the garden to burn my stinking anorak. Then the day she left I found a parcel, just in sides my door, with a note to say she hoped I liked it and it was made especial to go with the coat.

"You're not going for an interview in that *soppy* hat?" Gwen says.

The light changes in the room. I go to the window and look out.

"It's snowing," I says.

Detective Cooper slips. I reckon it's Roger with him. Looks like Roger, he feels the snow tween his fingers, smells it, don't know if it's true or not. I get back in bed and listens. Listens. Policemen in waterproof trousers come rubbing long the corridor, come rubbing down the ward. That's how come I get a shock and my hair gets up both sides to meet them.

"I've brought a friend in to see you, Catherine," Detective Cooper says. "Do you remember Sergeant Rawlings?"

I don't look at Roger case I nod and get him in trouble.

"Hello Lulu," he says.

I wishes he never.

Black Magic! Never even seen them coming. A big box and he puts them on my lap. Cellophane int on.

"Sorry," he says. "I've eaten all of the toffees."

Detective Cooper has a strawberry cream and walks off like looking for clues. My policeman has a chocolate clair. Roger has a caramel swirl and pulls a chair up closer to whisper me how everything is. The words is gnats around my face. I has to close my eyes.

"If you don't say anything, everyone will think you're guilty."

I open and close my eyes, see snow sticking outside on the winder and getting thicker. Like words, piling up. Little fingers start flowering pink up gainst the snowy glass, Baby Grady is on the ledge.

"It's a seagull, Lulu," Roger says. "A seagull with a bag of chips."

People is so confused. Detective Cooper comes back and has to arst me one more time. They wait. I don't say nothing. Stead I pass the Black Magic and wonders if policemen is really liars. The lady in the next bed is playing Scrabble with her husband. He's got triple-word score, VIADUCT; they can't work out how many it is.

"Well," Detective Cooper says. "We'll see you again tomorrow, at Red Roofs, Catherine. Catherine?"

"Her name's Lulu," Roger says.

But Sarah from Social Services comes in. She minds me of a rag doll, no nose and no backbone. And she int happy. They pull the curtain around the bed and stand behind it like it was a wall.

"I'm appalled—I can't believe you've charged her." She int quite whispering. "A) I should have been present; B) She's in no fit state, she doesn't know what day it is."

I does. It's Tuesday.

"I consulted with the court," Detective Cooper says. "If she's over ten and if there is sufficient evidence to charge her, then she must be charged. It's Parliament that makes the Law, Sarah, not me. If she's not fit to stand trial, then she's not fit to stand trial, we had to charge her; it's a serious matter."

"Come off it," she says. "Jesus Christ, she's hardly at large, she weighs three stone."

It's true, I int large.

"Has Catherine made a statement?"

"No, Catherine hasn't said a single solitary word, not to us or her lawyer."

"Her name's Lulu," Roger says.

"Then how the hell are you going to get a plea or an oath?" Sarah says. "Jesus Christ. I need a copy of the witness statements; I need to know what has happened to this girl. I've got nothing to go on, nothing, not a bloody thing. Out there Catherine Clark doesn't even bloody well exist."

"Lulu. Her name's Lulu," Roger says, folds the curtain back. They all look at me; I look at the coconut swirl.

"We'll see you again, Catherine," Detective Cooper says.

They walk way. Roger looks back from the door. He holds his hand up, more like hello than bye-bye. I lift my fingers, thanks for the chocolates, and then he's gone.

Sarah's hands is shaking.

"I've brought you some clothes to try on." She tips a bag on the bed. "Will you stand up for me, so we can try these on you?"

I hobble out of bed. She undoes the strings at the back of my gown. Nothing fits. The trousers is Rupert Bear and too short and needs a belt to stop them dropping down. Jumper's yellow. She puts it on me. I take it off. She puts it on me. I take it off.

"Lions," I says. "Yellow int no good."

"They'll have to do." She looks like she's going to cry.

I hold out the Black Magic tray but she don't want one.

Scrabble lady looks like dead, all the words on the board has slid. Her husband walks up and down, looks out of the winder; sits back down. The dictionary is by her hand.

"Psst," I says.

Husband steps over my policeman's legs, don't even wake him up. I whispers in the man's ear.

"*Dictionary*."

And he gets it for me. Every time surprises me, how many words there is. I look up what else Roger said. Premeditation. Murder. Manslaughter. Demolished Responsibility. Wonders about *oath*. Oath. Sworn? Sworn Oath. I promises to tell the f-ing truth?

Don't know how come the hospital done it, all this to make me live. I spects you has to be live fore they can kill you proper. Wonders if my mum will come to watch. She might run out of cigarettes and miss it, probably, or get doing a show stead. She might, I know how lucky I is. Still I listen all the time for her shoes in the corridor and everybody stopping to look. This policeman int big enough, case she chews him up. My heart bashes so hard hurts, panics, looking for the way out. My policeman yawns, stretches, holds his hat up over his head. Puts it on his lap. Picks it up, swirls it around on his fist. Puts it on the floor tween his feets. Puts his foot up on it. Reads gain the papers from his pocket. He looks at me.

"What does it say?" I arsts him.

"Child pro-theck-tion order from Thocial Thervices." He does it the shape of Donald Duck. "To thop your mum from coming in."

I wonders if it's the same as an injunction, won't stop nothing, not if it's coming. It's dark outside, ward lights shine on the winder glass. Smudged girl stares at me. Could get out of the winder, stand on the ledge and fly way. I get out of bed and hobble on my heels. Her fingertips presses on mine. I look down, at where she means. Can't, an Aston Martin is parked underneath. And the Sandwich Man smoking a cigarette, on the bonnet of his black Capri.

I'd run, girly, if I was you.

The building is one story, solid, winderless brick. We walk around the parked cars and raised beds searching for the entrance. It's spotlit brass: CASINO ROYALE. Silk shrubbery covered in snow sides the black marble steps. I spected curly neon and migraine-patterned carpet and a big space like a bingo hall, but this is a small Edwardian parlor with a sofa and a silk aspidistra on the counter. Receptionist has come around with a duster and polish to shine the mahogany coffee table.

"Do you think it's the uniform?" Gwen says. "I rather like it."

"Edwardian."

"It's rather fetching."

The long black skirt is ruched up high on the arse, gives an effect like a bustle. Front of the skirt is lifted though, as if by hands, to show shoes and ankles off. The receptionist sees us looking in, through slits in the etched glass. She goes behind her counter to get a set of keys. Her top is satin, black and gold in thin stripes; it's like a waistcoat at the front but spilling over the bustle behind. She lets us in, turns all the locks behind us gain. She's so beautiful, Princess Grace of Monaco, I gawps at her lips talking, don't hear nothing she says.

Smiling at me.

"Your coat?"

"Yes," I says. "It is."

Gwen digs me. Then I sees the row of hangers and Gwen's jacket going cross the counter. Keeping mine on.

". . . like a cross between *Bonnie and Clyde* and *The Railway Children*. Really suits you. Really does. My grandmother was a milliner."

"Are we too early?" Gwen says.

Princess Grace picks up a receiver hanging on the wall, looks up above our heads at a CCTV monitor; I can see the screen in the mirror. Sees a spotlit white collar and a pair of cuffs walk to pick up a phone on an island in dark space.

"More for you," she tells him.

He looks up at the camera. She presses a button and the camera zooms closer. He smiles stretching his arms, mimes what a massive yawn it all is. She loves him, can tell.

"The Pit Boss will be with you shortly," she says to us.

"Have you had much response?" Gwen says.

The man I seen on the screen comes through solid double doors in a white shirt and black dinner suit, blows the Edwardian theme.

"Who is who?" he arsts.

"I'm Gwen." She jigs.

"I'm Darren." He shakes her hand.

I feel like Gulliver, like Joan of the fucking ark or something. He looks up at me, shakes my hand. His is soft, catches slightly on my holly-prickled hand. Was specting a bull terrier but this Pit Boss, Darren, is like mild weather, with gray eyes and fair hair, clean-shaved and polished. The suit has got a satin collar and a stripe down the leg of the trousers. Soft-shoe-shuffle shoes. He smells loverly and clean. Talks plain and softly.

"Come through," he says.

The springs on the heavy double doors nearly snap my wrists. It's another world of mock Edwardian. A huge square room with a big clumsy circus of gaming tables looped together with red ropes. I spects the Pit is the dark bit in the middle, for dark staff with cuffs and a phone on a plinth. Customers go around the outside. None now, it don't open til two. The curtains are real but the winders int, the views has been painted on. Clifton Suspension Bridge, we came past it on the way to Bristol. Ships. HMS *Great Britain*; we seen it in the harbor. The green gaming tables glare flooded under the lights. A man in a blue overall is hoovering the table surfaces with an upholstery attachment.

"Baize," Gwen turns to say. Trips over the Hoover cable.

We follow Darren over the yellow-gold carpet, up and down slopes and shallow steps with lit edges. Carpets got a spring in it; I tends these boots int killing me.

An Edwardian bar is staged in the near corner with a couple of sofas and occasional tables. I nod at someone being an Edwardian barman, polishing glasses behind the bar. A pretty waitress called Dorit, in a shorter version of the girls' uniform, is sent to get us coffee. Seems friendly, wags her apron at us. The place int as big as I thought, whole thing is done with gilt and mirrors, stinks of cigarettes and polish. We sit on low red stools at a roulette table. Dorit brings us coffee and a side table.

"Cups and glasses aren't allowed on the baize," Darren explains.

He unclips a rope and goes around the dealing side of the table, tells us loads of things we didn't know. It's a beautiful thing, a roulette wheel, craftsmanship and engineering, random sequence of thirty-six numbers, alternating red and black cept for zero which is green.

"What wood is it?"

Darren's looking at the scars on my cheekbone, at the colors beaming long side my eye, and I know that the diamond in my ear has come alive under the lights. He's looking at that. It makes the one in his ring look silly. He members the question.

"Sycamore," he says. "Every day the wheels are polished and checked with a spirit level."

There are stacks of colored chips on the table, parked gainst the curve of the wheel.

"But if you have up to nine people playing, how do you know which customer is playing with which color?" Gwen says.

"It's your job to remember which color you've given to which customer. Sometimes you can have more than nine people playing at one time; some people play with cash-chips or even put wads of cash on the layout."

He pulls seven stacks of pink chips toward him, changes his hand position and zooms them cross the table for us to share. They don't stagger or fall over. He tells us about the outside bets, odd, even, red, black, low and high numbers, all even money.

"Cept if it drops in zero," I says.

"Oh yes," Gwen says. "What happens then?"

"Stuffed," I suggest.

"You could put it that way," Darren says.

We look at the layout and he shows us the valid betting positions and the odds for each. There's a brass slot in the table with a plastic plunger. Can we guess?

"Money," Gwen says, right answer.

"At four in the morning when the casino closes, the drop boxes are emptied. There's a rota for people to stay behind and do the count. Place your bets," he says.

Gwen tries to get everything covered; I put a whole stack on red. As the ball comes toward him he picks it up. A click of his fingers sends it racing around, tight up under the carved wooden rim.

"The ball is now spinning in the opposite direction to the wheel. If you listen you can hear the sound change as the ball starts slowing down and starts to descend into the bowl."

It does, changes key, pings off a stud, then dribbles slightly on the metal edge and drops with a clatter in 29 black. We lost everything. He picks up a dinky bottle made of white glass.

"We place this on the layout to mark the winning number," he says. "It's called a Dolly."

I sees me in mirrors all over the place.

"How long does the training take?" Gwen says.

He talks us through the details. Six weeks. Rubbish pay. They teach you to deal American roulette and the card games, blackjack and punto banco.

"And poker," he says. "If we feel you have the right qualities for it. How do you feel about it, now that you've got some idea?" he says last.

"Interesting," Gwen says.

I nod cos it is.

"Let me give you a tour and then we'll get to the paperwork."

We follow him back through the heavy doors and around the side of reception. The staffroom is full of people eating Pot Noodles and smoking and watching *Home and Away*. Makeup and hair dos and tons of diamanté, seems funny in the afternoon. Casino opens at two o'clock and the clock on the wall says twenty-five to.

"Say hello," Darren tells them.

"Hello," they says. Uniform, couldn't care less. Boys wear Edwardian suits with waistcoats, stripy to match the girls' tops. The girls' changing room has got lights around all the mirrors, and girls busy at lockers, stinks like a poofs' parlor. Then we push back into the gaming hall and walk the circuit, past high kidney-shaped tables that say *Blackjack* in a sweep cross them. We step up to a cash desk staged over in the far corner. Behind brass bars and a bulletproof screen, a young fat Edwardian bloke in a bow tie and glasses is counting sliding piles of money. The door is two-foot thick with a wheel lock like a submarine.

"This is today's float," Darren says. "And our newly trained cashier, we call him Eton Boy. Say hello, Quentin."

"Hello, Quentin," we says on cue.

Laughs, he's got fat red lips and a tash and his hair slapped down, wet-looking.

"Hello." He's shy but friendly enough.

If this is the float can't magine what the takings is like. Up in the seating area by the bar we wait while Darren gets the application forms.

"It is really rather exciting." Gwen's feet jig on the carpet.

When I look at the job application form it don't seem likely. I chew the pen at *Schooling*. Write O levels: English and Maths and what else, Geography. I give myself Cs. *Work history.* There's an ashtray on the table, I light a cigarette. I keep it simple. Farm worker, one year. Racing stable, two years. Garden center, two years. Never mentions the other jobs. *Skills*. Walking in wellies. Shovelling shit. Horse whispering. Naming trees. *Reason for leaving*. Sore points. *Current employment*. None. *References. Criminal record. Next of kin.*

Shame.

I looks up at a mirrorball turning, sees roulette wheels swirling in it.

LA-SO-SO-MAY YOU BLOOM AND GROW . . .

"BLOOM AND . . . GROW . . . FOR . . . ever"

She can't sing no more. I int got eyes, Auntie Fi. I want to lift my hand up.

"Auntie Fi," I try to say but can't find my mouth or lips or tongue. They gave me a tablit for a heart attack. I just got my brain and ears. My hearts int even beating. I'm dead. Auntie Fi. I'm dead and it int too bad. Auntie Fi, I'm dead but I int gone to a dead place yet, cos my policeman with the cough, coughs. And Auntie Fi is crying, small sounds h-h-h-h-h-h-h-h-h-h-h-h-all together sounds like the worst-ist crying of all, like finished all the way to the bottom. My mum's done her. I know it. H-h-h-h-h-h-h-h-h. Breathe, Auntie Fi. H-h-h-h-h-h-h-h-h-h-h. Breathe, Auntie Fi. H-h-h-h-h-h-h-h-h-h. I'm dead, Auntie Fi. H-h-h-h-h-h-h-h-h.

I got a nose and lilies breathing down it; got the smell so sweet it hurts my teef. I got teef but no jaws. I int got nothing can move. Can't open my eyes, Auntie Fi. While she cries I keep slipping way. I'm trying to stay, Auntie Fi, hanging on to the name and the lily smell.

Don't know how long.

Auntie Fi's breathing whistles like wind through graveyard trees. I know she is unwrapping the lilies cos the smell blasts from the trumpet flowers.

"I'll fetch a vase," a nurse says.

The nurse brings the vase back.

I see Auntie Fi with lily flowers. Members flower ranging in her shed. Auntie Fi, they is my favorite. Auntie Fi in the olden days learned me how to be a florist. Auntie Fi, say something to me.

Car keys.

I want to arst her who I is and how come Catherine Clark. I want to say her name. Her feeling is leaving, her shoes is clipperty-clop.

Auntie Fi!

Auntie Fi!

I has to fight with all my eyes to get a picture and hold it steady. Auntie Fi in the doorway looking at the floor; taps three times on the door frame and bows out, down the corridor.

"Catherine? Come on, love," the nurse says. "Come on, time to wake up."

My head rolls and my eyes roll. My tongue is sticky with lily smell.

"Your auntie came while you were asleep. She left the flowers and something for you."

She left me an I-Spy book. I take it out of the brown paper bag. *I-Spy Animals at the Zoo*. I look through all the pages and read all the words. Int never seen an Oryx or a Secretary Bird.

The night nurse has brung me jarmas from Sarah my Social Worker.

"Better than this scratchy old hospital gown," she says.

"Where is my conkers?" I arsts.

"Come on, love," she says, "slip out of that gown and pop these lovely fleecy ones on."

When she's gone, I take them off. I int pink or teddy bears. I int even Catherine Clark.

"What do you want for lunch tomorrow?" says a lady with a clipboard.

"She's going tomorrow," my policeman says.

The mirrorball turns. Gwen is reading my application form.

"Horse Racing Stable?"

"Yeah—Mick the Spit, he used to come in the pub and gob on the carpet, 'Jackie, come here,' he used to say. 'Come here, ya wooden cunt.' "

"Newmarket," she says. "But all of the times we've been to see Piggy. So you know about horses?"

"Uh-huh, dangerous at both ends, uncomfortable in the middle."

"Don't tell me you can actually ride?"

I look at Gwen's application form. Nine A levels. Bilingual: English and Welsh, she's written. Private Investigations. Well. Customer Service, I can't see it. The Pit Boss, Darren, is back with tests.

"Can you two sit separately, so that you can't see each other's answers? No calculators or written sums, you need to get the totals in your head if you can."

Gwen jigs to the next table. Earlier Darren told us the odds. Straight-Ups and Splits and Corners and Streets, and another one I forget. The sums is based on the odds and how many chips is positioned, where, on a roulette layout.

a) 14 x 35 =
b) 7 x 17 =
c) 4 x 17 + 9 x 11 =
d) 16 x 35 + 6 x 8 =

The sums continue down the page. Starts to tremble. Starts to sweat. Two thirty-fives is 70. Four thirty-fives is 140. Eight thirty-fives is 280. 280. 280.

280.

How many is two hundred eighty? I look up at the mirrorball, sees girls in *Railway Children* hats, all with a cigarette clamped between their teef. I shrug up at them. They nod their heads, slow, sure thing, sure thing, like diamonds winking. I shake my head.

"Have you got 490?" Gwen says.

Darren has wandered off.

"490," she whispers, "then 119, 167, 608, 384, 437 and 368? Have you got the same?"

"Has now," I says.

The girls in the mirrorball all wink at me.

SMALL AND WHITE—CLEAN AND BRIGHT—

(Latin crest, *some fearfulli solemni whatever*)

Mr. J.M. Lawson QC
Beaufort Chambers
Chancery Square
Lincoln's Inn
London WC1A 2PP

January 24, 1977

Dear Mr. Lawson QC,

Re: 2078: Your client, Catherine Clark

With regard to your letter of January 15, 77, I sympathize and whilst I do endeavor to act in your client's best interest, my duty is to the protection of the public and the enforcement of the Law.

The Ministry of Social Services and the Home Office require time to consider what they might wish to do with Catherine Clark. No specific time is indicated. I make no criticisms of those departments, but it is a most unhappy thing that with all the resources of this country, there is, at this time, no place suitable for the treatment and secure accommodation of this girl. Therefore I am unable to make the recommendation that I would wish to make.

In the case of a child of this age no question of imprisonment arises, I have only the power of detention left. To this end she will have to remain Remanded in Custody at Red Roofs Young Offenders Institution until such a time as she is fit to stand trial, or until the building of the new child psychiatric custody unit in Surrey is completed next year, or until there is a vacancy at the Girls' Remand Center in Battersea which is only ever short-term in any event.

Yours whatever,

Judge G. Reginald Witherington-Roycroft

Gwen's back, her headlights flood the dining winders. I still magines Piggy standing there even though he's gone to live in the field. Panda goes mad. I make tea. Gwen kicks her shoes off and feels if the carpet is dry fore kneeling down by the fire.

"It was interesting," she says.

She tips red plastic casino chips from her handbag onto the carpet and they roll off. I gather them up in a stack.

"I have to get the feel of a stack of twenty and practice cutting it down in fives. I have to learn my thirty-five times table, up to twenty, fluently, backward and forward, by tomorrow." She puts her hand over the stack but her short fingers are very hard pushed to reach the bottom chip.

"For God's sake!" She keeps leaving the bottom chip behind. "If you want to pay a customer seventeen chips, for example," she says, "you hold the stack like a pencil and wipe three chips off the bottom. See–twenty, minus the three, means the remainder has to be seventeen chips. Clever, isn't it?"

When she goes to the toilet I try it myself.

"How many people are there in the training group?" I calls.

"Six," she says. "So what did the lady of leisure do today?"

Can hear her hopping and hanging her suit.

"Panda, don't!"

The dog brings me one of Gwen's slippers.

"What's for supper?" she says. "I'm starving."

"Bacon. Sausages. Egg," I says. "Fried Bread. Beans. Tomatoes. Hash browns. A bottle of wine. The trifle is for me."

"You are joking?" she says.

"I've had a bit of a charmer," I says.

"What do you mean? Charmer. Where have you been? A charmer in Weston-super-Mare, surely not?"

"I went to sign on, which wasn't charming. Arst at the fish and chip shop on the corner in front of the pier, about the job in the winder. They said try Friday. Then I went out long the pier. The musement arcade at the end was deserted. Done fifty pence on the Sliding Penny machine, played for hours. Sat out on a bench and watched the seagulls flying til it started to—"

"Get on with it, get to the charming bit!"

"The white horse," I says. "Outsider, 11 to 1."

"You may as well be speaking Russian," Gwen says.

"The Six Horse Race machine. The white horse won, then it won, then it won. Winks as good as a nod, the mechanism was jammed. Every race ten pence was making one pound ten, times the six players, you can see what a charmer it was."

"But I don't understand! What does it mean?"

"Five hundred and ninety-seven pounds, in ten-pence pieces, that's what it means."

"Charming!" She rubs her hands and jigs her feets. "Then what happened, did the white horse pack up altogether, fucking collapse?"

"No, I fucking did, when the pier closed at three o'clock."

"You weren't joking then, about supper?"

"Well, you got the casino job, and I got lucky."

"Bring it all on then," she says. "Start with the wine."

I test her all evening on the thirty-five times table then she has to go to bed. I wash up, multiplying odds. Nod off in my coat on the sofa. Wakes up, gain, at three in the morning, sits up and smokes a cigarette, looks at the red training chips. I get down on my knees. Claws my hand over the stack, feels my fingertips on the carpet and where sactly twenty is, where the top edge digs into my palm. Index finger finds the bottom five, cuts the stack down. Piles it up. Left hand. Right hand. Left hand. Right hand is lazy and weak. I close my eyes, cut them down and stack them up.

Right hand.

Right hand.

I hear birds singing, then Gwen's larm and her getting up and ready. I make us coffee, she drinks it and goes. Can hear the car won't start, damp under the distributor cap. I go out and get it going for her and wave as she drives way. She's left the training chips behind. Warms up my left hand, then the right, cuts them down, piles them up. I prove twenty chips to the inspector, to the punter, to the camera. Wipes three chips off the bottom of the stack.

"Paying red: 17." I says it loudly and clearly so the microphone can hear it.

"*Ha rung, rung rung?*" the dog says.

I take the wheelbarrow, the dog sits in it and we roll down the prom and onto the beach, follow the curve of the shore and under the pilings of the pier. While the dog runs chasing the wind and seagulls, I dig up the ton of ten-pence pieces that I buried here yesterday. Then we go back to the chalet to wash them and count them. Last I leave the dog in the chalet and go to the bank. Has to back the wheelbarrow all the way up the steps of Barclays.

What did the lady of leisure do this week? Pick up dog shit in the hall. Learn the seventeen, eleven and eight times tables, the sequence of numbers around the wheel, clockwise from the green zero. We know the red numbers and the black and that some punters bet on certain segments of the wheel, called Orphans and Neighbors and Tier.

I've just been to the fish and chip shop by the pier, had a demonstration on battering cod, got some white wellies and a stupid hat. Start on Tuesday lunchtime. Always comes down to the same old thing, I has to be somewhere. I walk back long the beach, diamond and shantung lining flashing in the wind. Unlocking the chalet door I can hear the telephone ringing. Surprises me it's still connected. I magine that the fish and chip shop want to make a change of plan; I get to it in time.

"Hello?"

"Is that Kim?"

"Uh-huh."

"Ah," a girl says. "I really loved your coat and hat. I'd like to do millinery, my grandmother was a milliner."

It's Princess Grace from the casino. I bite my lip; wonders if Gwen is sick, had an accident or something.

"What I phoned to say is that someone has dropped out of the training this morning and you were next on the list. Darren wondered if you would like to take their place and come in on Monday morning?"

"Yes," I says, "I would."

When I get off the phone I sit on the sofa. Feels something start to spin. Sure thing. Sure thing, like I'm pinned to a mighty wheel. Feels sick and terrible scared.

Gwen rams the car into the muck heap. It's three in the morning. I knew that the training group was going for a Friday drink, but she's rolling, drove back the fifteen miles from Bristol legless.

"I've been promoted." She lurches in the hall. "They've decided I'm wasted, hic, on the tables, so now they're training me for reception, that's good, isn't it? I'm to be the, hic, face of the organization." She crashes through her plastic folding door. "Come in, come on, Chrissy Wissy," she says.

Bloke has been standing in the shadow. Gwen hauls him into her bedroom and the door crashes closed, fore he can say anything. I think about the training, it worries me, the maths. Six weeks' training, nine to five, is going to kill me; I work that out quick as a fucking flash.

"It's nice and bright and cheery, Catherine," Mr. Nesbitt says.

"Somewhere over the rainbow," I says.

A yellow path is painted on the floor and Mr. Nesbitt looks like a munchkin.

"Is this your dad, Catherine? Is this your dad. Is this your dad?" Toby arsts.

We follow the yellow brick road past the pool tables and the table-tennis tables and the dinner tables. Liam jumps in front of me, waggles his tongue through a V in his fingers. Wanker, I bounce my hand.

"How many boys are there?" Mr. Nesbitt ducks a chair, lucky cos it nearly got him.

"Twenty-six," I says. "The big boys is in the annex."

"How many girls?"

"Just me. Alison came but she went to court and never come back."

"That's a shame," Mr. Nesbitt says. "Did you like her?"

I shake my head.

"Why not?"

Becos, becos, becos, becos, becos.

"She set fire to my dictionary."

Husband at the hospital let me keep it.

"I can get you another one," Mr. Nesbitt says. "Is it ruined?"

"It int ruined, just half of it burned."

"Sorry." He shakes his head.

I look at his sorry face.

"It don't matter, Mr. Nesbitt," I says. "I had too many words, anyway."

"Is this your dad? Are you her dad? Are you? Is he, Catherine? Is he?"

Housemaster Jim calls Toby way, cos he int allowed bothering us.

We has to sit in a side visitors' room with the door open so staffs can see if Mr. Nesbitt gives me a gun, case I shoot them all. In real life he's brung a word puzzle book and pine tree bubble bath. I take the top off the bottle and smell the forest.

"Thank you, Mr. Nesbitt," I says, "smells better than cabbige."

I does a dab on my wrists and behind my ears. He folds his hands on the table and I sees the bandage has gone. He's got a scab. He's got a wedding ring.

"How is your wife Mr. Nesbitt?" I arsts.

"Still upset."

"Sorry," I says.

My finger follows the swirly stitches on the white tablecloth; yesterday I got a red one from in the . . . Fire larm starts ringing. Don't know if it's real or not. It int real it's just Liam, breaking glass gain. The larm is like a Chinese torture. Housemaster Paul gets a good idea and lets it ring for a punishment. When our ears start to bleed he gets up and goes to turn it off. Everybody claps. Then everybody is quiet cos the noise is loverly when it stops.

"Sorry, Mr. Nesbitt." I make my hands open and close on the table like a butterfly.

Red Roofs Detention Center
Dingles Farm
Dingles Lane
Egham
Surrey

Case File: Catherine Clark

Counseled by: Heather Bell (HB) and Jim Dent (JD)

Cont: page 36

Saturday March 12
She fell asleep during her visit from Mr. Nesbitt today. JD

Tuesday March 15
Home Office Psychologist, 2pm.

She didn't say anything. HB

Thursday March 17
In court: 2:45pm. Committal to Crown.

She wouldn't pick up the Bible and bit a court usher who tried to force it into her hand. No plea. Adjourned, pending. Sarah Waters (S. Worker)

Someone has been into Catherine's room and defecated on her rug. HB

Sunday March 20

ALL STAFF PLEASE NOTE: Catherine's mother phoned at 1:15 this afternoon to say that Catherine is a "pathological liar" and to mind we don't get convinced by her stories. Before I could respond she called me a "pathetic know-nothing teeny-bopper" and hung up. HB

We were concerned as to how she knew Catherine was here. The police are certain that the information was not given out. Her QC said likewise. I (HB) telephoned Janet Hobbs at Weybridge SS to report it to her. She says she had a very caring and plausible call from someone claiming to be Catherine's "Auntie Valerie."

I press the button for the lamp to come on but it don't work. The moon is big as another planet. Sideways out the peephole in the door, can see the oringe light and hear night staffs talking soft. Can't tell who it is. I sit down on the end of my bed. It int the moon. It's the round white light on the corridor wall, shining through the peephole and onto the winder.

Nothing is real.

While I'm waiting I sit down on the floor with my back gainst the radiator. Then I kneel up and warm my front, then does my bum, then sit down on the floor and put my feets up on it, I wishes I could get inside it. I undoes the bolt with my fingers and let hot water dribble on my wrists. Mop up what I spilled with my socks. Someone has stuck a poster on the wall over my bed. White horse, rearing up in the sea, looks scared case it gets drownded. I hear the squeak of shoes and a face comes up in the peephole, Housemistress Joyce doing the twelve clock checks. She don't say nothing, always looks at me like I was a bad bitter taste. When she's gone I get on my knees and feel underneath the drawers. It's where I hid the red tablecloth. I get undressed and wrap it around loose and tie a knot on one shoulder. I get up and the floor starts running. I keep running til I start to breathe. I run past pain til my heart gets up. I run toward the morning shining yellow in my mind. Every day I get more tuned.

Saturday March 26

She helped Gladys to prepare the afternoon teas and wash up. Gladys was talking about her daughter's wedding in June and what flowers to have. Catherine very distinctly said "Delphiniums with White Scented Stocks." She might like to help Mole in the garden over the holidays. Can we arrange this? JD

We drive around to look for the house. Find the rolling park easy enough, with all the streets like spokes coming off it. Park Lane, not as grand as it sounds, no trees, parked cars both sides, couple of motorbikes, gardens big enough for parking bins. It's a short street, leads from a mini-roundabout to the rusted ornate gate of the park.

"There," I says. "Green door. Number 3."

We sit in the car outside and wait for the letting agent. One thing's for sure, we can't stay in Weston-super-Mare.

"Here he is!" the dog says.

After the greetings the agent fumbles with sets of keys. Reckons the man that owns the house is an anthropologist. Wonders what one is.

"You're both working here in Bristol?" he arsts.

Gwen splains: we've been living in Weston-super-Mare and traveling every day to the casino but when training ends next week we'll be on different rotas. Late shift at the casino finishes at four in the morning but there int a bus til half past seven. Gwen's got the car but the day shifts starts at two in the afternoon and it's gas and traffic and hassle parking and a long way back at nine, if you're blind drunk. Twice I've had to drive us.

"Tzzz," the agent says. The keys keep trying him.

I liked it, driving the Quattro. Uh-huh, especial with all the winders open and the exhaust blowing and Gwen dead on the backseat. You know you is alive. I seen a barn owl in the full beam, first time ever. Its wings beat white same as playing cards do flying from the blackjack shoe. Sides, how can they take your driving license way if you haven't even got one? The agent still can't find the right key. I has a nap standing up, prop my elbows on the bin, got a new kind of tired on me. Keep poking myself in the eye and slapping myself about the face. I sink down in black blivion up to my waist, up to my shoulders, up to my diamond, spects my mouth is hanging open, dribbling, head is slipping off my hand.

"I can't take her anywhere," Gwen says to the agent.

Lucky I'm smiley kind.

"Can't *leave* her anywhere," I says. "I've tried."

"We're in," he says.

House seems nice, like somebody's actual home to rent. It's the cheapest we've seen and there int many will take a dog. We could walk to the casino from here, cross the park and the river and the city center. A skinny hall bends past the stairs, with dark wood planks and a loverly rug. There's a small front dining room with a gas fire and square table and net curtains, not especial friendly, like people tried but couldn't use it. The back room is done like a catalogue bedroom, for catalogue people with bedding. Chest of drawers and a wardrobe. French doors look past the side of the kitchen. L-shaped bit of garden. Next door's lilac tree hangs heavy in bud over the fence. White I spects, something to look forward to. Rest is broken concrete, forsythia and elderberry scrapping over it.

"You could do something with it," Gwen says to me.

But I int planning on staying that long. At the end of the hall there's a step down and light blue cold sac of a kitchen, cheered up though, with all the colors and patterns of clay pots and plants on the windersill. Old mother geranium lived here all her life. I find a pint glass in the cupboard and fill it to water the plants. Then I water myself, so tired makes a mess of drinking.

"Cooker. Washing machine. Fridge. Immersion heater."

Washer gone on the hot tap.

"No lounge?" Gwen says.

"It's upstairs at the front of the house," he says.

We follow him up. There's a plain bathroom at the top of the stairs, directly over the kitchen.

"They're rather fond of their foreign knick-knacks," Gwen says.

Back bedroom, same as the one below. The front lounge is the full width of the house, going over the hall.

"It's not to everybody's taste," the agent warns us.

"Good God," Gwen says.

I look at the lion skin pinned out on one wall, and the zebra skin on the back of the sofa, dark carved masks in one alcove, fists full of spears raised up in the other and other skins, drums of drums.

". . . deposit and one month's rent in advance," the agent says.

They go back down the stairs.

"We may as well take it," Gwen says.

"It's good value, I feel," the agent says.

We follow him in the car to his office in Bedminster, to do the forms. Wonder who Gwen will give as a reference. I wouldn't let her live in my place, if I had one. My references always turn out OK, once you get past the trouble with names. Will be glad to get to Bristol and have my own room, won't need Gwen for lifts. Rent and deposit up front for the house is all thanks to the white horse on the pier. Gwen says she'll give me her half on payday, don't spects she will. Don't know how I got myself tied up in this Gwen-Car-Dog-Horse fuck-up. Feel like I'm keeping the raft afloat, just til I can get off it. We was two loose ends got tied up together. Least with Gwen something always happens. She's on good form today, "foil" she calls it.

Never knew this kind of tired, comes from training the brain to do something it int natural good at. Five weeks now I've hammered the numbers and the odds, but last night my brain gave up, left me a smiling idiot. That's the trouble with the casino, no winders. Time-warped twilight zone. Daylight seems like medicine. We drive out of Bristol on a flyover. I love the colored hickle-pickle houses on the hill. Mazes me how the Clifton Suspension Bridge goes cross the gorge, so high up above the river mud. Isambard Kingdom Brunel. I seen his statue on a lunch break, little bloke, reckon he made this beautiful bridge cos he had a great big name to live up to.

"Bristol's Number One Suicide Spot," Gwen says.

Handy to know.

On the way back to Weston-super-Mare, we detour to see Piggy. I love going to see the horse. We whooshes long. Good driver, Gwen. Farmer's lane is radiant with blackthorn blossom like clouds of chalk and bitter-sweet smell. Everything else is fit to burst, holding off, sniffing last frost. Lets it wash over me. Sky is tirely white, magine that. And it's mild enough for the car winders open. Int ready to take my beautiful coat off though, without it I spects I would disappear.

"Isn't the May pretty?" Gwen says.

Cept it's April. And blackthorn flowers fore the hawthorn. They tirely different. I nods all the same.

Tirely tired, too tirely tired for whole words.

There's daffodils long the verge my side. Minds me, one time a lady came in the garden center with a picture torn from a magazine. The timing was perfect and she already had the grassy bank. I told her they was *daffodils* cos she really didn't know, said she'd need a couple of hundred bulbs. People always plant in rows; they can't help it. I splained this to her, said the best way to get the natural effect was to strew the daffodil bulbs around wildly. Surprised me, she came back in the spring, disappointed, with two hundred bulbs in a sack, they was all clean and dry and somehow rotted. Turned out she never understood that when you'd strewed the bulbs about wildly you was sposed to dig a hole and plant them sactly where they landed. Uh-huh. After work I went around her house, to help her out with what was what in her garden. Nice lady. Magistrate. Gave me cake.

Must phone Mr. Mac; tell him to put that fucking ball down.

"What are you chortling at?" Gwen says.

"Nothing."

Been Sheffield. Been Weston-super-Mare. Next week: Bristol. Next year, wonder where spring will be. Darren says a blackjack dealer like me can work anywhere in the world. He reckons my game is good enough now, but you need one year's experience fore you can apply.

"Now, about bedrooms," Gwen says. "I bags the one upstairs."

True, downstairs at Park Lane is kind of lonely but I like living close as I can get to the ground, and the kettle, and a door to outside. I think about that white lilac tree hanging outside the French doors.

"OK," I says. It int for long. I light a cigarette for Gwen and pass it. Hold mine in a pair of tweezers and smokes it, loverly, blows it out the winder.

"What on earth are you doing?"

"Has to get rid of the nicotine stains."

"The sensible thing would be to give up smoking, have you thought of that?"

"No never not for a second," I says. "Sides, the sensible thing would be for you to buy your own."

"Touché," she says.

When we turn into the field gateway, the horse is fine, waiting. Neighs.

I'm winning eighteen thousand on a roulette training game, when the lady from Personnel comes into the gaming hall. It's me she wants, waving paperwork. It's the job application form. Wonder if it's the next of kin, I just put "phone the council."

"I'm having trouble with one of your references. This one." The lady shows me what I wrote for Mick the Spit, the racehorse trainer. I never gave him notice, but I said there had been a sudden death and told him that I had to go.

"It *int* proper to give me a bad reference," I says. "I was a good worker and no trouble."

"It's not that," the lady says. "He's just adamant that he's never heard of you. In fact he was very rude. So rude. So insulting." Seems she still is holding the wound.

I shrug at Darren. He looks worried; he don't want to lose me after all this training. Then I get a dawning.

"No–no," I says. "Tell him it's *Jackie*, he'll know who you mean if you say *Jackie*."

"Your Christian name is *Jackie*?" Darren says.

"No," I says, "it's just what Mick the Spit always called me, I was too scared to put him right. He used to park his Merc long sides the gallops and shoot twelve-bore at us as we went past on the horses like a line of sitting ducks."

Darren loves it.

"I'll phone him back, Jackie, Jackie, Jackie." The lady goes off but I don't spect she will phone him back, she'll just tick the box that says "reference checked."

"They're applying for your dealer's license," Darren says.

My stomach flips; next week I'm doing it for real, with a uniform and proper night shifts and real punters placing bets. He's wanted at the cash desk. I go back to the training game with my dry tongue stuck in my cheek and sweat pouring down my back. Then Princess Grace calls me and I die another death. But it's only a parcel, with my name on it. Gwen is in the staffroom, on a break from reception, jigging about on someone's lap, don't know his name, int Chrissy Wissy.

"All right? Darren's Ace," she snorts her smoke.

The bloke sprays his tea. The joke is on me and it int proper nice.

"My uniform has just come," I says. "Best try it on."

The uniform fits nicely. Darren taught me blackjack himself cos he wanted to and everyone says he's the best in the world, sides Gwen was so bad at dealing they had to move her to reception, signing in members and hanging up coats. And we int allowed to fraternize or get chummy with punters. If we know a customer outside of work we has to declare it, so we don't end up being accused of dealing favors to friends. True everybody is fraternizing, all of the time, but not in the bloody reception. Yesterday some bloke, a punter, was over the reception counter, they were in the fucking cupboard, laughing and mucking about. Princess Grace had gone home sick. I could hear Gwen's hands slapping at him.

"In your dreams," she was saying. "In your dreams."

We look at all the shoes on the shop floor.

"Sorry," I says to the girl. "Fell on a pruning knife. Cut the nerves. My right foot is hypersensitive."

"Calf," she says. "Achilles. Outside edge." She's understanding. Shakes her head. Missing toe.

"That's another story," I says. "Every left shoe is loverly but every right shoe hurts. Maybe I should try the boxes on, stead."

Should ring Mr. Mac, about my compensation claim, I know that sometime never, they int going to pay me a single penny, it's just a matter of principle now.

On the way back I sit in the park on a bench. There's a newspaper in the bin so I get it out and read it. Smokes a cigarette with tweezers. Smokes ten, reads everything, sorts out all the junk from my pockets. Late sunshine is slanting golden through the trees on the hill. I get my new shoes out of the box, most spensive thing I've ever bought. Skint now, down to wages and hand to mouth. But I spects these shoes can do the job forever, found them in a dancewear shop of all surprising places. They still is handsome in tissue paper with soft straps and Cuban heels. The lady in the shop said people buy them for dancing flamenco. Said I'd settle for walking in them. I put them on and start back, thin-ankled and clipperty-clop. Horse-chestnut trees long side the path seems to be unrolling as I walk, leaves hanging limp with evening dew and the effort of being born.

I can hear the music from the corner of the park. 3 Park Lane. We finally got everything here, two loads in the car. Gwen has cleared her *belongings* from the hallway. Upstairs is full of Status Quo and seems like a hundred fans, deafening. The nice rug in the hall has gone somewhere, good idea cos the dog will only shit on it. Every nice thing has gone from the hallway and the kitchen sill. Bottle of Bombay Gin. Sticky. Three-quarters empty.

Hello?

The wood carvings? Gone from the stairwell. Bare. The music is so so so loud; the neighbors must be chuffed already. Rocking all over the world. I go upstairs. Gwen's bedroom door is open. There's a half-empty cardboard box in the doorway and a wardrobe half full of clothes, tangle of hangers and harness on the bed. I use the toilet. She's hung her Mensa certificate on the back of the door. Hello, a pair of Edwardian uniform trousers is bandoned on the landing, one new, size 14, man's shoe.

"Hello?"

Lounge door is open. Stereo tower where the drums was. Bare walls where skins was. He's on his knees. Gwen is chucking the length of her hair like buckets of water over his face. He likes it. He likes it. He lull lull lull likes it. Where's all the stuff?

HERE WE GO . . .

Oh.

"Hi. Quentin," I yells.

Quentin? Fat lips, red like he's wearing lipstick. Socks. No trousers. Where's the lion? Gwen jigs to turn the stereo down, always turns it up for an hour first. Uh-huh. Dog has stuffed its head under a cushion, can't listen or look. I grims. Quentin takes his glasses off, dries them on the bottom of his shirt. Reckon he's made of pure fat, int got no actual bones. Gwen changes the record, ripping into "Jolene."

Oh fuck, now she's rumpelling me.

Stereo tower. Calor gas fire. Paris painting. Sewing box. Wing chair. Plain navy sofa. Where's all the stuff? I swim off long the landing, vaults down the stairs in my new fleet-flying shoes. Fucking Quentin? I make a coffee, sees how my bedroom is, sactly. Peach. Never been a bed or pajama person. I just nap in my coat, dreams up my fluted cuffs. Pale. Spects it's a guest bedroom but nobody came. It int for long, it just needs something. Like a screwdriver so I can prize the hardboard off the fireplace, reckon there's a grate behind it. The wall lights work. The French doors bash open onto broken paving. I duck out, smell the lilac and it int even opened yet. There's a shed around the corner, dry, nothing in it. I sit under the lilac on an upturned bucket, smoke a cigarette with tweezers. Gwen's turned the stereo up. Listen.

. . . YOU MUST BE MISTAKEN, I'M SURE THAT YOU ARE,
THERE'S MORE THAN ONE CAR—WITH STICKERS ON . . .

Gwen's ex-fiancé, Ian, that took her to Paris the one time, is probably using a similar line to the new woman he wants to marry. Is there more than one redhead in a gray Audi Quattro with a kicked-in nearside wing and loads of straw in the back? Last week Gwen went to meet him at a service station on the M5. Rendezvous, she called it. The lengths she had to go to, to get Ian to agree, and then she wore a black basque and stockings under her mac. I get up and pick about in bricks and couch grass. We've got a washing-up bowl for a pond, bright with beads of duckweed. Pretty. We've got early rhubarb; I tug at a few young stems. Stand in the kitchen looking at the rhubarb on the counter, the ruby rub on the stems, the heavy veins in the flop of the leaves, the waxy shine on the white root cuffs, the fine lacy membrane.

The bed can go in the shed for starters and all the furniture. Or I can? I take my time thinking about it and then roll the bed base out the back, nice to think of something that int numbers and odds. When I've got my room empty I clean the glass in the French doors and run the Hoover around. Then go hunting, in the front dining room. Still int friendly. Something crashes upstairs; hear Gwen running long the landing from her bedroom to change the record in the lounge.

"Louder! Louder-louder!" Quentin begs from the bedroom.

At work they say his dad is so rich he goes about in a helicopter.

"Louder-louder!"

"How loud can you take it, boyo?" Gwen shouts from the lounge.

Where's all the stuff? Cupboard under the stairs? Uh-huh. Drums is piled, drums on drums. I get the lion by its ruff.

It's real.

And other skins.

And spears.

Brings back my kills.

. . . THE PHANT-TOM OF THE OP-ERA IS HERE . . .

Hang masks over the wall lights.

. . . INSIDE YOUR MIND

Red Roofs Detention Center
Dingles Farm
Dingles Lane
Egham
Surrey

Case File: Catherine Clark

Counseled by: Heather Bell (HB) and Jim Dent (JD)

Cont: page 42

Saturday April 16

> She laughed! Yes laughed—long and hard, at Laurel and Hardy on the television this morning. It does a heart good, doesn't it? "Funny," she said several times, "funny." It made all of the boys laugh. What a joyous place we are. JD

Surprises me, Miss Connor is coming to see me at two o'clock. Don't spect she'll like Red Roofs much. Sarah from Social Services brung me a pair of sneakers and a brown skirt and a brown top. Sneakers is both left feets. Sarah said make do for now, next week she'll buy the two right feets and then I'll have two pairs. Everybody else is over in the classrooms cept me. Even though the boys int here the noise they made still is and the mess. I go in the dinner room so I can see Miss Connor coming. I hope she don't tell my mum where I is, wonders if it's a trap, that's how come

I get the drumming and my hands start sweating. I sit up on the windersill to watch and wait.

She's still got her blue Morris Minor. It stops at the gates. She gets out to ring the buzzer and talk to Mr. Jim and he presses for the gates to open and closes them up gain behind her. It's just Miss Connor on her own; she's got a greyhound dog in the back. She sits in the car with the winder open finishing her cigarette. When she gets out her skirts gets caught and then she drops her bag. Everything has fallen out, files and papers. Quick she sprays some odorant under her arms. And a different spray on her tongue. She don't like smelling of cigarettes, flaps her hands around her head. Then tucks her blouse back in and pulls up her socks. Then she goes back in the car for a tissue and blows her nose and makes sure her nostils is clean. Then she shuts her skirt in the door and when she opens it gain, the dog jumps out and runs around the garden. She whistles it loud with two fingers and it comes straight back, that's how come I love Miss Connor and she still int got no ears. I wishes the boys don't come and smash her car up. She rings the doorbell. Mr. Jim lets her in.

"Lulu!" she says. "Class hasn't been the same without you!"

"Hello, Miss Connor." Words is thin, squeezed out past my tonsils.

I spects us to go in a visitors' room but stead we sit in the kitchen, long as Miss Joyce don't find out. Mr. Jim makes us a pot of tea cos there int no boys to piss in it. I want to drink mine quick, but can't cos it is too hot. My tongue is furry. Shivers run up the back of my legs. My hands is trembly on my lap.

"What's your dog called, Miss Connor?" I arsts.

"Thomas Hardy," she says.

I reckon it's a good name.

"Do you remember this?" She gets a folder out of her bag. She's got mud under her nails and the polish is all chipped off. Then I see it writ: *mountins of the moon–part two*.

"Have you written any more?" she arsts.

I shake my head.

"What you need to do is write down what happens next. What happens next?"

"Don't know, Miss Connor," I says. Wonders if she thinks this place is Butlins.

"Just make it up." She minds me of my grandad. Don't spect he knows nothing, even where I is. Don't want him to be upset case it gives him headache. I look at my words: *mountins of the moon*. Grandad invented the whole world.

I don't feel proper, got snot. My head does a swirl. I bite my lip hard and sit on my fingers, sees the kitchen cupboards coming in and out and Mr. Jim itching his head cos everybody got the fleas.

"She's under a lot of stress," he says. "No one gets any sleep; she's got a bit of a fever."

Things is trembly, don't know how come. Miss Connor puts her cardigan around my shoulders. Wonders if you can die from tired. Fleas. I has to sits on my hands case I scratches, they makes me worster than a nutter. The telephone rings in the office and Mr. Jim goes to answer it.

"Would you write to me, Lulu?" Miss Connor arsts. "And I'll write back, letters are the best thing ever."

She does her address on a bit of paper with a swirly pen. It int her house cos it's St. Paul's School.

"I saw Mr. Draper in town the other day," she says.

"Is he a teacher?" I arsts.

"No," she says. "I thought he was a friend of yours, he asked me if I'd seen you, wondered if you'd moved or if you were still at school. I told him I was coming to see you today and he sends his love. He says he'll see you soon."

"Mr. Draper?" I says.

"He said you were good friends?"

My hearts start beating backward. My fingers make me a prayer. It's the Sandwich Man. It's the Sandwich Man.

Ten. Nine. Eight. Mr. Jim comes in the kitchen.

"I has to go to the toilet," I says.

Seven. Six. I run up the stairs quick. From the winder on the top landing I look out cross the road. He's in the black Capri; his arm comes out the winder and waves. Then I knows. He int never going to stop cos now I is too good, like a game.

Sporting chance. I hang on to the wall and follow it back long to my room. *Coming—ready or not.*

"Catherine?" Mr. Jim comes in my room. "What's the matter?"

I can't say nothing, all these peoples is killing me.

"I'll tell Miss Connor that you don't feel well, she can come another time."

I try to say sorry but it won't come out, gets tangled around my tonsils and down in my guts. Mr. Jim grabs at me and I flaps like a bird in the corner.

"It's all right, Catherine," he says. "It's all right."

It int all right. Int nothing all right. He's got me clamped, walking up and down. I got Mr. Jim inside my face. He looks like terrified.

"I can't read your mind," he says. "Can't read your mind."

I kick hard and he drops me.

"Stay way from me," I says, "cos I'll kick your teef in."

Mr. Jim looks stonished. Like I done a disappointment. He goes out of my room, looks back like a naughty dog. Int proper, he's more scareder than me. I slam my door and rip the picture off the wall, this int fairy tales and horses int never got a horn. Don't want sneakers cos I slings them off. I get the drumming and start to run, til stitches on both sides is killing. Come on. Sweat drips off my fringe, makes me blind. Ha-ha-ha!

"Come on, then!" I yells up at the ceiling and the gods. The drumming comes together like the sound of people clapping. Then Miss Joyce turn the keys in the door, locks me in case I kill her.

Bed has moved all wonky cross. We been in a fight. Eyes can't get open proper, feels like a fat lip and hair pulled. It's early, mist and birds lifting. I got blood on my fingers, some of my nails is off. Got blood all on the skirting boards. Around the winder. Poured down the door. Got crusty under my nose and on my chin. Got lumps of hair on the bed. I careful touches my head. Uh-huh.

Keys turn in the lock. My door squeaks open wide as a yawn. It's Miss Joyce.

"Mr. Lawson is here with Detective Cooper to—"

She can't come in, table from sides my bed is upside down and in the way, from where I smashed the ceiling down. Wires from the light dangle down and fizz where they touches together. The wardrobe int a wardrobe no more. We listens to the small sounds of rubble trying to get comfortable. Miss Joyce shifts. A piece of broken glass from the bulb breaks smaller under her shoe. I done a shit on a bit of plaster and left it by the door, balancing nice on a table leg.

Miss Joyce looks at it.

I look at Miss Joyce.

"Have you got anything to say for yourself?"

"Fuck you," I says. But my voice int there, total gone, from all night screaming, screaming, screaming, *Miss Joyce, I needs the toilet.*

"Fuck you."

"No need to thank me," she says. "Let's have you downstairs. Put your shoes on first because of the glass."

She int real. I walk over a piece of the wardrobe to get my sneakers. I pick one up and pour the piss out like from a teapot. We watch it splash on the broken drawers and soak up in the plaster dust. I sit down on my bed and put the sneakers on. In the corridor I stop at the bathroom door, spects I can wash the blood off my face.

"No time for that," she says. "They're waiting for you."

I follow Miss Joyce. Walking rips the scab on my knee and a line of blood trickles down, sounds is squelching out footprints. Boys is like wallpaper waiting to watch me coming. Night staffs and day staffs. Nobody don't say nothing. Even Liam don't say nothing. Boys all follow us down the stairs. Mr. Jim tends he don't know me.

"Does it hurt, Catherine?" Toby is running long sides. "Does it, does it hurt, Catherine, does it?"

They stand up when I come in. I has to lock my knees case they does a dip. Detective Cooper's a sausage, cooked in the sun yesterday. Mr. Lawson is being my barrister, he always is brand new. Words is scared to come on their lips, case they would arst me how I is. Mr. Lawson looks at his watch and his cufflinks shine two suns on the ceiling.

"Sit down, Catherine," Detective Cooper says.

Mr. Lawson pulls a chair out for me but my knees is locked, that's how come I stay where I is. They looks at each other. They looks at me. They looks at their fingernails, sees if they got any dirt. Mr. Lawson looks at his watch. Detective Cooper looks for clues up Mr. Lawson's sleeve. We all look up at the two suns. We all looks down at my bits of knees and two left feets. I got a flicker in one eyelid and blood pumping a lump of lip.

"We wanted to ask you about this, Catherine." Detective Cooper puts my scrapbook on the table, fat with leaves and pressed flowers.

Housemistress Julie is on duty tonight. Mr. Jim is with her, lucky he int my friend no more. Noise is worster than hell on earth, that's what Miss Julie reckons. Boys don't want to go to bed, bashing and shouting til they get locked in. Then they yell out through the spyholes a game called Who's a Twat, and anybody can join in. They gave me this room now cos mine int no good. Toby is next door. Crying gain. Sounds like stuck.

"I want my mum I want my mum I want my mum."

Makes me cry cos I don't want mine. I wonders who to cry. Can't think of no one so I has to stop. I got stiff and ouch and everything swelled up.

"Catherine?" Miss Julie says. "Do you need anything before I lock? Did you have paracetamol, for the pain?"

I don't say nothing. I hear her shoes come in and breathing looking down at me. She makes the blanket over my shoulder, tucks it around my neck. Her warm hand presses on mine and she kisses my ear, don't know how come. The lamp button clicks off. I peek. She reaches tween the bars to pull the top winder shut. Then I see her black shape in the corridor light starting to close the door.

"Miss Julie?" I got a slippery voice, sounds int proper mine.

She stops closing the door and comes back in. Her face is a little bit kind.

"Will they hang me?" I arsts.

She comes down by my bed.

"No, love," she says. "They don't hang people any more, especially not little girls."

"Will I have to go to prison?"

"Not prison. You might stay here. I don't know, love, maybe for a very long time, until you've grown up. You can't go to prison until you're eighteen. You should try and make the best of it, Catherine."

I slow nods my head.

Does a tap dance, sounds good on the changing-room floor. Done it, finished my first proper shift, feel light with tiredness and relief, anything now could blow me way.

It was funny. Nobody knew who I was. Edwardian style sits on me nice and they got my skirts made extra long. I got a chestnut hairpiece from the market all piled up and false eyelashes that come out sideways, not black, conker brown and soft. Wrapround eyes, Moonface calls them. Darren laughed, was ever so proud, said I'd make a beautiful whorehouse. I dealt roulette to Mr. One-Chip most of the afternoon, the Camp Inspector weren't even watching, scraping varnish off his baby finger with his teef. The last game of blackjack was good with four players and all nine boxes open. No mistakes.

Gwen comes in the changing room.

"I've been waiting for you out there, come on," she says. "We're going down the Cellar; everyone is going down the Cellar. We're celebrating."

"Are we?"

"Yes. End of training. Dealer's license. Come on."

Nice of her to suggest it since we don't get together much and actually now I'm wide wake with relief. I like it down the Cellar, feel like lying back in my moon and having a drink and watching the nutters go on.

"Let's drive home first and get some supper, and then come back out in an hour."

"OK," I says.

We has cheese on toast and then get ready. I scrub all my makeup off, clean my teef, drag my fringe out with a bit of spit, cuts a lump off here and there.

"Is it too much to ask, a little effort?" Gwen don't reckon I can wear my jeans and T-shirt to a nightclub.

"You can't dance in flip-flops" she says.

"Sactly," I says.

"Why can you do it so spectacularly for work but not now? I don't understand. I really don't." She wuthers case I look bad on her.

Work is different; I has to turn up and be a dealer. I int got dressed up in real life since the Ritzy in Sheffield. Even now it makes me purple. A bloke from a group came over especial to arst me if I was a man or a woman. Niver, I said, I'm a serial killer. Lucky Gwen was gone to the toilet.

"Come on," she says. "Let's get there, it's half past bloody eleven already." She's been two hours taming her hair to get the wild effect. I don't know why she bothers; she always looks like a gasoline sales rep, at the end of a day. Stinks of diesel and Poison perfume.

"Keys?

"Check."

"Purse?"

"Check. Paper down for the dog?"

"Never mind that—have you got cigarettes?"

"Check."

"You don't need the coat, it's June," she says. "Nearly June, will be June in a few weeks."

"Keep it on," I says.

It int really a nightclub, just Davros has got a bar and a bit of a dance floor down in a cellar and lethal steps. Everyone from the casino treats it like a private lounge, to meet up after work and muck around in. Loads of blokes come down here chasing the casino waitresses and dealers and casino customers come down as well, it makes a joke of the fraternizing rule.

"Been on a sunbed?" Davros arsts me.

"No—spent my day off in the garden."

I pass me in mirrors at the bottom of the stairs. The ultraviolet lights bring my eyes and teefs and pale broidered cuffs screaming loud into view. And the white bars on my dark cheekbone. Diamond is alive sides my eye. A big crowd has come in behind us. Sees Quentin. He don't come over, sat on his own. At work the other day he was crying cos he loves her.

"Sulking," Gwen says.

She always goes to the toilet so I can pay for the first drinks. I wait patient for my turn at the bar; a great oak tree of a bloke is standing in front of me. He looks over his shoulder straight in my face. Turns around to see if I'm real. Case I'm a hologram. Been beamed down. Or something. Gwen comes shoving through.

"Do you know Peter Eden?" she says to me.

Never seen him fore. He looks at me.

"My mate," she says.

I look up at him, red end of a matchstick stirs around slowly in his lips. I get a cigarette from up my fluted sleeve like magic and he tends to strike the match on his chin. But he's got a matchbox in his pocket. But now some loud joker is mucking around and falls backward into him.

"Do you mind?" the Oak Tree says. "We're trying to have a conversation here."

The Joker grims. Sticks his tongue out. Tips his head. Gwen smirks at the Joker, starts jigging, ready to rumple. I see: Gwen and the Joker.

Oak Tree turns the matchstick with his fingers, winks at me.

"I'm Heath," the Joker says. He turns his back on the others. This Heath, he's got my face, got my name, shaking my hand, steering me off, he's whizzing, great big silver crucifix swinging in one ear. Does I work out?

"I work in the casino," I says.

A crowd has come with us, all talking at once and laughing. Lot of hugging going on, most of it Heath and he keeps them all going like spinning plates on poles. Could even wear you out. I see Gwen left behind, this int what she had in mind. Or me. I shrug at her and the Joker's arm falls off the back of my neck.

"Heath, are you going to dance?" a ratty bloke says. "Do that thing with the strobe again."

Can't see Gwen now.

"With the strobe, Heath. Go on, Heath."

"I'll give it a spin," he says. "Excuse me a minute." He passes me his jacket. It's heavy green leather with red leather sleeves, number 9 stitched on the back. He's wearing faded jeans and a black T-shirt with cap sleeves. People cheer and gather around and I can't see for the crowd. The concrete wall tween the dance floor and the bar has got a big crescent moon cut in it. Normally I climb up and lay in the curve of the moon, it's my spot, can see everything both sides. I take his jacket and go around to climb up in it. So comfortable laid in the curve. Smokes a cigarette with tweezers. Heath sticks his tongue in the DJ's ear, rifles through the record box looking for something particular.

"Heath! Heath! Heath," the crowd says.

Don't know what the music is but it sounds like the sea pulling and crashing. Heath stands in the middle of the floor, seems to pray and bow to the mirrors. DJ puts the strobe light on and this Heath moves. He's so fine-tuned like someone trained in ballet is, there int no shake or tremble, no limit. He holds perfect arabesques, turning in the strobe like his arms is swinging a heavy sword. He could even be on ice, changing legs as if his hands and feet had blades. The strobe light seems to fix him up and I sees seven turning blades swirling all at once. He lands turning still and those seven swords catch up and come to rest as one. Final he knights the floor. Everyone cheers and claps and bored now gets back on with their own bitching and attempts at dancing.

I've still got Heath's jacket. He jumps up on my moon to rest, with his hands on his skinny hips and his chest heaving. His skin is so white it's almost blue, flawless. He's got a beautiful face in profile, with carved eyelids and an armour nose plate. The big silver crucifix dangling from his ear casts a swinging shadow on the back wall of the club. He's almost see-through. Few moments I glimpses a peacefulness like still water, fore he starts revving gain, cracks his big swollen knuckles.

"I'm on fire," he says. "I'm cooking on gas; I'm sweating like a nigger on Election Day, as my old dad used to say. Ah—got cramp," he says. "I've got to stretch it out," he says. "I have *got to* stop smoking."

The dance floor is empty so he sits down on it, does the splits by the rivers of Babylon, swivels to face forward, bends flat over his knee. Gwen has been and brushed her hair. She sees Heath down on the dance floor and comes over, starts whipping her hair and swirling devilish around him, smacks pissed into the wall. Heath laughs, so hard like a bastard, gets up to see if she's OK.

"No sense no feeling," she says, stunned.

Heath laughs more, runs way with the slapstick theme, ducks planks, makes me laugh so hard I nearly fall out of the moon. Running commentary. He's such an arsehole but he int having none of Gwen; every time I look at him I finds him looking at me. Sticks his tongue out and tips his head. Joker.

"Forgive me," he says, "I'm getting overzealous."

"Who's Zealous?" I give him his jacket.

Gwen slaps at him.

"You," she says. But her hand keeps missing. He floats like a butterfly, stings like a bee, int taking his eye off me.

"Come down here at once." She points back at the floor where he was sitting. Some other clown from a different show takes her up on it, and so she rumples them, stead.

"Vodka?" Heath arsts me.

Davros sees me sitting in my moon, comes to say hello, always does.

"Lap-dancing club," he says. He's still trying to find a way for the Cellar to make some money. "I was in one the other night," he says, "And do you know what? A black girl came and stood on the table, I looked up, like that, straight up her skirt and she didn't have any knickers on, just like a ham sandwich, I thought, honest, cunt like a ham sandwich."

Then the barman calls him and he's gone.

Heath brings me vodka, strong, double, treble. His arm is around my neck. He smiles at me, like it's a surprise, it is a surprise, surprises me. I wonder if he's having a joke. Look around to see if someone has bet him.

Do I want to take my coat off?

No. We stand on the dance floor talking, close so we can hear each other, same height. Karate has made him fit and deadly as he is. He's been training since he was seven years old and won the European Championship when he was eighteen. Now he's twenty-four, three years older than me. Started smoking and hasn't trained for months. He still looks and behaves like a kid but he knows about a lot of things. Clever, I spects. Over his shoulder I see the Oak Tree, watching, leaning gainst the wall by the archway. I grims at him—don't know how come I'm with Heath, six foot two albino tree frog.

Oak Tree grims back.

I sees through a gap in the crowd that Gwen is hanging off Quentin's belt, rolling her face in his crotch, keeps looking up to see if I'm looking. Wonder if she's jealous, it int ever happened fore. Now Davros has got me a drink as well. A wave of tiredness goes over my head. I sway, can't shake it off. I glug the treble vodka down, hopes the shock will keep me wake. Bwah-ha-ha-ha! When I go to the toilet Gwen follows me in.

"So," she says, "you've finally caught something."

I shrugs.

"Heath seems to like me, Gwen, I int sure why."

"Well do you fancy him or not?"

I don't know.

"Don't be such a freezer." She sounds angry, slams a toilet door. "I'm sick of you always sulking around because nobody wants you, and now somebody does, so you might as well just go for it, have some fun. He likes you, what bloody more do you want?"

"He's ever so funny. Is he a customer at the casino?"

"What has that got to do with anything? Get a couple of drinks down you and get on with it. What is there to lose?"

I int going to get on with it. The Oak is in the corridor, I has to get over his roots.

"I want to be a tree," he says.

It don't surprise me. I has to swing under one of his branches, put my hand flat on his chest. I look up at him slight in the eye.

"Can feel the sap rising," I says.

Gwen comes and shoves me.

"Move along now," she says. "Peter Eden is most definitely, most assuredly out of your league. Heath Crow is just what you need."

And here he is, the Joker, waiting for me, wants the last dance. Gwen virtually pours my drinks down my throat, slaps me on the back like a go-get-him-kiddo.

The music stops and Gwen comes yelling that a taxi is outside waiting.

"Am I coming with you?" Heath says.

He arsts me gain, in a what-do-you-say kind of way. I int got the heart to say no. As we leave I keep my head down, case people think I'm a desperate measure. Gwen tries really hard to get Quentin in the taxi but he's so drunk laid out on the pavement we have to leave him there. Gwen sits in the front. We pass the casino still open for another two hours. Heath reckons he knows how to card count.

"Is it a plus-minus system?" I says.

It is. He chirps on big-eyed about the beauty of the card-counting system. About the man who invented it and how it cost Las Vegas casinos a couple of million. The card counters he trained even wore disguises.

"Obviously, the faster the game is dealt, the harder it is to count."

"So the dealer will see sudden heavy betting when the count is favorable?"

"Yep," Heath says, "usually in the last few hands before a new shoe."

"I've got some cards indoors," I says. "Can you teach me how it works?"

Gwen makes a bored sound, makes a change cos normal it's me.

At Park Lane I has to pay for the taxi. I magines the three of us will go upstairs in the lounge but Heath leans on my ear in the hall.

"Where's your room? Show me."

It's like he wants to tell me something and he don't want Gwen to hear, sides my room is the nicest place for sitting and learning how to card count, I've got the fireplace open now and a few bits of chair to burn. He shuts the door behind him and brings me straight down.

"Don't bother now with the cards," he says. "It's you I want."

Makes me laugh. I roll around like Norman Wisdom.

"Int true," I says.

"No?" He wants to take my coat off me.

"Keep it on," I says.

He int joking. Takes my flip-flops off. His sneakers stink.

"Hup," he says. My jeans is off.

Makes me laugh. And him. Makes me laugh. I'm just a girl who caint say no.

"Just relax." He reranges my everything. "I don't want you to hurt yourself."

Funny thing to say. We rolls around laughing.

"Ow!" I yells. Laughs loud, half nelson int necessary. "Ah!" I yells. He's kneeling on my hair; I looks up at his balls swinging over my face. Makes me laugh, don't know what I'm sposed to do with them so I put my hands in my coat pockets.

"You're not taking this seriously, are you?"

"No, course not," I says.

"Relax. Just relax, relax."

"I is relaxed."

"Something feels nice and furry," he says.

"Zebra skin."

Makes him laugh, we roll around. I spects we both is drunk. He wants to undo my shirt, I won't let him, has to keep my body covered.

"OK," he says. "Fair enough. Just relax, here comes a Heath Special."

I'm so surprised it's for real, I lays still like the wooden cunt I is. He's naked-white and see-through with twanging veins and sinews and big smashed and swollen knuckles. I clenches everything up, case my cunt is like an allotment.

"Relax. You aren't relaxed. Just relax, just drop into my hands."

He slaps my thigh, digs my ribs, tickles my feet, I laughs, he pulls me closer, gripping the severed nerves in my leg, makes me scream out the pain.

"That's it," he says, "make some noise."

But now he's in his stride like someone allowed and deadly and direct and I got a fast feeling of Rosemary's Baby growing inside me. That's how come I starts crying.

"You don't have to be embarrassed, most women cry when I've finished with them." He pulls his jeans back on. Laughs. "Sounds arrogant but it is a fact. They get overwhelmed with my technique and sexual expertise."

Makes me cry more, so underwhelmed.

"What you have to understand is this: I've got five black belts, in five different martial arts disciplines. I'm a master of the mind and body. Seriously, physiology is my specialist subject; I've dedicated my life to it. Back in a minute," he says. Sticks his tongue out, tips his head.

Wonder if he has gone to make me a cup of tea. Through the French doors can see that the kitchen light int on. I stand up on fucked legs. Heath's sperm gobs into my pants. Rosemary's Baby. Fuck, fuck, fuck. I shiver and shake and wrap my coat around tighter. I open my door and listen.

. . . NO MORE TALK OF DARKNESS
FORGET THESE WIDE EYED FEARS . . .

Can hear Heath upstairs, larking about in the lounge with Gwen. Went up for the toilet and got collared. No one is in the bathroom. I go up and lock the door, hang me and then my coat on the back of it. The light bulb has gone, moon through the winder sees me shiver naked into the dry bath. My hands are too weak to press the safety lid on the bottle of toilet bleach, it click and clicks and clicks and clicks. It clicks and opens. I lie back in the bath and twist sideways, my feet slide up the wall, my legs follow, my hands help lift my pelvis to follow. The bleach is thick and gobs into me. It burns. It burns. I'm raw. It gobs and gobs, it burns and burns and I bite and bite and bite on the corner of a towel. The bleach burns and gobs into my womb, I bite, it burns, it gobs, and fills, and gobs in my pubic hair, I gag and it gobs and pours, over my bars of body scars, tears run down my face and burn, burns me clean, back to bone, back to the backbone.

Kills all known germs dead. I bite the burn of the bleach, stupidity makes me sober and white. I burn red with shame and shake. My white skin, my black coat, the lambskins slip over my bones. I face the bathroom door. Straighten Gwen's Mensa certificate. Straighten my coat, my face and backbone.

I'M HERE—NOTHING CAN HARM YOU
MY ARMS WILL WARM AND HOLD YOU.

Hear Heath and Gwen, still talking and mucking about in the lounge. They don't hear me going down the stairs. In the kitchen I light a cigarette, rattle it to my lips, the nicotine is urgent. I swallow the smoke and hold it. Burning still. While the kettle is boiling I open the back door. The smell of bleach is stuck like a fish bone in my throat. My knickers are fisted in my pocket. I try to burn them with the lighter, on the concrete outside the back door. They won't burn. I know there is an old can of paint-stripper under the sink, I get it. I gob some of the paint-stripper onto the knickers then set fire to them. The flames rage, red in my face, burning up, I feel sick. I stagger into the dark garden, does a swirl, throws up under the elderberry. Sit burning still, trembling on the upturned bucket waiting for my flooded eyes to drain. I don't know what I has to do now. Breathe heavy on the lilac smell. It's no big deal. Make the three of us coffee, take it up. I'm with Heath, he chose me. We were having a laugh. I was just overwhelmed. Underwhelmed. Drunk. Out of control. Surprised. I'm out of proportion, wired with tiredness. Don't know what to do with a *boyfriend*. Talk about card counting. Rosemary's Baby. Stupidity, that's all. Heath int a monster, well, what did I expect? It's bigger than that though, the feeling. My guts know something I don't. The white lilac smells sweet; I hang on to that, snap off a spray of it. Put it in a jam jar on the tray with three mugs of coffee and carry it up. When I get to the top of the stairs a gap comes between the songs.

"In my dreams!" Heath laughs. "Let's face it, Gwen, I'm only a plasterboard wall away from your bed; it can't be more than half a day away now."

"I didn't expect you to stoop quite so low," Gwen says, "but I'll grant you it was well executed."

"She's all right actually," Heath says. "But Quentin, Gwen?" He laughs like a bastard. "Quentin!"

"Quentin is a very, very rich boy as it happens. You obviously don't know who his father is."

I take the tray back downstairs and leave it on the side. I put my keys in my coat pocket and my cigarettes and let myself out. Feel like nothing, nothing at all. I look left and right, either way there's nowhere to go. I walk to the corner of the park. A big white van walks behind me. The grass in the park is cold and heavy with dew, wets my jeans up to the knees. I watch my bare feet whiten and swell. The big white van is waiting for me on the other side of the park. Following me, or someone lost, maybe wants directions, no one else about, so I stop and turn. I look left and right, surprised to find him here.

"You could get in," the Oak Tree says.

So I does and slam the van door. He int wearing last night's beautiful clothes, he's got stubble and look likes a hedge backward.

"I don't do a market on Monday," he says. "It's my day off. I was looking for a friend of mine but I couldn't remember which street."

He grinds the van past Temple Meads Station. Words don't seem necessary. It's barely light. The city center is empty; he swirls around the statue of Queen Victoria who int amused and stops the van underneath the awning of the Royal Swallow Hotel.

Brambles and barbed wire. Underneath. I rips through a gap. Down in the ditch. Splashing. My legs is streaming. Streaming down in the stream in the ditch and the dandelion splashes. Something coming. Whooshing. Shushing car coming. Meadowsweet smell. Shush. Stingers. Scratching. I is fine-tuned. Can hear music coming in a car. Humming. Violins. Starts me itching. The car has gone but the music stays, I got it on the tip of my tongue. Climbs up out of the ditch and runs ripping cross the field, up the hill, way, way from the road. Eyes is prickling. Thistles. Purple scratches. Patches. Black and white.

Cows. Trees. Trees on the top of the hill. Run straight in. Weave, weave, weave the trees, fast tween the dark and light, saying the names.

Ash.

Alder.

Birch.

Beech.

Chestnut, sweet.

Bluebells hit me like a wall. Don't know if it's all a dream, drops down on my knees, looks at them all looking at me. My breathing comes together with the trees. Something snapping makes me turn and drop down flat in the blue sweet smell.

Tiny snap, gain, lifts my head a little bit.

A deer. She int sure. We stop breathing. Her eyes is kind like understand. My mouth goes twisty and eyes burn, cold trickles down my cheeks and drips on the bluebell leaves. I close my eyes. Open my eyes. The deer int there no more. I has to be like her. I has to disappear.

Red Roofs Detention Center
Dingles Farm
Dingles Lane
Egham
Surrey

Day Journal
Cont: page 48

Friday April 29

Catherine Clark absconded between 9:15 and 9:20 this morning (probably through the vent in the wall behind the compost bins). She was last seen wearing a red tablecloth and sneakers. I've notified the police and Ian West (duty officer) at Social Services. Sarah Waters isn't in until Tuesday because of the bank holiday. HB

I don't look back. I listen for the sound of him starting the van and driving off. But the sound don't come, he watches me walk, up over the brow of the hill. I don't look back; I'm blinded by whitebeam trees in the park flashing their mirrored leaves.

3 Park Lane. I put my key in the lock. The opening door spreads a dog shit on the mat. Heath's leather jacket is still on the stair post. My clean uniform is on a hanger; it rolls and goes in a bag with my shoes and

chestnut hairpiece and makeup bag. The taps in the heels of my shoes strike nail heads as I cross the landing, the stereo speakers spit.

Bookends on the sofa.

Her face is red raw, her dressing gown is gaping open. He's wearing her towel and his back is screaming with pink clawing. Needle scuffs at the end of a song. The dog growls and then starts yapping, she don't know me. Gwen slaps it down. I wait for one of them to say something.

"Sorry it's worked out this way," Heath says. "It's just there's a spark between Gwen and me and we kind of got it together while you were out."

"What a state," Gwen says. "Where have you been? You've got mud on your face. You've missed out on crumpets."

"I don't know that *crumpet* is the appropriate word given all the circumstances," Heath laughs like a bastard.

"You." Gwen slaps him.

They look at me. They look at each other. Gwen lights a cigarette, flaps the smoke way.

"Why are you such a wreck?" she says. "You've got leaves in your hair, fucking bluebells, whatever is going on with your lip?"

I dab with my tongue on my canine tooth, bitter taste of bluebell sap. Watch them both get taken aback. I lap at my swollen lump of lip where an Oak Tree bit and we made savage sound and fed off each other.

"Suits her, doesn't it?" Heath's hands open in his lap. "I did enjoy it, though; I want you to know that. You really are a great girl."

"Maybe if she put on some weight?"

"God, no," Heath says. "Her physique is beautiful; believe me, there isn't anything wrong with her body."

"What are we going to do with her?"

"Cheer her up."

"I'm off to work," I say.

"Well, wait for half an hour and I'll give you a lift," Gwen says. "I'm on a day shift as well."

"I'm happy to walk," I say.

"Suit yourself," she says to me. "Oh dear," she says to Heath.

Can hardly carry the false eyelashes; my eyelids limp. I scrub peat out from under my nails at the sink and swallow a handful of Pro Plus. Then go out to perform the afternoon matinee. Memorize my lines and move as directed. Gwen is on reception, taking the old Greek's coat. I was sure she would phone in sick, half of the afternoon shift has.

Darren sees who he's got.

"Blackjack Table 2, please," he says to me.

Wissy is on Blackjack Table 1 sides me. We wait for Mrs. Herrington to climb up on her perch. It's agony to watch, the pencil skirt don't help or the eight-inch spikes she's got for heels.

"Are you a bit of a tippler, Mrs. Herrington?" I say, but it's just my magination.

Her name's Barbara but everyone calls her Mrs. Herrington cos she's virtually a God, with a black suit and a blonde bob. Spider's eyelashes. Black widow. Normally she comes over to make me stupid and clumsy but today I int got any nerves left for her to play on.

"Afternoon, Babs," I say.

She turns to see my empty hands fluttering. She sucks at the air like a night-feeding fish, casino suck; the sound brings a God and Darren over to witness the opening of the table.

"Are you OK?" Darren says.

"Whiplash, bit my lip," I lies.

The other God brings the cards from the safe in the cash desk and slings the four packs on my table.

"Thank you."

I peel the cellophane seal from the first pack, the cards are newborn slippery, you have to hold them firm and square. And yourself. I fan the deck flat on the table sweeping from left to right. Spades then hearts come pouring out and clubs and the diamonds wink one behind the other. I flourish the fan at the end with a flick on the diamond ace. And the joker stands to one side. The second deck comes below it, sweeps back the other way. The joker stands to one side. For the third deck the arc is closer to me, tighter, but it lays down for me fluid and flawless, and the fourth, they hold their breath but mine sighs smooth to the end, put that in your pipe and smoke it, Barbara, I think.

Makes Darren smile.

"I'm glad we've got that on camera," says the God in the shadow.

I look up at her.

"Check," she says cos she has to. "Where's your other earring?"

"I've only got the one," I say.

"Well, you can't wear just one," she says, "take it out."

I feel for the butterfly.

"Not here, you stupid girl, do it when you go on a break."

I close my eyes; suck in a wash of bluebells ringing. Darren unlocks the cash-chip tray in front of me and the table is officially open.

The old Greek sauntering around dismisses Wissy with a smile and comes to my table. He raps three times on the baize with his knuckle, OK's the four full decks and my handiwork. I flip the two furthest fans and watch the cards turn over, running the arc, passing each other midway. I do the same with the two nearest fans so all the cards are face down then blend and stir them all together, for three-point-five minutes.

Or til Mrs. Herrington says stop.

The old Greek is patient with her. When she says so, I gather the cards in, square the four decks into a block, then rifle through the shuffling procedures. I slide the red plastic cutting card to the old Greek and he cuts the block a viable quarter. While I settle the block into the shoe, he slips a crisp twenty from his wallet.

"Buying in—twenty pounds," I say.

"Check."

"Eleven—double or card? Eleven doubles one card only. Thirteen. Blackjack. Nineteen. Nineteen stands. Thirteen. Card. Fifteen. Card. New shoe. Twenty-five bust. Eighteen or split nines, splitting nines, one card only. Sixteen. Eighteen." The words ring mental in my mind. "Twenty-one. Blackjack pays two to three."

"Check."

"New shoe." I prepare to reshuffle. Someone taps me on the left shoulder. Squid.

"New dealer," I say to the microphone.

I show my empty hands to Barbara and the mellow old Greek, and stepping backward, bow out.

I didn't notice but Roulette Table 2 has got a crowd around it. I has to squeeze through it to get out on my break. The staffroom is full of smoke but no actual people; the extractor fan is sucking so hard my uniform pulls out from my body. I go into the changing room, walk light through the scene with the blue flowers and into a toilet cubicle. Rub the crown of my head on silver birch and woodland floor, on the back of the toilet door, tasting gain the blood on my lip where he bit and we lapped it up. Bluebells snap. Someone coming; the changing-room door swings open.

". . . even think she's all that attractive. Hook nose, un it? Blobby. On her chin. On the tops of her legs. Pigeon-chested. She is though, un it?"

Moonface. The other one coughs on hairspray, think it's Dorit the waitress.

"Apparently she likes it up the arse," she says, smacking her lippy. "And now they all want a go."

I wait, case she gets shamed, talking about my treacherous ex-best friend like that.

"I'd better go out—give us a dab," Moonface says. "R2 is down ten grand, you should see the crowd around Mr. Abdullah now. Darren's doing his tank."

The changing-room door swings twice. Gone. Someone else comes in humming. It's Lois, can smell her Amarige perfume. She does a double take.

"What a transformation! When they designed these uniforms they had you in mind. Who did your hair—pinned up like this? It's beautiful!"

"No," I say. "It's just a hairpiece."

"Are you enjoying it?" She hitches up the leg of her tights.

"This is only my second shift, just small games."

"It's mental out there now; R2 is down twenty-two thousand. Aw fuck it! Now I torn them."

"Sorry," I say.

I look in the mirror, bluebells fill half of my vision. Mrs. Herrington, I think, my one earring. I feel for the butterfly. My diamond drops in the sink, my diamond flashes, bounces, dribbles on the rim, disappears down the plughole.

"I'm having a boob job on Friday," Lois says.

I'm under the sink. The plastic U-bend fitting won't unscrew.

"Twins," Lois says, "36 double D."

I kick the fitting.

"I thought 36 double D but now I'm not so sure."

I wrench the pipe off the wall, off the sink; smash the U-bend fucker to bits with my heel.

"My husband wanted 40 double D. I'm not so sure."

My diamond winks pleased to see me; I free it from limescale and hairball. I think of where to put it safe. I look at my coat. So black and splashed with bluebell sap. No one will take it, it's *my* coat. I feel for the tiny hole in the pocket and poke the diamond earring through; it drops inside the shantung lining.

"Had best go back out, Lois," I says.

Everyone is around Roulette 2. Everyone cept three dealers standing at empty tables, looking to see me coming back and if it's them next for a break. As I pass through the crowd, the ball drops. Crowd roars, stands up, cheers, throws arms and beer mats up in the air and whistles. Someone picks me up and puts me down, people is even standing up on stools to see. Any minute Mr. Abdullah could leave and would want to take his winnings in cash. I see the cash desk is full of Quentin and sombre Gods preparing. Course Mr. Abdullah could take a casino cheque but it wouldn't be as satisfying as an empty vault and a Securicor van parked out the front.

All of the Gods has come down, standing in shadow at the head of the wheel. I report back from break. Darren takes my elbow and leads me off, to the far side of the Pit where the lights and microphones int switched on til the evening crew comes in. Wonder if I done a mistake. Don't think so. Hearts bashing. I int got the stomach for another wrongdoing.

"I want you to go on R2." Darren gets drowned out by the roar of the crowd.

Good joke.

"I don't want you to go in unprepared." He int joking.

We turn to look over at the crowd. Darren leans into my ear.

"The effervescent Mr. Crow, in the jeans and the red and green leather jacket, see him?"

"Number 9?" I say.

"He's a thief—but he's stealing from Mr. Abdullah not us. Now is not the time to challenge him if you see a sleight of hand. Quite a character Heath Crow. I would ban him but he's so much fun he's actually good for business. The table is down sixty-three thousand pounds." Darren's eyes wobble on the impossibility of it.

This isn't meant to happen, especial not on a Monday afternoon.

"The ball keeps dropping in the Tier section of the wheel," he says.

In theory it can't happen.

"We've changed dealer three times, I wouldn't put you in there Duchess, if I didn't know how lucky you are. Don't be intimidated by the sums of money. Don't hang about. Your commentary needs to be loud and clear."

Uh-huh.

Crowd roars. Gods watch me pass from dark to light. I tap the dealer on the satin shoulder. The crowd jeers and hisses, case changing the dealer breaks the spell. Mr. Abdullah himself don't seem to mind. He's so lucky today there int nothing on earth can touch him.

"Paying: seven thousand nine hundred and forty-three?" The dealer's voice is so tight it squeaks.

"Check," says the Camp Inspector.

"Check," says Mrs. Herrington.

"Check," says a God in the dark.

I stand to one side while the dealer prepares the payout. He can't leave the table til he's done it. The chip-sorting machine is choking on the overload gone down it so I make myself useful and unjam it. Put stacks handy for the dealer to move. He's in a terrible mess.

"Wheel," I whisper to him.

He leans over just in time and saves it from an illegal standstill. A God comes from the cash desk with a briefcase full of cash-chips to top the table up. The payout is finally prepared and spread out and right, I reckon.

"Seven thousand nine hundred and forty-three." The dealer still sounds unsure.

"Check."

"Check."

"Check," Mrs. Herrington says but her eyes don't quite tally.

Takes nine journeys cross the table to get all the winnings over there. The dealer is shaking so badly stacks keep collapsing on the way. Looks like he's going to faint.

"New dealer." He shows his empty hands and steps back to let me in.

It's my table now and I don't give a fuck. I hold my empty hands up for everybody to see.

"Good afternoon. Gentlemen," I say for irony. "Place your bets please."

Mr. Abdullah can't get the chips on the layout quick enough or high enough, he gets those in the front line to help him. I see Heath's cuffs and broken knuckles helping to straighten the towering chips. He takes a few chips off the top for his pocket. I pick the ball up and flick it.

"Place your bets please," I say a second time so they know that the ball is spinning.

Heath is as loud as hell, whooping it up, running a commentary. *Tier section on the layout looks like a dinosaur's backbone.* He int wrong. The ball changes key.

"No more bets," I say. "That's all now, thank you."

Mr. Abdullah is well behaved and sits down and the crowd takes back all of its arms. Everyone is holding breath. Gods must look but can't. Ball drops. Pings. Clatters.

Every light in the world goes out.

"Game void!"

"Game void!" Gods shout out in absolute darkness.

There int even a sliver of daylight in this place, all of us is so blind we could be down a mine. I know in the darkness fingers is squirrelling chips off the layout, searching out the cash. The crowd is mental, yelling objections. *Bang*. A gun goes off. Mirror explodes. I drop down and under the table.

Silence says *anything breathes I'll kill it.*

Somebody is moving. A paler shade of black in blackness. Other hearts machine-gun around me, all cowering down under Roulette 2.

Listens.

We all listens. Someone can see, to move, to unclip the brass hook on the Pit boundary rope. I smell Darren's aftershave close by. Two people? Moving. They can see the Pit phone on the plinth. Pick it up. Listen. Nothing. Put it down. Magines the Gods, close, dived down flat on the carpet. Mrs. Herrington still up in her high chair.

Stopped. Now coming closer, stepping over.

"Keys," a voice box says like a Dalek.

Kick of an instep says *yes, you.*

"Don't shoot! Please don't shoot me!" The God's knees crack as he stands up. Keys jingle-jangle on the way to the cash desk.

I sign the bottom of my statement *Kim Hunter.*

"Thanks for this." The policeman squares the pages on the desk. "Send the next one in, would you?"

I nod and close the office door behind me. In reception a couple of electricians are working on the wiring for the alarms and camera systems. The gaming-hall double doors are propped open, can see a huddle of Gods in the Pit and forensics still taking fingerprints and looking for the bullet. Everyone is quiet; shocked and still deaf from the blast of the gun. Gwen is in the staffroom with Betty-Boo and Moonface waiting for their turn, and Princess Grace who wasn't here this afternoon or yesterday. Seems like they called her in especially to shed some light on something.

In the changing room I put my coat on, skid on an oily patch of exhaustion and hang on the hook for a minute. I has to get out of here.

"Aren't you going to wait for me?" Gwen says as I pass back through.

She thinks this afternoon's robbery has wiped out last night's treachery.

"What's the matter with you?" she shouts.

Her, I think; she's what's the matter with me. Darren is outside on the marble steps, smoking a cigarette.

"I didn't know you smoked," I say.

"I don't," he says, coughing. "Have yourself a day off tomorrow; everyone needs it. We'll open again on Thursday."

"Thursday is my day off."

"Come in on Friday," he says. "Where's your taxi? Everyone is having a taxi."

"I'm happy to walk," I say.

"Are you all right?"

"Uh-huh."

I turn right stead of left, turn left stead of right. Walk.

Sway suspended up on this beautiful bridge, with strings of lights above and below shining in the estuary mud. Everything stays behind me.

On the main road, between the street lights, I jump the wall into Ashton Court Estate, dark with boundary trees. Blow out into the open meadow. The sweep of light from the city below makes my shadow run up the hill. Catch a flapping wind on the ridge, my shantung lining flashing like a distressed signal. I stop to breathe in the open on the edge of the stony car park, find the tire tracks in the grass where Peter Eden swung the van around. Then blow over the golf course and slide sideways into the woods. A tree takes me up into its arms; I balance there with my forehead on bark and sleep with one leg dangling down.

First light finds me up, flying up on the wing of the city, on the edge of a promising sky. Shush.

Shush.

I breathe through the scene with the blue flowers, glancing off silver-birch trees, slowly and lightly tracing back the footprints of a nine-toed animal.

Has to squeeze my mind, to find him, find him, find him last in lights of cabbige whites, and puzzled eyes, his baby lips, sounds small and fluttering. *Int no god.* I open my eyes. Colors is painted on. Sky is too blue. Clovers is too purple. Buttercups shine too shiny. Wonders who I is? A ladybird. Who is I. Who I am. Close my eyes. Sees a meadow in my mind. I hovers. Open my eyes. Fingers read the lines done down on my cheek.

Lulu. Grady. Pip.

Waves wash words up in my mind. Seed grass talks Chinese. Words come plain as truth, *int seeing Baby Grady no more.* Swifts cut dashes cross my body. I got knuckles and knees in the dirt, sounds like a night-time wolf howling in sunshine and buttercup stalks.

Screaming wakes me up. I got the taste. Purple clouds. Got thirst worster than sand. My skin is Six Weeks in the Bahamas Brown. It don't look like the same day. Dandelion clocks has growed up around me. I look up in the sky. Wonders if I made it up and got me stuck inside a story. I think the story from the beginning, see if I told any lies. Ants tickle around my toes. Sees where my baby toe int. I looks at sneakers in the grass sides me, both left feets. Cornflakes where I was sick, wonders if to eat them gain. Breathing through my skins; something . . . snapping.

Shadow.

Man with a dog. I crawl through a gap in the bushes and get out on the road. Run long on the verge. Posh houses both sides with tall walls. When cars come I hide in driveways and in gardens under laurel bushes. A police car drives past and a dog starts barking in the house. Scared case it's big and gets me. I look out at the road, too many cars. The dog is loose, coming. I run at the big wooden fence, get up on nothing. That's how come I panics over the top and drop down on the other side, next to a car, nearly trips over some feets, sticking out from underneath.

So surprised.

Can't move.

"Pass me the big spanner, would you?" says a man's oily hand.

So I pick it up and give it to him. The barking throws itself at the other side of the fence.

"Bloody dog," says the man under the car. "If you're looking for Suzy she's gone shopping with her mother."

"Sorry," I says tween my beating hearts. I listen to the dog and a lady calling it Bruno. Police car drives back past the gates.

"Wait for her if you want," he says. "There's some cake and lemonade in the porch."

Word lemonade does me a swirl. I look at the house and two garages. Underneath the car I hear the spanner slip. *Ouch*. He's sipping in a fist, spects his knuckles has gone. I kneel down and look under to see how it is. Uh-huh.

"Sorry," I says.

"It's OK, it slipped, that's all. Suzy will be back soon. Just go on in and help yourself."

The porch is like a glass room, the door is slided open. Smells all the red geraniums. The lemonade is in a glass jug, real lemons floating in it and bits of thin ice. Tall glasses shine with orange stripes around. Jug is too heavy for one arm, muscles has set like concrete from running. I got shakes bad, try not to slop it. Legs is twitching, I has to sit down on the furnitures. Bamboos and cushions done with cabbige-rose chintz. I look at the four cakes; they got white icing and cherries on. Int proper to take a cake, case someone is coming especial for it; they got four glasses and four plates. I spects Suzy is a princess, she's got a dad and friends come around for lemonade and cake. He rolls out from under the car, wiping his hand on a bit of rag.

Don't want him to see me proper, case they done me on the telly.

He int coming over, stead now he's gone under the bonnet. Rovers int too much trouble. Lemonade int fizzy, it's got bits of lemon, better than bubbles. I dab it, dab it with my tongue. Wishes I could glug it down but can't case the ice cuts my throat, case my stomach gets oversited and chucks it all back up gain.

If Suzy comes with her mum I has to say *hello*. Then run. Or just run. Could say *sorry got the wrong house*. Could arst them if they got a spare room or a shed or something, only if I does the ironing and the decorating and gardening and fixes the cars. I spects if they seen my fingers they'd know I'm good at fiddly and I always clean proper and hoovers around the edges. My mum learned me everything case one day I has to be a slave. Car on the gravel.

Empty glass on the glass table.

I'm down the steps and around the side, quick I'm up in a lilac tree and quiet over the fence, case they want me to clean the oven.

Handbrake. Car doors slamming.

"Your friend was here, Suzy; I think she must have gone."

I spects if you live in a great big house you has to learn how to shout.

"Which one—which friend?"

"I don't know, darling. How would I know which one?"

"I hate you! You're never here!"

"I've bought tuna, darling, to barbecue," shouts Suzy's mum.

I run stripy cross the next-door grass. The road int safe, too many cars, wishes I never come this way. I try around the side of the house, see a shed and get up on it. Behind is a footpath. I drop down. Don't know. Left or right? Right is always best with me just cos my sneakers is facing that way. I run past people walking dogs, I is a little girl out jogging, does it bouncy with a tend ponytail, don't know how come.

This bit int posh. Somewhere on this state an ice-cream van is doing its tune, sounds pink and sticky, same as my tongue, and running out of battery. My legs don't want no more, muscles is burning in spots like cigarettes. I spects my arms is stuck up running, don't know if I can get them back down. My eyes is first to give up, can't make sense of all the blurring. Hungry is biting at my sides. I start chewing my own fat tongue, tastes the blood fore the pain. I has to get something to drink. Something to eat. I has to. I has to.

The path comes out in a small field with gardens around it and back gates. Been around it three times, no way out cept where I come. No point going back, I never passed nothing to eat. Hungry pains is chewing me up. Knees is screaming for a rest but they int allowed to stop case we lays down dies. Corner house is the best chance, on its own with big grass and apple trees. No apples, just bits of leaf and leftover blossom.

Kids was playing.

I heard them squealing with the hosepipe and the paddling pool and all the stuff out of the shed, but there int no kids here now. Everything looks bandoned. The garden path is straight, the back door is still open. Someone was in the kitchen washing up fore but I can't see no one now. Probably gone to the ice-cream van. Can see right through the house cos the front door is open and the front gate. I climb over into the garden. Crawl long by the fence. Crawls past a boy hiding in a bush. Makes us jump.

"I thought you were Nuptials!" he says. Looks terrified.

"Sorry." I keep on crawling. Stand up and squeeze long behind a shed, comes out by a water butt where a girl int hiding very well. She's got jeans and a red top.

"Sorry," I says cos I made her jump. I stay low and spy where to go next. The girl comes kneels sides me.

"Gerry's in the canoe," she whispers. "Barry's in the tent. Chantal is in her usual place."

I see how the garden is, they got sheets and blankets pegged out from a line, been doing a show. I spects the shape behind the sheet is Chantal waiting in the wings.

"Rory the Story is in the Wendy house," she says. "Tina went indoors. Flea is down behind the wall."

Cept he int cos when she blinked he jumped cross, now he's laid down in a curve tending to be part of the paddling pool.

"Where is Nuptials?" I whisper. "Who is we hiding from?"

"Me," she says.

Surprises me. I look where everyone is hid.

"Who is you going to get?" I arsts.

"You!" She shoves me so hard nearly fell through the cold frame. She don't know. How much trouble I got.

"I int *playing*," I says.

No good cos now she's walking backward shouting and pointing at me.

"She's It! She's It! She's It!"

That's how come kids come out, got me surrounded. They look like for some reason I int standing straight.

"Sorry." I sees all the eyes sliding sideways. Uh-huh.

"It! It! It! It!"

They does me swirling, around and around, ring-a-ring-a pointed fingers. Kids int no good. They int proper, they int.

"It! It! It!"

I has to get a good idea. I has to, fore they take me hostage, case they seen me on the telly.

"It! It! It! Let's chain her up!"

I get a good idea.

"OK," I says. "I'm It."

They int sure if I said something, that how come I has to say it louder.

"I'm It."

They still int sure if it's true, so I does them savage claws and a roar. Then all is screaming and running way bottoms of feets.

Chantal is in her usual place.

Flea is being a paddling pool.

Tent has got an elbow.

Canoe rolls over on the slope, makes a thud and a slide and says *ouch*. My feets nearly leave me behind, through the kitchen and through the hall and out through the front door. Rude but fastest way.

Down the road I is a blur in colors of green, light and dark and camouflage bark on all the plane trees flying past. Ha-ha-ha makes me laugh. I is lucky. Uh-huh, I is. I grabbed a bread bag on the way through the kitchen. When I get to the end of the road it's one way or the other. Has to get off the roads. I run past some cottages, up a dirt track and over a farmer's gate. I sit down in a corner huffing and see what I got.

Six slices and a crust. I eat two slices and a half, save the rest for later.

I is the wind, fast as stitches in lines of green wheat. Trees is thick long the top of a ridge. I run with sunlight into the woods, run downhill, come out by a church in a village.

Int proper to lock a church.

The moon is starting to shiver and shake. In a garden, sides the graveyard, is a sailing boat, on a trailer next to the house. I duck low through the gravestones and go over for a proper look. The boat has got a blue plastic sheet over it, to stop it leaking, I spects. Too cold for scared. I has to get in. I hop the wall. Climbs up, one, two, three, and slips in underneath, listens for someone to shout, or come out of the house. There int no sound, just my hearts bashing. I feel my way inside and creep long, wonders if the trailer will tip but it don't.

Surprises me I'm on a boat with a tiny ship's steering wheel. It's all hogany wood. I keep the blanket wrapped around me and peek out the curtain. Now there is two cars parked, right next to where I was sleep and a light on in the hall. It's coming daytime, birds getting up. I look quiet in the cupboards see what there is. Just tools and paintbrushes and tins of paint and cans for gas and ropes and sailing things. I find some scissors, that's how come I cut all my hair off, short like a boy. Don't know what to do with it so I leave it curled up in the sink, case they thinks it's a cat. I eat one slice of bread and fill me up with water then I slides out nice and quiet, frightens a thrush out of the hedge.

On the lane there's a bungalow with grass around it and fields behind. I run through their garden and jump the back fence. The sun is coming up, turning the low mist golden colors. Far way on a hill can see a tower, standing up, taller than a castle or a palice or something. I try to keep it in my eyes, so I know I is going somewhere. After while the running don't hurt, it gets like normal, running so smooth and easy as breathing. Reckon the tower has got a bell, can hear it ding-dinging in the wind, in the rushing of the leaves in the trees.

Ding—takes time to swing.

Ding—like calling people in.

Ding.

Sometimes I lose the tower, villages and houses and hills get in the way, but I always find it gain. I run through trees sides the road, saying the names. Beech. Beech. Beech. I pushes my legs faster, til everything burns and blurs. I listen for the sweet sound of the bell.

Ding—calling me.

Ding—calling me the way.

Gwen's car is outside the house. A container lorry is reversing, trying to park in a gap that don't look big enough. Surprises me, Heath is driving it. Sticks his tongue out, tips his head, then bends the lorry inch-perfect into the space. I stand on the pavement with my hands in my coat pockets and my shoes hooked under my thumbs. He jumps down from the cab.

"What happened?" he says. "Gwen and I were out all night looking for you."

"I went for a walk. There was a robbery at the casino yesterday."

"I know," he says. "I was there, remember. Are you impressed?"

He means with the lorry.

"What's in it?" I arsts.

"Washing machines," he says. "You haven't taken it personally, have you, last night?"

Last night I slept in a tree at Ashton Court.

"Night before last," he says. "Morning after the night before last. It was just a game. That's your trouble, you don't play the game, nothing about you plays the game."

"Ah," I say. "I didn't know there was a game going on."

"I meant what I said, though; don't take me for a total cunt. If the truth be told I actually *like* you more than Gwen, but it's her I want to be seen with, it's her I want to fuck. What you have to understand is this: there's nothing like a bit of upper-crust to make a man feel less like a peasant."

Makes me laugh. All the way to the front door. Stead of waiting for me to open it with my key, he bashes hard three times with the knocker. Panda is yapping and stripping paint with her claws. Every day kisses bye-bye to the deposit on this house.

"Heathee! Heathee!" Gwen canters to open the door.

I look at Heath. He looks at me. He's smiling utterly toffed. But Gwen's elocution drops off, with an afternoon bottle of Scotch. And her knickers.

"Heathee!" she says.

Then she sees me.

"Oh." Queen-sized contempt. "Where have you two been? What is so funny, pray tell?"

"Hello, Gwen," Heath says. "How's about a Rubber Duck?"

"Talk sense, boy," she says.

"Ten Four to Rubber Duck, we got us a convoy!" He rapids off some kind of hillbilly dialogue from a film, I spects.

I go down the hall. Dog shit slalom, leave Gwen and the dog riding Heath's thighs.

"Where the Dickens to?" Gwen says. "In a lorry? Don't be ridiculous. Well, of course not. Why would I conceivably want to spend eighteen hours sitting in a lorry? Just be a good boy and come and see me when you get back. Isn't it?" she says.

I put the kettle on. Cold treacherous coffee for three and the white lilac sprig in a jar are still on the tray sides the sink. *In your dreams.*

"Fair enough," Heath says. "You don't want to come; I haven't got a problem with that."

Given the choice of two evils I don't know how come I got *both* of them. No tea or coffee in the cupboard, there int any milk, there int any money til payday. Loads of Indian takeway cartons and empty bottles though. I take a glass of hot water to my room and close the door, lies down on zebra skin. Hole in my chest like someone shot me, took out a double handful of heart. I get up to look at my bit lip. The girl in the mirror don't know me, looks away mistaken, she's total deaf to the sirens and the loudness of the drumming.

Listen.

Emergency. Emergency. Get out of here. Get out of here. Go anywhere. Go anywhere. I haven't got any money. I haven't got anywhere to go. *Go anywhere.* It's a fervent fucking prayer like demented bells ringing and it makes me cry. My bedroom door opens; Heath comes in.

"Knock, knock, knock," he says. "I couldn't interest you in a drive to Scotland, could I?"

"But you simply can't." Gwen's hot on my heels down the hall. "What about work?" she yells on the doorstep. "What about me?" she screams up at the lorry. "What about me?" She swings on his wing mirror.

"See, that's what I find sexy. Her spirit," Heath says.

He means gin. The bottle was in the kitchen. She bought it and the takeaway with money I left for the rent and horse food.

Heath reckons this Scania is the Rolls-Royce of lorries and the last one of the fleet of ten he had. He got his sales training at the top of IBM, youngest highest earner in the history of the company.

"I was married to Leanne then," he says. "I meant it when I married her, I was eighteen, I'd got my first three Scannies, was driving one of them myself, but do you know what ended that marriage? It only lasted four months. One day I turned a lorry over on a roundabout and she was in the passenger seat, somehow in the shake-up and fall, the fat cow landed on my head, nearly suffocated me to death. The minute they got me out of the wreckage I went and phoned a solicitor. It was only at that precise moment I noticed how fucking fat she was. And what did she get? Half."

The second marriage lasts as long as Birmingham to Manchester, long as two toddlers and ten Scanias and a forged banker's draft for a yacht.

And the last Scania rolls on. Acrimony. I minds myself to look it up.

"It didn't help that her father was head of the CID," he says. "It cut me up; I don't mind admitting I was in pieces. It still hurts but it is easier now. Now I'm walking in the light of the Lord."

Makes me laugh. Bit too loud. But his eyes is rapt by the motorway lanes and the contraflow. His crucifix swings in his ear, silver in wing-mirrored light of the Lord and fast-lane traffic.

"How do you balance armed robbery with your Christian beliefs?" I arsts him as we passes Liverpool.

He stares at me so long and hard he swerves the lorry out of the lane, a car horn blasts, furious. "All right—you pillock," he says and turns back to me. "I think you're . . ."

"Dead?" I suggest.

"Guessing," he says.

My magination. Makes me smile. But the girl in the wing mirror don't smile, can hear the drumming, think I see me running in trees sides the road. Double handful of pain wrings out my chest. I plan to die, first chance I get, and closes my eyes, giddy with relief.

"Where did you go the other morning anyway?" Heath says. "Where did you go last night?"

I close my eyes.

"Gwen seems to think you're a prime candidate for a disappearance, she said nobody would notice you were missing."

Cept her, when her car won't start.

"She was pretty sure you had nowhere to go." He looks at me. "You got yourself a fat lip somewhere."

Spinning with my eyes closed, I open them. Hang on a telegraph wire. Crows like notes on the stave. Murder. I put my feet down off the dashboard, sit forward and light a cigarette.

"Gwen said once you cut your wrist with a razor blade; the bath was full of blood."

I flip back both of my fluted cuffs, hold my hands up.

"You're telling me Gwen is a liar," he says. "She says she's got nine O levels and three A levels, is that true?"

"Probably."

"Has she got a horse?"

"Yes."

"I know it," he says. "She's a classy woman."

He means Welsh slapper. Flashes another lorry in ahead of us.

"Did you know that Gwen's mother tried to drown her when she was six?" he says.

Didn't try hard enough. In the kitchen sink; in the washing-up water.

We pass a buzzard sitting on a post. Once I went to Swansea with Gwen and met her mother. The double sink and the draining board were gleaming polished metal, saw my face in one tap and Gwen's in the other.

"I don't want to come between you and Gwen, I mean, up until two days ago you were best friends."

Her mother made us all a fillet steak with pâté on it and wrapped it up in flaky pastry. Kept saying how nice it was to have young girls in the place. She couldn't get over the size and shape of me, twirled me around in the kitchen, had me walk to the door and back. Turned out Gwen's dad got crushed when a lorry skidded off the road and plowed him into a wall. The insurance money bought the bungalow with the marshy paddock behind it, bought elocution lessons, a private education and a horse that Gwen couldn't manage. Spects she thought Gwen might bag herself a Lord. A doctor, Gwen told me once, a solicitor would do. I look at Heath Crow, mesmerized by the dusk lights.

Has to close my eyes.

"So where did you get the split lip?"

Rewind.

At the far side of the park where he picked me up, Peter Eden stops the van, turns the engine off. It judders, the cup and saucer we stole from the Swallow Hotel rattles deep under the seat. High up in the van, we can see over the park wall.

"I live with a woman," he says, pitter-patter. "I've got a daughter who's three."

The bluebell posy dies in my hands.

"I won't ever leave them," he says.

I lean over to kiss him good-bye and he turns his lips away.

"I kiss my daughter with those," he says.

I didn't quite hear. I didn't quite hear.

Gear change of motion wakes me up fast-forward. Roundabout? Dark A-road? Doomed hills. Died and gone to somewhere unpleasant.

"Cumbria," Heath says. "It's Oh–three hundred hours, what does the Oh stand for—Oh my God it's fucking early! Light me another one of your cigarettes. How long is it since you last went fishing?"

Fact I'm still alive knocks all the wind out of the death of me. It hurts to breathe, to keep breathing.

"With a rod?" I say. "Never."

The lorry is parked in a hot lay-by. We snap through a copse with clouds of wild garlic and gnats. Midges. Mosquitoes. Call them what you like.

"Bastards," I say with my mouth closed.

Heath knows this place, this darkness; moves like he's got night vision. Skin prickles. Gnats nip. No free hands to slap. He's got the fishing box and the rods and a manky quilt over his shoulder. I've got his holdall bag, and a fire-blackened pan and an empty army jerrycan. Somewhere I spects is a fucking great sign says: Private Keep Out.

We int sactly sleek.

Even though I'm burning up, hot on the decision to die, I stop to do up my beautiful coat case the shantung lining gets ripped. Eyes adjust to flat shine of night water through the trees. Can hear running water to the left of us.

"Spring," he says.

Then we come to cross it and stop to fill the jerrycan. At the bottom of the slope we come out into a cove. Tread careful cross the tabletops of rusted rocks to a sheltered drop and a gravel beach and a small fire pit. Can't see the moon but the lake can. Heath's skin is so white, the lake light bouncing flickers on it. Tiredness, wiredness, prizes our eyes and mouths open, concentration of seeing and breathing. Ears filled with blood drumming.

Da-doom.

Man makes fire with two sticks, even though there's a lighter in my pocket. Heath's eyes burn on the friction, as if they can scorch, as if he can breathe a flame into being. The kindling flares up sudden, flames in each of his eyes.

"I'm wasted," he says. "I'm totally fucking wasted."

Makes him smile. I know how it is to be calm, sailing straight past caring. The lake takes us off. Listening. Doom. Da-doom. Da-doom.

"You make the coffee," he says, coming back, "it's in my holdall. You have the cup; I'll have the pan, put tons in. I'll get the rods rigged up."

I pick about on the shore finding twigs and driftwood to feed the fire. He sits on his quilt in the lotus position, tilting into the firelight, threads the fishing line through eyelets on the rods. He sees me with the spoon and the screw top in my hand.

"That's not coffee," he says. "That's my dad."

Surprises me.

"Sorry," I say into the canister and screw the lid back on.

"Every time I try to scatter them, I can't bring myself to do it." He bites on a lead pellet to close it on the line. "He wasn't actually my dad. We weren't related; just I went to a residential school."

My hand in his holdall finds the glass jar of coffee.

"He lived in the folly that used to belong to the grounds. He didn't have any kids, there was me and another boy, we hung about there all the time."

I wonder what he is telling me. Heath's eyes are cast out across the lake. A memory of something suffered makes a mist slip over his eyes.

"He bought us stuff. Bought my first karate lessons when I was seven, first black belt at nine. At a school like that you had to wise up. You had two choices: you were either the hunter or the hunted."

I think he means borstal. I put the cup of black coffee by his knee. Lift a flaming stick toward him so he can see to thread a silver barbed hook.

"When I was ten he bought me a motorbike." He tugs the knot in the line with his teeth to tighten it. "The other kid was into guns; we only had to call him Dad and he bought us what we wanted."

An owl fills the bowl of silence. Heath's mind has gone to the lake shine. I feels the life in him.

"Me and this other boy, we used to terrorize each other in the woods. He shot me once. Only the once." Heath lifts the side of his shirt, firelight shines on a puckered fist of a scar. "Smashed a rib, glanced off through the soft tissue, I was a bit too quick for him."

"Why did he shoot you?" I says.

"I fucked him over at the tuck shop."

We sit for a long time.

"Was that the end of it?"

"Nope," Heath says, "that was the start of it. I went to see the old man at the folly. *Dad*, I said, can I have a crossbow? One night . . ."

The story is on the skin, bristling and booming and whispering. Our frightened eyes hang on to each other. The story breathes over our shoulders, keeps poking us in the back. The crossbow bolt parts my hair and thwaps behind me into the tree. Terror hangs on every word, on every stood-up hair.

"So what did I do?" Heath looks over his shoulder, back at me, the heels of his hands tread back through the woods; they do not make a sound, he leans close to whisper, lest all of the ears in all of the leaves come closer to hear him speak, "I doubled back to the witch's house."

"Hold on, hold on," I says, "I has to piss."

"I'll come with you," Heath says.

We didn't catch anything, no bait. Heath lies down, loving one of my cigarettes.

"Share this quilt with me, if you want," he says. "We've got time for a quick one."

I'm on the opposite side of the fire.

"I'm all right, the gravel fits me nice."

"It is a pretty impressive coat. I wouldn't mind getting one like that for Gwen. Where would I go to get a black sheepskin like that?"

"Lambskin," I say. The word sounds strange, as if I don't know it.

The owl sounds like a wolf.

Heath is asleep. I take the smoking cigarette from his fingers and wander down to the water, follow the shore to the next cove. I leave my coat and clothes on the beach. Moonlight bouncing strikes my patterns white. New ones have still got threads of scabs. The lake water is not that much colder than the air. Soon as the water is deep enough I give up my legs and swim soundless to the silver middle.

"Take me out," I arsts the lake.

I give it my last breath.

But it won't take me, it throws me back. There's nothing down there to hold on to.

I leave Heath sleeping on the lake shore and go back through the woods to the lorry. I find the rope behind my seat; climb up on top of the container. Get in knots with knots and tie it on the strong branch. I put the rope around my neck; stand on the edge looking down at the drop. I'm afraid. Afraid it won't slip, afraid it won't slip tight enough. I'm afraid I'll shit my pants.

I'm afraid to live. I'm afraid to die. I'm afraid it lays me down, in the recovery position, one leg out in space. A car whooshes past. Hear Heath coming, snapping back through the trees with all of the stuff.

"*Where are you?*" He does the voice of the witch. "*I can feel your heart, beating through the door handle.*"

"I'm on the roof," I calls. "Just seeing how it is."

"It's Oh–seven hundred hours."

"What does the Oh stand for?"

"Oh my God I'm fucking late—roll 'em up–roll 'em in–roll 'em on–Rawhide! If it stays clear like this we'll see Ben Nevis on the way across."

Blink. We drive off. Leave the noose hanging down. Handy for some other poor bastard.

Welcome to Scotland.

Splatt. Gnat-smack. And smear. Girl in the wing mirror hates me. Disappointed. One day though, I promises her, I am going to take her out. If you practice often enough, you can train yourself to do anything. We know that. I know that. I know that.

"I know you want to," Heath says.

It's true, I does. I wait for him to pull the lorry over but he sails past the next chance, undoing his belt, then his jeans and unlacing a basketball boot. *Welcome to England*. Gnats all stop at the border.

"Oh baby let's do it, let's do it right now!" He's on the rumble strip.

I take my coat off; hot on a rush, knowing somehow I am already damned, somehow in a damned skid. I've still got a fat lip where an Oak Tree bit, got bluebells filling one third of my vision. I got Park Lane and Gwen waiting, seven hours down the road. How many dog shits in the hall? I slide over the top of the engine cover, step aound the gearstick.

"Over or under?" I say to Heath.

"Now slide, baby, just slide onto my lap, of course if you wanted to take your clothes off first that would be fine by me," he says. "Hang on a minute; we'd better let this pillock pass."

The pillock passes and another dark motorway mile and another three minutes on the dashboard clock. I slip over Heath's thigh bone, tilt my skinny pelvis down the gap in his lap and final get my hands on it, the wheel of this beautiful, beautiful Scania. He just slips out from behind me, disappears up on the bunk behind the seats.

Hear his clothes coming off. *Lake District* a tourist sign says. Then he comes to sit on the wide engine top. Albino tree frog. It's the huge knuckles and the way he folds his legs, in a pair of karate trousers. He hates driving, fucking hates it. Now he smokes with his eyes closed, sings about what happened one time, when the devil went down to Georgia.

Pillocks come and pillocks go. Keep driving a bluebell strip.

Blink. In your dreams. Heath disappears, gone back on the bunk to sleep. Fast asleep.

Me and the Scanny keep rolling on south. In and out of the slow lane. Two bright sidelights winking and blinking. Someone somewhere forges his tachograph, so Heath says.

Cold.

I reach for my coat and drag it over, get my arms in the sleeves and it around me. Light another cigarette and hold it in my teef, gives an overtaking laundry van a wave with my fluted cuff. We went ice-skating in Manchester. I've got bruises on my forearms from blocking, shoulders wrenched from punching, groin strain from taking off and holding up the leg position. Heath is thinking about starting up karate lessons, self-defense for women. Reckons I'm natural-born at it. He taught me how to do a reverse-turning butterfly kick. The trick now is to do it on land, where you haven't got the speed and the lift provided by flying on the ice. We got chucked out of the ice rink for mucking around. Overcited. Going the wrong way. Next to the seat is a box of tapes. I slip any old one into the machine. Press play.

FEED THE BIRDS, TUPPENCE A BAG
TUPPENCE, TUPPENCE

Wonders whether to put my foot down and smash us face first into a motorway bridge.

AROUND THE CATHEDERAL THE SAINTS AND APOSTLES

Ding—that's where the clock bell is.
Ding—at the top of the tower.
Ding—but it int a church or a castle.
Ding—red brick and white fancy bits.
Ding—wonders if it's a palice.
Ding.

Twelve. Twelve clock. Thirst is worster than cramps or stitches. I go around the edge of green grass fields with oak trees and white painted fences. I crawl long sides a hedge and get out onto a lane. Thirsty worster than a sparrow in the winter. Looks up at oringe rocks, climbing high and steep to a terrible wall and the bell tower standing up behind it.

Car coming.

I jumps fast on the verge, crashes down deep-deep in the ditch, grabbing wild at stingers and gnats.

Splash!

The ditchwater rings around my ankles, see pretty poisons floating on it. Can't drink it. Int nothing can drink it. I sees a flash of red in the green. A robin has come to see what's red and happening in his ditch.

"Can't drink it," I says.

He blinks his eyes. That's how come I starts crying.

At the top of the hill is traffic lights, sign says Egham or Virginia Water. Wonders if there is any *water,* if they named the place good and proper. Thirsty worster than a man in the desert. I turns right, follows long sides the terrible wall. There's big old trees behind it, hanging over making shade. Saves me from the sun's thumping. The road is busy but not too much. I try to walk like a normal, tends I is a little girl, going somewhere for tea and cake. Then the wall curves in and I sees through the gates.

It is a palice!

The grass is like a beach. Don't know how many peoples there is, sitting underneath the trees and on the palice steps. The gates int open or closed, halfway, too big and heavy for shifting. There's a man in a little gate hut, looks like a guard, so I tends to look at all the creatures, climbing up on the gates. Dormice and squirrels and men with leaves for hair. Still bits of colors in the rust. Blue on a kingfisher's wing. Toadstools red. Silver on the fairies' wings. Thirsty, thirsty worster than rabies.

Ding—the bell fills the world.

"Are you in or out, love?" the guard says.

Ding—

"In," I say.

"Only the cars come too fast over the railway bridge, we had one killed last year."

"Sorry," I says.

He herds me in case I was a last lost sheep.

Has to find a tap or a hosepipe or a gardener's toilet, could get some water from the cistern. The driveway is wide and glittery white, sweeping toward the palice steps. All the trees long side the drive is round and square and triangle shapes. Hedges flap up sudden in the shape of birds. The people on the grass lie flat, arms out like nailed on crosses, or dropped in chairs out of the sky. I seem like moving slow motion. An old lady comes toward me in a nightie, arms up case she floats way. Spects there int much gravity. No talking or people sound, too stonished by the sun and words has dribbled down chins. Wonders if this is a deaf place. A crow keeps hopping, looks around to see me still coming. It takes me through a tunnel done with burnum trees holding hands. The yellow flowers hanging down splash my eyes like pouring rain. Other side blinded, feels the boom of angels' wings. Two angels, sprinkling white light. I look up at them.

"Sorry," I says.

But they is made of stone, white feets gripped on a rock. Water pours from their hands and splashes into a pool. The colors of kaleidoscope tiles keep shifting underneath the water, sees my mum lying on the bottom. Bubbles comes running from her lips, like a string of tiny words; I get a panic to get her out.

"Int real," I blinks.

Blinks, scared case the water int real. I kneel up on the crumbly stone edge, sees a stone angel under the water, drownded with a broken wing. Spects the other two elbowed her in. It is water. It's cold and wet, gone tween my fingers. I sniff my hand and lick up a drop. Then I sees a girl in the water, got nutter hair all chopped. She puts her fingertips up to mine.

"Drink it," she says.

I cups water from an angel's hand and pour some over my head. I put my face down in the pool and drink it like a horse. Ha-ha-ha makes me laugh. I lay down flat and slop water over my body. Has to take my sneakers off and dangle my feets right down in it. I is lucky. Uh-huh. I is. Then I see the lions, roaring out of stone, guarding the steps and the stone arches up to the palice doors. One lion is looking down over the wall, to see where his paw dropped off. Still there, too heavy to glue back on. Kids bigger than me sit with people on the grass, all looks like best behaviors. Sun makes my red cloth steam. The stone edge is hot under my back. I close my eyes.

Something swings, falling feeling wakes me up.

Ding—

Everybody stands up, all of the peoples sitting on the steps.

Ding—

All of the peoples cross the grass.

Ding—

They come around bushes and out from under trees. Everyone is going in, thick up the palice steps. No one even sees me sitting here by the pool, they just walk past. Wonders if I is invisible. I put the wet sneakers on wet feets. The driveway does a swirl around the angels' pool and then goes off both ways, maybe all the way around the back. Think I has to go and look for some shed or place to sleep.

"Coming for tea?"

I look around cos he is talking to me. Newspaper folded under his arm and soft gray clothes, a beautiful velvit gentleman.

"I hate having tea on my own," he says. "Would you be my guest?"

I look at the velvit gentleman, poppies broidered on his waistcoat. His hair is dark gray and heavy, shining in the sun like a metal. It flicks up pretty. He don't magine me saying yes cos his eyes is a shame like holes in knitting. Spects it's all right.

He smiles and his teefs is nice.

He tucks his hair behind his ear and puts his hand up to help me down. Then his arm is a triangle and I has to put my hand up on it and walk sides him like a lady. I tries to keep my spear tidy. We stop and look up the palice steps.

"How many do you think there are?" he says.

"Pigeons or steps?"

"Steps. Forty-eight," he says. "Four lots of twelve. The tower is one hundred and forty feet tall and can be seen for miles around."

True. We stop at the top of the steps and turn around to see how it is, cross the parkland grass and trees.

"This terrace is forty feet wide and stretches east and west for almost a quarter of a mile."

We go under the middle stone arch and into the palice through arch-shaped doors. The hallway is a shock, sact same colors as Truly Scrumptious.

"Outrageous," he says.

The floor is chess; got dog-ends squashed all over on it. Stinks bad of piss. Behind the door a man is standing with his nose gainst the wall and his toes curled up the skirting board.

"Don't mind Arthur. He's catatonic."

The wall patterns jump out. Creatures squashed up in boxes. Fox-fish. Kitten-pig. Rabbit-snake. Dog swallowed its own leg makes me get a hick-sick feeling. Int proper.

"Int proper," I says.

There int no sounds. The velvit gentleman int scared. Smiling, looking up at the ceiling. Blue painted angels flying with clouds, look scared case they fall down.

"The man that built it wanted to make a huge impression but he couldn't decide what style to have," he says. "Early Italian Renaissance on the ceilings," he says, "classical Greek in the middle, and down here, a grotesque, ghoulish mix of Italian, French and Flemish Gothic."

His teefs is nice, he does a swirl, that's how come I does one, well.

"Feel sick yet?" he arsts.

"Uh-huh," I says, "I got ghoulish."

He puts out his triangle arm and we go up the middle stairs. An old man in a black cloak is sitting at a table on the landing; he's got a candle and a red apple. My legs is springs, case I int allowed, case he wants to know who I is, case I has to run.

Int real.

The old man in the painting looks surprised, case we is coming up out of the floor.

"Afternoon, Isaac." The velvit gentleman nods at the painted man.

We turn and look up.

"East stairs or west stairs?"

"West," I says.

There int no sounds, just our feets on the white rock stairs, small squelching from my sneakers. On the top landing a sign says *Grand Hall*. Every now and then hear a sound, like people screaming down in dungeons. Makes me jump, man comes on the landing from a sideways door. He's got a green shirt and two books.

Is real. Coming down, smiling cos he's got glad teef.

"Hello, Anton. Beautiful day. How's the diamond business?" he arsts.

"Sparkling," the velvit gentleman says.

I look at the wall-pattern monsters. They got white bulging eyes with black dots and sharp teefs smiling, wicked. Tortoise-fish. Fox-lizard. Don't know how many there is, thousands, spects. Hare-toad. Red man with claws and sharp wings, stuffing his tail down his throat.

"Hhhuck!"

The men is looking at me. We all look up. The hick-sick sound I done is still going around with angels on the ceiling, that's how far my guts chucked it.

"Crikey, Mitten?" the velvit gentleman says. He don't know how come I done it.

"Sorry," I says. "Fly. Or something."

The other man is smiling now he knows there int no need for an amblance.

"I see you've got a visitor."

The velvit gentleman looks at me.

"My niece, Mitten," he says.

My face burns ghoulish pink. Int *Mitten*. Int.

"You've come to cheer our Anton up?"

I nod my head.

"I'd best be getting along," he says. "The library."

We lean over the banisters to watch him going down.

"A sad, sad story," the velvit gentleman says.

We don't go in the *Grand Hall*, stead we turn through the west door where the sad-sad man come out. *Ward 14* says a plastic sign. The velvit gentleman smiles and opens a door for me.

"Battenberg on bank holidays," he says.

Don't know what it means. The corridor is dark wooden, fitted together like a puzzle. Our legs cut through stripes of sunshine, don't know how many doors there is. I spects this is a hospital. Bad smells hiding worster smells. We pass rooms like hospital wards, beds and stuff on chairs and bedside drawers. Some beds has got bodies, buried under pink blankets. The velvit gentleman smiles at me.

"The ladies are this end," he says.

A cleaner man is in the corridor, shining the floor with a machine. He's got a stone or something under it cos it's ripping swirls into the wood. Another man is on his knees, tending to polish, but he int got a cloth. Stripy jarmas on.

"Derek," the velvit gentleman splains.

A lady comes out from an office, with keys on her belt and a white uniform. I look back where we come, case.

"Saint Lizzie," the velvit gentleman says.

She smiles, sees us coming.

"Anton!" Her eyes is twinkly. "A visitor?"

"My niece," he says.

"Wonderful!" she says.

The man on the floor comes crawling over, tends to polish my knees. Still got scabs and grass stains.

"Thank you, Derek," Lizzie smiles at us. "Better have some tea, Anton, before they take it away."

"Can you shift him?" the cleaner man says. "He's in my way."

Derek crawls over, tends to polish Lizzie's feets.

"I see you're ready for bed, Derek?" she says. "Shall we find you a dressing gown?"

He smiles but he int got no teef. Lucky, he don't know it.

We keep on walking. The corridor gets double wide sudden with a big sitting room, armchairs and plastic chairs and wooden chairs. People sit all wonky, old peoples falling forward and sideways practicing for dead. Some of the people is visiting, chairs pulled up close together, but nobody knows what to say. The other side of the corridor is three round tables with chairs and some people sitting at them. Sees a metal trolley. Sandwiches. Biscuits. Cake. Milk in plastic jugs with colored lids. The velvit gentleman pulls out a chair for me. Another man is at the table. He's got a sandwich in one hand and a cigarette in the other. Tends we int here.

"Don't mind Charlie."

I look at the velvit gentleman, his name is Anton and it don't sound like English or Anthony. He brings a teapot and does me a cup and saucer.

"Milk, madame?" he says.

Makes me laugh cos nerves. He int French though, don't think.

"Sugar?"

I look at my plate. Ham sandwich. Egg sandwich. Chocolate cake.

"Not everyone likes Battenberg. Do you like marzipan?" he arsts.

Don't know. I look at the slice of cake with pink and white squares. Man called Charlie taps his sandwich over the ashtray. Blows out smoke. I got hungry worster than double daggers. Looks at the chocolate hundreds and thousands sprinkled on the chocolate cake. Goes deaf sudden like a faint. I look up at the ceiling, sees angels looking down and monsters in the corners with fangs and pink tongues. On my plate, got cress and wet slice of tomato. Charlie don't want his cucumbers cos he puts them in the ashtray. Don't know what to do. In the metal teapot shine I see a little girl.

"Eat it," she says.

Anton is watching me.

"Hungry, Mitten?" he says.

My stomach does cartwheels, got the taste of staying live. So stuffed with water and food, can't hardly move. A lady is coming cross the lounge and then cross the corridor, walking like her slippers is skis. Oringe hair and gray roots, coming to me, especial. My legs twitch. But it int me, it's Anton, she int happy, shoves his shoulder.

"Shut-up. Shut-up. Shut-up," she says, spitting.

"Shut up yourself you batty old cow." He smiles ever so nice.

"Shut-up. Shut—" She stops. Don't know why she come. We watch her go back to her chair. Nurse Lizzie is talking to the peoples, going from group to group. When she comes over her tea has gone cold.

"I'll have one later," she says, "when Leonard gets back. Did you show your niece your room, Anton?"

"That would be all right, would it?"

"Yes, of course," she says.

That's how come we stand up and put our chairs nice tidy back.

"Bye, Charlie," I say.

He don't say nothing.

"I'm right at the far end," Anton says. Longest corridor in the world filled with the sound of a somewhere man singing in a shower.

We get smaller and darker. Bad smells has all blown down this end. Anton's door is last on the right side, open. Little room with a bed made nice with blankets and a table sides with the Bible on it. Minds me of me; he int got nothing. But there is a door in the side wall. He puts a key from his pocket in it and turns the lock.

"Nothing is sacred," he says. "Lizzie and Leonard know of course, they don't mind me using it."

Surprises me. This is an end tower room, int square, they done it half a moon, with curving winders waving and shining, all the way. They got flowers being marigolds sploding in petals of colored glass.

"I'm glad you like it," he says.

I look around the room, still got marigolds in my eyes. Smells of polish and sawed-up wood. He's got a grandad clock.

"Can you keep a secret?" he arsts.

I nods cos can.

"I got the floor from the East Wing. I fetched it square by square."

I look at the floor, white light in it like ice.

"It took me a year, nearly killed me."

"Sorry about the edge," I says.

"I can't cut the marble to fit the curve. I thought I'd put sand in the spaces and grow some thyme."

I listens the grandad clock. Tick-tock. Tick-tock. He's got a fireplace and a pile of sawed-up chair legs. His bed is wooden in the shape of a sleigh; got rugs on it. I walk long the curve of the winders; look out through marigolds at the back. The shadow of the giant tower is running way with smaller towers. We is taller than cedar of Lebanon trees. The palice has got a terrible wall and rocks that go down steep, to the lane where I came up. Farway fields, green and downhill yellow. Don't know if the red roofs sitting in the hills is Red Roofs or just farms. Hair stands up, members the trouble I got.

The velvit gentleman gets a pole with a shiny hook and opens the top row of winders with it.

"Listen," he says.

People sing-songing words like praying.

"In the chapel, choir practice," he says. "They modeled it on the Vatican."

I wonder what a Vatican is. He's got a rocking chair on a rug and books piled up. At the bottom of his bed is a wooden chest with black metal handles and a lock.

"Has you got treasure?" I arsts.

"Yes," he says. "Soon the sun will turn and start to come in."

"Like a tide?" I say.

"Exactly. I recommend the rocking chair."

"Uh-huh." I sink down in the rocking-chair cushions, make a gentle nice rocking.

The table is a wooden box turned upside down. He's got a loverly desk, I spects he sits at it looking out, the arms of the chair is polished smooth from all the sitting and standing up. Nice lamp with green glass. He goes to a little fridge that's tending to be a chest of drawers. Brings a bottle and two glasses and puts them on the box table.

"I've been saving it for a special occasion." He shows me the label on the bottle. "I'll just check the corridor, make sure the coast is clear," he says.

The bottle makes me nervous case it splodes. He comes back, smiling. Don't know if to tell him, case I int especial enough. Too late—POP makes me jump. Wine does tick-tock in the glasses and fizzes up bubbly. Cold and slippery.

"The sun is coming now," he says and it's true.

Marigold flowers come out of the glass and set off marching cross the wall and floor. I dabs my tongue in the wine. Gets fizz in my eyes.

"How long has you been saving it?" I arsts.

He counts on fingers for years.

"Nine."

"I like your room, all your things is wood and nice."

"They brought it all in a removal van and left it in the pouring rain, outside on the steps. The champagne bottle was on top of the clock with a label saying *Anton: Ward 14*. It nearly caused a riot. Bob Stanwick ran across the lawn with the bottle like a rugby ball. The others brought him down. There was a scrum; old Arthur broke away with it." He's smiling membering olden days. "There wasn't so many of us then, we couldn't get away with as much. We were all scared of Vera because she was little and mean and kicked your shins. There was no tea or biscuits for two weeks; she confiscated the bottle and locked it up."

"Lucky she let you keep your furnitures."

"She did. It took all day to get it up here. I didn't have this room then, A-Level is in my old room. It was so small we couldn't get everything in. We had to lay the wardrobe flat and put the bed on top of it. Either that or move into a shared dormitory, which—"

A telephone is ringing sides his bed.

"Excuse me." He goes to pick it up.

"No, I'm not coming today, George, I've got a visitor as a matter of fact. The new caretaker's daughter."

Surprises me, who I is. George's voice is bigger than the phone, sounds ho-ho-ho.

"I've got to go, George, the sun is coming in. Yes, tomorrow night, definitely deal me in. The Billiards Room? The window is open, is it? Good, see you then."

Now the sun is coming fast. Anton pulls the chair over from his desk and sits the other side of the box. He picks up his wine and members his story.

"So. When Vera left, five or six years ago, she unlocked her filing cabinet and smuggled the champagne back to me."

His trouser leg has ridden up, he's got a dent in his shin, I spects where Vera done him. He is a velvit gentleman, got black monkey boots all soft and velvety. His broidery waistcoat is beautiful, poppies in all the colors of green.

"How long has you had this room?"

"Since Peterson Roth died. Some people say that I killed him for it."

"Oh," I says. "Was it you that done it?"

"No." Makes him smile. "He had a heart attack, at home on weekend leave."

Ding—

Dong, says the grandad clock.

Ding—

Dong.

Ding—

Dong.

Ding—

Dong.

Marigolds go rushing bubbly over my head. We sit side by side in the sun. Growing time. Watch marigolds flower in the air and all cross the wall and floor. He tells me about the olden days fore they closed the East Wing down. I don't hear no dings or dongs or fast passing trains cos listens the sound of Anton's voice rocking me same as the chair. I know how come his mouth is nice; he got little dimples at the sides.

"We're a bit cramped but I don't mind too much," he says. "Life is better with women in it."

Someone tap-tap-taps on the door. He hides the bottle and our glasses quick, down the side of the bed. Nurse Lizzie comes in and marigolds shine on her face and white coat.

"I'm sorry, Anton," she says, "visiting hours are over now."

"Ten more minutes?" he says.

She looks past him at me, rocking in the chair.

"Your uncle's room is wonderful, don't you think?"

I nod cos it's true. It is.

"Ten more minutes?" he says.

Her face does rules is rules.

"I'll tell you what," she says, "I'll come back when I've herded all of the others out."

Sides, someone is yelling her name and she has to run. I stand up, feels sure on this hard hard floor just how heavy I is. Feels sure. I is real.

"I wanted you to see the sunset," he says. "It's the perk of being west."

I look out at the sun, running down red in the marigold sky. Members all the trouble I got. He is looking at me. Teefs is nice.

"Thank you for being my guest."

"Has I done it proper?" I arsts.

"You're the finest guest I've ever had."

Int true.

"It's true," he says.

Int.

We listens to the tick-tock. And birds outside chirping fore bed. Train coming. Dead fast. Loud and shaking the floor, sudden gone, like it never was. And the birds is quiet after. I spects he is beautiful. I like his furnitures. Wonders if to marry him cos I could keep everything polished.

"Shall we make Lizzie walk back or shall we go of our own free will?"

"Free will," I says. It sounds nice.

We pass a long line of people, waiting in the corridor. Nurse Lizzie is with a man, same in a white coat. His badge says Leonard. They got a metal trolley like a desk with medicine and tablits in little plastic pots.

"Anton! Be sure to come straight back up."

"Five minutes," he says.

Everything is much darker now. Last people leaving on the stairs.

"Bye, Isaac," I says to the painting on the way down. The velvit gentleman holds my hand. Something wrong with my eyes makes monsters double in the ghoulish hall. I get the goose bumpoles. Feels wobbly. Tired, like a swimming pool inside me.

"Have you started your new school?" he arsts.

I tends deaf.

"Half-term, I expect, yes, half-term. Are you doing anything tomorrow?"

"Int sure," I says.

"I hope I haven't got you in trouble. What time were you supposed to be in?"

Surprises me.

"Thirty-two o'clock?" I says case it's a joke.

He opens the palice doors for me. The angel fountain has been turned off.

"Do you know where you're going?" His teef is nice.

I grims at him, shake my head.

"Follow the driveway all the way around the back." He has to come outside. "Actually the other way is quicker. Follow the terrace along the East Wing and around the back. Then down past the tennis courts and bowling green. Through the archway in the wall, past the greenhouse and the vegetable gardens and that's where you are. OK? Do you know which house you are? Is your father the maniac with a hedge trimmer?"

Makes us laugh. We stand on the palice steps and then we sit down, talking so long like getting old.

"Anton!" It's Lizzie, ever so angry. "I have to lock the ward."

"Sorry," he calls up. But he int, not really.

"Bye," I says. Wobbly, misses the step.

"Crikey, Mitten," he says.

"Now, Anton!" Lizzie says. "It's ever so late; is someone picking her up?"

"Uh-huh," we says. Both naughty and confused, sactly who I'm being and sactly who I is.

"Bye." I hold up one hand. Whoops. Walks a wobbly walk, shivering white, past winders and winders of bashed-up planks and sheets of wood. My hearts and the palice doors bang.

Tzzz. Tzzz. Ha-ha-ha! I is a python. I shake the ladder on the palice wall.

"Go on then," I yells at the gods.

Ha-ha-ha, I is a rattler! I got another skin, growing underneath. Bubbly wine has done me wobbly. I take the sneakers off so my toes can grip the tiles. Shivers in the shadow of the sunset nearly finished, sees monsters with wings biting on the edge of the roof. Blinks.

Int real.

The wind has grounded down the teefs but they could still suck you to death or slap you straight off the edge. *Tzzzzz.* The tower makes me small and dark. It's another world on the palice roof, east and west, sliding Mountins of Moon and dark triangle shapes. Wobbly. My spear can balance me. *Tzzzz.* I look down over the edge at the palice steps and the pool, dark shapes of angels with moon on their wings. Lions, they work best in the dark. Shivers. The moon is up and round, shivery silver, hurts my eyes. There int nothing to hold on to but I is brave up the slope, frightens a line of pigeons sleeping under a ledge.

"Sorry," I says.

Ding—

Feel the air swing.

Ding—

A warm wind is blowing on the back of my legs.

I turn to face it and it blows way my eyes. A warm wind is lifting up my chin and holding on to my face. I lay down in the dip where two roofs meet and the warm wind comes out from a vent.

"Good girl," I says and hiccups.

I make a pillow with my sneakers and get my legs up under my cloth.

So nothing as a leaf. Blowed way.

"Any chance of a slurp?" I says.

They both blinks, so surprised.

"I int a monster," I says. Tries to shift a chink in my neck.

Terrible stiff. They looks at each other. Looks at me. Looks around them case I got them surrounded.

"Thirsty," I says. "Been sick."

The man that looks like a white rabbit holds up his cup of tea.

"Whoops," I says. "Careful case I slip and slop it."

I spread the tea around in my mouth so that everything what's dry gets wet, slops it side to side, tips back my head and gargles with it, then I swallows it.

"Don't spect I could have a ciggi?" I says.

Both of them hold up open packets.

"Thanks, one for now and one for later," I says. "Beautiful moon, int it?"

The white rabbit strikes a match for me to puff the ciggi light.

"Minds me of a vamp," I says.

They both look sactly same, total stonished.

"Vamp?" they says together.

I hold the ciggi with long stiff fingers and get balanced careful on the slope.

"Now you," I says to the white rabbit. "You has to say: puff-puff-puff, only when I nod my head."

"Puff. Puff. Puff?"

"No. Quicker—puff-puff-puff."

"Puff-puff-puff."

"Uh-huh. And you," I says to the man with the top hat. "You has to say: smoke-smoke-smoke."

"Smoke-smoke-smoke."

"Puff-puff-puff."

"Now I'm a girl with a heart of gold and the ways of a lady so I been told, the kind of a *gal*," I says, "that wouldn't even harm a flea."

They is stonished. Stonishes me.

"But just you wait til I get the guy who vented the cigarette, I'll shoot that son of a *hick*—believe you me."

They believe me. I nods my head.

"Puff-puff-puff."

"Smoke-smoke-smoke."

"It int that I don't smoke my self, I don't reckon they harm your health—I've smoked all my life and I int dead, yet." I does one cough for the song, lucky, gets three real ones added on. Whoops.

"Puff-puff-puff."

"Smoke-smoke-smoke."

Feels sudden ever so tired. Tile skids out from under my foot, skids down the roof, goes flying off the edge. We listens. Waits. Waits long time. Then hear it smash on the terrace below.

"Shush!" we all says.

"Sorry," I says. "The velvit gentleman has done me, wobbly."

"I'm Fiddler," the top hat says. "This is Mick."

"Nice to meet you," I says. "Had best get going. Bye."

"Don't forget your cigarette, for later."

"Have the packet, love," Mick says.

"And the box of matches."

"Thanks," I says. "Whoops. Careful."

I waves them from the edge with my spear. *Tzzzz*. Disappears down the side of the chimney.

The moon is perfect round and drumming blue, sees easy down the fire scape. I run long the black edges, East Wing and West Wing, then climb a tree, get up on the terrible palice wall. The green lamp on the velvit gentleman's desk is shining behind the marigold glass. *Hick*. I drop from the palice wall and down onto the railway line. The silver tracks shine and disappear in the tunnel's black. Listens. Booming. Around me bats is ducking and diving, I shake my spear at them and get on my toes, warms up the warrior song til good and proper int scared of nothing. Then I scream down the tunnel same as a train, running my spear long on the rail, that's how come I know where I is but it knocks and bounces.

Flewed out of my hand.

I has to stop and get down, read with my fingers the railway stones, fat concrete slabs and the cold smooth rail. Light at the end of the tunnel is blue with the moon. Same size both ways. Has to close my eyes to listen. Ticking clock. Water dripping and trickle. Int sure now, case I turned around, don't know which way I come in. Booming. I hear it coming, trotting light. Listens, sorts out boom from blackness and sweetness, breath warm as hay. I blow back soft and kind as can.

"Hello." I sees tiny horseshoe shapes, trot way silver in the dark. "Don't go."

Listens booming. I find the knot in my red cloth and the cigarettes and matchbox. Careful, don't drop all the matches, tries to light both ends of a dead one. Next one works. The rails curve off to a smaller tunnel blocked up with bars. Good place for staying live if a train was going to kill you. Match burns my fingers so I drop it. Light another one to find my spear, then I run on gain trusting the dark and the rail to take me out. Nobody in the station cept a lady fox, standing on the platform looks like waiting for a train.

"Toot-toot," I says.

She's so surprised she don't do nothing, just watches me run past. I drum long the tracks. Then off up through a night-time woods. Owl's woo shivers with the moon. The drumming comes so loud and so clear. I sees the signs and the tracks of heavy plants been crossing.

On top of the hill I can see it. I stalks to the edge, then sit down and look at the sky. Listens. Everything held still by the moon. I hear it first and then see it. Red light, green light, white light winking. It slopes down cross the moon. Uh-huh. I run at the fence, climb over the Keep Out sign and then skid down and down. I stop at the bottom. Look left and right and back up where I come. Listens. Long and wide and deep. I know it, I sniffs it, every stir of wind and air and sand settling down. Every hair stands up to feel in the air. Ears listen for something to get hold of. I has to stay up wind, I pick up dust and trickle it, has to *know* where he is. Eyes int the best thing for shadows running wild in moonlight. His feeling starts to burn on my skin and membered ice.

"Go on then," I whisper.

No. The air is dry and warm, and the dirt, daytime sun still laid on the ground. The Sandwich Man, he int here. I shake his feeling off me, sets off running left, through sand rolled out smooth, leaves strides short but sure behind me. Sees the moon is running with me up onto purple stones, rolled out more wider than a road. Got agony from my bit-off toe, members it and starts to cry but we has to grit over it and run on with staggering stitches. I hang on to the sky, sees three stars go out and the moon turning to burn yellow. Sees the ground black and silky smooth come racing up under my feets, steaming, burning hot, leaves tracks behind in the soft tarmac. Joins up the white dotted line, pulls into the fast lane, past giraffes with wires dangling down and signs covered in plastic. I look around and up at the sky. Can hear one. Uh-huh. Comes over my head, winking, I hammer left up a slope. Airplanes is showing me the way and that's how come I track them.

I got it now, road sign says this way Heathrow. The road is terrible, high up and bright with barriers and middle night lorries passing bedtime winders and I best had get off it. Then I'm running on a thin grass slope around the side of a concrete lake, surprises me, airport sheeps. They panic where to go with just the lake or the fence, next thing I've got a mile of sheeps all running long in front of me.

I got it now, all the airplanes circling around waiting for their turn to come down. Int easy to hide, with the road and the fence and full moon on the Serengeti. Every time a lorry comes I drop down flat on the grass, or blows up gainst the fence, tends I is a bit of red plastic. Gone. I has to get over the other side, can see the shapes of airplanes coming in. The fence is five times bigger than me with barb wire rolled on the top. Int easy cos it wobbles. Three lorries go past one behind the other while I wobbles about in their headlights fixed up on the barb wire. I fall down long on the other side, got holes in the middle of both hands. Hurts bad. Way from the road the world is darker. I lie down, watch for the next airplane coming. Sure thing over roofs, I jump up and head straight for it. It comes thousand miles fast, screaming down with engines and wheels, I roar and shake my spear at the driver and the wings slice over my head. Ba-boom the wheels hit the ground and I bounces up in the air. Makes me laugh. Makes me laugh so rude. Then I see all the headlights coming, fast, making stars and bouncing over the grass. Got me every way. Total blinded cept for ring-a-ring-a engines running and fumes and the big N's of trouble knocking.

He opens the door of the jeep and I get up in the passenger seat. All the others circle around us and turn way, headlights racing outward. Man does his walkie-talkie.

"Ground Control to Air Control. All *bzzz*. Receiving?"

"What the *bzzz* is it?" walkie-talkie wants to know.

"A small African *bzzz*, sir, shall I take *bzzz* to the *bzzz*?"

"Take him back to fucking Africa for all I care, just get the *bzzz* off the runway."

"Right." My man turns the walkie-talkie off, shakes his head. "I'd better take you home," he says and puts my spear careful nice tween the seats. "You're ever so brown, been on your holidays? Somewhere hot?"

I nod my head.

"Well, you look very fetching in red; I like your beads, very nice."

Jeep is nice, warm yellow moonshine and winders open. Stinks of gasoline and burned chocolate. Got twelve cigarettes left. I light one and blow the smoke out the winder. Cold comes out of me sudden, teefs and knees start going same as the jeep's tappets.

"Give us one of those," he says. Then steers the jeep with one elbow so he can scrape the match.

"Power-sisted?" I arsts.

"Light as a feather." He does a shape of eight to prove it. Then he drives us cross and cross and cross bouncing headlights on the grass, sees a leopard's spots. Tired, closes my eyes, turns spots into marigolds. Could lay my head down now and go to sleep behind the seat. Driving in circles, I reckon.

"There they are," he says last, "somebody keeps moving them."

I look at the airplane-sized gates while he gets out to open one. He has got a key for the padlock. Then he drives us out and closes it gain.

"Where are we going, where's home?" he says.

I suck on the holes in my hands.

"Nestles Avenue," I says.

"Just around the corner. I want you to listen carefully though." He changes gear. "It's not safe, running around alone at night, I wish it was but it isn't. It's not safe. The little girl on the telly is still missing, little Ellie Smithers. And that other older girl, what was her name, the one they didn't have a picture of? I wouldn't want that to happen to you. What if you disappeared? Your family would be devastated; they'd never get over it. Down here, is it?"

"Uh-huh."

Nestles playing fields is blue-green from the yellow moon; vultures still sleep up on the rugby posts. Factory lights in stripes and lorries loading chocolate up and chimneys smoking clouds of black. Tastes same. Trees is still London plane, army bark, lighted up by lorries coming out of Nestles' gates.

"Here," I say.

He stops the jeep outside the Pennywells'. Houses is fast sleep and curtains closed.

"Can you get in?" he says.

I nod my head.

"Can go around the back."

"Back to bed?"

"Uh-huh," I says.

He passes my spear.

"Remember, serious trouble if you're found again in the airport grounds. It's a criminal offense."

"Sorry," I says.

He waits til I'm in the gate and it makes an agony squeak. I wave my spear and he drives way.

Scared, case I'm a burglar at Nanny and Grandad's. I tiptoe the front path. Planes has blasted all the petals off all the newborn roses. I slow crunch the gravel down the alley, dragging fingers long on the pebbledash. The side gate latch is high, Grandad done a shoelace to pull it, but it snaps cos now it's glued with rust. Snaps til there int none left. I get my toe up in a knot-hole and climb quiet over the gate. Weeds has growed up wild through the cracks in the path. Back bedroom curtains is closed. I stand underneath. Listens if I can hear them snoring, hog-chewing. Got nerves. I light a ciggi and walk down the back path, duck under a pair of Nanny's bloomers hanging on the line. Grass is always high and wild; Grandad int got the back to mow it. Daffodils all the way long the margins of the garden. We went to Woolworths on the bike and come back fast to plant them. Then Grandad got a good idea and we planted mirrors side the wall to get us a thousand at a glance. The daffodils is shriveled up and dried like tissue paper, under growing love-in-a-mist. Got sick feeling, sudden, case Grandad don't know me, case he knows and don't want me. I look at the back door. Airplane goes over the roof and I duck. I keep looking at the back door, and upstairs at the bedroom winder. Got sick sides citement, case Nanny phones the police. The back door was never good at locking. Don't know if to go in the house, could wake them up, say "member me." Can't case they get scared and drop down dead with burglar fright. Magines in a minute, *ting-a-ling-a-ling*, Teasmade waking them up and newspapers dropping on the mat. Could wait til Grandad comes downstairs and opens the back door for light so he can shave. Stand on the path so he sees me like a morning surprise when he opens the curtains up. Might fall downstairs, if he comes too fast. I best had get a great big breath, case he squeezes it all out of me. Maybe just knock on the front door. Polite. Wishes I could run and jump and get up in the bed with them. Can't case Nanny does a steric. Tired, does a yawn so big it nearly swallows me. Cold. I move the wheelbarrow into the first sunlight on the path, sit in it and smoke another cigarette.

Blue greenhouse looks littler, the wooden door is stiff when I pull it. Int proper. Seeds that me and Pip sowed died flowering cross the greenhouse roof. Tall coleus bent over double, dead. My writing is on the lolly sticks done with permnant ink. Everything dead. Sensitive plant turns to dust when I kiss it. Everything is dead, cept cactus. The watering can is full and the water butt outside. I has to water them careful nice, one by one from tops and saucers

"Come on," I whispers, "come on."

In my body everything shifts, to make room for a big new feeling, I spects I just died standing up.

"Lay down," my grandad says, "lay down, pet."

But my grandad, he int here. He int here. The plants gasp all at once, then an airplane comes over the house and we has to lay down case we break.

They int got bobboldy glass, don't know if someone is coming or not. They got gnomes on their doorstep. *No place like gnome.*

"Hello, trouble," Mr. Pennywell says. "Vi!" He yells up the stairs. "It's the girl from next door."

"Who is it?" she says. "Hold on, I'm in the airing cupboard."

"We haven't seen you for a while." Mr. Pennywell says. "See you're still doing your African thing."

Vi has got high-heeled slippers with pink fluff and looks at me like trouble on foot. They stand in the doorway looking at me. They int sure what I want them to do case it's complicated. They look at each other. At me. I has to make it easy for them.

"Is my grandad dead?" I arsts.

"He went with your Auntie Valerie, dear; she came and took him away after the funeral."

"Still got her white Triumph Herald," Mr. Pennywell says.

"We wouldn't know, dear," Vi says. "Bill went with Valerie."

"I remember you," Mr. Pennywell says, "under the bonnet, fixing it once."

It int true, never done a Triumph Herald in my life.

"Valerie took Bill."

"After Rose's funeral."

"Oh," I says. "Thank you, I'm sorry to bother you."

"No bother," Mr. Pennywell says.

"Where's your mother?" Vi says.

I fling an arm down the road, close their gate gain behind me. Left or right don't matter cos there int nowhere to go. I get a good idea; Grandad might be at Cranford Park, still being a park keeper.

I seen every tree, seen park men marking a cricket pitch with a white-line machine, but my grandad, he int here. I get up on the roof of the public toilets and cries to sleep. When I wake up I sees a mum with kids and bikes and ice-cream cones come into the park. Little boy drops his ice cream on the path and she drags him way to leave it; when they gone I get down and eat it. I watch going-home-time traffic and night coming.

Wonder what I has to do. Could go the police station and say boo—here I is. Could go to Powys, try find Pip, but I don't spect there's anything to eat in Wales. Cept coal. I think about that velvit gentleman, in his marigold room. I squeeze my eyes tight closed, if I can think it hard enough can make his rocking chair rock by itself. The velvit gentleman turns around from his desk and magines me still sitting in it, rocking soft on the rug.

Act Three

There's a dawn hush and a stirring. These people wear green and have soft edges, step in and out of the bamboos, whispering. Fifteen, twenty guides and porters have arrived, sitting around the office steps with bare feet and woolly hats and sweaters, in various states of unravel. The village is waking, rug-slapping sounds, a cockerel crows; a bell dings on a Brahmin cow. The men and boys must come here every day, hoping for climbers, hoping for work.

But it looks like it's just me.

They've got some chai on the go. Soft blur of words and laughter. Ah—now that is nice. One lad is bringing the kettle over, held in the bunched-up sleeve of his cardigan.

"Mzuri." I hold out my enamel mug. "Habari?"

He's happy, fine; he fills the mug for me.

"You are wellacome," he says. "Wellacome to Uganda. Wellacome to the Ruwenzoris. Wellacome to the Mountains of the Moon."

An ancient Greek said he'd seen ice, miles high up in the sky. High as the moon. Mad as ice, thrust up from the hot jungle heart of Africa. I can't see anything, just the yellow dawn cast like a spell and shapes of sheds in cobwebs of mist. The chai is hot, milky and sweet, very, very wellacome.

The Bajonko call the mountains the Ruwenzoris, the Rainmakers. Main reception is a shed with steps up and a boot-worn path to the counter. I pat and stroke the timber. There's something reassuring about forest people, they build things to last. I expect the trees have taught them to take a long-term view. It's the same man with a blue woolly hat and soft whorls of chinny beard.

"Your night in the tent, it was wet or dry?"

"It was half and half," I say.

"Ruwenzori tsk," he says. "Today, you are ready to climb; you are ready?"

"Yes," I say, "I am ready."

I pay the fees for entry to the National Park and fees for a guide and two porters. He gives me a receipt and a disclaimer to sign. Then he slides a large book across the counter.

Mountain Climbers Log.

Makes me smile.

Nationality: British.

Next of kin: I write Danny Fish and make up a phone number.

Duration:

In the logbook the prewritten dates have dashes beside them, where nobody has gone up for weeks, except: Robertson, UK, who went up three days ago. I see what they mean by duration, intended days in the mountains. Three. He takes my surplus stuff to the storeroom and comes back.

"That is everything. Come with me, we will get your guide and porters organized."

Outside, I look around at the sky, all around, try to detect some high land mass distant in the mist.

"Where are the mountains?" I say to the chinny man. "Which way?"

He points, up, directly up above our heads. The enormity of my mistake—the image is so overbearing, so foreshortened—I actually recoil from the punch of two black fists.

"Wha!" I say. But the image has vanished, like something imagined.

"It is the Portal Peaks," he says. "The gateway."

The boys, the porters, are shy, smiling. One carries a black plastic sack tied with sisal rope on his back: firewood. The other carries my pack. I feel a bit naff but it seems like no burden to him; it is probably much lighter than most and will get lighter as the food is eaten. Once loaded, the porters disappear, going on ahead to the first camp. This leaves me with my guide, Emmanuel; he's wearing a trilby and a brown pinstriped suit. A tall knobbly staff of a stick is planted beside his bare feet. He looks at my bare feet. I reach and shake his official slip of hand.

"Ninitwa Louise," I say.

He nods his head. We will begin. He points the way with his staff. I had thought I'd follow Emmanuel or we'd walk together but he falls silently into the mist behind me. I look back; see his faint outline and a banner of mist trailing from the top of his staff. The roadway is wide and sandy-stony, follows a man-made watercourse lined it seems with aluminium and supported on a heft of wooden trellis work. Yesterday, coming up the foothills, I passed high-security cobalt mines; imagine that somewhere down the line this watercourse turns a turbine, for lighting underground. The sun is breaking through. I sense a sherbety fizzing dell and then drop steeply into a cool green hollow. I feel that my guide is in front of me, that the way is already known, but whenever I look back Emmanuel is still there, never gaining ground or losing it. I walk on, fording stream after stream. The sun comes out. The sky turns black. The Portal Peaks boom and disappear. The rainmakers clap. It goes pitch dark. The sun comes out. A rock wall appears in front of me. I look up at ladders of water staggered up through vertical shafts of light. Everything at first rejects the climb. I cough my guts up. Spit. Snatch at breath and foliage. The light turns on and it rains. Pours strings of pearls. The light turns off; the pearls turn into slender rods. The spectrum lights turn on and off, passing always through black and bloodshot. It rains in the pale. It rains cellophane. It rains rice and panel pins. It rains, pours, frozen peas—first appearance outside Chile.

Why "chilly?" I arst.

At the top of a steep rise we look distant, cross the landing at the bathroom. It rains, pours, drenching like a shower fitting. It stops. The plateau before us is flat and black in the acid light.

What are those things?

Bog humps.

Tussocks. The light switches on and off, on and off. In the caverns beneath our feet the rainmakers are smashing on anvils. Forging. Manufacturing. Pans crash in the sudden larder. Lightning throws a sky net over us, filling the air with static and net curtain. The rainmakers launch a thunderbolt; it cracks the world, our skulls and the wall above the fireplace. The rainmakers have high pressure and hosepipes. My guide knows the way to the Mountains of the Moon, I follow the splashes left by his feet.

The splashing becomes a squelch. The plateau stretches for miles across the Bigo Bog and the garden. Is we twits? Turning slippery pirouettes, windmilling our arms, making spectacular leaps. The wet-mattress bog comes up, swallows my legs whole. In a chomp my arms is gone. The bog takes over my mouth, one nostril, one ear; I look up sideways with my one surfaced eye. Sees my guide smiling, dry-eyed, and Nanny sobbing on the path.

"Oh Biiiiiillllll! Bill! Biiiiillll!" she says.

The mess is like nowhere else on earth.

The fire is devilish, hell hot, cracking out carbon splinters of bark. Keeps changing shape and direction, the wind is a black thing, we all smart through the woodsmoke. Firelight blowing the other way leaves my face in a private blackness. Today has left them short of nothing. These are a soft, pretty-eyed people. The porters are children really, alive in the flames. Mountain boys, goat-legged, kid-skinned. Emmanuel is honored with a log to perch on and a dry blanket around his shoulders. The rain is petting on the roof of the shelter. They talk; seem to make polite enquiries, about families, the whereabouts of acquaintances. There has been some event, recently, up above our heads, something to do with ice axes, something slipping, a rope getting caught; something the boys can't bear to imagine. Emmanuel shakes his head, smiles at the life that passed before him. He feels inside his suit jacket and produces a tiny leaf-wrapped parcel, tied up with banana fibre. Inside the wrap is a dice of raw red meat. He skewers it on a stick. I think of my onion to peel and chop, my rice to rinse and cook, my distant bag in the adjacent barrack-sized hut where I will lie down later, in my wet sleeping bag and my wet dry clothes and my saturated skin and water-swollen bones. When I went into the hut my flashlight beam caught a scatter of mice among the ten empty bunks. It was so cold in the shed my breath made solid shapes that melted. Endorphins are pumping still inside every cell. This stillness, this bliss of stillness could tip, my head does. I've been in training for this all my life but I had to keep stopping to empty my soul, couldn't raise my foot to another foothold, couldn't lift a leg to step over, couldn't shift my own weight forward, against the incline, against the rain. My knees couldn't take another slippage, my hips not another boulder smacking; my hands couldn't grab at another nothing or pull up on another tooth edge. When I hung blind, by the crook of my arm, sobbing from a hoop of root, my guide sat on a boulder sides me, said, Pet, it must be time for some dinner, said, Pet, your story is beautifully written.

"Hello."

My stomach does a backflip.

"Nice surprise." He tucks his hair behind his ear. "Fancy some lunch?"

I jump down off the angel pool. The velvit gentleman sticks out his elbow and I has to be a lady gain. Lady with a spear and holes in her hands; got rips in my red cloth, stitched it up with thorns. The palice hallway is still ghoulish. Arthur is still behind the door, int moved since last time. We go past the stairs, then turn and turn and go through a door says *Dining Hall*. It int proper, not with mouths full, and chandeliers. I skid on a slice of carrot. The velvit gentleman knows the way through the cigarette smoke and tables and hands waving knives and forks about dangerous. Everyone knows him.

"The caretaker's daughter," he splains.

We keep moving. The line int very long. I get a faint from all the food, looks up at the roof, a hundred thousand angels I spects is flying about in gold up there. A plate is waiting. And a dishing spoon.

"Fish fingers? Liver and bacon? Cornish pasty?" he says.

"Yes please."

"Is that one after the other or all together?"

"With cabbige," I says.

Anton goes around behind the counter and I has to follow him. The dinner lady smiles at us.

"I didn't think you were coming today, Anton," she says. "A visitor?"

"Mitten," he says. "The caretaker's daughter. Can we nip through, Beryl?"

Cept we already nipped and she don't mind cos now she's yelling seconds. In the back is a big kitchen, loads of metal tables and trolleys and sinks and shelves and towers of white plates. The back doors is open wide and I follow Anton out to a little corner of sunshine and paving stones and a white plastic table with chairs. Anton puts the tray down on it. Blue wisteria is flowering full pouring down the palice walls.

"Hang on." He goes back in the kitchen, comes out with a dustpan and brush and sweeps up all the dog-ends. I wait with my fork ready. He takes off his gray velvit jacket and hangs it on the back of the chair. His black waistcoat is broidered with violets. Warm in the sun, he rolls his sleeves up out the way, case we is getting messy.

I never seen the sausages.

"Beryl cooks a few for me," he splains.

"Oh," I says.

My Cornish pasty int got no filling that's how come I has to put my cabbige in it and pick it up with my fingers. He chops his sausages up and parks his knife on the side of the plate and does his dinner with a fork. His eyes is white and flashing, colors of pebbles underwater. He eats slow, chewing. He's got girl's hair, flicking up, and velvity lashes and eyeshadows. The lines on his face is especial perfect like someone chopped wood on it. I spects he is beautiful, looking at me, eating slow and chewing. My eyes is conkers, I rolls them. We listen to a train, fast, coming, makes a terrible scream.

"It's to warn workmen in the tunnel and at the level crossing," he says. "Sometimes I think the pitch will crack my windows. The four minutes past is the worse, going straight through so fast."

We both has a glass of water.

"A hundred years ago supplies were brought in underground along a track from the main line. Steam engines then. Pit ponies used to pull the loaded wagons through from the station."

He piles his fork up careful.

"Sometimes, when I meet George and some other friends to play cards, we hear a horse neighing under the floor of the Billiards Room."

"Is there one stuck down there, case we can get it out?"

"We went and checked. We were so sure of what we kept hearing. But the tunnel is blocked with bars at both ends and we shone a spotlight straight through it."

Don't know if to tell him I seen a pony ghost. He's looking at me.

"You were going to say something?"

I rub on the side of my mouth, where he's got a bit of bean juice. He does a dab and rubs it off.

"The man that done this palice," I says. "Who was he making a big impression for?"

"Thomas Holloway was a quack; he made millions from a health tonic. Having amassed a great fortune he had no idea what to do with the money so he advertised for ideas. It came to his attention that there was nowhere for mad rich people to go, to be cared for, to *recuperate*. King George had gone mad, you see, and they got interested in the subject, the Victorians built a lot of asylums."

The holes in my hands is itching terrible, has to smooth the itches way on the edge of the table.

"Is asylums for nutters?" I arsts.

"Yes. But, they started to *differentiate* between the *chronically insane* and those who, given *treatment and relief*, were confidently expected to recover."

Treatment and relief is tiptoeing words, one behind the other. I members my dinner, stabs a sprout. Still froze in the middle so I has to suck it.

"So, Holloway agreed to finance a sanatorium for the rich and ran a competition for architects to submit a design. He chose an architect called William Crossland to work with and they both got carried away."

He lifts his plate way, lights a Benson Hedges with his flip-top lighter and blows the smoke way sideways.

"It's all hand-painted. Apparently only the House of Lords was equal to it in *splendor*. The plan was to accommodate two hundred wealthy patients, in luxury, none of whom were to be *epileptic*, *paralytic* or dirty."

"Epileptic. Paralytic." I chews on the words and a bit of liver. I love the sun shining on us and the way Anton talks, picking words especial for me.

"They couldn't decide about the Gothic." His hands love each other. "Some people believed that Gothic decorations lead to a cure by the *distraction* method." His eyes cross over a wicked monster's smile. "Others thought that they might *weigh heavily* upon a *diseased mind*, that the classical or romantic was more soothing, more appropriate. They couldn't decide, Mitten, so they just had all of it. "

"Same as me with my dinner," I says.

"George is writing a book about it, he's dug up all of the history. Now of course the East Wing is falling down and the West Wing is full to its hammer-beamed rafters, a fine example of Grade One overcrowding, neglect, filth and ruination."

"Ruination," I says.

A dinner lady comes outside with a packet of cigarettes, looking in her apron pocket for her box of matches. She sits down at the table with us.

"I'm all in," she says. "Heat's terrible coming off those cabinets. Have you had enough? There's fish fingers left? Sure?"

We is sure. I'm still doing my liver and bacon, eyes was bigger than my stomach cos they int used to doing food. She takes her sandals off, puts her feets up on the spare chair and lights a No. 6.

"How's things, Shirley?" Anton arsts.

She shakes her head. Things int good. Anton moves his chair around closer, pulls her in gainst his shoulder. Hanky-chief comes out silky, like a long trick from his top pocket. Int no crying sounds, just hunched over, shrugging her shoulders, all snot and fingers and silky green paisley. Things int good. Takes two trains to come and go fore she takes a deep breath and comes up like from drowning. Lashes is wet stuck together. She sniffs hard, tries to smile, wiping under her eyes with her thumbs.

"I've had to stop wearing mascara." She looks up in the sky. Then she looks at me. Long time she looks at me. One tear races down her face and hangs on her chin.

"What are we going to do?" she arsts.

Don't know. Spects something will happen cos something always does.

"Is there no hope, Shirley?" Anton arsts.

"We went yesterday. There isn't anything else they can do."

"How did Trevor react?"

"He made jokes about it all the way home, 'Could be worse,' he said, 'could be you.' But in the night he woke me up. 'Shirl,' he said, 'when I'm gone, I want you to marry Anton.' "

"Well, at least he's still got his sense of humor," Anton says.

And she's all upset gain. The corners of the hanky-chief is twisted up terrible.

"Now he wants us to sell the house and get a Winnebago. 'Think about it, Shirl,' he said. 'See how far we can get?' "

She was going to say some more but another lady comes in the doorway barking.

"Some of us are still working in here!"

Shirley looks at the gods, has to put her sandals back on. She don't know what to do with the hanky-chief.

"I'll wash it, Anton," she says.

"Wash it and keep it," he says. "I'll call around later to see him. About seven?"

She nods her head.

"Good-bye, love," she says to me.

"Bye, Shirley," I says.

We sit through five trains looking at the chair where Shirley was. Sounds and colors come slow back into the world. Wishes I had my cigarettes but I left them in my place. Don't want to arst him cos he's only got two left.

"Fancy doing some painting?" he says.

Uh-huh. Wonders what color it is and if I'm doing mulsion or gloss. Doing the ceiling drips in your eyes and makes your arms an agony and if the light int proper you can't even see where you been. I is good at careful and edges, never get paint on the carpet or the light switch. Anton puts our tray of dirty plates on the trolley inside the kitchen then comes back out. Then he hangs his jacket on his finger and swings it over his shoulder. We walk around past the underground slope and the bins and then cut cross the grass past the chapel. This is a busy place with lots of people, staffs and patients and visitors, int sure which ones is the nutters. Anton walks left-right so I does a shuffle to change my legs cos in his shadow I int even here.

Down an overgrowed laurel path we get to a building like a classroom standing on its own. In the hall is a noticeboard empty cept for drawing pins and a sign says: *Welcome to Re Creation.* Nobody here. Long one side is pegs with old shirts covered in colors of paint. I spects we'll have to sand everything down first, int nothing worster than dribbled gloss.

"Has we got sandpaper?" I arsts.

"Cartridge paper. Sugar paper. Crêpe paper. Tissue paper. Newspaper."

"Sandpaper? Toilet paper?" I arsts.

"Do you mean tracing paper?"

"No—toilet paper."

"You want to work with sandpaper and toilet paper?"

"Uh-huh. Case you cut your finger on a splinter or bit of nail you never seen."

"Crikey, Mitten." He holds up a painty shirt for me to get in. Someone left a daisy hat so he slaps the dust off on his leg and pulls it down on my head. Edges is floppy. He folds his arm, sees how I is. His front teefs is like two little girls, knows how pretty they is. Under his bottom lip he's got a scar, looks like one time he got hit from behind and accidental bit it.

"Is you growing a beard?" I arsts.

Makes us laugh, don't know how come.

"No. I keep forgetting to buy a razor. Shall we go in?"

We swing through the double doors like cowboys. Surprises me, peoples. No one looks up, cos busy around the tables making baskets. All the ceiling is made of baskets hanging down off the pipes. I follow Anton around past the backs of chairs. I sees they got machines and clay for swirling pots. By the winders they got a line of heasels. Someone done paintings, still wet, don't know how many, all swirling red and black. A lady with a brown curly perm comes out of a cupboard with some big sheets of paper. She's got big boobies down in dungarees and a blue vest.

"I thought if I pegged some paper up, it would surely bring Anton in. I see you've got a friend with you."

"Mitten," he says. "It's all right, is it?"

She smiles at me.

"We've had a lot of children in over the holidays. The more the merrier! I'm so pleased to see you, Anton; I moved your portfolio into the office." She leans closer, does us a whisper. "We've got one or two jealous people."

I look around the people. Can't tell. Most is ladies weaving the basket stuff in and out. Crossed fingers and eyes. I see a great big beautiful person like an angel sitting down making a basket, int proper a man or a boy. Wonders if he is a statue, but then his eyes come down from the ceiling and he pinches and tucks the basket stuff in. Is real cos when he moves his curls bounce. Nobody can sit sides him case they magines trampling on his wings. Wonders what a portfolio is and how to be more merrier.

"You're very welcome, Mitten. I'm Amy," she says. "Do anything you like."

I does a swirl inside. Anton hangs his jacket on a nail bashed into the wall. He ties his hair up with a lastic band, at the back it flicks all up and fans out like a Chinese lady. Then he hangs a ciggi in the corner of his mouth and with a little stub of pencil makes a curving line on the paper. Draws fast. He's got a rag wedged in the heasel to keep the smudging finger clean. Good cos only smudges what he wants. I sit up on the windersill and watch Anton's hand and the lines flash. The drawing looks like

Shirley, with her cigarette and feets crossed on the chair. Last he does the wisteria and the paisley hanky-chief twisted in her hands. The pencil makes the picture look silver, like bossed on silver metal.

"That's me started." The ciggi in his lips don't fall out or get wet, that's how soft his lips is. He unclips the drawing, lays it flat on a side table. Then he starts a new big page. A small face comes out on the paper. One eye is squint, other one big, looking straight up at us. Mouth has a sideways grim and shiny skin. Prickle feeling. Fingertips is cold on my face.

Lulu.

Grady.

Pip.

Gets a side swipe feeling. Has to close my eyes.

"Some people get away with murder." Amy comes back laughing. "How are you getting on? Oh my goodness, Anton," she says. "You are so clever, Anton."

He keeps drawing, does his girl a floppy hat, with daisies on it. Legs like a deer. Words go over her head, *Welcome to Re Creation.* Anton is smiling cos he likes it, rubs a little winder of light into my open eye.

"Is you really a camera?" I arsts.

But then a chair falls back sudden, loud. Someone getting up. The angel man-boy is tall standing up, in a long white hospital gown. Arms is up and back, like he's done a perfect landing. Anton draws him quick as real life, sides me on the paper. Then the angel boy's arms come down, and he hangs his head and one hand inside the other.

Fallen down! On the floor int proper and all his body is electric shock. Terrible. And Amy and Anton has to hold him case he smashes his head on the floor gain. Lucky cos Anton got his tongue. Int no good.

"Nine."

"Nine."

"Nine," people says.

"It's OK, Michael." Amy talks tween his golden curls. "It's OK, Michael."

But it int. It int.

"Michael! Michael!" they shout cos he twists all stiff.

"Ambulance is coming," someone says.

"They're coming," Amy says.

"Michael! Michael!" His angel face is going purple and his lips. Then Anton does him the kiss of life. In my mind I make it true, I make the angel boy Michael breathe. Anton's hands is piled up, pushing all the air back out, cept now he's getting red and tired cos he int had air his self.

"Shall I take over?" Amy says.

But Anton int going to stop. Long time, fore the table legs and chairs shift and the amblance men is here.

"How long has he been gone?" they arsts.

"About fifteen minutes," Amy says.

"Pains in the chest?"

"A fit. Then stiff. Then still." Amy's voice snaps. "He didn't say anything."

"Do we know who he is?"

"Michael. From Ward 6."

"Eight," a lady says.

"I've seen him up on 12."

"Oh dear," Amy says. "No one really knows where he's from. He just comes in every day."

The amblance mens is all around. I see thumbs pulling eyelids up. The angel boy's eyes slide sideways, looking at me, arsting me something. Then the thumbs let go and his eyes is closed. His lips is black. I look for where Anton is. Some people is still making baskets. Anton int in the room. I look out in the hallway case he's in the toilet. Int. I hang up the painty shirt and run down the laurel path. See Anton walking fast cross the grass, like nowhere especial, just into the rhododendrons. I has to run to catch up with him.

"Is you all right?" I arsts.

He shakes his head. He don't know where he's going, doing shapes of eight in the bushes.

"I spects we've had a terrible shock and needs a cup of sweet tea."

"We need a bottle of bloody brandy, Mitten, that's what we need. Look at my hands." He stops to show me how shaky they is. He int no good cos upset. Int got his hanky cos he gave it to Shirley. Now his hands is on his hips, he don't know which way to walk or look.

"I could weep. I feel so sick. Do you feel sick?"

I could weep and sick no trouble at all, cept my tonsils is too big in the way.

"Christ, Mitten," he says.

Never knew mens cried. I has to hold his hand and take him by the wall so we can sit down on the grass cuttings where the lawnmower man comes to dump it all. I gone icy with the taste of dead and it's cold and dark in here. Grass smell is sweet and warm underneath us and we breathe it. Anton's hand pressed together with mine makes us a prayer. We close our eyes to make it true, case we can make the angel boy breathe. Then we hears the amblance leaving, goes down the driveway fast and screaming and we know that the angel boy Michael is breathing, the angel boy Michael is trying to live.

That's how come we does a kiss.

A porter crumbles a handful of sugar into the kettle. We get lost in the swirl and the stirring knock of the stick. The fire is sending embers streaming up through the hole in the tin roof. Fire flying. I think of Tony Gloucester Road. My eyes slow shutter. Emmanuel picks charred meat from the edges of his morsel then returns the exposed pink flesh to the fire. Morsel, is that the right word? A shrill whistle sounds. Not a bird. Nothing with sense lives up here. The sound makes us all turn around. Again—the shrill whistle. Emmanuel and the boys share ideas, send a response, whistled out into sudden green fog. A few minutes later from the blackened wing two lads arrive, porters. Glad to be here, they dump their loads, firewood, a European backpack, skeins of rope and climbing equipment. There's hand rubbing and knee warming; the porters are full of talk and gesturing. The word "England" jumps out. Across the fire they smile and nod to greet me. There is debate. Yes, I am coming from England.

No.

An England person is coming.

Makes me smile, it's so far-fetched. English man and woman meet on a different planet. Christ—I hope he isn't a romantic. There is only one proper thing to do in these circumstances. The rise to the hut is lethal and steep. A porter takes a flaming stick to light the ridge. A National Park guide shows first. And. Surprises me. It's a buxom wench in a swimming costume. One of her front teeth is missing.

"Robertson, I presume?" I say. And offer her the mug of tea.

She takes the mug with one hand and shields her mouth with the back of the other.

"My tooth plate hurts," she says. "I've been leaving it out. I wasn't expecting company." She drops her hand, revealing a black gap in the front of her smile, and then covers it back up again.

"Shame." I grims at her. "Well, it gives you somewhere to park your pen. Where did the tooth go?"

"I lost it." She shakes her head at the memory, at the carelessness. "Lost it on the Matterhorn."

"What—your tooth or *it* generally?"

She laughs a sudden wholesome bray, then seems shocked, as if she doesn't know it, and covers her mouth up again with her hand.

"Hard, isn't it?" She means the Mountains of the Moon, the terrain.

I nod.

"Thanks for this." She lifts the mug.

"If I'd known you were coming," I say, "I would have baked a cake."

She laughs, makes a little self-mockery, the absurdity of the swimming costume, but we both know it is the perfect garment for a Bigo Bog. Her laugh is very infectious, I see it spread to everyone present. It's probably all part of the bliss, the bliss of arrival, the bliss of a tumbledown mountain shelter; we all shifty around to let them all in at the fire. First she wants to sort out her equipment. Her backpack swarms with plastic bags, everything is organized so that she can't find anything. It doesn't stop her looking, though. She finds the "dry sock"section.

"Want a pair?" she calls to me.

"I'm airing foot rot; thanks, though."

I lose myself in the flames of the fire and the sound of people at home. One of her porters is a clown, the others egg him on. I don't understand the language but I know the pad of a shaggy dog story. My army of wet cigarettes, standing up to dry in ash around the fire, are ready for an about-turn. When Robertson comes over she's wearing dry fleece trousers and an olive sweatshirt. Somehow she has combed her hair and performed an immaculate French plait. Complete smile, with the tooth in place. She is blonde-haired but brown-eyed, handsome, wholesome, like the Bionic Woman.

I make space for her to sit.

"Wellacome," I say.

She laughs that bray, cuts it off short, gets instantly lost in the fire too, mesmerized by the flames. The brew in the kettle comes to the boil; we all kneel to worship at the spout.

"How do you know my name?" she says. "I've never met you before, I would have remembered."

"I just guessed."

"You guessed my name?"

"Uh-huh."

"But you could have guessed anything," she says.

I feel along the hot front line of cigarettes for a candidate to smoke. Robertson doesn't smoke.

"What, you just guessed?" she says.

There's some hilarity among the others as her porter delivers his shaggy dog punchline.

"You're making it up." She pushes me, laughs, brays, long and loud out into the mountain range. Then there is silence. Everyone is smiling.

"I haven't laughed like that," she says, "since . . ."

"Grandma fell off the roof?" I suggest.

Beyond the shelter, lightning flashes.

"I'm really glad you're here," she says.

There's a candle on the floor between our beds.

"This small!" Robertson says. "This small."

A long-necked beaky shadow bird flies across the wall behind her. The dry acoustic in the hut seems to draw the sobs out. I look at her hanging lower lip and slick chin where tears have mixed with snot. It's not anger or self-pity, more of a bitter disappointment, twisting her lips, pulling up at her cheeks. The ruin of her face was so unexpected, the flooding of her eyes so sudden. We seem to have come so quickly to this.

I shone the flashlight around the hut for Robertson to see the mice scatter. Pete's white vest, hanging under the slats of a bunk in the far corner, threw her for a moment.

"I thought you were by yourself," she whispered, sounded disappointed.

I showed her my wet clod of sleeping bag and the writing on the wall: *Jesus came here to learn how to walk on water—after five days anyone can do it.* She chose the bunk next to mine and had a spare, dry everything. This sleeping bag is filled with feathers; she produced it like a dove from up her sleeve, in the dark empty barrack hut it took flight in the beam of my flashlight. She had an inch of candle which she lit and placed on the floor between us. I was finally warm in the feathers; lay listening to her talk about the ice caps and how she saw the lunar eclipse mirrored in the glacier. Then this.

"I've never told anyone before."

I swallow a lump in my throat and for lack of what to say wait for her to continue.

"I didn't mean to say all that . . . now you think . . ."

"What about your dad?" I help her out.

"He's wonderful. I was always my dad's girl . . . I don't know why I told you all that . . . I think that's why I'm so upset; it's such a relief to talk."

"It's this place," I say. "It draws out everything. Are you an only child?"

She lies down again, propped on her elbow.

"I've got a brother," she says. "He tries to mediate, he's OK. Have you got any?"

"Two. Philip, he's nearly forty now. Graham is twenty-seven years old but I still call him Baby Grady."

"Do you see them often?"

"All the time."

"I'm really glad you're here," she says. "Have you warmed up?"

"A bit. I'm finding it quite hard to breathe actually, like a weight on me."

"It's me, I've burdened you."

"No, I was burdened before you got here."

"You might be feeling the altitude. Have you got a headache?"

"A bit. Are we very high up?"

"Four thou'."

"What does it mean? Four thousand what? Are we bigger than Ben Nevis?"

"Here, about three and half times Ben Nevis. I've climbed mountains all over the world but this . . . this is . . . this . . . this is . . ."

"Like nowhere else on earth?" I suggest.

"Beautiful," she says. The knowledge, the word, cheers her up. "Isn't it beautiful?"

"Is it?"

"You'll see," she says, "first thing in the morning. Just for a few moments. Beaut . . ." She falls asleep, falls clean off the top of the word.

I sit up and light a cigarette, leave it suspended in my mouth, haven't got the energy to draw on it or lift it up and down. Hear the rain knocking on the side of the hut, woodwind. Robertson is so innocent. So sincere, so dear. Frightens me. I gasp at my own existence, it frightens me, it frightens me.

What am I doing here?

"I don't know, Lynn," I said.

"Have you come to try and find yourself?"

"No." I tried to lighten the mood. "I've come to try and lose myself."

She tried to laugh but it tipped into tears and how small her mother makes her feel.

She's dreaming. I imagine snowfields, chipping into ice, bashing nails into rock, trusting a harness and a rope. Her eyes will be puffballs in the morning. I *has* to be kind. Could have done without the emotion, though; the lump in my throat has slipped painfully to my chest. Feel hollowed out and afraid suddenly as the candle pisses itself out. A double handful of feathers rise. Afraid I'll rise. My breath shorts, throws back its head, paws twice at the floor with a small round hoof. Darkness takes my breath away, gives me Pete's vest, Pete's chest, booming. Imagine I have shouted his name, Peter, across a mountain range and an ocean. Listen. His voice comes back to me pitter-patter with rain on the roof. *I'm night-blind. In the dark I can't see anything.*

Robertson hasn't moved. It's only just coming light. No sounds. Soundless. No rain. Nobody called my name but it seemed so close and clear. The floorboards make no sound under my bare feet. I open the door to lasers of twisting colored lights. Water drops on moss, cushions and pillows and bolsters of moss. Moss climbs scant trees, spectrums of green and yellow, pinks and purples. I pass our guides and our porters still asleep in the shelter by the ashen fire. Boom! My heart! But it's only Emmanuel's trilby slipped on the top of his staff. The trees seem related to heather, the roots ground hugging, foot tugging and slippery. They lean crippled, tripping over long sage beards. There's a pathway of rotted logs braced to carry weight over the swamp, they sink and roll under my feet. The colors keep starring in the light. There's a level clearing in the rot of sloping woodland, great sweeps of everlasting flowers. I know this plant, helichrysum, but it is unimaginably huge.

Christ, what are those things?

Plants. A rank phallic display, their blue-green solid color seems to throb. Rude. Guessing by my height they are eighteen feet or more. They guard a ring of rock seating, a meeting place for giants. Moss couldn't resist it, overflowing masses, inviting touch with colors like a fabric shop. I sit back on a giant's chrome throne. I sleep for a minute or an hour, wake up with beads of rain streaming down my face.

Robertson.

Robertson is coming, picking her way toward me with two steaming mugs.

"Worth getting beaten up for?" she says. "Tea. I thought you might want your cigarettes with it."

I dry my face on my wet pajama sleeve. She's in her swimming costume and shorts and flapping remains of boots. Black mud has curled up between my bare toes. She smells of toothpaste and soap.

"I was thinking about my grandad." I take a mug and the cigarettes from her. "He used to tell me stories about the Mountains of the Moon. I thought he invented it all, but he didn't; he must have read about it in the *National Geographic* or seen something on the television. A tussock army protected the swamp; giant plants guarded the slopes and wandered about, searching."

She's bent backward looking up. I light a cigarette and blow the smoke sideways.

"What are they?" I ask her. "They look so familiar."

"Groundsel. The microclimate fosters giants, gigantism."

A great shadow steps over my head, but it's only the passing black eye of a cloud.

"Is that what's going on with the beards, and the moss? What do they call this other stuff again?"

"Lichen."

She ruffles water from the turquoise moss and sits down on the giant's footstool. Around us beads of water sit cupped in frills and whorls. Lichen patterns rock, blooms in limy stars and peachy roses and blue-gray spots.

"What were they looking for?"

"Sorry?"

"The giant plants were searching, you said; what were they looking for?"

"A kiss."

"What happened if they found one?"

"I don't know. They never, ever did."

"Kiss one," she says, "see what happens. Might turn into a prince."

"That's what worries me."

She puts her tea down and stands up to try it. Which plant and how to approach it? Her hair is perfectly combed and plaited. She sinks in bog and beanbags and bolsters of moss, climbs up a staircase of mounting blocks and gives the plant a puckered peck.

Nothing happens.

"You mustn't kiss them more than once."

"Why, won't it work if you keep on trying?"

"They get wore out," I say, in my voice, except smaller.

The forecast is bleak. Every crevice and crack in the black rock is billowing green steam. My pajama top has stuck to my back and my tongue to the top of my mouth but there is no sun, just a midday night and rain with teeth regrouping. We take a route up the middle of a river, stepping on boulders, shoulders above the swell.

Robertson looks like an ad for "go faster" swimwear. *Don't go with the flow.* She spends a lot of time in Scotland, by the lakes and forests, runs up and down Ben Nevis on a weekend just for something to do. She does hill running in the Lake District and sea canoeing around Mull, wherever that island is, with o'mist rolling in from the sea. All day she has been turning to share something with me, a wave, a smile, a hand-picked detail; segments of a miraculous orange.

"Did you see that?" she says so bright and breezy.

Only thing flying up here is Jurassic imaginings.

"When we get back down to base tomorrow we can look it up. I've got a book, *East African Flora and Fauna*. Tell you what I've got as well. Chocolate eclairs. I have. Two of them. And I might let you have one of them. If you're lucky."

Emmanuel, her guide and the boys have stayed at the hut so that we can explore locally. Lynn finds the sopping echoing bleakness beautiful; me, I long for greenery, for the life in it. It's very quiet, unnatural. The rainmakers are up to something. We head back up a steep branch stream, happen upon a mountain pool with blue-green other-worldly water and a slim powdery waterfall. The altitude has turned my blood to treacle. I kneel down on a rock by the pool and lap water up like a big cat.

"Do you swim?" Lynn says.

"Only if I'm drowning."

She brays with her hands on her hips, it's so instant, with the gap and all. A woman in the water looks me in the eye. Over my shoulder Lynn's face is reflecting in the water too. She'd like to ask about the four scars on my cheek, but she won't, nobody has ever dared. Any minute now—mountain pool waterfall nymph.

"Will you?" she says.

"There's not enough light," I say with my camera to my eye.

She takes off her boots, rolls her swimming costume down. Nakedness comes easy to her. I look away, find breasts and fannies revolting, something too mumsie about them. She snaps her one tooth into place. Smiles at me.

"Power shower, nice and refreshing," she says. "You don't fancy it?"

"I'm not all that warm to tell the truth." I lie, have to keep my body covered.

"Ready?" Lynn says. "Can you take one of me under the waterfall and—"

A thunder drum roll interrupts.

"And one in the pool? Ready?"

"Ready. Now the tricky—" She slips, falls into the pool with a side slap. Zoom in on her cold, winded grimace. Click. Wind on. A lower angle draws her legs out pale and lifeless, distorted by the depth of the water. Click. Luminous white bosoms, floating and spread, click. Hhuck!

"What was that?" Robertson gasps. "Did you throw a rock?"

Click. Daylight is being wiped out. Click. Like an eclipse. Around my feet pink static leaps like fairies over the stones. She can't stay in another second.

"Did you get me?" She shivers blue-lipped and bullet-nippled back into her swimming costume. Slips her feet back in her boots.

"Do you think the pictures will come out nicely?"

"I think Moss Nymph this morning was more successful," I say. There is a terrible sound to the left of us, hell's hounds. We turn to see a black pack of rain, coming baying toward us through the trees.

"Oh–Woof-woof!" I says.

Then Lynn and me run for our lives.

Hours ago we said goodnight. Hours ago we blew out the light but I keep shuffling backwards and forwards through a deck of dreams searching for a place to sleep, beneath a grand piano . . . an elderberry . . . a greenhouse bench . . . shush . . .

"Are you awake?" Robertson swirls in summit cloud. Her voice comes and goes. The wind pulls and flaps at her words, climbing walls, mountains, walls, mountains, walls.

"Ravenous," she says. "It can't reach me here."

Lightning strikes the tin on the hut, my heart gets up. Scarlet running on the edge of a blade turns me over to spades and corridors of doors, of door, of doors and of beech trees and arms and arms and of window bars . . . knock three times on the door frame . . . ha-ha-ha, joker . . . cup of tea? I look in the lions' eyes, back at my digital watch; my spear turns into a bamboo cane with a peeling tinfoil blade . . . champion, pet . . .

"It's no good," Robertson says. "The floor is drenched this side."

Place your bets . . . on a cracked tongue . . . hello, Mum. Ace—*I'd walk a million miles for one of your* . . . come on then, I scream down the tunnel, but the train takes me back to marigolds and burning sparks and into a blizzard of searing pains . . . coming, ready or not . . . the fly agaric screams when I pick it . . . I think you done it this time . . . I sees Pip walking down the road, whistling and drumming on change in his pocket. Red double-deckers. No-no I'm ram-jam full . . . I don't want to know your name I just want to get on the bus . . . I went to the doctor the other day . . . We could go and eat up the road . . . no thanks I'm sick of tarmac. Thank you very much you've been great. I sees the double doors swing on a pub. And I know it I know it. He's still a piano man.

Oom-pah-pah, oom-pah-pah. That's how it goes. I sees Pip walking down the road, whistling and drumming on change in his pockets. I have to run to keep up with him. Philip. Imagine I've shouted his name, Philip, across a mountain range and an ocean.

"Are you awake?" Robertson says. "Have you got cramp again?"

Everything whites-out and I rise, transcend, transcend, on some high white plane out of this world, a warm wind is singing coloratura.

DAWN'S PROMISING SKIES
PETALS ON A POOL DRIFTING
IMAGINE THESE IN ONE PAIR OF EYES
AND THIS IS MY BELOVED

I run cross the grass past the chapel, pigeons fly up sudden and he sees me coming.

"What's happened?" he says.

Int sure what he means.

"Why did you come running like that?"

I shrugs. Shrugs gain. Grims at him.

"Crikey, Mitten," he says.

He stops walking; looks at me like a disappointment. My heart starts knocking.

"How come the rhubarb?" I arsts.

"I want to draw it. I called for you earlier. The interesting thing is that none of the caretakers have got a daughter your age."

Surprises me. Never spected he would call for me. He int sposed to call for me.

"You're not the caretaker's daughter?"

"No," I says.

"Who are you, then?"

"Your niece?"

"I said you were my niece to get you on the ward. I thought you were the caretaker's daughter."

"Sorry," I says.

"So who are you?"

"Who does you want me to be?"

"Where have you come from?"

"Around."

"Do you live in the village?"

"No."

"Your parents, do they work here?"

"No."

"It *int* proper." Anton throws his arms up disgusted. "Not when I always tell you everything."

"Sorry," I says.

"You must live somewhere nearby, you're always about."

I nods. True. He's looking at me, case I was a picture.

"Your hair is crawling with lice," he says.

"Terrible," I says. "How does I get rid of these bastards?"

"What's your name?" he says.

"Mitten," I says.

He pinches the top of his nose. I is sorry cos he is my friend, every day we has breakfast and dinner.

"Does you want to come to my place?" I says. "Case you can be my guest?"

"Your place?"

"Uh-huh."

He thinks a bit. Stands with one hand on his hip.

"Are there any grown-ups in your place?"

"Just ghosts and the Angel Michael."

His face is trigued.

"Have you got water, in your place?"

"Uh-huh."

"Let's go to the chemist first. Then the off-license. Then your place."

"There int nothing sacred!" We stand in the silly laurel. I arst them proper nice not to take my fire scape. Anton looks up with me at where it was, wisteria all torn down.

"Was a pretty fire scape. Sorry," I says. "Now we has to go the long way around."

He comes with me through the Dinner Hall and then up the ghoulish stairs. We listen at the Grand Hall doors, case there's a meeting or something. Nothing so we can go in. Always is a surprise, the size how big the Grand Hall is. Spects you could get a football pitch in it. The painted people around the hall look to see us coming in. They is sactly the size of life with names writ underneath.

"Shall I compare thee to a summer's day?" Anton says.

William Shakespeare, standing with his pen, actual seems to write it down. The Duke of Wellington looks in agony leant on his own sword through the top of his own shoe. We walk around the edge of the hall so Anton can see the paintings gain. Florence Nightingale has growed a beard. Sir Walter looks like knelt on a stone.

"That's him," Anton says, "Thomas Holloway. And his architect, Crossland."

"Nutters," I says.

"Where has Queen Victoria gone?" Anton looks at the space on the wall.

"Same place as my fire scape, Fiddler and Mick."

The sun comes out from behind a cloud and slices through the Grand Hall winders. Angels on the ceiling sprinkle golden dust down on us.

"Kingdom of Heaven, int it?" I says.

"More angels here," Anton says. "I haven't been in here for ages."

He stands looking at a painted lady, she int got a name. Then he opens the bottle of vodka and has a swig and then it's my turn. Burns my throat, then warms my belly.

"Bwah-ha-ha!" I says.

Anton's face is dreamy, looks at everything long and careful cos later he will draw something seen. Now he's smiling at the white statues, standing up high on the Grand tall walls.

"Ancient Greeks," he says. "Philosophers. Geographers. Aristotle, Socrates, Diogenes."

The Grand Hall doors swing open. It's a man nurse in a white coat.

"Have you seen Mr. Clew?" he shouts cross.

We shake our heads and he goes gain, lucky never seen the bottle.

I walk the sun ladders on the floor all the way over to the stage. I get up and stand on it. Bwah-ha-ha! We looks up at the old Greeks and angels on the ceiling. The painted people all go quiet and look at me up on the stage. They waits for me to say something. Bwah-ha-ha!

"Meine Damen and Herren," I says, "Madam et Monsieur, Ladies unt Shentlemen." I walk upstage and back.

"Vhere *are* your troubles now?" I arsts them. Bwa-ha-ha! "Verboten."

Makes Anton smile. He slides his thumbnail tween his front teefs.

"We were going to your place?"

He meets me at the side steps of the stage and waits while I shift the hatch.

"Your place is under the stage?" he says.

I flick the switch for him to see, lights around the mirrors and costumes hanging on a rail. He climbs down the steep steps and ducks his head.

"It's where I get my *school* clothes from. See. St Trinian's."

"I did wonder about the Dorothy shoes," Anton says. "And the hooli-hooli skirt."

I knock, knock, knock the heels together.

"Nothing happens," I says. "Can't put the lights on night-time case it shines through cracks in the stage."

Anton's face is beautiful. He's got the paper bag from the chemist in one hand, bottle of vodka in the other. Follows me crawling through a trap door.

"East Wing," I says. "I'm on the top floor same as you, cept my side most of the winders is broke and covered up with boards. Don't be fraid of the dark."

But it int actual too dark today, the sun is splintering in through hundreds of cracks and open doors. Anton stops to look. Dormtrees. Beds still the shape where people got out. Dusty sock makes me jump. Drawers and bedside cupboards left open, nothing left to hide.

"Look at this." Anton goes into a dormtree with eight baths stead of beds. Rails go around for curtains once and water pipes go about in the air. The sinks slope hanging off the wall with lumps of plaster in them. Anton turns a tap, it's stiff.

"No water," he says. Then we hear it coming, bashing. All of the pipes start swaying and spraying out umbrellas. Puddles run out from under baths and toilet doors and skirting boards. Water comes so hard in the sink, jumps back out for Anton to catch it. Wet, good and proper. I look under the closed toilet doors case somebody is hiding in there. Big fat spider runs out, stops, up on tiptoes. I spects he knows where he wants to go but don't want to get his feet wet.

The walls are black and green with mold, all plaster bows and loops and bunches of grapes. One long piece has smashed down, broke over a bath. Angels flaking off the ceiling float down on us. Jumps.

A sparrow flewed up! Fast. She goes out through a hole in the winder glass.

Further long the corridor I show Anton the office, with the filing cabinets and the flat board with plugs for telephones. In a cupboard they got machines on wheels. Battery chargers I reckon, dials and needles and electrical switches. They int got clips for car batteries though, they got rubber pads. I put them on Anton's brain and turn the dial for a joke.

"Tzzzz," I says.

Anton tends Frankenstein. The office stinks of mold from old magazines and files piled up high in boxes.

"An old doctor left his bag." I get it out from the desk drawer. Anton loves it, tries to read the labels on all the little tablit bottles. He wants to put the light on.

"No lectric," I says.

I get the temperature stick from a silver tube and put it under Anton's tongue. Holds his wrist.

"Uh-huh." I shake the stick. "You int well."

I hang the doctor's things in my ears and Anton opens his shirt, chest is warm as a nest and hairy. His heart is bashing so hard, wonders it don't knock him over.

"Uh-huh. You is definite still live."

I listens my own heart. Terrible, makes me sick. I tear a wrapper and get the wooden lolly stick out. I press it down on Anton's tongue.

"Say aaargh," I says.

"Aaaargh!" he says. That's how come I love him.

"You mustn't ever take these medicines," he says. "What's that noise?"

"Fiddler and Mick, up on the roof."

"What are they doing up there?"

"Taking all the gray stuff way. Reckon it's dangerous."

We tiptoe around a stinking lake in the corridor by the lounge and stacks and stacks of plastic chairs, past the big space with empty shelves, spects it was a library once. The Angel Michael never shuts his door. He int in.

"Michael's room," I says.

Anton stops to look in the dormtree.

"Michael lives here?"

"Uh-huh, bed number five."

Poor Michael. He keeps trying to get *sectioned* so he don't have to hide and stalk about the palice like a nutter. He wants to live in the West Wing proper like Anton and all the others. Anton's got a cobweb on his gray velvit jacket, flakes of angels in his hair. Right at the end we get to my door.

"It int too bad," I says. "Morning glory winders this end, only half of them is missing."

Surprises Anton, my place. He lays his velvit jacket on my bed. Good job I made it nice. The whites of his eyes is so white. He turns a circle, looks up at angels.

"Early Italian Recognizance," I says.

"*Renaissance*," he says.

"What does 'recognizance' mean then?"

"It's linked to 'recognize.' During the war, planes flew 'recognizance' missions, spying from the air at things below."

"Renaissance recognizance." I looks up at the angels.

Anton smiles, picks up the dictionary on the table.

"I got it down Ward 7, nobody there."

He puts it down, looks at the curving wall of winders, most boarded up rough with wooden sheets and planks. Gaps for air and chinks of light and ivy growing in. The top winders is beautiful though, morning glory flowers twisting with heart-shaped leaves in the glass. Flower color is somewhere true in the middle of blue, like dying I spects.

"Had to clean the glass three times to get that shine. Wishes you could see them in the morning, Anton."

He looks at the photos of people I found, smiling over my fireplace. At the books on my shelfs. At the floorboards.

"Have you sanded these?"

"Done them with Vim and a wire brush. Then after when it was dry, sandpaper til my arms dropped off."

"White cotton walls," he says.

"Sheets," I says. "It was brown and oringe wallpaper pattern done especial for a headache. A flap was hanging down in the corner but when I tugged it the whole room made of wallpaper came down in one piece. Had to wrestle it."

He looks at all the wooden ladders I've sawed to make the arch, up and over the bed.

"What's the idea, with the ladders?" He rubs his eye, got a flake of angel in it.

"I got four jasmines coming. Wilf is growing them on a bit in the greenhouse for me. Does you want a cup of tea? A sandwich?"

"I didn't think you had electricity for a kettle."

"Beryl in the kitchen always gives me a flask and a sandwich box. She think it's for the gardeners. Terrible, must mit."

"I'm all right with this." He tips the vodka bottle. He loves the dentist chair. It's shiny white metal with brown padded arms and all the stuffing coming out where people dug their nails in.

"Couldn't shift it," I says. "But it's brilliant."

Anton lays down on it and his hair splashes out.

"Ready?"

I tip the chair back sudden and his toes fly up.

"Open wide," I says and he does. Can't see proper, puts my thumbs in his dimples and my hands cupped around his chin, has to get half up on the chair. Uh-huh. I look at every tooth, both sides case trouble is hiding, gives them a wiggle one by one, sees if he got any loose.

His hands shoot up.

"There's your trouble," I says. "Now spit."

Surprises me. He laughs, sounds like something heavy falling down the stairs. I spects he is beautiful. Then he looks sad and a knot grows tween his eyes. I rub the knot with my thumb, sees if I can loosen it. My fingers stretch to hold his face case it rolls way. Uh-huh. Terrible lumpy, int so much pushing it, just arsting it nice to leave. Magines my thumbs is tiny irons smoothing skin and sadness way up and over bone. Then, gain, his breathing comes soft, in through his nose and out through his mouth. Shadow around his eyes is velvit. He opens his eyes. I sees water running over stones.

Ding—

We blink.

Ding—

We blink.

The tower bell is a sure thing.

"Your hair," I says. "It's so cold, could splash my face in it."

He makes a little whimper and closes his eyes like a dream. We listens. The lawnmower coming. Going. Chucking up grass. Smell it. Tick, tick, tick, tick. Tap dripping in the sink. Tiny rumble in the East Wing floor from a fast train, long, screams into the tunnel.

"The four minutes past," Anton says.

Gone.

Wonders if Anton is sleep. Sun slicing in through the open bathroom door is burning hot on my legs. Burning on half of Anton's face. I blows a breeze cross his skin, blows from his parting to his chin and then from ear to ear, case I can make it a blessing or just even something nice. I lands a butterfly kiss on his eyelid and he flutters inside the sun. Sound he makes is sactly the same as wood pigeons in the chestnut tree. I squash his lips up with my fingers.

"Say television," I tells him.

"Telli-wison," he says.

I irons the last bits of sadness way, chases them off into his hair.

"Oh fuck," I says.

"What?"

"Just seen a lice and its friend, went around behind your ear. Shall we shampoo?"

My bathroom is beautiful, got honeysuckle coming in. The floorboards is white so bright with light from the middle-day sun, dashing in.

"You've got a chaise," he says.

He means the sofa under the bathroom winder, perfect for lying and looking out.

"It was down on Ward 3, nobody there. Michael helped me to carry it up here. Loverly, int it?"

He loves it.

I open a cupboard and show him my stash of white sheets and towels and hospital gowns. If I throw dirty ones down the chute, clean ones come back up in the hatch. Surprises me every time. Anton looks long my shelf, at hand cream, body cream, lip cream, eye wash, tweezers, nail scissors, soaps, shampoos, bath smellies and toothpaste. I got lipstick and massacre and eyeshadow palettes.

"Found everything," I says. The big winder is open, up-down sort. Me and Anton kneels down on the chaise and look out. Smells of summer-cut grass and honeysuckle.

"Heaven," I says. It's my turn. "Bwa-ha-ha!"

Sideways long the East Wing can see the palice steps and people sitting out on them. This is a busy place with all the patients and the staffs and peoples coming and going and visitors. Some go to the village in groups, nurses has to go out with them. The lawnmower man has to go fast cos by the time he mows this side, the other side has growed gain. Anton tries the chaise proper, laid back. I shift to show him the best miracle. I turn the bath tap and sure enough hot water comes out.

"And the toilet works." I pull the chain to prove it. "Wouldn't believe all the yuck I tipped down it."

Anton goes to my bed to get ciggis from his jacket pocket. Then he leans in the doorway, looks over his shoulder at my loverly room, at angels swirling on the ceiling and the sweep of my Glory sky.

I lean back on the wooden chair and tips my head back in the sink. The side of his hand guards my eyes and the warm water pours through.

"Keep them tight closed," he says. "Is it too hot?"

"Loverly," I says.

Then I sit on the chair in the sun with my feets up on the bath while he sorts out my tangle with the chemist comb. Then I wash his hair sactly same, shampoo and fingertips on every inch of brain. Afterward we run a bath. Yardley: Lily of the Valley, found twenty boxes of these bath cubes down on Ward 9. Nobody there.

"One for you and one for me." I drop the bath cubes in the water.

Anton kneels down to crumble them in.

"I'd forgotten that these things ever existed," he says.

Bwah-ha-ha!

"Have you had many other guests?" he says, ciggi hanging in his lips.

"No." I take the ciggi from his mouth, has a puff and blows the smoke way. "You is my especial secrit," I says.

He nods his head.

"What will you do in the winter? The gateman, someone, someone will see smoke from the chimney or flame up on the windows." He unties my red cloth knot.

"There's a blanket cupboard behind the boiler room on Level D." I has to unbutton his shirt.

The black fists of the Portal Peaks boom and shake in my upturned face. They disappear.

"Who's Quentin, then?" Robertson says.

They boom. They disappear.

"Quentin?" I say.

"Last night in your sleep you called it out, five or six times."

"He's a friend, from a long time ago," I say. "I'm going to see him in South Africa, when I finally get down there."

Our guides and porters are leaving the National Park office now. We were both generous with our tips. We wave. They wave. They don't look back. The Portal Peaks boom in my face. They disappear. Stuff is us, her stuff, my stuff, all out on the grass, we're having a repack, getting ready to leave and go our separate ways. Robertson's plastic bags are swarming. She is religious with her thousand little routines; imagine if one thing were to slip her entire life would fall off. The stuff I left in the shed reminds me who I'm supposed to be. I reread the letter from Danny Fish.

> The apartment below is empty now. The boom-bass fucker downstairs moved out three weeks ago. They've been and fixed the boiler in the basement so the apartment is toasty. Rats? I see no rats, hear no rats, and smell no rats. The landlord got arrested for drug trafficking and the pub has closed down.

He went up to London to visit a friend.

> We went to see "Cats" in the West End, never seen so much old pussy in all my life.

"What's funny?" Robertson says.

"Nothing."

I was surprised to find the letter waiting at the Post Restante in Kampala; I'd gone to post a letter to him and one to Tim and the pottery peeps.

"What's in the little box?" Robertson says.

"Couple of used films; I've been sending them back to the apartment."

"What's in the canister, rice?"

"Ashes."

She picks up the gold plastic canister with the black screw-top lid and reads the small fold of paper attached to the side with tape.

Thanks for your letter. Something's come up so I can't make
it. I know you'll do the right thing for my old
dad and the top of Kilimanjaro is where he always
wanted to be.

Heath

It was also waiting for me in Kampala Post Restante. Gwen will be camped in Manchester now, outside Sharon's house. Can see Gwen dragging along the pavement attached to Heath's leg, hanging like a gremlin on his window wiper; she'll make it so he has to run her over. Sharon's sisters will come running through the garages and alleys with ponytails and buggies, to see the spectacle. They can't believe that Sharon bagged a brilliant bloke like Heath; the local kids have never had so much fun, the neighbors are so happy for her. Little bastard boy Gavin will shut Tarka the dog in the garden shed and then set fire to it. Jennifer will say nothing and continue sucking on her lollipop. Heath will throw Gwen by a twist of her long red hair into Sharon's car, he'll dress it up as one last, final chat, then he'll drive Gwen to a beauty spot and they'll fuck like bunnies in the back.

"Are you going to take the ashes up there?" Robertson says. "Up Kilimanjaro?"

"No," I says. "Not on your nelly."

"What will you do with them, then? Scatter them somewhere else?"

But our attention is diverted by the arrival of the little people. We get glimpses of their movements, through systems of tracks, around the backs of huts and bits of plots and towering growth of this and that. Here they are. My heart still booms every time. See half a ring of sumptuous skin and washed-out pastel rags, they leave one side open, don't know what we might do if they get us surrounded and trapped and cornered. Cue representative.

Titter.

Cue representative. Here he is, chubby, blue pants, pink sweatshirt shredded to decorous rags. Comic timing. Shakespearean stance.

"Muzungu—give me money!" A breathless rush, to squeals of laughter, he slaps on his own fat thigh, tickles us all to tears. They can all come closer and sit down now.

What have we got in our bags?

Well. We get it all back out. They show us what they've got. Good sticks. Scars. A football made of strips of cloth, wrapped up in an orange fruit net.

"Mana-chuster," the lad says. "Oo-ah-Cantona."

Mickey Mouse washed out off a T-shirt. The contents of Robertson's backpack are up for consideration. There's a swarm of her plastic bags and wonderment at the revealed contents. A boy dismantles her head flashlight.

"If these batteries are going to be finished," he says, "do you have got some more?"

"Two spare ones," she says.

I wonder if Christmas is like this. Another lad is fully absorbed in the workings of Lynn's Swiss army knife. She shows him the tiny tab where the tiny tweezers pull out. The medical kit is explored; we do small surgery on a splinter, deep in a septic finger. A soft leathery leaf is found and a shake of antiseptic powder is wrapped up in it for continued treatment. The map of Africa is spread out; they understand direction. East: sun up: six o'clock. West: sun down: six o'clock.

"Where is England?" a girl asks.

Kids always ask. I crawl and place a relative pebble out in the dirt. They tell us the names of local villages not shown on the political map. Sometimes I can find what they want on page maps in the guidebook. They love that, proof that they are in the world. My boots are tested, laced up, dragged around in. What they want most is the pen and a sheet of the lined A4 paper. Sun sweeps across the page. The Portal Peaks are free of cloud. Terrible terrible black towers. The sun is scorching on my shoulders, so I put my umbrella up. Of all the things I brought with me it has proved to be the most useful, instant shade for every blistering occasion. It's black, the umbrella, a compact thing, doubles up as a baboon basher. The Portal Peaks disappear. The children talk among themselves, among our stuff, interested in everything. Robertson smiles at me. I suck on the chocolate eclair.

"There!" she says.

I look up and see what an ancient Greek saw, ice mile high up in the sky, mad as the moon, mad as ice, thrust from the jungle heart of Africa. The Ruwenzori stand up, then bow out, in a super-trouping flash of light. A heavy black curtain drops and everything, everything begins to crackle.

THREE MONTHS LATER

"It's not malaria." The doctor is holding my chin. "It's hard to know if you're pale or not with such a tan."

"I am pale, I am definitely pale, underneath."

"You do look quite dewy." His thumbs smooth across my eyebrows and temples, this sickness has a soft powdery texture. Same as this room, whitewash dashed with brilliance like his tunic. The ceiling fan shivers the palm fronds growing in through the glassless windows. A vine has made use of the shutters to climb in over the sill. The rattan couch is calling me.

"About four days, you say, since you arrived on Zanzibar. You didn't have it on the mainland?"

"No."

Thwump! Pain chops my brain in half.

"Can you make it stop?" I reel in my chair.

He shines the flashlight in my mouth, under my tongue, up on the roof of my mouth, under my gums, back behind my epiglottis.

"No tonsils," he says. "You're traveling alone?"

"I was supposed to meet my friend in Dar es Salaam but she didn't turn up."

"Are you worried?" the Doc says.

"Yeah, it's really distorting my vision; everything is super-eight-ing."

"I meant about your friend."

"Robertson. No. Just surprised. We were going to travel down through Malawi together. Her flight goes back to England from Zimbabwe in six weeks, she has to be coming along soon or she won't do the distance."

"Maybe she is just—"

Thwump! My mind splits, he holds my temples together, I hold his hands on my temples together. The nurse, his African wife, comes back in with a china jug and bowl, puts them on the mosaic dresser by the couch.

"Hop up," he says. "I think we should get your temperature down."

I stagger to lie on the couch. Sunlight cuts through the palms of palms and the doctor and his wife's hands. A mangy ginger cat super-eights across the sill. Thwump! He pushes gently on my shoulders to stop me folding longways in half. He talks to her in a language. Who knows where she is from, with her round face and eyes and mouth, her skin so totally black?

"We will make you more happy," she says.

I rest in the crook of her shoulder while she peels the wet pajama top off me. Buck away from the sponge, twist with the trickles, steam into a whimper. The doctor lowers a blind.

"You need your friend," his wife says. "You need your friend Livingstone."

When I wake it is evening. Still Zanzibar. Sultan hot. The surround sound of prayers echoing down the alleyways and Michael Jackson's "Thriller." I have slept all afternoon, feel a bit better. While I've been asleep the doctor's wife has washed and dried my white pajamas. Kind.

"I don't know what's wrong with you," he says finally. "I've no painkillers stronger than what you've been taking. I think you should get the night ferry back to Dar es Salaam, there's an excellent hospital there, should things worsen."

The hospital doesn't know what is wrong with me either. In the bus park, in the exhaust fumes, I look for space spinning; bend to vomit between my own feet. The mob bends over with me, sees if my scattering on the ground has anything in it they can use.

They push me. They pull you. They're all yelling *Kilimanjaro—Kilimanjaro—Kilimanjaro*.

Pain ruins one side of my face, the smell coming back up makes me—Hhuck! Kilimanjaro. I'm wracking on the current of some cold voltage. I raise my head to look at them. A trickle of sweat runs into one eye.

"Do I look like I could climb a mountain?" I stagger. "Do I? DO I?"

They're deaf, fixed on my white skin, their voices on a tourist loop—Serengeti–Ngorangora Crater–Kilimanjaro–Zanzibar–Serengeti—

"Get off!" They're pushing me, always pushing me.

Malawi, I've gleaned, is very relaxed. Thirty-six hours away on this bus.

"You're crying."

I shake my head. But a tear gets out and trickles down.

"What has happened?" Anton says. "What's happened since last night?"

All of my breath is kicked.

"Has somebody come down the corridor?"

No.

"Michael, has Michael fetched you trouble?"

No.

"Do you know why you're crying?"

Good question. I stop crying to think about it, don't know. Makes me cry even more.

"Have I upset you?"

Idea upsets me worstist of all. I flaps my hands to keep it way.

"Christ, Mitten, you're setting me off, whatever is it?"

My ribs is crying, my shoulders is shrugging.

"Tell me," he says.

My face crumples into his sleeve and then he scoops me up, gets out his campanula hanky. I suck in the coldness of his hair, breathes hard on the lavender oil in it.

"Can you show me?" He smooths my nail edge with his thumb. I point to the book on the floor, cross the room where I slung it.

"Ah." Anton sits us down and rocks me tight in his nest. "They killed Piggy, didn't they?"

"I wants to be sixteen," I says and cries for years.

Sun comes in through the bathroom door and drenches us on the bed. We don't even need the sheet with the sun burning on our skins. We stretch out long so it can kiss us all over. First hot sun this year, dashed with happy rain. Spects there is a rainbow somewhere over the palice roof. Some rain has sprinkled in through the gaps and dotted the floorboards dark yellow. Normal we sleeps in the afternoons like twin babies breathing each other. Surprises me how lucky we is. This is the third summer coming. We just grow time the best we can. Now it's the spring term I has to disappear in the day, sposed to be at school. Anton comes to me in the mornings and learns me everything, stead. At four o'clock after school we can go out and walk about in the grounds. We chin wags on the palice steps. On the weekends we scape and go to the beech woods and Virginia Water lakes. Sometimes I be Anton's niece and go to Ward 14, has tea and cake with Lizzie and Leonard. Everyone knows us. After Anton has his ECT he always is a little bit shocked and they let me sit in his marigold room ready to say welcome back.

I get up and go to the bathroom. Eyes still red from crying. Glad to be in my place gain. I stand in the bathroom doorway looking at my beautiful room. The jasmines are starting to flower, climbing halfway up the ladders, they been all winter in the greenhouse. Wilf don't mind me coming and going for pots and a bit of compost cos I helped him to level the floor and now we is making an orchid house. He thinks I'm Beryl's daughter. Terrible. When it was agony cold at Christmas me and the Angel Michael bandoned the East Wing and moved into the boiler cupboard down on Level D. Was all right, warm. Beryl in the kitchen done us proud, reckons she can fatten me up. Don't spect she can. Was OK in the cupboard cept Michael snores like one of them machines for cracking up concrete. But in the daytime me and Anton always came to my place and done lessons warm in bed. One time the wind brought beech leaves in on us. Another time snow. We had so many blankets on us it was almost rude, we tended they was buffalo skins and sang home-home on the range. Last week we got smothered in blossoms. He makes me smile, so beautiful it is when he smiles, I keep on trying case I can get one. Sometimes we can't tend, so we hold on to each other's heads and take turns crying. All these years and we never arsts, where we come from or who we is.

I climb back on the bed and recover on Anton like a coat.

"You're killing me," he says into the pillow.

My lips is little for kisses. I tends they is sweet-pea seeds and sows a row long his rib. Then he slides me under his arm. His nose wants to play with mine.

"Feeling better now?" he says.

Don't know. Still got tears lined up. He lies on his back to fly me on his knees in the sun that streams in through the bathroom door. So beautiful he is. Tear drops out of my eye and splats onto his cheek. I crashes softly into his chest, never knew nothing so hairy and warm. Then he rolls us over, recovering me, and his cold hair splashes over my cheek. He always holds my little finger and kisses the tiny nail.

"The question is: Are you going to continue with it?"

He means reading *Lord of the Flies*. Still there, on the floorboards cross the room where it dropped, feel sorry now for the crumpled pages.

"I wouldn't have given it to you if I'd thought it would upset you so much." His chin is on top of my head. "Will you continue with it, though?"

"Seems rude not to," I say. "Was a shock. How bad I believed it. You said it was *fiction*, lies, but it int. It int." Has to be careful cos I still got more tears lined up waiting.

Anton's chin nuzzles my hair.

"Good," he says. "That's the point; stories tell lies in the service of truth."

His thumb wants to feel my teef edges; I tends to bite it off and swallow it.

"I've bought another book for you to try," he says. "It's a story about a seagull."

I push his thumb out with my tongue.

"Does the others kill it?" I says.

Makes us laugh. His lips know my wrists. I think about the seagull, though.

"What's its name?"

"You'll see," he says. "How is your story coming along?"

"Don't know what happens." Massive yawn nearly swallows me.

"A job for the Imagination—*un devoir pour l'Imagination*."

"That's it." I snuggle down. "Whisper me gain, in French."

Anton is sleeping. Magnolias in the grounds below the winders is flowering, the smell comes through the gaps in the planks and the broken winders. Newborn wisteria is feeling about for something to get hold of; when it can't find nothing it bends back on itself. Through the top morning glory winders can see the house martins keep coming and going with bits of straw for weaving. Proper basket cases. Sometimes think the angels on the ceiling can smell this new spring life and closes their eyes and smells and listens. So quiet, Anton breathing sides me. Angels on the ceiling mind me of Michael, blowing about in all directions. He's back in his dormtree now, forty-four doors down the corridor. Anton is always scared case Michael gives me way, thinks he is a *liability*. I trust him though, I would with my life, and Anton says my instinct is probably much better than his. Sides, I int no good at early nights, and when Anton goes back to Ward 14, Michael comes to see me, always frightens me to death. We put blankets over the table and sit under it like a tent. Under there we can light a candle and the flame don't shine on the dead wing winders. Needs to make some black curtains.

Poor Michael. Yesterday he done the newsagent's in the village but the police just thought he had scaped and led him back through the palice gates. He don't understand, the West Wing is so full of people now they has to serve lunch and dinner twice. Staffs say it's hopeless, dangerously out of control. They can't *section* anyone new, not til a few more kill themselves, sides, it int no good behaving like a psycopath here, where it's total normal. I told him he needs to go into Staines and put his foot through a winder there.

"The border?" I say to the conductor. We have just passed a branch road, clearly signposted; I don't know why we haven't turned down it.

"We will go first into the town and then some person can bring you back to the border," he says, tying the end on something stitched up.

They send you in the wrong direction; run you around in circles, so that more people along the way can get a chance to fleece you. The border closes at six o'clock and now the bus has overshot it by twenty minutes and about five miles.

In town the man-animal mob is on me as I step off the bus. They make me mental. Demented. A big bull-necked man is shouldered up closest to me.

"How much to the border?" I ask him.

"Twenty dollars," he says. "Come, come."

These *int* poor people, they're too strong for hungry people, too well watered and fed. They're pushing me, they're pushing me; they are always fucking pushing me.

"No," I say, "I'm not going to give you twenty dollars. Tell you what I'm going to do, I'm going to give you *fifty dollars*, that's what I'm going to do, give you fifty dollars, no, fuck it, *one hundred dollars*. That's what I'm going to give you, *one hundred dollars!* Jesus Christ what am I saying, what am I saying, what am I saying, let's just call it five hundred, uh-huh, *five hundred dollars*, that's what I'm going to give you, no, no, no, Jesus, not five, not five, not five, a grand, let's call it a grand, *one thousand dollars* for you? My friends?"

Thwump! Pain nearly knocks me over. I can't make anyone understand I went over to Zanzibar and picked up something like a brain tumor on the way.

"Five dollars," the Bull says. "Five dollars, we go, come, come."

Africa can make you ugly. It's making me ugly. It's making me really fucking ugly. I spit in the dust. Follow the Bull across to a blue pickup truck; topple my bag into the back. He leans over and opens the passenger door. Not so poor they can't afford a tidy pickup, with gas in it.

"Five dollars," I say.

"Five dollars," he says.

We take off, throwing an orange blanket of dust behind us. His watch says five thirty.

"Will we make the border?"

"Yes, no problem," he says.

A couple of buses and four-wheel drives are coming from the border but nothing else is going to it, just a few No Man's people striding out to beat the darkness and cattle being herded home. It's so wet hot, oppressive. Thwumping, thwumping Tanzania.

Malawi is, I've gleaned, very relaxed.

Very, very relaxed.

Malawi sounds friendly, like a sing-song. Bye-bye, Tanzania, you total fucking cunt. My nerves twitch with border anxiety. Just have to get through passport control and immigration this side, and that side. I gather my pajamas and all my sick wits about me. Put my penknife handy in my pocket. Have to get across No Man's Land fast. Fast through the money changers.

Tanzanian shillings into Malawi kwacha. U.S. dollars into Malawi kwacha. Approximately? I sort out my passport and amounts of currency. Daylight is struggling with night clouds gathering over the border huts and barriers. I see No Man's Town ahead of us, in No Man's Land, between the two borderlines proper, kerosene lamps lined up both sides ready and waiting for darkness. The Bull's fancy watch says five fifty. He swings the truck around on waste ground just before the barrier, parks facing back the way we came. I haven't got a five-dollar note. Tanzania has demanded so much money from me; I've been totally deprived of giving anything. I hold a ten-dollar note toward him and waive the change with goodwill.

"What is this?" he says, overacting a script with no context.

"Ten dollars for the journey." I urge it into his hand because he's delaying me. The man in uniform is limbering up ready to lower the border barrier.

"But this journey is one hundred dollars," he says.

We *int* in the mood.

"We agreed five dollars, you've got ten dollars." I get out of the truck and slam the door.

Thwump! Shiver a response to the heat outside. Can't reach my bag from this side, as I turn the corner of the truck I see his face in the broken wing mirror, watching me. Wanker. I put my toe up on the back tire and step up to lean for the straps of my bag. But the tire drives out from under my foot, crashes me down to hang by my armpits on the side metalwork of the truck. He starts to drive. Gaining speed, my legs are tangling, my boots are bouncing high off bumps in the road, I can't hold on any longer, I let go, falling hard and ugly in the road.

"Hey! Hey-hey!"

No Man's people, a crowd of them, have seen this happen. My bag is bouncing away on the back of the truck. There's a bye-bye touch on his red tail lights. There's the sweep of his one headlight. I know that I am covering ground, at this moment quicker than he is. Cattle crossing the road are going to force him to slow down. No Man's people are running behind me.

"Hey!"

The cows are in his way; he rages two wheels up the bank trying to get the squeeze past them. I'm only a stride off his tailgate. He slips a gear, it's all I need, enough to get beside his open winder. Enough to grab for the neck of his shirt, enough to get a twist in it, enough for me to hang on, enough twist in it for him to turn purple, his hands tear between his throat and the steering wheel, enough to slow us down, enough loss of life, to make him, to make him, to make him . . . stop. Stop.

Finding my feet I tighten the twist around his throat with one hand, turn the engine off with the other and throw the keys. No Man's children bang heads to catch them. He is a fat black man, bulging purple, his fat fingers trying to remove the squeeze, I am so far possessed there *int* anything can touch me now.

"One more squeak out of you, you fuck, and I am going to kill you. Do you understand?"

Wise man.

I loosen the twist, throw the neck of his shirt back at him and leave him to live. Flaming flaring torches and a crowd part to let me through with my bag. Could lay face down on the dirt and sob. Because he's still alive. Sickness weeps out of my skin; tiredness buckles my knees, hot sweat mixes with night shiver. Only fury keeps me moving.

"Hey! Hey!"

Turn to see the Bull's head as it rams full speed into my stomach. Knocks the wind out of me, sends me sailing, reeling backward. Thorn bushes break my fall; tip me face down under them.

"Hey! Hey!"

He's walking away with my bag, held up like a trophy for the crowd to see, but he hasn't bargained on me. I unhook my cheek from a thorn. I take off from ten yards, land on the back of his knees, it takes us both straight down. I'm up quicker than he is and I want him to die. Stupid man down, kicking up dirt with his knees, his eyes are defiant, his mouth is defiant, his throat is offered up like a final gesture. I decide to cut it for him and open out my penknife blade. It flashes silver in the headlight beam.

"Hey! Hey! Hey!"

Flashes silver against his fat throat. He buckles down under the blade. Blood sprinting down his neck changes the expression on his face. It's not enough, though, to cut his throat, there's nothing in it for me. My elbow jabs his fifth rib, sure enough to bend him forward. Piece of shit. My boot connects under his jaw, his bottom lip explodes. Fury gets him up, snorting and blinded with blood, he spits out the bitten off end of his tongue and he comes for me. Stupid man. Stupid man. Can't resist his exposed groin.

"Awah! Ooo!"

He drops back onto his knees, perfect height for a perfect treat. I've been practicing this one. I measure my three strides.

"This one," I tell him, "this one is especially for you."

The reverse-turning butterfly kick takes his face out like an ice skate. He sounds like nothing on earth. But he is amazing, defiant, roaring, trying to stand up. I'm tired of him now. I'm going to kill him. He's got the headlight in his eyes. And defiance. I'm holding my knife blade pinched at the tip. It's the natural thing to do, looking at his wide open chest. I lift my arm, feel the weight of the knife, loaded to spin through the air, loaded to slam straight in.

He grabs at his heart with both hands.

Drops back to his knees.

Falls sideways like a dead man.

I step forward, look down. See plainly in the light of the flaming flares that he is plainly dead. See several hundred No Man's people holding their heads on, silenced in violence, and among them Robertson's face, white with horror. The crowd cowers, shows me its empty hands; I see that the knife is still in my hand.

I look at the dead fuck on the floor.

I look at my purple backpack, go quickly and open it. His bulk flays over as my boot shoves his hip. I open my medical kit. The freaky polythene bat opens out, I squeeze the orange oval mouthpiece into his bloody busted mouth. I blow down the tube, his chest comes up. My hands kick the air back out.

"Breathe, you piece of shit," I says. Beats seven sorts of life back into him. Until his eyes flicker and my effort is interrupted by six uniform pairs of boots with uniform trousers tucked in. A man in a purple frock comes between the muzzles of guns and an African woman with a toolbox.

"We are doctors," she says.

I shift out of their way.

"Border Police," a uniform says. I stand up, helped on all sides by the tips of the six guns.

I look at Robertson's face. I wish she hadn't seen all that. It wasn't pretty; you couldn't chuck it under the chin like a wayside violet.

"Wrong daisy," I says to her.

Thwump!

"I'm not going to leave you," she says. "I can go to the British Consul. Are you all right? Are you hurt?"

"Nothing that twenty-five years in a Tanzanian jail won't fix."

Rifles propel me forward. Robertson is coming along beside us. She turns on the uniform with the biggest epaulettes and the red feather in his black beret.

"Are six guns really necessary?"

"Your friend is a very dangerous lady."

They've got that right.

"She has killed this man," one uniform says.

"And then she has made him come back to life," says another.

Somehow a far worse crime.

"Exactly so," the chief says. "The dangerous lady cannot decide if she wants him to be dead or alive."

The No Man's people are coming with us, all having the same debate.

"Everybody is shutting up," yells the chief. Everybody does.

Looks like it's just me, booming under the bare bulb, in this wooden scout hut.

And the Border Police chief sitting behind the barren desk.

And the six uniforms standing behind him.

And the No Man's people that have followed us in with boxes and crates to stand up on. And Robertson with her backpack and mine, white-knuckled ride. Can't look at her face, she doesn't know me. My breath climbs over a wall of panic, could run, no where. Thwump! Nearly knocks my head off. Sweat stings, pouring over the carpet burns I got on the bus. The pajamas wet with sweat have stuck to my back. My breath swims in the shallows, around a couple of broken ribs.

The chief knows what he has to do. None of his keys fit the desk drawer. A uniform points out that it only needs a yank. Nothing in it. He holds his fingers up to receive a pen, snaps them as if magic will produce one.

Nobody has got one.

"Do you want a pen?" I ask him.

He waves the idea off—no paper.

"Just give me please your passport."

My white pajamas are tie-dyed with blood in sprays and drips and heart-shaped splatters, wonder if it's mine. I produce the passport from my money belt and lay it on the desk stiffly so my rattling hand doesn't show. He reads all of it, admires the border stamps.

"You were in Zaire?"

I look at him. Yes I was.

"How is it there?"

"I was made offers I couldn't refuse."

"I don't understand," he says. "What is your meaning?"

"Well. For example," I say, "I got a lift on a beer lorry. I agreed to pay the driver and we traveled the first day together happily. On the morning of the second day he picked up five soldiers at the side of the road."

No Man's people are interested to hear about this place Zaire.

"Two soldiers sat in the cab with me, the other three sat out on top of the cargo."

"Beer!" the chief says.

"My bag was also on top of the cargo, out of view, and I was worried about the soldiers taking things from it."

No Man's people can understand that.

"At the end of the journey, a lonely spot, we all got out of the lorry. My bag was handed down from the roof. I gave the driver the twenty dollars we'd agreed and he was happy about it. But when I tried to walk away the soldiers ran and stood in front of me. 'One, two, three, four, five,' the talking soldier said, counting himself and the others. 'Twenty, twenty, twenty, twenty, twenty,' he added it up, 'one hundred dollars,' he said, 'you must give it to us.' "

The chief makes a clicking sound with his tongue.

" 'Why?' I said. 'Why must I?' 'Because,' he said, 'we did not take anything from your bag.' "

No Man's people laugh.

"I tried to walk away but they came again and stood in front of me. So I had to pay them one hundred dollars."

"Aye!" the chief says. "Zaire was in this condition?"

The generator outside dies. Darkness snuffs us out.

I lift my head from my arms on the desk. Wonder if I've been in a bus crash. The chief's chair is empty. The uniforms are in charge. No Man's people have bedded down across the entire floor of the shed. And Robertson. When I ask, I'm taken outside to a toilet. The uniform in shorts, with overdeveloped calves, leads the way, parting growth with the tip of his rifle. The one with the cough follows behind. Robertson stays to mind our bags. No Man's people line the route all the way to the shithouse door. Inside I throw up a spoonful of burning yellow bile. Then smoke a cigarette. Stare down the black shithole.

There's something not right about me being here.

I think about what I did yesterday; in any law or language: throw away the key.

And so many witnesses. It's the bottom line; I write off the rest of my life.

The chief is back, with the bull-necked fuck from yesterday. He's sitting forward on a chair that has been added next to the chief. No Man's people shove and strain to see him. The heart attack has stroked down one side of his face. My reverse-turning butterfly kick has spread his nose on the other. The doctors have stitched up the nick in his throat. What's left of his swollen tongue lolls in his open mouth. His jaw is broken. In any language: savage. His eyes are bloodshot, defiant; they want me punished.

An American ten-dollar note is on the desk. It seems very large, fingerprinted with brown blood. Robertson is left of me, sitting on her bag. I can't look over at her face.

"Yesterday," the chief says, "you have agreed to pay this man one hundred dollars but when he had brought you here to the border you only paid him ten. True?"

"Not true. We agreed five dollars, I paid him ten."

"This ten dollars?"

No Man's people have a laugh among themselves, like how many other ten-dollar notes are there floating around in these parts?

I nod that it probably is the selfsame ten-dollar note. He's pleased that I am so willing to enter into the spirit of the prosecution.

"So! You will now pay this man ninety dollars."

Makes me laugh. I laugh so hard and it hurts so bad, makes me rock in my chair. No Man's people join in laughing. Above it all I hear Robertson's great wholesome bray, elated at such a cheap conclusion.

"No," I say.

"No? You will not pay this man ninety dollars?"

"No."

"But you have paid the soldiers in Zaire so now you can pay this man. How much will you pay him?"

"Nothing. We agreed five dollars, he's got ten dollars."

The chief sucks air through his teeth as if I've made a very painful decision.

"Madam, you do not understand. You are in serious trouble. If we cannot resolve this matter here it will be passed on to the courts, you will have to be detained, in prison, here in Tanzania maybe for many, many months, maybe many, many years, here in Tanzania, tut-tut-tut." He doesn't recommend it, the Tanzanian judiciary.

"Good." I light a cigarette. "I've got all the time in the world. I love Tanzania."

"Give me one of those," the chief says. "So, you will pay soldiers in Zaire but not this man here. Aye! I do not understand it. Tell me please, how is it so?"

"This was different," I say.

"How so?"

"Well. This was only one man. You can argue with one man and a pickup truck but not with an AK-47 and five bloodstained machetes."

I see Robertson out of the side of my eye gnawing on her wrist knuckle.

"Eighty dollars is a good price," the chief says.

"No." I put my heels up on the corner of his desk.

The Fuck snorts.

The border closes early.

Darkness comes on the dot.

A uniform is sent outside to crank up the generator. We wait. We listen. We listen to insects throbbing and the Fuck's breath, whistling past the swellings in his nose and throat. The generator doesn't want to know. We listen to it trying. No Man's people who can't fit in the shed light up flares outside, filling the black windows with flames.

"Seventy dollars," the chief says.

I look at the bull-necked Fuck, see two of him; don't know which one is real.

"No." I sleep a while, smiling with my eyes wide open.

Sickness crawls up and down the back of my legs. My lungs labor. Thwump chops my head off; I catch it between my knees. A rolling bottle of drinking water curves toward my waiting foot. I nod my thanks to Robertson but can't meet her eyes. I drink half of the water down. I look at the three Fucks. I look at the three chiefs. I look at the eighteen uniforms, don't know which ones are real.

"Fifty dollars, come, come, madam, we are all very tired."

"No." I'm starting to hate him. "Lynn?" I say.

She ducks over and crouches down by my chair.

"*Anything*," her eyes say.

"Can you nip over to No Man's Land and get me a packet of cigarettes?"

The crowd catches the words.

"Can one of your uniforms go with her?" I ask the chief.

He nods.

"Which brand?" Robertson says.

An impulse makes me reach out and chuck her under the chin. She stands up and is about to go, cowed by guns and uniforms and limelight from a green moon on the black faces of the crowd.

"Lynn?" I say and she turns. "Better take this with you." I pick up the ten-dollar note on the desk.

"Hey! Hey!" Riot breaks out in the shed. A thousand fingers at a glance are not pointing at me, but at the center space on the desk, where the exhibit should rightfully be. The bull-necked Fuck stands up suddenly, sends his chair crashing. He snatches the ten dollar note from out of my hand and storms out, knocking No Man's people sideways. We all stare at the route he took out of the shed. Listen to his pickup starting, wheels spinning, reversing. Well, he *int* gone to get me some cigarettes. One of my shoulders shrugs at the chief.

"You are free to leave," he says.

"Oh thank you!" Robertson says. Starts crying into her hands.

I get up, stand swaying, sirens in my middle ear tell me I am going to faint. Didn't want to make Robertson cry.

"It's OK," I says.

She sobs.

"Come on, old chum," I sway. "It's OK. It's only a cabaret."

I look at all the purple backpacks lying on the floor. Robertson lifts the real one up for me and I get a shoulder through the harness. I'd like to collapse but my knees are locked. Robertson is stopping me from toppling, my arm is around her shoulders and her arm is around my waist.

"One foot in front of the other." She taps my left foot forward with her boot.

"Padam, padam, padam," I says. "Da-da-dum, da-da-dum."

Da-da dum.

The border is closed; we've got seven hours to kill us. We go with the No Man's crowd under the barrier and into No Man's Land. They wing off, leaving us. We topple with our bags up onto the wooden porch, outside the closed Immigration Office. Robertson walks around me, sorting out the angles of my tangled limbs.

"Recovery position," she says.

A shiver shakes through me, pneumatic. Mosquitoes whine around my head. At the other side of the lorry park, the No Man's party is starting;

the pissheads and the prostitutes come out to play the night away. Techno music is dragging on a flat car battery. Robertson's plastic bags are swarming. I hear and smell the insect repellent spray and her hands rubbing together. Her cold palm sweeps across my hairline, my brow, my cheekbone. Stings in carpet burns from the bus and thorn gashes, makes my eyes water. A sleeping bag is laid over me.

"Thanks, Lynn," I say. "I just need to lie still for a minute."

She is sitting on the step, close by. I open one eye to check. The starlight is painfully bright, casting shadows.

"Where did you learn to fight like that?" she says.

"In prison."

She absorbs the news. I can feel her gaze on the side of my face.

"That kick, that thing you did flying through the air—did they teach you kung fu in prison?"

"No. Someone taught me the butterfly kick; I had years in the prison gym to practice it."

"So violent," she says. "I don't know what to say."

"Goodnight, sleep tight, see you in the morning?"

"It was beautiful, though, in the headlights. Beautiful. Violent. You're *so* lucky," she says. "Ten dollars!"

"I was still robbed."

Night frogs, loud as they are and insistent, remind me of lambs calling. I roll over, recover on the other side. She is still sitting up, hugging herself against the night chill.

I wait for her to speak, to ask, what I was in prison for.

"STRANGE SPICE FROM THE SOUTH . . . HONEY THROUGH THE CONE . . . SIFTING . . ."

Baby Grady is on the kitchen floor. I squashes him to death with beloved ness and put him back down with his racing cars. I has to hold on to the sink. The drumming is so loud.

"Brrmmm, brrmmm," Baby Grady says.

Sick taste, sandpaper-dry from scared and making sense of everything.

"... AND THIS IS MY BELOVED ..."

"Mum," I says.

She slams her hand down on the piana keys, makes me and the photographs jump.

"What do you think this is—some kind of joke? Do you think Borodin was having a joke when he wrote these birdsong melodies?"

"No," I says, "only—"

"Do you think Rimsky-Korsakov was making a joke when he stole them from Borodin?"

"No," I says, "only—"

"Well, that just goes to prove how much you don't know. I'm not interested in your mundane little existence; I'm an adult and you're ten." She lights a ciggi, smoke all comes out one nostil.

Wonders if to say "eleven."

"Do you think Rimsky-Korsakov was interrupted all day long by people calling him *Mum? Mum mum mum*," she says.

Bryce comes in the front door and makes a wind and all the sheet music takes off flapping like seagulls in the room. They drop and slide from out the sky when Bryce closes the front door. He nores us, goes down the hall.

"Daddy?" Grady in the back room laughs, belly tickle.

Hands is shaking when I pick up the pages and put them all the proper way around. The bashing is so loud. Baby Grady is laughing in the back room.

"No, Daddy!" He laughs harder, starts squealing cos he loves it.

I look at Mum. Wonders if to call her Vivienne. Or Joan.

"Mum," I says. "Ellie Smithers has gone and I seen what the Sandwich Man done."

That's how come I starts crying.

"Boring! That's all now, thank you! PETALS ON A POOL ... DRIFTING ..."

"Oulu! Oulu!" Baby Grady is on the side in the kitchen.

Bryce is leaning, reading the *AutoTrader*.

"Take him," he says.

I put Grady on my hip and go out, down the alley. We wait on the triangle grass for a gap in police cars. Then run cross the road, disappear in the bushes. Shivers darkly under the beech trees in cold left from yesterday's winter.

"Monkey," Baby Grady says. "Oo-oo-oo."

"Shush." I tie him tight in my red cloth and climb up the tree. The Sandwich Man's blocks int so safe. Then run the planks through the treetops, long the end to Africa Tree Camp.

"Superman?" Baby Grady says.

"Shush," I says.

Listens. On Lowry Lane, heavy plants still crossing. Tinker's horses galloping scared. Down in the Humps, police radios crackling.

"Shush." I rock us backward, forward, filling up with cold.

Baby Grady presses his fingertip on my eye, tries to stop where the tears come out. He catches one of mine and wipes it down his chubby cheek. Tree Camp is creaking way with cold wind getting up and panics in the gold leaves. I want to go to sleep; sleep is heavy, on me like a coat. Underneath, through the gaps in the floor, I sees a transit van park, then four policemen in white suits, carrying stuff cross the Humps. They put up a tent over Sheba's grave.

"Gone way," Baby Grady says.

I look through my binocliars at vultures in the sky. Herds and herds of policemen herding in Lowry Lane, spreading out down in the Rift Valley. I has to go and tell them. Tell truth. Say he took Ellie into the Masai-Mara but then he come straight back without her. Makes me cry cos it's my fault. Cos I never went down and kept her safe.

"Superman?"

"No," I whispers. "We has to go and tell the policemen."

"Roger?"

"Shush." I hugs him tight. "Back down."

When I turn around I kick my scrapbook, it skids and tips half off the edge, I grab it but loose pages of my story Mountins of the Moon go swooping down through the trees and over the Humps and Leafy Lane. I pick Baby Grady up and run back through the trees with him on my hip but a wood pigeon clatters and makes him scream and kick his legs, how bad shock it is.

"Shush."

Past my feets down in the road sees the lady from 97 holding one of my pages and looking up, through the branches, through the trees, in my eyes, eyes to eyes.

"Have you got that baby up there?"

"It's all right," I calls. "We is just coming down."

"You've got that baby up there–oh my God!" she shouts and starts to run.

"It's all right," I yells.

But she runs, she runs up our path and bashes on our front door. And Bryce comes out and looks cross and Mum as well comes running and Mr. Baldwin seeing what it is. Trouble, coming, running. Everything is drumming.

"You are dead!" Bryce yells up at me.

"Stay still, just stay still!" the lady from 97 is shouting.

I sees my mum in the road. We is the gods, strings of terrible words catch up in the trees. Baby Grady is strangling, hanging on the knot in my cloth. *Ladder.* People is shouting. *Ladder.* Bryce is running back with Mr. Baldwin to get one. The Cortina parks and two more police cars. Uncle Ike swings long on his crutches, Auntie Fi runs long sides him. The Smithers family come back with all the searchers in a pack. Words turn into a slipping wind and blue police lights and Baby Grady is slipping and my hands is sweating, my feets is sweating, bark under my toes don't know me.

"Stay still, stay still!"

The branch is snapping, the wind is cutting me; the dark is pushing me. I sees the fright of eyes caught up in headlights. Mr. Baldwin's ladder comes up longer and longer and the top of it leans on my branch. Bryce comes bigger and bigger up it.

"No, Daddy! No, Daddy! No, Daddy!" Baby Grady turns way, clings scared on my hair and knot.

"Come on, son." Bryce holds out his arms.

Baby Grady won't look.

"Give him to me," Bryce says.

But I can't.

The other four tapes are signed and sealed; this last one is just a formality.

"This is Interview Room 2, Trinity Road Police Station, Bristol. It's November the 8th 1986. The time is 2:57 a.m. I'm Detective Inspector Wilson."

"And I'm Detective Inspector Webb."

"I am also present, Thomas Book, duty solicitor on call, here at the request of Kim Hunter."

"Will you please state your full names?"

"Kim Hunter. Beverley Woods. Jackie Birch. Dawn Redwood. Catherine Clark."

"You have at one time or another used all of those names?"

"Yes."

"Remind us. How old are you, Kim?"

"I was twenty-one in September."

"You have come into the police station of your own accord this evening?"

"Yes."

My leg rattles the table. Spills all of the coffees. Soaks all of the cigarettes. DI Webb pauses the tape.

"Do you need to see a doctor?"

"Have you got a habit, Kim?" DI Wilson says. "Something that you've not told us about? Do you need a doctor?"

"No." I put the plastic coffee cup down with both hands cos it's hopeless, my hands and legs are storming; nerves can't handle the sea of calm inside me.

"It int *cold* turkey, it's *frozen* fucking solid."

"About that blanket?" Mr. Book says.

I know that soon, when we are final finished here, in the morning, tomorrow, day after, there will be a proper place for me. Lots of coal making lots of heat. Lucky we int in America really, one enormous electric chair.

"Can we turn this fan off?" DI Wilson wonders out loud.

Mr. Book tries the control panel on the wall. DI Webb comes back in with a blanket, stinks of piss.

"Put this over your legs, flower." He kneels down to tuck my frozen bare feet in.

We all has a nap. Wakes up just fore my nose touches the table. Tips back my head; shoulder blades come up to hold it.

"Shall we get it over with?" DI Wilson says. "Are you OK to continue?"

I keep my eyes closed and nod my chin onto my chest, bones shift in my neck like plates.

Resume.

"Why have you come into the police station tonight, Kim?"

"To confess."

"What is it that you want to confess to?"

"The kidnap and shooting of Quentin Sumner at number 3 Park Lane, the night before last."

"Do you know which day that was?"

"Firework Night."

"Did you act alone in the kidnapping of Quentin Sumner?"

"No."

"Will you name the people you were involved with?"

"No."

"Kim has been offered witness protection and has declined it. Is that true?"

"Yes."

"Why have you declined the offer of police protection?"

"I don't believe the police can or will protect me."

"Why should you take all of the blame?"

"I'll take the blame for my part."

"What was your part?"

"The ransom note was made with words cut out of my dictionary. I knew he was hostage in the house. I shot him."

"Who did you shoot?"

"Quentin."

"Why did you shoot him, Kim?"

"I was aiming at someone else, Quentin got in the way."

"Who were you aiming at?"

"I'm not prepared to say."

"Was it your gun?"

"No."

"Where is the gun now?"

"I threw it off the Suspension Bridge."

"When you pulled the trigger did you know what you were doing?"

"Yes."

"You intended to kill?"

"Yes, the person I was aiming at."

"Why did you want to kill the person you were aiming at?"

Mr. Book shakes his head and throws his cigarette packet down. His lighter skids. We've been all over this, how a court will regard my lack of cooperation, how many extra years it will cost. But any minute now, how many years will be irrelevant.

"I'm not prepared to say."

"You shot Quentin Sumner by mistake?"

"Yes."

"You were aiming at someone else?"

"Yes."

"Quentin's condition is critical; he's not expected to last the night. How do you feel about that, Kim?"

"Sorry."

"Is there anything else you'd like to add?"

"Yes," I say.

All three men look at me, we haven't rehearsed this bit. I rattle the plastic cup to my mouth, lap at the lukewarm sweetness.

"What is it that you'd like to add, Kim?"

"Kim?"

"I'd like some other deaths to be taken into consideration."

We listens to the recording machine, crunch and whirr and stop by itself. Finished chewing up the entire tape.

"Bollocks!" DI Wilson says.

A policewoman lets Mr. Book into my cell. I didn't hear them coming over matey in the next cell, kicking off and rattling his cage. Drunk and disorderly. My solicitor, that is. He's brought me forty Silk Cut, though, and a bottle of Lucozade from the chemist.

"What time is it?" I ask him.

"I don't know," he says. "Does it matter?"

"No," I say.

He wants to sit on the metal bunk but there's a rubber fried egg and folds of boozy puke in the blanket on it.

"It's about 2, 3, 4 a.m., something like that. That's disgusting," he says.

"Wouldn't mind if it was mine," I say.

He's in jeans and a sweatshirt, scratches at stubble on his jawbone. He leans one shoulder on the wall. The concrete floor is numbingly cold but the steel pipes are hot behind my back. Mr. Book has caught hailstones in the top of his moccasins. The orange cellophane wrapped around the bottle squeaks as it untwists; the glucose bubbles race to escape.

"Thanks very much, for this." I drink it shaking like a junkie.

Silk Cut filters are perforated.

"Have you got a light? They've taken my lighter off me."

He hasn't, he's having a nap, with his head tipped to the wall.

"About the first one," he says.

"Shush," the beech trees say.

The branches is snapping, the wind is cutting me, the dark is pushing me, thick with frightened eyes shining up in headlights. The ladder bounces on my branch. Bryce comes bigger and bigger up it.

"You are fucking dead!" he shouts.

"No, Daddy! No, Daddy!"

"Come on, son," Bryce says.

But Baby Grady won't look.

"No, Daddy! No, Daddy! No, Daddy!" He screams and kicks and clings to me.

"Give him to me," Bryce says.

I change my hand grip on the branch above and move a little bit nearer to him.

"Good girl!" someone shouts.

"No, Daddy! No, Daddy!" Baby Grady squeals.

"You motherfucking cunt," yells matey in the next cell.

Memory fills my ears with the sound of Sheba's punctured lungs. With the sound of the belt on Pip's back.

"I'm going to kill you," Bryce said to me.

I put my foot on the top of the ladder and shoved it as hard as I could. It skidded sideways and off the bough. Bryce turned, jumping out from the fall.

Forward.

Catching hold of nothing, of nothing. His arms went out like on a cross, his head dropped onto his chest; the fence post passed up under his ribs and came out between his shoulder blades. There was agony of wind in trees and lights and silent screaming mouths. He kicked and jerked and his neck twisted, oh God, he might have said. A hot stream flooded down my legs and splashed on and off my feet. Everything emptied out of me. A fire engine came, spinning blue lights through the trees and blackness. Spotlights waved about and fixed me up blind in the beam.

"Shush," the beech trees said.

Baby Grady was tight and warm against me. I turned my head; saw through razor blades of light shining wet streaks on his chubby cheeks. But his blue-gray see-through eyes were floating away, high up with lights on the golden leaves.

"Stand back! Please! Everybody back!" the Sandwich Man said. "Let's let the firemen do their job."

The metal fence post screamed, sprayed out a wheel of burning sparks.

"Pretty," Grady said.

I heard the hum of a hydraulic lift and Baby Grady's chortled delight. I kissed my baby brother good-bye and handed him to the fireman.

"The charge against you was dropped," Mr. Book says. "There was insufficient evidence. The prosecution lost their two main witnesses."

What was his name, my barrister then? He always was brand new. I remember Red Roofs and Detective Cooper; my scrapbook was on the table fat with leaves and pressed flowers. *Dead.* It didn't seem like the right word, I wrote the word big and small copperplate, wrote it swirly-wirly joined up. There it was stuck on the page, the torn photograph of Bryce, wagging with a stick in his mouth. I sent the half with Sheba on it to Pip.

"The charge against you was dropped, Kim." Mr. Book thinks I didn't hear. "The prosecution lost their two main witnesses."

"Will you do it?" I arsts him.

"I'll do it," Angel Michael says.

I forgot him up on the laundry yard fence. White angel in a hospital gown. He's got blood all down the front and zigzag stitches up his arm, from Monday and his fist through the winder.

"You int old enough, Michael," I says. "For the part."

Anton's clothes on the washing line is an English cottage garden. The buckit is overflowing with bubbles, splashing on the paving and his bare feets. He's got friendly toe beards and especial stuff for hand washing, can't trust his silk and broidery down the laundry chute. This new drug has made him beautiful gain, his shirt is so white and his eyes and teefs, with his hair tied up and fanning out he minds me of a gray orchid. He reckons the new drug stinks, though, in his blood, in his sweat. But he smells sactly same to me, lavender and linseed oil.

"Shame Shirley isn't still about," Anton says. "Reminds me, we got a postcard yesterday, it's in my jacket, in the inside pocket."

I get the postcard out.

"Morocco!" I says.

The Winnebago broke down in the Atlas Mountins. I look at the picture gain. Probably sand in the air filter. It's all right now. They seen a room full of human skulls. Shirley fell off a camel, then it spat at Trevor. Trevor spat back.

"Morocco," I says.

"Burleigh?" Anton is still thinking on the other question. "Never heard of the place. What's he like, your boss, this Bernard?"

"Sideways a bit like a golden eagle."

"I mean, what does he do for a living?"

"He's got a car showroom in Egham, sells Silver Shadows and Jaguars. His wife died last year, found him loads of times crying and shining the horses. I just said chin-chin, Mr. Ripley, and it always cheered him up. Cept now I call him Bernard, we is a proper good team. Look," I says.

Two butterflies has landed on Anton's candytuft hanky-chief. Red admirals.

"Red admirables," I says.

"And what is it you've got to do?" Anton pours soapy water down the drain and fills buckits for the rinse. I wait for him to turn the taps off.

"Has to wear a costume with an apron and a black bowler hat, and sit on the back of the carriage, nice and smiling, and hold the horses' heads for the judging."

Int sure about the hairnet.

"So what's the problem?" Michael comes back from out of the sky.

"We has to be there for *two days* and stay in a hotel. Bernard wants to come to my house *in the village*, wants a *mum or dad* to say: *yes*."

"You're killing me, you know that, don't you? After dinner," Anton says, "shall we go down there?"

Yes!

Blacksmith is coming at seven.

Anton loves the tack room, sniffs it in, the leather polish, metal polish and hayloft sweetness. Even the straw on the floor is shining; last sun comes in the barn door. I been all week cleaning the harnesses ready and the carriages side by side is gleaming. Sees Anton's face in the coachwork, smiling.

"It's Victorian, this one," I says. "Me and Bernard has been restoring it. Once upon a time it was Queen Victoria's. Her arse was right here, on the selfsame cushion. We got a photograph to prove it, on the wall behind you."

Anton looks at it.

"Sepia," he says. Every word he says is beautiful.

Then we go around to the stable yard; Misty always neighs when she see me.

"She's beautiful, int she?" I says. "Her real name is Mistress Dappleday."

"Huge," Anton says.

"You can stroke her nose, she don't bite, she's gentle, kind and always willing. Was half dead when Bernard got her."

"She won't like the smell of me," Anton says.

"Come and see Fritz, he's around the back. He int big like her, he's a little pony stallion. Especial thing about Fritz, he's total, absolute black. Uh-huh. Most times a dark horse has got brown hairs mixed in or brown shading somewhere, but not Fritz, he's total black."

Blacksmith's van is parked outside the stable door, he's got a gas furnace in the back. Air smells of the hot shoe burning onto the hoof.

"Give o'er," Blacksmith yells. "You little shining shitbag!"

I smiles at Anton, shakes my head. Bernard is surprised and happy to see us.

"Fine evening, welcome," he says to Anton. "We're having a bit of a struggle, I'm afraid."

"Don't be fraid, Bernard." I take the rope off him.

"He'll stand for you," he says and it's true.

"Twat," I whispers in Fritz's ear. He likes the word, stands still, listening, case he can hear me say it gain.

"I'm pleased you've called by. I was going to call on you later."

Anton shakes Bernard's hand.

"About Burleigh," Anton says. "I'm quite happy for Mitten to come but I wondered, naturally, about the sleeping arrangements?"

Surprises me, how good Anton is.

"I'd worry, if you didn't worry," Bernard says. "Now what I had in mind is this: my sister Ellen will be there with her two daughters and a room is booked for four girls to share. I can give you the details of the hotel. Perhaps I could have Ellen telephone you?"

"No need," Anton says. "I'm sure Mitten will love it, she's very happy working here. Thank you for giving her the opportunity."

"Well, I'm thrilled to have her. We'll need to leave at the crack of dawn, day after tomorrow, we'll be back very late the following night, is that OK? I'll drop her home, of course."

"In a Silver Shadow, I see," Anton says. "Beautiful."

"Thank you," Bernard says. "She is a fine one. Nineteen thirty-two."

They go off, talking. The blacksmith files down the last hoof and the job is done.

"Now aint he dainty?" He slaps Fritz's arse.

Anton and Bernard is still talking, leaning now on the paddock fence; it int dry, only painted it this afternoon.

Me and Anton walk back up the hill, with the tower dinging high up above us. When they test the palice fire larms Bernard always says same thing, watch out a lunatic is loose. Eight o'clock. Last sun is oringe on the steep oringe boulders. We pass two people in a car, kissing in the lay-by.

"I feel a bit bad," Anton says.

"Sorry."

"Genuine, Bernard, isn't he? Christ, how will he drop you off?"

"It's OK," I says. "I live at number 7, second left. I go down the side of the house and climb over the back fence."

"You've done it before?"

"Uh-huh. When it's dark in the winter he drops me off."

"I didn't realize that, I thought you walked back. There was nobody there, in number 7, you never got caught?"

"One time a man seen me, said 'Hey, you,' said 'Sorry, lost my cat,' then he came outside with a flashlight and helped me to look for it."

"Crikey, Mitten."

"Donald, he's all right, I done the clutch on his Mini. He thinks I live over the back, can't never find the cat. Terrible."

Terribleness makes us smile.

I spects my room smells sweet with the hoya bella, and the gardenia, and the jasmines over the bed flowering. Yesterday was my day off and we went on the train to Chelsea Flower Show. I had my wages and twenty pounds, won from George at poker. I got an eight-foot hoya bella and a gardenia tree and the Dutch man arst to marry me. Lucky, Anton said I was already his. On the train coming back the carriage smelled like heaven and people got petals in their hair. Sleepy, we was drugged with flowers just like bees and Anton forgot the rules. I got inside his jacket and he kissed my parting all the way back. When I get in I can mist the leaves.

Can have a bath, with miles and miles of hot water.

Thinks about the pots I made on Sunday in Re Creation, don't know if they will bake nice or splode inside the kiln. Amy says tomorrow we can get them out and see. Anton smiles at me. Sometimes reckon it's a fine, fine life.

"How are you getting on with the cassette?" Anton says.

"*Le garçon est dans le jardin,*" I says.

I loves it. I loves the French, makes me sound pretty, like someone else.

"*Cheval,*" he says. "Horse. *Chevaux*. Horses. *Les beaux carrosses.*"

Little sparrow in the hedge says it back. We walk and talk and collects some stems for the vase in my bathroom. Int no pavement. Careful cars. Anton picks tall buttercups; the bunch likes butter under his chin.

"You're going to have trouble with the next bit of French unless we can sort your English out. I mean, when you think, do you think *int*? Sometimes you say I *is* and sometime you say I *am* and I wonder why."

"Just cos can."

"But you know which is correct?"

"Uh-huh, int deaf or stupid."

"You quite often drop the beginning off words."

"Saves energy Henry Higgins."

"Who's Henry Higgins?" he says.

"Rex Harrison."

"You've got me." He trips over a cow parsley stalk.

"Careful," I says. "Tripped over your Antipodean Twang?"

And he laughs, the most beautiful sound I've ever heard. Been saving it especial.

"My *Antipodean Twang*. Where did you get that from?" he says, best mused.

"George," I says.

By the traffic lights at the top of the hill, we wait to cross the road.

Les beaux chevaux.

"George says all of Ward 11 are being transferred to somewhere in Staines, next month," Anton says.

The traffic lights turn oringe, then red. Beau int so thorny as beautiful. We look to see if the next car is stopping. I sees the sun on the windscreen, the bonnet of a black Capri, looks straight at the Sandwich Man's face. Looks straight at me. I cover the scars on my cheek with my hand. We cross the road in front of him. My legs is starting to tremble. The Sandwich Man turns right, same way as us. He points at me and wags his finger, laughs. Laughing.

"We'll have to go and visit George, Mitten," Anton says. "We'll miss Old George and he'll miss us."

We walk in through the palice gates.

"Evening," the gate man says.

The Sandwich Man is throwing me kisses through the gate, tending like he just dropped us off. Can't hardly walk or see for red.

"The horses are magnificent. I see why you like it down there."

Red. I hears the fly-garic screaming.

"Something stinks. Is it me?" Anton says. "I've got this horrible dry tongue and this metal taste in my mouth, it's like—it's like fear, without the emotion attached."

Still got the red cloth I was wearing when I left Red Roofs. Somewhere in this village the Sandwich Man is waiting for me, waiting for the game to start. I has to get dressed up for the part. The Sandwich Man learned me the frightened game. This time first move is mine.

Here I is, standing waiting under a tree. Here I is, at the traffic lights leaning on the post. Here I is, the only thing standing on the roundabout. Here I is, up on the wall standing in front of the village shops. Here I is, on the railway bridge. I sees all the people in passing cars wonder if they magined me. But he int driving about, he must be sitting somewhere in the Capri. The lay-by in the lane. I pass back through the palice, climb up over the back wall and stalk down the steep oringe rocks.

Uh-huh. Below, the Capri is parked. I look up at the clock on the bell tower. Sit on my heels. Wait eleven minutes. He is in the car, can see his elbow.

Listen for cars coming.

Nothing.

Coming—ready or not. I jump down, heavy on the roof of the car, the metal crunches and bends in. He gets out ducking to see what happened.

"Sporting chance?" I say.

He chuckles; he loves me. He grabs for my legs. I jump over his arms and onto the bonnet. He has to get around his open car door. I smash my spear through his windscreen and it shatters. Skipping up the rocks, I know that he is following, laughing, I sees red, sees black, sees yellow and Ellie broken, sat on a shelf in the underground sewerage.

I stop at the top of the rocks, lean on my spear waiting for him to catch up. I look up at the clock on the bell tower. He tries to grab me but I jump. The Sandwich Man lands behind me. He laughs. He loves me. I jog, he jogs almost with me. Up the West Stairs. Down the East. He loves me, walking through the ghoulish hall. Out of the main doors. Down the palice steps. Once around the Angel pool. I squeal like a girly should and he laughs. We does shapes of eight around people sitting on the grass. They laugh, good game, mad man and his visiting daughter. I listen and squeal and flits with my spear and looks up at the clock on the bell tower.

Ding—

Good game.

Ding—

He laughs.

Ding—

I hear the fly-garic screaming.

Ding—

When I picked it–I wanted to die. I died.

Ding—

A thousand times cradled in Mr. Nesbitt's arms.

Ding—

"Come on, Mr. Draper," I says. "Getting old?"

The Sandwich Man laughs, he loves me, his little savage. He loved me so much he had to let me live. But now I int a little girl. The search parties int gone off home. I int half dead from cold and starved. Ice int bitten off my toes.

I int in the foxhole. I int in the long narrow pipe. Me, me, I int in the hollow of a tree, int dug in under a rock. I int under the bucket of a JCB. I int buried in the ground breathing through a piece of straw. Here I am.

"Here I is," I says. "Boo!" Come on, I thinks, we've got three minutes.

He loves me, skidding down the railway scarpment. He loves me, running long track. I run deep into the tunnel and stop. Can hear him panting, see the daylight behind the shape of him.

"Come on!" I shout. "Just you and me, in the dark."

His laugh booms in blackness. Listen. Water dripping. The rails fizzing. Hear him swallow his Adam's apple; feel all of the air sucked out of the tunnel. On time, the four minutes past.

"Shall we say a prayer?" I arsts.

The headlights of the train shine on the back of his eyes. On the back of his open mouth. Then all of the brakes on the train scream and fill the darkness with burning sparks spraying out from all the wheels.

Pretty.

I find the Angel Michael on the edge of the angel pool. A crowd is going out through the gates.

"Someone's been killed on the level crossing," he says.

"Can I have a puff on that, Michael?" I sits up sides him in the sun.

"Its wacky baccy." He lays his head in my lap.

Don't care if it's camel shit. I see through smoke the blue, blue sky and water pouring from angels' hands, the shifting colors in the pool from the kaleidoscope tiles. Smells honeysuckle and cut grass. This is my heaven. This is my place. Girl in the pool puts her hand up to mine.

"Where's Anton?" I says. "Is it poker tonight? I made me a Love for Lydia dress."

Michael don't say nothing, starts lulling a song about strawberry fields. Baby pigeons is learning to fly, flapping one leg at a time. A big square amblance comes in the gates, flat tires on it like square wheels. It comes slow long the drive, parks next to where we is sitting. Fight going on inside it, lady sounds madder than this place put together.

"They took him away, they took him away, they took my little boy away, help me, help me." She don't want to go in the spaceship. Driver gets out, winks at me, tells me with his hands that the lady inside is as mad as a ram. She's shouting and screaming and kicking. I grims at the driver, he walks around and opens the back doors of the amblance. A man is in the back with the lady.

"Calm down," he says. "Don't do that, Mrs. King! Calm down! You're all right, Mrs. King! Can you run in, Sid?"

Sid can run in and does, comes back with a straitjacket for my mum.

I've got the tune in my head and hum it.

"Mr. Draper was killed by a train, Kim, the inquest recorded Misadventure." Mr. Book starts to pace. "There is no case to answer."

I hum it louder. Mr. Book goes around in circles. I want to confess. I want a clean sheet. I want to be punished. I want to be free. I want to blow the lid of this shitter.

I hum it louder.

"Puccini?" Mr. Book says.

I hum it louder.

I find him behind the door, in the ghoulish hall, with his toes pressed gainst the skirting board.

"Arthur," I says, "do you know where they took that beautiful blonde lady, Mrs. King, came in this afternoon?"

His eyes slide sideways. I curls my hands, mad as a ram, sticks my tongue out sideways.

"Ward 2," he says. "They took her little boy away."

I fly the stairs. The ward doors is wedged open for fresh air, can see the long corridor. I move a plastic chair and sit to watch the comings and goings. Drugs trolley and a line. People on Ward 2 walk like they got bricks balanced on the top of their feets. Can hear the television, *Some Mothers Do Ave Em*. Everybody is in the lounge watching, int nobody thinks it's funny. Corridor is empty cept for two shufflers and a going nowhere. I nips long, keeps my head down past the staff office and lounge. Waits for someone to call me back, say hey, but nobody does. I stand in a doorway of a dormtree. Listens, long the corridor, follows my ears to the frothy and babbling sound.

She is tied to the bed, thrashing her head, splashing pink foaming words up the wall. Nobody is coming. I go in the room. The bed is rattling and shifting.

"Shush." I pats the air. "Shush."

"This is where they round you up," she says. "This is where they come to collect you. No!" She bucks and shakes the whole bed.

"Shush." I creep closer.

I try to hold her skeleton hand but she grabs my wrist and digs her long nails in.

"Give back to Caesar what is Caesar's." She spits words then starts a prayer. "Our father who art, in this, the winter of our discontent, I have to get back to Mandalay."

"Shush," I says.

She looks at me.

"Help me, Rebecca," she says. "I have to find my daughter." She starts to cry. "They took my little boy away."

My heart falls to bits.

"Amazing Grace has gone," she says and sobs. "They took my little boy away."

I wonder how Baby Grady is. Idea of his name makes me cry; don't know if someone is feeding him.

I nods and tears drip, wipes snot on my red knot.

"Shush," I say. "Shush."

"Help me, help me," she says, gets terrible scared, "I don't want to go on the spaceship."

"I'm going to help you," I says. "I'm going to help you now."

She smiles and tears start pouring down her face and dribbles of words in strings hang off her chin.

"Shush," I says.

She lays still while I climb on the bed. Starts to cry.

"Help me, help me."

"Shush," I says. I lean close over her ear, hum softly the tune of "One Fine Day." She lifts her head nice and I pull the pillow from under it.

"On the sea . . ." She cries and nods her head, smiling.

"On the far horizon . . ." I says and puts the pillow over her face and leans on it heavy with all of my body. She bucks but I keep on singing softly "One Fine Day" til Pinkerton calls Butterfly and then she is perfect still and the performance is final, finished.

"Mr. Book," I say, "I tucked the pillow under her head and spread out her hair. I left the ward as easily as I arrived. I waited til dawn then got in a horsebox and went off to Burleigh Horse Trials."

He shakes his head.

"There is no evidence," he says. "She was deranged; she choked on her own phlegm."

Can't stop the tune in my head. I hum it. I hum it louder.

"About the death of Jonjo O'Brien. Kim. Kim! His car went over a precipice called Devil's Leap in Newmarket, a bomb crater, I gather. He wasn't a very savory fellow, he was blind drunk leaving the pub; the road was known to be dangerous; locals were campaigning for barriers. He was blind drunk, he drove off the edge."

"He didn't have any brakes," I say.

"Accidental death. There is no evidence to support what you say, Kim. What about this last chap? In Sheffield you say?"

"What about him?"

"His name?"

"I didn't know his name."

"So how did it come about?"

"I was reading my horoscope, in the paper, on the grass in the park with Patricia. My neighbor Patricia, she was a lovely lady. This bloke comes along. 'Look at you,' he says to Patricia, 'sitting there with your tits out and your legs open.' "

Mr. Book waits for the rest of the story. But that is the story. He paces three times around the cell with his hands behind his back. I swig some more of the Lucozade.

"What happened to him, Kim?"

"Gasoline," I say.

Mr. Book squeezes his temples with his hand. Pulls on one of his long eyebrow hairs.

"Later today, in court," he says, "we'll just deal with Quentin Sumner."

"Is he dead?" I arsts.

"No. He's in a coma, on a life-support system."

A passing policewoman lets Mr. Book out of the cell and lights my cigarette for me.

"I'll see you later, Kim," he says through the bars. "They'll probably take you to Holloway straight after. Do you want me to notify your friends and family?"

"I don't want to know," Robertson says. "I really don't want to know. How was it though, in prison?"

I think about it, no one has ever asked me before.

"It was dangerous. Very, very dangerous."

There was something not right about me being there. I can smell fruit? When I open one eye her hand is there, offering a knife blade with a slice of fruit on it.

"Pawpaw," she says.

I haul everything up to sit propped sideways against a post. Get lost in my own fingers and lips and pawpaw juice.

"Fucking hell it's heaven, Lynn," I say. "Where did you get it from?"

"Arusha." Another slice arrives, goodness on a knife edge. She is my friend but she doesn't know me. It's a start, I suppose.

"Do you want a banana?" she says.

"I'd kill for one," I say.

"Would you? Would you kill me for it?"

"Only if I was really hungry. Have you come down direct from Arusha?"

"I was offered a lift with a Franciscan monk. Comfortable Land Rover."

There's no such thing.

"There was a tent on the roof rack and he let me have it. Dar es Salaam was miles of a dog-leg in the wrong direction."

"Fair enough," I say.

"We had the most amazing journey down through the middle of Tanzania. The people were just so friendly."

I nods. Heaven and hell is same place, Africa has learned me that.

"Have we got any water, Lynn?"

She shakes her head. I look across to No Man's Land, kerosene night life moving about. Lace up my boots, wincing as scabs on my knuckles crack. I stand up in installments like evolution, with muscle knots and stomach cramps and a couple of cracked ribs.

"Remember the Mountains of the Moon?" I say.

She laughs. I think about the two steps down from the porch and the movements required. Make a total mess of them.

"Do you think it's safe?" she calls. "Should we go together?"

"Stay with the bags, Lynn, I think it will be OK."

Nobody in No Man's Land is going to want to tangle with me. Even this illness is sick of me now. I feel much better. Much better actually. Wired to within an inch of my life. Half blind with tiredness. The stars are in my face, dropping into my open mouth.

Judy Garland nights. Bassey. Sinatra–tosser.

Malawi side. Malawi. I'm in Africa. I'm still free. I'm still half alive, scuffing over the lorry park. An African nightbird calls out *careful.*

Finale and Reprise

The lamplight puddles in the wet-looking floor. My frozen face and fingers sense serious heat, apparently there's a problem with the heating thermostat in the basement. The apartment is still vacant like a stage set with painted miles and a promising sky, a huddle of floor cushions and some candles on a low table. Everything that can shine, does. The rent is paid up to date. The windows are open, heat escaping from the apartment steams into the cold outside air; drifts and disappears through the bare arms of trees. The pub across the road is boarded up. No phone box below. It's a filthy evening, darkness lightened by sleet. The woman in the mirror startles me, blows out of the glass in colored cloths and white pajamas. Damp, filthy, white pajamas. She is as brown as a year in Africa. The sun has bleached her teeth; nutter's hair: hacked here and there and backcombed by a side wind, salt and sand and thorns sewn in it. Cold wet nose like a dog. There's a letter for me from Scotland, Robertson I presume.

Danny Fish left me some supplies. There's an electric cooker and a fridge, from the Sofa Project he said. I make coffee. No Techno downstairs, just sleet slapping on the open windows. The apartment is hot, seriously hot. I take off my walking boots and socks. My feet are the color of teak. The Skeleton Coast has polished my toenails brilliant white like nine opals. Out of habit I check between my toes for jungle jiggers. No brown fleas buried; no pus pockets of maggots. I left a chink out of my right shin on the good ship *Ilala*, in Malawi, five months ago but the scab still isn't ready to drop. The photographs are all developed, I sort the twenty-seven packets of pictures in sequence.

Kenya: Masai Mara. Lakes: Naivasha, Nakuru, Baringo, Turkana.

Mombasa, the steamy turquoise coast. Uganda. Mountains of the Moon. Moss and waterfall nymph, the pictures of Robertson came out well; I'll write and send them to her. Lake Victoria; Murchison Falls. Chimpanzees at Fort Portal. Rainforest mountain gorillas: I wanted to scream "Run, run, run for your lives!" I was standing there with a camera but it could have been a gun.

Zaire. Volcanoes and refugees. The body reassembled in the grave I dug, couldn't find the head or the left leg. Couldn't find it.

Tanzania.

A car door slams.

"Sit down," I say.

Ah, Malawi. The good ship *Ilala* was sailing through a blue-black galaxy, full of stars. The storm didn't give any warning, it didn't come from any of the compass points, it came up out of the water and swallowed the *Ilala* whole. The cargo came loose and storming seemed to have a mission to kill us. Waves crashing onto the deck picked us up and threw us. We just missed a hundred certain deaths. Then the storm sunk and disappeared back below the surface. We were black and blue and bleeding. Neither of us could walk on land for a week, *Swashbuckled*, Robertson called us. Even then we couldn't get to land and had to wade waist-deep through a mile of water hyacinth with our backpacks on our heads. Malawi. The lake and the sky, they loved each other. There was something all-consuming about the blue, the language of blue. The blue rocks and the blue lizards, the blue water and the blue fishes, the blue enameled Fabergé crabs with little gold-rimmed glasses and lilac claws. Baobab trees and swathes of wild flowers.

Zimbabwe: Victoria Falls. Yellow irises and rainbows.

Botswana: Bushmen in the Kalahari. Okavango Delta.

Namibia: Sossusvlei, the apricot moonscape. Oryx tracks. Etosha National Park: mirages and salt pans. This photograph is the one. Like someone emptied an ark in a puddle. A car door slams.

"Sit down."

Fish River Canyon. Diamond fields and ghost towns. Skeleton Coast. South Africa. The batch of photos I want, the last film. Stellenbosch: châteaux this and that, wine tasting and duck ponds galore. It's only three days since I was there.

Their home was beautiful, a white-painted farmhouse in the Cape style. The driveway was eight miles long, level and straight between acres of ripening grapes. Even when I was some way from it I could see a figure standing in the middle of the road ahead and knew it was Irene. She couldn't have known I would arrive that day, but something had made her leave her garden and look down the lane with her hand shading her eyes. She walked a little way to meet me. I hadn't expected to cry but her face, the posy of English spring flowers, had not wilted. Me, I could not forget her eyes. She called me Kim, of course, and as I bent to take her welcome hand and as I cried and knelt to kiss it, the perfume was there on the wrist, hers, mine. It would linger through all time. I didn't recognize the bones of Quentin. His slap of wet-look hair didn't quite cover the scars, where surgeons rebuilt the top of his head. One eye was blind but the other one knew me. Memory kept hearing the sound of suffering he made, while I held his brain in with my hands until the ambulance arrived. One evening after dinner when Irene and I walked down to the dam I asked her what it was that had made her disbelieve the verdict. She said Quentin had been heartbroken when a girl called Gwen dumped him. He was struggling at the casino to keep his feelings contained. In the weeks before he was shot he had written in his diary seven different references about how kind *Kim* had been to him.

Memory kept hearing the sound of my lungs tearing. When Quentin was in the hands of the ambulance men, I ran. Heath and Gwen had disappeared. I ran. I ran. I left behind my coat, with my diamond in the lining. November the 5th: fireworks and bangers. Thirteen years ago.

"Sit down."

I fan the South African photographs on the floor.

Dear Louise,

Hello dear friend—I hope the end of your journey was wonderful and you saw mind blowing things. I'm f----g freezing. You have never been far from my mind and I've thought of you lots but the last three weeks have been HARD—emotionally etc, etc. After learning how to feel good about myself while traveling and learning to stay calm–I come home and I'm back to square ONE–God have the tears rolled–felt totally unable to cope–the first few days were OK–novel–baths at my brothers, CDs to listen to–went swimming with my mum, bought some Nike Air running shoes + sports bras–it was OK. My brother's new girlfriend was lovely. My mum picked me up from the airport–unexpectedly–but we never talked–no understanding–no *real* communication + she started on me again. Tried to bite my tongue. I got panicky–jobs, my life, self-confidence. Yuk. Bloody awful–my dad can't cope with me being sensitive and emotional (reminds him of my mum I think) so he was rather abrupt with me–my stepmum was supportive–fed me–made me tea and bought me Rescue Remedy. Well I had a grim 12 days–went for runs–sorted my gear in the loft and panicked about loads of applications I'd rung up for–my word processor broke and generally I had to call on all my resources to keep the fear down–*not* the same person that had such a wonderful time with you.
Anyhow I'm now at my friend's in a cardboard box room with no space to swing a cat + surrounded by bikes–my gear and all her spare stuff. Not v. good. Also I don't think her boyfriend wants me here. I've written off applications for teaching jobs. I'm trying to change my thought patterns–fuck it's hard–all my self-hate lack of approval, belittling thoughts, feelings of jealously, loneliness + fear well up continuously. I just feel SO sad. BUT I am trying. Christ people

> don't realize how hard it is to get up + face each day + pretend to be happy. But I am trying. Found some anti depressants + I'm taking 1/2 a tablet at night, but afraid to go to the doctor's, all the teaching posts are subject to a medical report from the doctor's + they ask if you have mental illness.
>
> All my love Lynn XXXXXXXX

I've had a bath. The other letter is six months old, from Tim, to tell me that funding was withdrawn and the pottery has closed.

"Sit down."

I'm back at the photos again. Margaret and Vernon Pennsylvania USA and me on safari. The Masai Mara, the spin and swirl of it, projected, superimposed. Clouds created the flashing, the strobe, zebras know. I was sure that there weren't any elephants there, they're big things, if there were elephants you would definitely see them, but then from a ridge I understood that elephants are six inches tall and china blue in the yellow grass, they come and go in numbers, in hundreds, and the whole threshing force of it bowled me over and over. There's photographs of us in the campsite at Samburu. Trees full of monkeys. Lake Nakuru's million flamingoes, acres and acres of pink, flapping and high-stepping. I remember I remembered my mother. You couldn't imagine a show like it.

"Yes, Nigel, yes! From the top please, Philip."

Mr. and Mrs. Trickett is on the sofa and Sheba and she int allowed, they got hair on them. I put the tray down careful nice.

"You're a credit," Mr. Trickett says.

"Get down Sheba."

"It's all right."

"She don't like *Carousel*," I says.

"Stop. Stop!" Mum says. "What are you building there, Nigel—eh? A little shithouse? Out the back, a little fucking shack? If you were a RICH MAN, Nigel, if you were a WEALTHY MAN."

Mr. Trickett does noughts and crosses with his finger in the velvit cushion then he rubs it out.

"A bungalow now, is it? A prefab? Listen to the words! Listen to the words, Nigel, Great Big House. GREAT. BIG. HOUSE. WITH ROOMS. BY THE DOZ-EN . . . I'm only seeing two rooms, Nigel."

Mrs. Trickett picks lumps of hair off her skirt and tries to stick them back on Sheba sactly where they come out from. I sit back down on the floor with my pile of pink and frilly, pick up the needle, gain.

"Crêpe paper," I says.

"How many aprons are there?" Mrs. Trickett says.

Don't know how many.

"Boys is having neck chiefs," I says. I weaves the needle in and out and push the pink frill long the cotton. "And Stetsons."

Mr. and Mrs. Trickett is looking at me.

"Blister," I says. "From pinking scissors. Mum got one sactly same."

"Now build it! A GREAT BIG HOUSE, Nigel. Philip! Stop tinkering, when I'm trying to think!"

Pip keeps on playing the overture for *Carousel*, case he can mind Mum back to the right show. Mr. Trickett yawns.

"I spects you is ready for bedtime?" I says.

"Well, it is nearly three hours past Nigel's bedtime." Mrs. Trickett checks her watch. "I think it really is enough, now," she says. "He is only nine; I think you should fetch him, dear."

I shakes my head. Lucky, Mrs. Trickett is talking to Mr. Trickett and he stands up. He coughs, checks all his pockets, goes down the hall sideways, past all the pink and white crêpe-paper aprons and butterfly bows, hanging from hangers on the banisters. Knock, knock, knocks. Mr. Trickett coughs. Sheba covers her eyes with her paw. Pip slides off the piana, I spects his fingers is bleeding.

"Dad!" Nigel says. "I forgot you were here!"

"We've been here six hours, son," Mr. Trickett says.

Memory saw Pip running up a ramp, into the school assembly hall with sand in a wheelbarrow. Was it me, was it us, with rakes spreading it out?

Is it deep enough, will the chorus kick it up? Lunchtime is the dress rehearsal and every kid in the school is outside on the netball courts, dressed in pink and white crêpe paper, and they have to be careful case they tear it. Am I five or six? My badge says *Producer*, Pip's says *Musical Director.* My mother, our mother, in jeans and a knotted shirt, flies up two flights of school stairs with a megaphone in her hand. Leans out of the upstairs windows.

"READY?" she says.

You couldn't imagine a show like it. Looking at photos of flamingoes on Kenya's Lake Nakuru I remember Vernon Pennsylvania USA.

Soda. No, not drinking soda.

"It's a real alkaline mineral, they use it in glass-making. The only thing that can grow in the lake is soda adapt-ated algae. The flamingoes have gotten a way to get the algae from the lake without actually drinking the caustic water."

You couldn't imagine a show like it. I remember I remembered my mother.

"I CAN'T HEAR YOU!"

WHEN YOU WALK THROUGH A STORM . . .

The doorbell blasting shatters the past. Peter. My skin knows it's him. Woman in the mirror stabs out a cigarette in the ashtray. I press the intercom button; the main entrance door slams below and he comes flying up the stairs. Who is the fairest of them all?

"There you are," I say.

The mossy smell of him tips back my head. He sniffs air beside my neck, what's there, on my neck, in the hall, in my apartment? Man smell? One eyebrow queries the timing.

"You look well," he says.

"You've just missed Danny. He took care of the apartment while I was away."

"Nice bloke," Pete says. "I called around a while ago to see if you were back."

"He's moved just up the hill," I say. "We're neighbors now."

Pete's shoes splash in the shine on the floor, step around my empty backpack, the few things I brought back from Africa. He sits down on the floor cushions, next to my camera and the Stellenbosch pictures. Puts down his keys and cigarettes.

"I thought you might have married a Masai or a Zulu," he says.

Habit takes me in to the kitchen to put the kettle on. Lean my forehead on the wall to get control of breathing. In and out. Hear my heart flicking over and him fingering photographs. When I bring the coffee in, he stops looking at the pictures to watch me walk. He looks at the cup, sitting firm on the saucer. All the way to the floor beside him. He cocks his head. The radiator is booming out heat, the open windows are slapped by sleet. His eyes listen, his lips, his skin detects some wind of change, in the room. Danny Fish's guitar is still here, some chords on a scrap of paper. Pete lights a cigarette. A tremble shows up in the flame. The pack skids across the floor toward me, with the matches on the top. It is Zanzibar hot. He parks his cigarette in the ashtray, pulls a moss-green sweater over his head. It leaves his hair tugged. He rolls the cuffs back loosely on his blousy shirt.

The fridge starts to hum. A car rushes up the hill spraying sludge in the gutter. We look at the white telephone on the floor; Danny has had it installed. A wonderment. Who would phone me? I tip my head back against the wall. An outside air breathes in. A small gasp escapes me. He looks at the woman in the mirror.

"No rattle," he says.

He picks up a handful of photos, the yellow-gold sequence; sun rising on the swell of ocean. The Transkei. Coffee Bay.

"The dolphins and gannets follow the sardine run along the coast. It's an annual spectacle."

He hasn't heard of such a thing.

"Are you on a boat?"

"A fishing boat, the dolphins just kept coming, hundreds and hundreds and hundreds of them."

Now he's holding the Stellenbosch wine lands, the jeweled colors of ripening vines.

"Nice people?" he says.

"That's Quentin and his mum, Irene."

He looks closer at the picture.

"How is he?" The loaded question is light.

"Quentin? He's confused about a lot of things," I say. "Absolutely sure on others."

The woman in the mirror looks at me. Pete looks at her.

"I've always loved you," he says.

I feel sick and stand up to go to the bathroom. He follows me up. His hand on my wrist whips me back, he tries to clamp me against his chest and I hammers on it. When my arms are useless and I can't stand up he buries me carefully into the wall. He's angry, really angry.

"I've been trying," he says.

I thrash.

"I've been trying to kiss you for twelve years." His jaw is hard in my cheek. "You *always* turn your face away."

"Can you stand me up please?" I say. "I feel like a carpet roll."

I turn my face away. Twelve years. I was in prison for ten of those. He goes in the lounge, picks up his keys. I feel sick and faint.

"You don't even know my name." I put my head down between my knees. Have to sit down. I have to sit.

"Whatever else you think, I have always loved you," he says. "And I know, I know that you have always loved me. You loved me so much, you even went to prison for me."

What a wonderment. The wrongness of it. I didn't have my coat. I didn't have any money or shoes. I didn't have any nerve left, there wasn't anywhere to go. I didn't have any nerve left. Underneath the railway arches I was sitting on a sub-zero fortune, every passing pimp stopped to tell me so, to help me out with a place to stay, with a few thousand little credit card crimes and a shoplifting spree. A little start-up tab from the Crack boss.

"I didn't go to prison for *you*, Pete."

"You knew. You knew," he says.

"I had no reason to link you with Heath. No motive."

"You didn't see me?"

"No, I heard the gunshot; thought Heath had let a firework off in the house. I didn't see anything."

"It's good to talk to you," he says.

"So talk. Tell me about the witch's house, Pete."

He flinches as my words thwap like a crossbow bolt into the tree beside his ear.

"Quentin tells me you and Heath go back a long way, all the way back to tuck shops, all the way back to the woods."

Pete cuts his thumb pad with an imaginary knife, presses the scar there on a small thumb of air.

"We're brothers, me and Heath," he says, "blood brothers."

"So why this time, why were you *gunning* for him?"

"He fucked me over for the robbery money." He picks up a match to chew on, looks up in the corner as if something magical is occurring there. "Heath's instinct was so quick he anticipated the bullet. I didn't see Quentin there, tied in the chair behind him."

"Time to go," I say.

He didn't quite hear me. The fridge changes key.

Hum-hum.

Hum-hum.

It is a wonderment to him.

"Are you sure?" says the woman in the mirror.

I look at him. He looks at me. My head is going to explode. My heart.

"Bye," I say.

He picks up his keys. One last look back. A pause. Am I sure? I nod. He lets himself out and closes the door.

I run to the door and open it. Down the stairwell I can see his hand sliding along on the banister.

"Peter!" I call down.

He comes back up, four steps at a time. I push the gold canister into his hands.

"Take your *dad* with you," I say.

Recovery positions.

... THOUGH YOUR DREAMS BE TOSSED AND BLOWN ...

Listen.

Listen to George, Old George, kneeling down in the Grand Hall. George holding my shoulders so tightly and his face flaming and his eyes welling, trying so hard to impart courage. Listen to my heart stop. Memory plays the wheels of the trolley, like a tram on the parquet flooring. I didn't see them cut him down from the hammer-beamed rafters where they found him hanging. I saw his empty body go past on a trolley. I felt the life die inside me.

Listen.

It starts to rain. It starts to hammer on the grand windowpanes, starts to drip from light fittings, the hammer-beamed roof starts to rock. In the kingdom of heaven, every angel heaves, every angel on every ceiling starts to sob and weep. Every cherub starts to wail. Tears splash down William Shakespeare's face. Elisabeth the First dabs her cheek. Thomas Holloway starts to cry and the ancient Greeks; monsters bite their own cheeks and weep. The dinner ladies and the gardeners weep.

And George. Old George.

The Angel Michael turns, with his wings up and his arms up weeping. Angels rain down on us, weeping. And Fiddler and Mick. And Leonard and Lizzie. Arthur comes away from the wall. Amy drops down on her knees. Shut-up waves a stick up at angels, shut-up, shut-up, shut-up, she says. Anton left an envelope for me, said *Mitten* on it. The brilliant cut stone dropped into my hand like a tear. And glistened. Everyone's tears filled my eyes.

I went home to die.

Storm flashes and water falls, thunderous in the dark corridor. The East Wing heaves and shifts and sinks deeper into the mud. I slam my door on life and lie down on my bed to die. The corridor starts to fill and floods rush in under my door. Beech leaves swirl around my bed legs and water slaps at the skirting boards. The kingdom of heaven rocks and cries and falls to pieces but nothing can move me.

Listen.

Ding—

Autumn turns to winter. Everything dies. My eyes roll, with the night and the day and the winter glory skies. Siberia howls through gaps in the planks. Snowflakes can't settle in the room, not quite green not quite white. Michael brings me food on a tray. His ice skates whoosh down the iced-up corridor. Sheets of ice beside the bed splinter under his blades. My head rolls way from his hand, from the spoon, from his eyes, my cracked tongue pushes the food back out over my cracked bottom lip. He leaves the food and the rats tip the spoon, clattering in the bowls and gnawing at the soft rot. Gasp how close I am.

Ding—

Winter turns to spring. I smell the linseed and lavender oil. I starts to hear him calling. Blossom collects in my eye sockets, sticks to my blistered lips. I turn as thin as an idea, a morning-glory feeling, I'm happy. Gain. Laughing at the clouds, high up above. Angels are crying, glad it's time. I reach up for an angel's hand.

Ding—

Somewhere true in the middle of blue.

Ding—

Mitten. The angels know my name.

But it is Michael, come to say good-bye, winders of light rub into my eyes. I sees Michael's angel face, one last time with tears and twisted lips, trying to swallow something too bitter.

"I've brought these people to help you," he says.

I see then over his shoulder the solid shapes of strangers. One face comes closer and I know it, the sweet, sweet smell of the horses on him.

"Dear God," Bernard says.

My lungs refuse air, my ribs is an empty bird cage. My voice cracks with my lips.

"This is my place, Bernard," I says. "I wants to stay here and die."

"The baby came too soon," Michael says. "It's in the sink. Nothing to do with me."

Angels come down from the ceiling and stand all around me.

"We're going to take you out," they say.

My backbone lifts up off the bed.

"Hold on."

"Hold on."

We sit in the car at the traffic lights.

"They're very nice people," Maud says, "a very nice family." She sits watching the lights change, must be one color she likes. Social workers int fit to drive; I learned that much.

"They're all looking forward to you coming." She goes on red.

Maud took over my case from Sarah Waters, who lost me for three and a half years and never got me the two right sneakers. I look down at the two left ones, falling to bits with the heels trod down. Maud indicates with the winder wipers.

"One of the girls is just fourteen, the same age as you, so you'll have lots to talk about. I think the others are seven and five. When I spoke to Mrs. Smith earlier she said they'd baked you a cake. I think you might be going to Wimbledon on Sunday, Center Court, strawberries and cream. Lucky you."

Here we is freezing in a June cold-sack. House with the weeping willow and a blue Peugeot estate under the carport. Bastards to fix. Here they is, all waiting on the lawn. Mr. and Mrs. Smith. Hope and Faith and Charity. They got names from out of fairy tale. It don't matter which one is which, all the same, white-haired princesses with light blue pinafore dresses and braces on their teef. Useless legs, can't hardly hold them up.

Maud holds me out like I was material for them to see. I don't say nothing.

"Let us not all stand here staring," Mrs. Smith says.

"It's not going very well, is it?" the little one says.

I look at the sky. At the lawn. At cars passing on the getaway road. I look at these people.

"You're most welcome, Catherine," Mrs. Smith says.

"Yes," he says. "On behalf of all of us we join together with thanks and welcome you to our happy home. Now should it be Catherine, or Cathy?"

Puffed-up little twat.

"Or Katie?"

"Or Kit?"

"Or Kitty?"

"Kitty-Kat, no," the littlest says.

"Is it spelled with a K or a C?" arsts the middlest.

"I don't know," I shrug, "with a C, I think, C for Car, C for Cunt."

"That'll do," Mr. Smith says. "I'll not have you bring that filth into my house; you can go back to where you came from."

"I'd love to, Mr. Smith," I says, "but they won't let me."

"We're not off on a very good foot," Mrs. Smith says. "Come in, Catherine, come inside and let's get you settled in."

"When you've got three girls in one room, another girl is neither here nor there," Mrs. Smith says. She squeezes around the bunk bed and the single bed and my camp bed in the middle. "There!" She leaves handprints in my new fluffed pillows.

"We made this space for you to put your things." Littlest bites her lip.

"Now where is your bag? Did we leave it in the sitting room? In the hall?" Mrs. Smith goes off searching. I lean on the door frame, looks at all the posters.

"We love Abba," Littlest says. "We do, don't we? We love Abba."

Suddenly all three of them is up on the bed, snapping their fingers and doing a dance and singing something about Waterloo. Wonder sometimes if I'm real. When they finish I'm sposed to clap.

"Do you know, I think Maud must have driven off with your things? I'll ring Social Services now and get her to bring them back."

"There int a bag, Mrs. Smith," I says.

"You don't have your own personal things with you?"

"I int got personal things," I says.

"I see," she says. "I see, I see, I see. Now why don't you and I make a cup of tea and go and sit in the front room and get to know each other a little bit?"

I turn the bright cut stone in my pocket, follow her to the kitchen.

"How are you feeling now, Catherine?" Mrs. Smith says. "Maud tells me you're a very, very lucky girl."

But the littlest comes in the kitchen.

"Shall I show you everything?" she says.

I shrug, why not. The back door is open. There's a small grass garden with a plain high fence. They got a tennis ball, on a string, on a post, Mr. Smith whacking it around, Biggest missing.

"Dad," she says, all loop-da-loop.

Middlest is trying to skip but can't.

"Garage," Littlest says.

Three pink bikes, two with stabilizers. Big doll's house, all the furniture in the attic. Paddling pool. Trampoline. Roller skates. Workbench, loads of tools hung up on the wall, saws and drills, rows of chisels and sizes of hammers, a full metric set of spanners, none of them done a job in their life. They've been drawed around in black, so you know the shape of something missing.

"If it's raining, Catherine, you can come and play in here," Littlest says. She picks up a baby doll from a pram, wants me to hold it but I can't. We go back in the garden. The tennis ball is still whacking around, now with the middlest.

"Dad!" she says.

"Your turn, Catherine," Mr. Smith says. "We might as well see what you're made of."

I was only there ten days. Sometimes wonder who broke who. The school didn't ask my mother again, after "You'll Never Walk Alone." And now I'm here, off the coach walking down Buckingham Palace Road, following signs to Victoria Station and the Underground. The air is so cold it's granulated. Head full of multi-purposes and snot. The arcade coming into the station reminds me it's the week before Christmas. One thing at a time.

District line—Westbound—South Kensington.

The Underground is warm and packed with Saturday-morning Christmas shoppers. They've used the photograph on the posters, advertising the exhibition. I go up past them on the escalator. Apparently the printers have had trouble reproducing the red. *Arresting* is the name of the picture, coined off the top of Tony Gloucester Road's head, when he was filling in the entry form. He's a film cameraman, works for the BBC Nature Department. He came around again last night. Stayed over. Still don't know what he looks like. I feel ever so unlikely, like a terrible mistake. We were doing all right til we got to his dick. My guts flutter just thinking about it. He was OK about it, well, as OK as a bloke could be, opened the windows, got me some air, put a blanket around my shoulders, fetched the bucket, case.

"Sorry, Tony," I said.

He gave me a white gardenia that turned into a tissue.

"I've never had anyone react in this way before," he said.

"I'm ever so sorry," I said. "It's a . . . hhuck! . . . dick thing and fannies are . . . hhuck! Out of the fucking question."

Has to turn my face from the memory. Remember to breathe. Think instead about the pavement passing under my feet. Think about railings. Bars.

This is the place. I stand and smoke two cigarettes on the steps. I take off Tim's anorak and stuff it in a carrier bag. A security man inside the building glances in the bag and lets me through. I wait in the long line for general inquiries. Tiredness adjusts my ears to the echoing din of kids and dinosaurs.

"I have an appointment, eleven o'clock," I say, "with Chris Plum."

Someone takes me to him, through the Jurassic Period and a gallery full of precious stones. We turn down some stairs and then down again and through some corridors with coded doors.

He's a quietly spoken man, used to handling fragile things. It's been so interesting. The vault is cool and dimly lit, just one spotlight over a metal table. He slides a shallow drawer from a cabinet and puts it gently under the light. It's under glass but I'm scared to breathe. A tiny label names it.

"January the 10th 1797. Mozambique." Mr. Plum's glasses blow up his eyes, like a pair of duck eggs. "Last seen two hundred years ago, almost exactly."

"I'm amazed, Mr. Plum," I say.

The Camera magazine is on the table, *Arresting* is on the cover. The other twenty-three photographs from the same film are more interesting to him. Two are particularly sharp and close up on individuals. There's no denying the sameness of it, its tufty head and swallowtail and blue-black iridescence.

"Very importantly, can you remember when?"

"December the 17th," I say. "My second day in Africa. My first roll of film. Everyone else photographed the view."

"Unbelievable," he says. "Thrilling."

"They disappeared as quickly as they came," I say, "in a series of rapid blinks."

Starts crying. Don't know how come.

I leave the museum with Mr. Plum; he only works half-day on Saturday. He wraps his scarf around his neck and claps his gloved hands together. I wrap my arms around my ribs.

"Keep the photos, Mr. Plum," I say.

"I can send them back to you?"

"Keep them, Happy Christmas with love from me."

"Well thank you," he says and nods. "Are you going to the Tube?"

"No, I've got to go around the corner, to *The Camera* magazine's exhibition. The launch lunch. I've got to shake some hands and get my prize."

"Is it worth having?"

"According to a friend of mine, it's the best camera ever made."

He nods.

"And, a paid freelance assignment to go back to Africa," I say. "Fuck that. Nearly killed me the first time."

Makes Mr. Plum smile.

"Bye," I say.

In three strides he's swallowed whole in the pavement rush. I put Tim's anorak on and stuff the carrier bag in the pocket. I'm an Englishwoman, I've decided. Even without leaves, I know the name of everything. Sycamore and London plane. Size you can get your head around. Stepping off the plane at Heathrow I thought I had so much African heat in my marrow it would glow in me for the rest of my life. But here I am with frozen blocks for feet. I ask a passerby for directions. Ask four people, none of them lives here.

It's a very posh side street. This is the place. Glass-fronted. I cross over the road and crouch down opposite between some bins, to smoke a cigarette out of the wind. Some people arrive in a taxi and the doorman opens it for them. So tired. I close my eyes and rock a minute on my heels. When the cigarette is finished I fold a chewing gum into my mouth, something for my nerves to chew on. I take Tim's anorak off and put it in the carrier bag and get up and cross the road. At the top of the steps, through the glass door, can see a party in the foyer. Christmas party dresses, yards of white linen and sparkling glasses; tinkling piano; scarlet pompoms and black butterflies, exploding out of every wall. My booming heart. I walk up the steps. The doorman is a solid thing standing in my way.

"Come on now," he says. "Back down. We don't want your sort in here."

I don't say anything. Just chew, produce the folded invitation from the top of my sock.

I don't know how they could choose a winner. My guts are churning now, watching the clock. The best camera ever made is on my hip like a sharpshooter, seems fangled-dangled to me. Can't remember anyone's name, everyone looks the same. The wine makes me shudder. And this creep. He's so pissed he can hardly stand up, bow tie on the wonk and the back of his shirt hanging out. Staring at me.

"*What?*" I lift an eyebrow.

He toasts me with a wine glass swaying with his knees dipping.

"I'm trying to make my mind up," he says, "if you are actually attractive or not."

"Probably not," I say.

Every day I meet a candidate.

I should leave, if I'm going to get the seven ten to Chester. People are starting to leave. Everyone is red-faced, on the occasion, on the wine, in the glow *Arresting* makes. Butterflying eyes. I find the main man to say thanks and good-bye.

"You're off," he says. "We're all going on to party in Piccadilly if you'd like to come?"

"Thanks," I say, "but I have to go, I'm meeting my brother later, I haven't seen him for twenty-five years."

Baby Grady didn't want to communicate with me. He asked the Salvation Army Missing Person Service not to make contact again on my behalf. Philip, he's a biochemist. Went to university. Married a girl he met there. I'd like to ask him if he knows how I got to be *Catherine Clark*, if he can remember the man who went and registered my birth. I'm an auntie it turns out, two nephews and a niece. Thomas, Lulu and Jake. In the photograph he sent, they seem complete, with each other and the swing in the garden. They live in Chester. Have always lived in Chester. I can't see myself in their picture.

"Yes please," says the ticket man.

"A single please," I say.

The tannoy is blaring. My nose is dripping.

"A single. Where to?"

"Sorry?"

"Where do you want to travel to?"

The tannoy is blaring.

"Sorry, I can't hear very well?"

"Where do you want to travel to?

"Portsmouth," I say.

Encore

Portsmouth, depart from Platform 9, eight minutes. Tim's anorak is wrapped twice around me. I'm shivering Siberian on the platform bench. A pigeon with one foot asks me for something to eat.

"Sorry," I say.

It shrugs, goes off to ask everyone else. There's a big crowd on the opposite platform, spread out and minding the gap. A Christmas crowd, with gifts and luggage and hats and scarves, all knocking against the cold. I open the zip on the case and lift my prize camera out. Super-zoom over the tracks. Viewfinder. Pan left along the platform on the other side looking for a picture in the crowd. And there she is—what a picture. An old friend. Click. Unmistakable. My old friend.

Streaming ribbon of corn-colored hair.

And the sleek train on that side, snaking in to take them away. I'm up. I'm running, the camera bag banging on my hip. There's a blockage of Portsmouth people with prams at the barrier. I hurdle over the railing, sprint the distance to the stairs, fly them with the thwump of train doors slamming below. Hammer across the footbridge looking down at the train's roof, and the empty platform and the whistle-blower.

"Hey!" I scream. I leap the stairs in three bounds. "Hey!" The whistle blows. The last guard steps up into his train. I hop and step and jump right up into his chest.

"You're lucky!" he says.

I'm hanging off his sleeve.

"I'm a sporting person," I rasp. "I like. To give. A train. A chance to get away. Without me."

I sway through the silent carriage, checking each seat, through carriages A, B, C, D, E, F and G. Clickerty-clacking, I rattle through the buffet car, through H and I, J, K. Climb over an army camped between compartment doors. Now the train is flying, L, M, N, O, P.

"End of the line," a voice in a sleeping bag informs me. I turn around, go back. A woman in the window glass looks over me. She's looking for someone.

"At ease," I say, but the army shifts its knees again.

Wonder if I'm mental.

"Ticket please," says a chirpy chappy.

I slide the ticket from my trouser pocket. Scan the backs of heads. Scan around all the tables.

"I think you're on the wrong train, love," he says. "This ticket says Portsmouth."

Scan every seat facing.

"Either you've got the wrong ticket or you're on the wrong train. Did you want Portsmouth?"

"Portsmouth," I say. "Why would I want to go to Portsmouth? This is the train I want. Where's this train going to?"

"Calais."

Surprises me. I count the cash from my pocket.

"Looks like you're having one-way," he says.

"Thank you," I say.

Sway back through the alphabet, stop at the buffet counter.

"Yes!" says the spotty lad.

"Can I have a carton of milk please?" I say.

Between D and C I open the milk, swig and sway through B and A.

"Hello again," the guard says. "Lost something?"

I spin about. Doors slide open and closed behind me. Calais. I lean rocking by the toilets, on the rocking carriage join. Look through glass doors to the back of the train. Through glass doors to the front, can't remember which way I've just walked. I feel for the butterfly. The toilet door opens beside me. Uh-huh. Here she is. I put my hand out, squeeze her shoulder. A ribbon of corn-colored hair swings around to face me.

Doesn't know me.

"I'm sorry," I say. "I don't know where you got it from, or how long ago, but you're wearing my coat and I want it back."

I have a swig of the milk. Lick my lip. Can hardly wait for what happens next.

CREDITS

VIKING PENGUIN PRODUCTION: NEW YORK

PRODUCER/GAMBLER: Carole DeSanti
BACKSTAGE/FRONT OF HOUSE: Christopher Russell
REPRESENTATION: Zoë Pagnamenta
COVER DESIGN: Eric White
AUDIO EFFECTS: Nina Wakeford

I. J. KAY PRODUCTION: MADE IN ENGLAND

ORIGINAL SCRIPT STAGE MANAGED AND LIT by Anthea, Becky, Jason, Jenni, Pam, Richard F., and Sam

SPECIAL AGENT/VISONARY: Anna Webber
PRINCE OF PUBLISHING/KING OF COPY: Dan Franklin
BACKSTAGE/FRONT OF HOUSE: Tom Avery, Kathy Fry, Sally Sargeant, and Neil Bradford
FOREIGN RIGHTS: Jessica Craig and Zoe Ross
ANGELS: Arts and Humanities Research Council Arts Council South West

EARLY PROMPTS: Tim, Nicola, Tricia, and Richard K.

PROPERTIES/CATERING/TECHNICIAN/DRESSER/SHAMAN/RESEARCHER/SUPPLIER OF HERBS AND WORDS: Johnny Meadows

GASP IN THE LIBRARY/LAUGHS: Daniel Brookman
AIR IN THE KENYAN HIGHLANDS: Karen Blixen's *Out of Africa*
BACKGROUND STRINGS: Thom Thomas-Watkins and Richie Taylor

DOCTOR/FAN CLUB: Keith
BONE-CRACKER: Martin
ALTERNATIVE MEDICINE: Chris
CHAUFFEUR/AMBULANCE DRIVER: Jamie Nelson
COAL/GAS/SOLAR POWER: Digger
PEACE: Good peoples of K and A

MY THANKS TO THE CAST AND ALL OF THE ABOVE

Songs

Lulu's musical renditions are drawn from the following works.

"Wouldn't It Be Loverly": Alan Jay Lerner and Frederick Loewe

"Swanee": music by George Gershwin, lyrics by Irving Caesar

"Toot, Toot, Tootsie! (Goodbye)": Gus Kahn, Ernie Erdman, and Dan Russo

"My Mammy": music by Walter Donaldson, lyrics by Sam M. Lewis and Joe Young

"Baubles, Bangles & Beads": Robert Wright and George Forrest

"Willkommen": John Kander and Fred Ebb

"Padam, Padam": Henri Contet and Norbert Glanzberg

"Cabaret": John Kander and Fred Ebb

"Summertime": George Gershwin and DuBose Heyward

"We Saw the Sea": Irving Berlin

"Bali Hai": music by Richard Rodgers, lyrics by Oscar Hammerstein II

"Happy Talk": music by Richard Rodgers, lyrics by Oscar Hammerstein II

"Something's Coming": music by Leonard Bernstein, lyrics by Stephen Sondheim

"Money": John Kander and Fred Ebb

"Rockin' All Over the World": John Fogerty

"Stranger in Paradise": Robert Wright and George Forrest

"Edelweiss": music by Richard Rodgers, lyrics by Oscar Hammerstein II

"Take That Look Off Your Face": music by Andrew Lloyd Webber, lyrics by Don Black

"The Phantom of the Opera": music by Andrew Lloyd Webber, lyrics by Charles Hart and Richard Stilgoe, with additional lyrics by Mike Batt

"I Caint Say No": music by Richard Rodgers, lyrics by Oscar Hammerstein II

"All I Ask of You": Andrew Lloyd Webber

"The Surrey With A Fringe On The Top": music by Richard Rodgers, lyrics by Oscar Hammerstein II

"Feed the Birds": Richard M. Sherman & Robert B. Sherman

"Oom-Pah-Pah": Lionel Bart

"And This Is My Beloved": Robert Wright and George Forrest

"It's a Fine Life": Lionel Bart

"If I Were a Rich Man": Sheldon Harnick and Jerry Bock

"You'll Never Walk Alone": music by Richard Rodgers, lyrics by Oscar Hammerstein II

"Singin' in the Rain": music by Nacio Herb Brown, lyrics by Arthur Freed

"Arrive": music and lyrics by John Meadows